I0613752

Xenotech
General Mayhem

A Novel of the Galactic Free Trade Association

The Xenotech Support Series

Dedication

To my amazing daughter,
for her creative inspiration.

Copyright © 2016 by Paul David Schroeder

All Rights Reserved. This book or any portion thereof may not be reproduced or used in any manner whatsoever without the express written permission of the publisher except for the use of brief quotations in a book review.

Cover design by Dan Paulson

Image of Crab Nebula on the cover is courtesy of NASA, ESA, J. Hester, A. Loll (ASU)

ISBN-13: 978-0-09978319-1-7

Spiral Arm Press
1725 Carlington Court
Grayson, GA 30017
www.spiralarmpress.com

Prologue

*"We are made wise not by the recollection of our past,
but by the responsibility for our future."*
— George Bernard Shaw

"When are you going to tell him?" asked Shepherd.

"When I work up the courage," said the man.

"No time like the present," said the Påkk.

"I know," said the man, "but I don't want him to hate me."

"It may be too late for that."

"Perhaps," said his companion, "though Jack's a better man than I am."

"So tell him and give him the chance to find that out for himself," said Shepherd.

"Soon," said the man. "When his life's not so complicated."

Shepherd laughed.

"What?" asked his companion.

"That *won't* be soon."

Chapter 1

"Cliffhanger: noun, a situation of imminent disaster."
— WordReference.com

I hoped the piton held—and wished I hadn't had such a big appetite over the past few days in Las Vegas. My extra pounds were making it harder for me to support myself and putting more stress on the small sliver of metal my life depended on. I was three-quarters of the way up a vertical rock face five hundred feet tall. It was sandstone, one side of a big butte not far from town, and I was scaling it to rescue my son, my lover, the mother of my child, her brother, and his girlfriend. They were all being held captive in an oligarch's villa at the top—except that it was more of a fortress than a villa and was dug into the side of the butte, not really on top.

The fortress villa had a great view of the lights of Las Vegas and was nearly impregnable. It could only be reached by lighter-than-air transports, and then only when a docking platform and mooring mast were extended from the villa by powerful motors. The top of the butte directly above was liberally seeded with anti-personnel mines and security cameras covered all the approaches from the front and the top.

Approaches from the rear were a different matter. That's why I was climbing—or more accurately, given my current situation—*not* climbing. I'd say "I like big buttes," but I'd be lying. I didn't like this one at all—especially because the sky looked like rain. Climbing dry sandstone is challenging—climbing *wet* sandstone is suicidal.

I'd done a little mountaineering in Alaska and New Mexico with my stepdad and had learned how to climb clean, using chocks, not pitons, to protect the integrity of the rock. The piton my rope and I were attached to—the one I wasn't sure would hold—was probably close to a century old, a legacy of some forgotten adventurer from the nineteen-thirties.

I was looking for a spot above me where I could plant a chock, but nothing appropriate was in reach. Then a drop of rain decided to have a party on the tip of my nose and invite its friends.

"Jack," said my phone. "You're running out of time. Once the sandstone gets wet…"

"I know," I said. "It will change from stone to mud. Can you spot a crack where I can set a nut?"

"Maybe," it replied.

My phone scuttled up my back from its usual spot on my belt and followed my right arm that was hanging onto the rope through the well-aged piton. It was carrying three chocks of varying sizes and a length of climbing rope on its back. When it reached my hand it grew a dozen new pseudopods with sharp points, jumped a few inches, and made its way up the cliff face by digging them into the soft rock.

"Here's a spot," it said, setting a chock into a crack almost out of sight above me.

The rain was changing from scattered showers to torrential downpour, which wasn't good. It hardly ever rained in the Las Vegas basin, but hardly ever is not the same as never. The rope my phone carried wiggled and I grabbed it.

"Ready for a test?" I asked.

"Ready," said my phone.

I pulled on the rope, putting weight on it to confirm it would hold. It didn't.

The new chock came free and I watched the rope sail past me with my phone using more pseudopods than I could count to hang on to it. The rain was soaking the rock around the piton— it had probably never been wet *and* had a load on it over the decades—and the piton picked that moment to pull loose. The chock I'd set below the piton also came free from the rain-sodden rock and I was regretting the fact that this might truly be a cliff-hanger ending for yours truly.

I fell. It seemed like I was falling for a few hours, but it was only a few breaths. I expected to leave a Jack-sized hole in the desert floor, like Wile E. Coyote after a failed attempt to take out the Road Runner. Instead, I smacked into something well before reaching terminal velocity. It was painful, but my protective Kevlar-like pupa silk shirt stopped me from breaking any ribs. I still held the rope my phone had been clutching and maintained a secure grip on it as I examined my surroundings.

I was in a large, bowl-shaped depression made of a dark, somewhat resilient material. Five tall pillars, topped by spiky formations were on one side and a long, green slope of regularly patterned rocky ground stretched above me on the other. I hadn't remembered seeing anything like it on my way up, but then again, I'd been focused on the cliff in front of me, not looking behind.

The torrential rain stopped as suddenly as it started and the hot Nevada sun dried me out. A few seconds later my phone crawled up the rope and joined me in the bowl. It was displaying a yellow smiley face on its screen with black oval eyes so big there wasn't much room left for yellow.

"What?" I said.

"Look up," said my phone.

I tilted my head back and saw another cliff, covered in the same scaly green rocks. A huge overhang loomed above us and my monkey brain was afraid it would collapse and crush us. Giant pale stalagmites and stalactites were arranged in an even pattern on its near side. I was so slow on the uptake that I wondered what geological forces could have formed them.

"Now look down," my phone suggested.

I leaned so I could see over the edge of the bowl and saw several hundred feet of empty air below me. Two strange symmetric green hills had mysteriously appeared nearby, leading to a pair of massive green pillars stretching up toward my refuge. Then the huge overhang tilted towards us. The stalagmites and stalactites separated and an eye the size of an adult Dauushan's head appeared even higher in the rock face.

The overhang wasn't a natural rock formation—it was the snout of a green scaly monster, hundreds of feet tall. Its massive mouth, with dozens of sharp teeth, not 'tites and 'mites, opened wider. Then it roared—with a noise like a thunderclap and a rush of unpleasant-smelling wind like a tornado in a sulfur factory.

"Sorry about that," said a voice that was deceptively normal-sounding, given the size of the being doing the talking. "I knew I shouldn't have had extra onions on my burrito."

I felt myself being lifted closer to the monster's jaws and saw a huge tongue, larger than a politician's ego, moving inside its mouth. It would have been licking its lips, if it had lips.

"Don't eat me!" I squeaked.

"He doesn't have good taste!" added my phone. "That is, he doesn't taste good!"

I was strangely comforted to know my phone was as weirded out as I was.

"No worries, guys," said the voice. "I just ate." Then the creature belched again, as if to emphasize its point. It lifted us even closer to one of its huge eyes.

"Are you okay?" the gigantic being asked, sounding sincere, not scary.

My brain had trouble taking everything in, but my gray matter finally managed to integrate the details of what it had felt, seen and heard. I was in the palm of some sort of creature out of a Japanese monster movie, or a Tyrannosaurus Rex with a major pituitary problem. The arms were wrong for a tyrannosaur, though. They were too long. This big guy's arms were so long it could probably touch its toes—which were likely at one end of those mysterious new hills below me.

"We're okay," I shouted. "Thanks for the save."

"You don't have to be so loud," said the voice. "My ears are big, too."

I stared up at the humongous eye again and saw a giant scaly green bunny ear flick straight up, then fold back down against the creature's neck in what I took to be a nervous gesture.

"Would you mind putting me on top of the butte?" I asked.

It looked like the giant's arms would reach that far.

"No problem," said the voice.

The enormous entity didn't lift me up—it grew until it was taller than the butte and able to place me, and my phone, gently at the top of the cliff. Thank goodness the antipersonnel mines were supposed to be concentrated on the *other* half of the butte's surface.

"Wow!" said my phone. "You can violate the cube square law!"

"It's no big deal," said the voice. "I was told my species can manipulate our size and mass using internal congruencies."

The giant proved its point by planting its arms on top of the butte, shrinking down to human size, and levering itself over the cliff edge.

"I'm Gustávish, by the way," said the saurian, "but you can call me Gus. I have a gig for Kingsworth Electronics at GALTEX later this afternoon. I'm supposed to play a really big threat to network security."

"Typecasting," said my phone, its words tinged with awe.

"Jack Buckston," I replied, extending my hand to shake with Gus. Thank goodness his claws were retractable.

Then a loud and irreverent voice spoke up two inches from my left ear.

"Are you tellin' me *your* species has a built-in congruency, too?"

"Chit, be nice," I said.

"Is the bug on your shoulder talking?" asked Gus.

"Dang right I'm talkin', buster. Murms are the only species in the Galaxy that evolved with a built-in congruency," grumbled my little friend.

"I don't think so," said Gus. "Though maybe you're right. Gojons don't have *a* built-in congruency. We have *three* of them. One for mass, one for temperature control, and one for energy."

"I've never *heard* of Gojons," said Chit. "And I've heard of *everybody.*"

"My apologies, but Gojo was only recently discovered. Our star is out near the end of the Sagittarius-Carina spiral arm. We're the newest member species in the Galactic Free Trade Association."

My phone bleeped and blooped a few times, then reported.

"Gus is correct," it said, "according to the latest report from the Joint GaFTA Exploratory Corps, they were found by a Nicósn scout ship six months ago."

"It's a pleasure to meet you," I said. "I've never run into anyone from a species that can radically change size before."

"It comes in handy when you're dealing with the local flora and fauna on Gojo," said Gus.

I made a mental note not to put visiting Gojo high on my bucket list. Then my phone chimed in with an inane and borderline-impolite question.

"Can you breathe radioactive fire?"

"Only when I eat too many jalapeños," said Gus.

I knew the feeling and was beginning to like the Gojon. Like a lot of big guys—and actors—he seemed to be shy and insecure underneath a blustering façade.

"How come GaFTA had to discover you, instead of you discoverin' GaFTA?" asked Chit, belligerently. "Didn't you have congruent space travel?"

"No, we hadn't developed space travel on our own," said Gus, "but we have *internal* congruencies, so we could join. The scout ship's first officer said there was a precedent for that sort of thing."

"Murms *are* that precedent," grumbled Chit. "Gol' durn giants with *three* internal congruencies…"

The rest of her rant faded into mumbles.

"Terrans didn't develop congruent space travel," I said. "How did *we* get in?"

"Space travel's optional," said Chit. "It's discoverin' congruencies that's important. Besides, the galactic networks couldn't wait to get their hands on your content."

"Just how long *had* you Galactics been observing us before we got our invitation?" I asked.

"You don't wanna know, buddy boy."

Maybe I didn't. I distracted myself with another question.

"Why are you wandering around out here in the desert, Gus?"

"Nerves," said the Gojon. "I get anxious before I perform and walking helps me calm down."

"Good to know," I said. "I'm glad you were nearby."

"Me, too," said Gus. "You seem like a nice guy and if I can estimate Terrans' ages correctly, you're too young to die."

"You've got that right, my friend," I said.

Then my phone made a bleep and a comment.

"Poly and Max and Rosalind and Cornell and Sally aren't going to rescue themselves."

It wasn't a completely accurate statement. I gave odds of better than fifty percent that Poly and Rosalind, at least, could pull off their own rescue. Still, it was smart of my phone to get me back on task.

"Thanks again for your help, Gus," I said, "but I've got to get moving. People's lives may be at stake."

"Is it going to be an adventure?" asked the Gojon, bouncing his kangaroo-like tail. At human size, his enthusiasm was more endearing than frightening.

"Based on past experience…" said my phone.

"…the odds are good," said Chit.

Chapter 2

"The best fortress which a prince can possess
is the affection of his people."
— Niccolò Machiavelli

Gus asked if he could join us and I said "Sure." Having a size-changing saurian on our team seemed like a plus. Chit and I had a plan for getting into the oligarch's fortress villa, but it had room for improvisation.

Our new Gojon friend wouldn't be able to fit into my Blend Into the Scenery coverall with me, and I was counting on that to get me past the security cameras above the villa. The B.I.T.S. coverall in my backpack tool bag had been a gift from one of my clients. It was made from Orishen morphabric and bent light to make its wearer effectively invisible. Originally designed for stage hands who needed to be unseen when moving sets during performances, it had saved my life on more than one occasion. I'd also found some spare B.I.T.S. cloth, but Poly had that now and used it as a poncho. I wondered if Gus could curl up and imitate a rock for the cameras. I explained the situation to him.

"...and that will make it very difficult to sneak up on the fortress villa."

"No problem," said Gus.

He grew until he was twenty feet tall, leaned over me, and shrank to the size of a praying mantis, landing on my right shoulder. Chit, on my left shoulder, did not sound happy to have company. The two of them started an argument on either side of my neck, debating the virtues of their respective species—with particular concern for their internal congruencies. Chit pushed for quality over quantity, while Gustávish couldn't understand how any species unable to change size could be worth much in the galactic scheme of things. It felt like I had an angel on one shoulder and a devil on the other, though I couldn't tell you which one was which. While their words echoed back and forth through my empty skull—

at least it would have been easier if my skull *had* been empty—I found my B.I.T.S. coverall in my backpack tool bag and started to put it on. Chit and Gus put their discussion on hold while they found places to nestle next to my ears that allowed them to see out the thin face-panel on my coverall.

"You can continue your conversation about the merits of your species later," I said. "Murms have instantaneous communications and Gojons can change size. Apples. Oranges."

"More like apples and kumquats," muttered Chit.

"Or raisins and watermelons," said Gus, giving as good as he got.

"Table it, please," I said. "This next stage is tricky and I need to focus."

I put the climbing rope back in my backpack tool bag and found the small B.I.T.S. cloth covering that rendered my backpack invisible as well. Then I put on my pack by feel and followed my phone as it crawled toward the opposite side of the butte.

The best way to handle land mines is not to step on them in the first place. My phone used only six legs for movement and devoted most of the mass of its mutacase to extrude a three-foot rod with a sensor on the end. It panned the sensor back and forth in front of its path, mapping out a safe course through the minefield.

We had to backtrack several times when we ended up in cul-de-sacs where the mines were packed in too tightly to navigate around. The top of the butte had been extensively mined and I was *very* glad my phone knew where I should go to avoid being blown up. After a few minutes, it became mechanical to shuffle my feet forward along ground that my phone noted, like food additives, was generally recognized as safe. I thought back over the last few hours and marveled how I ended up in this position.

* * * * *

My mind and my psyche had still been recovering from several major shocks. I'd been in the house in western Las Vegas where we'd tracked Cornell and doing what one does in the first-floor powder room when I'd heard the sound of the front door opening. Shortly thereafter came the loud, distinctive *Soooo-eeeeet!* of sweetener blasts, then five heavy thumps. By the time I'd pulled myself together, stepped out, and moved from the hall to the living room, everyone had vanished. I'd raced to the open front door and saw an airship disappearing toward the north.

The vessel had an uncommon design. It was some sort of blimp that looked like an overinflated upside-down clothes iron inside an aluminum frame, with wings and silent congruent engines on top. It was moving fast. The side of the gasbag closest to me was painted in the black and purple crenelated and crowned hill logo of Chapultepec & Castle. I needed to follow it.

I must not have been thinking straight, or I would have contacted Tomáso or Shepherd or even Martin to get Queen Sherri's huge dirigible, the *Matriarch of the Skies,* to follow the C&C ship. But Tomáso was still recovering from being drugged and I was lost in non-cognitive action mode. I ran to the garage, got in Cornell's large, silver Mercedes-Kia, overrode the autopilot, and burned rubber trying to keep the odd C&C airship in sight.

I followed it—with plenty of help from my phone's telephoto lens function—until I saw it moor to the dock at the oligarch's fortress villa in the butte whose upper surface I was now trying to cross without turning into hamburger. My phone briefed me on the villa's security profile, so I drove Cornell's car around to the rear of the butte on a collection of conjoined potholes pretending to be a road. I was prepared to free-climb the back of the butte in my best navy blue pinstripe suit and was surprised to see a vehicle already parked up ahead, waiting for me.

I looked at my phone.

"Initiative," it said. I could have kissed it.

Martin got out of a rented Jeep Land Rover and shook my hand.

"I've got your backpack tool bag and suitcases," he said.

"Thank you."

I changed into a comfortable pair of black pants and a long-sleeved black shirt—the outfit I liked to use when playing ninja—and traded dress shoes for sneakers, frightening a prairie dog or two in the process.

"You might want this," said Martin, pressing a bundle into my hands when I'd finished tying my shoes. It was a bag with with rope, a small hammer, and mountaineering supplies.

Machismo be damned. I hugged him.

"Thank you!"

Martin hugged me back and gently pushed me toward the base of the cliff.

"Get moving. I'll mobilize the appropriate resources," he said.

"We don't want to spook the people holding Poly and…"

"Duly noted. Dauushan Drop Marines won't be storming the villa. We'll be ready—but only when you give the word."

This time I didn't hug him. I just nodded, walked to the cliff, and prepared to start climbing.

* * * * *

I pulled myself back into the present. My phone had stopped. We were at the edge of the butte, directly above the windows of the oligarch's fortress villa.

The oligarch who owned the place—Nikolai Ivanovich Lobachevsky Komanev, according to my phone—had made billions selling natural resources when Siberia declared its independence from Russia back in 2018. He'd moved to the United States, renamed himself Nicky Stone, and hobnobbed with American corporate royalty, playing bridge with Bill Gates and poker with Mark Zuckerberg. Stone had been smart enough to sell his companies *before* Earth's business community realized just how cheap access to asteroid mining and teleportation would make raw materials. With billions in cash, Stone bought the NFL's Las Vegas Raiders, the NBA's Pittsburgh Inclines, and the NHL's Mexico City Aztecs, turning all three franchises into champions in less than a decade.

Stone was a fanatic about privacy and security. His fortress villa, carved into the side of a butte, was his ultimate sanctuary. He also rented the place out through Airbnb. Go figure. I didn't know if that meant Stone might be The General, the secret master behind EUA Corporation, or just an astute businessman trying to monetize an underutilized asset. Either way, the mines would kill me just as dead. I wondered about the rental agreement's fine print for injuries if any renters stumbled into the mine field.

"Where's Nicky Stone right now?" I asked my phone.

"He just finished giving the Commencement address at Harvard Business School in Cambridge."

"Oh," I said. "That takes him off the suspect list for being The General."

"Don't count on it," my phone retorted. "Maybe he just wanted an alibi?"

"What does Chapultepec & Castle want with a Russian— pardon me—Siberian oligarch?"

"Low off-season rental rates for fortress villas?" responded my phone.

I stepped forward to stand next to my helpful communications device. Unfortunately, I must have strayed from its carefully selected path. I heard a click underneath my foot.

"You didn't," said my phone.

"I think I did," I said ruefully. I was sure triggering a land mine was not on my bucket list. In this case, it would be more like my kick-the-bucket list.

"Oops," said my phone.

"It will go off when I lift my foot, correct?"

"Uh huh," said my phone. The fact that it was behaving unlike its usual loquacious self convinced me I was in deep trouble. There was no way I could outrun the blast wave from the mine's explosives— and I was quite fond of my lower extremities.

"Is something the matter?" asked Gus from his perch near my right ear.

"You might say that, bub, if you was payin' attention," growled Chit.

"If that *click* was a mine being triggered, don't worry. I can shrink down and put myself between your foot and the mine, then grow fifty feet tall so the blast would only tickle," said Gus.

"Don't bother, bozo," said Chit. "You'd only set off every security alarm for a quarter mile doin' somethin' like that and screw up the rescue."

Gus let out a practiced actors' sigh and my little friend pushed her way out through the space where the hood met my neck on the B.I.T.S. coverall. She tickled. I couldn't look down far enough to see what she was doing but felt Chit land on my tennis shoe through the canvas. I didn't need to worry about following her actions—she kept up a running commentary.

"I'm inside the housing," said Chit. "These babies are *old*. Third Gulf War-era conventional explosives. If they'd been modern congruent black hole mines we wouldn't stand a chance."

"Good to know," I said, trying to encourage my little friend's troubleshooting.

"There's a little stirrup I can put over the trigger mechanism to hold it in the down position," she said. Her deep voice echoed inside the mine's casing.

"Be careful," I said, regretting my words as they left my mouth.

"Don't teach your grandma how to suck…"

"Jack," said my phone, distracting me. "Poly is in the room directly below us. I can pick up her voice through the rocks. If the plans for the fortress villa on Airbnb are correct, she's in the room with the picture windows on the front of the butte."

"Roger that," I said, "but first things first. How's it coming little buddy?"

"One stirrup on," said Chit. "Now I'm fastenin' the other one…"

I held my breath for three beats.

"Done," said my little friend.

"You're sure it's safe now?"

"I ain't exactly out of the blast radius myself, bucko. Of course it's safe."

I stepped off the trigger plate and nothing happened. Nothing went boom. Chit flew back to my left shoulder, on the *outside* of my B.I.T.S. suit, this time. Thank goodness she was too small to register as more than a tiny blip on the fortress villa's security cameras. I started breathing again. Then I heard a mechanical voice below my feet. It was counting down.

"Ten. Nine. Eight…"

My fingers scrabbled in the soft dirt below me. They found the edge of the mine and I pulled it out of the ground.

"Six. Five…"

Using both hands and a discus-tossing spin, I launched the mine over the near edge of the butte. I could hear it continue to recite as it fell past the top.

"Three. Two…"

I threw myself on the ground as a blast loud enough to wake a sleeping teenager assaulted my ears. It was accompanied by the sound of tinkling glass. Fine reddish dust settled over my body. I brushed it off when I stood up.

"You guys okay?" I asked.

"I've had better days, buddy boy," said Chit.

Gus sobbed theatrically and began a soliloquy, *"'tis not so deep as a well nor so wide as a church-door, but 'tis enough…"*

Thespians. He must be okay, too. I pulled off my backpack, removed and repacked my B.I.T.S. suit, and got out my climbing rope. After the blast, the idea of trying to sneak up on the fortress villa went out the window with the shattered glass.

"Hold this," I said to Gus, now returned to human size. He understood what I was doing and increased his mass to be a better anchor.

I tossed the rope over the side of the butte and scrambled down it until I was even with where the windows had been. Poly grabbed me and pulled me inside, past a sprinkling of safety glass on the floor. As I'd expected, the windows had been armored and substantially resisted the blast, turning into powder, rather than shrapnel.

Rosalind was holding a mini-sweetener on a dozen frozen thugs and henchmen piled up against the left hand wall. Cornell was standing at a well-stocked bar, fixing himself a drink, and Max was sitting on the floor in the back of the luxuriously appointed room playing with Verne Wells & Company models of the Nautilus and Martian tripods on the plush carpeting.

"Where's Sally?" I asked.

"Guarding the prisoners," said Cornell.

Prisoners? I thought. *Weren't all the prisoners out here?*

"What took you so long?" asked Rosalind.

"Who cares about that?" added Poly with a smile. She gave me a hug and a more-where-that-comes-from kiss. "What a way to make an entrance!"

* * * * *

It all started when…

Chapter 3

*"Fatherhood is the most amazing thing that
could ever have happened in my life."*
— Corey Feldman

Small arms wrapped around my knees and my universe changed forever.

My mini-sweetener fell from my fingers and clattered to the porch.

I reached down and hugged the boy back. I had a son.

My brain was a jumble of emotions. I felt joy like fireworks exploding, since I'd always wanted children—just maybe not so soon. I felt pain like knives stabbing, since Rosalind had hidden Max from me and I hadn't been part of his life. I'd never known my own biological father and that lack made it hurt even more not to have known Max from the day he'd first come into the world. I felt anger at Rosalind for manipulating me and spared a moment of lucidity to wonder whether or not she was telling the truth about Max, though one look had been enough to know that he was my child. I felt concern for Poly. She was my business partner, my lover, and—I hoped—would someday be my life partner. She hadn't signed up for a relationship with a man who'd had a child with another woman.

None of that mattered now. I went to my knees, so I could be at Max's level, and looked him in the eyes.

"Hello, Max," I said. "It's wonderful to meet you."

"Are you really my daddy?" said the boy. His eyes were shiny.

I looked up at Rosalind. She nodded, and shrugged a half-hearted apology, as if trying to make up for years of subterfuge. We'd have *that* conversation later.

"Uh huh," I said, giving him another hug.

We didn't say anything for a minute—we just held on to each other, neither one of us wanting to let go.

"Jack," said my phone, making a throat-clearing noise to get my attention, though it didn't have anything remotely resembling a throat. It had jumped off my belt and was on the porch beside me, waving half a dozen pseudopods.

"Later," I said. I had more important things to do.

Max and I broke our hug.

"What do you like to do for fun?" I asked.

"Take things apart," said the boy, "and put them back together again."

"Me, too," I said.

Max was looking at my phone. I could almost read his thoughts. He wanted to figure out how its mutacase worked. My phone noticed Max's gaze and scuttled closer to Poly.

"It's really important, Jack," said my phone.

"Tell *me*," said Poly.

I looked over my shoulder and saw Poly staring at Max, then at me, then at Rosalind. Poly and I would have *our* conversation later, too. I could hear Poly and my phone talking, but wasn't paying attention to what was being said. It was much more fun to talk about taking clocks apart with my son. Then Poly leaned down and tapped my shoulder.

"You need to hear this," she said, holding my phone near my ear.

I squeezed Max's hand, rolled my eyes to ensure he knew I'd rather be talking to him, and listened to what my phone thought was so blasted important.

"There was a plane crash at Hartsfield Port," it said.

"So?"

"Just with felt and yarn," said Max, "but Aunt Sally says she'll teach me how to use a needle and thread when I'm five."

I returned my focus to Max for a second and smiled. I had a cool kid. I also couldn't give him all the time he deserved right now.

"I'll show you some tricks with leather and waxed thread soon, Max."

"Thanks, Daddy."

"It was a private jet," said Poly, interrupting.

"Owned by Chapultepec & Castle," continued my phone.

"Scott Winfield and Josephine Johnson were on board," said Poly.

"There were no survivors," said my phone.

I heard a noise in front of me and looked up to see Rosalind holding her hand near her throat. Her face was white.

"You'd better come in," she said, turning around and heading inside.

Max took my hand and led me into the house. Poly tapped my shoulder, returned my sweetener, and followed. Chit distracted me by flitting over from the door's view port to my ear.

"I knew I should-a had that birds 'n' bees talk with you when you were younger, bucko," she whispered.

I didn't reply. I just shook my head slowly from side to side and rolled my eyes again, this time for my own benefit. I reached back with the hand Max wasn't holding and squeezed Poly's. She squeezed back.

We stepped into a square three-story foyer with a marble-tiled floor. Rosalind shouted to the balconies above.

"Sally, Cornell, please come down. We have company."

Without waiting for an answer, she led us into a large living room furnished in Galactic Modern. It was filled with eclectic pieces from a dozen worlds and species. Poly and I sat on a black, white, brown and tan Tigramm faux-hide love seat and Max sat on a matching ottoman facing us. The bottoms of his sneakers were a few inches off the floor. Rosalind sat across from us in a wingback chair covered in light blue Nicósn vine-style upholstery. She looked worried and distracted, like someone at the wrong end of a Hellfire missile lock.

Max kept up a non-stop chatter. He told me all about the books he was reading and web series he was following. He was a particularly ardent fan of the Muppet Avengers and loved it when Kermit Hulked out. I told him I liked it when Ms. Piggy did Black Widow's martial arts moves, which always tended to break important pieces of the set. We both giggled as I tried to imitate one of her punches.

Poly nudged my elbow. I looked her way and realized I'd forgotten to introduce her to Max. *Mea culpa, mea maxima culpa!*

"Sorry, Sweetheart," I said. "Poly Jones, please meet my son, Max."

Max held out his hand with a child's exaggerated politeness and earnestly shook the hand Poly extended.

"Pleased to meet you, Ms. Jones," said the boy. I was glad to see that Rosalind had raised him with good manners.

"I'm very glad to meet you too, Max," said Poly. "I think we're going to be great friends."

She smiled at Max using the same high-energy expression that made me glad to be her lover and partner. Max was clearly taken by Poly as much as I was.

"Do you work with my Daddy?" he asked.

"Uh huh," said Poly. "We're partners."

The boy looked thoughtful.

"We're also boyfriend and girlfriend," I said.

"Oh," said Max. He turned to me, seeming even more thoughtful.

"What's your last name?" he asked.

"Buckston," I said. "What's yours?"

"That's my last name, too!"

I hugged Max and we both smiled, pleased to have more in common. I made a note to add that to my list of topics to discuss with Rosalind.

Our discussion was interrupted by the arrival of Sally and Cornell. When they entered the living room they froze, staring at us, staring at Max, and staring at Rosalind's pale and fearful expression.

For a change, Cornell wasn't wearing one of his signature suits. He was dressed as casually as Rosalind in jeans and a black *Astaire-Way to Heaven* t-shirt. Sally was beside him wearing a similar outfit, though it looked better on her.

When he saw us, Cornell reached for a weapon but came up empty. He must keep them in his suits. Sally did a similar double-take, but was also unarmed. Poly held a mini-sweetener, pointing it in a non-threatening direction.

"Put that away," said Rosalind. "You won't need it." She turned to her brother and Sally. "Come in and sit down. They won't hurt us and there's something you've got to hear."

Cornell and Sally kept a wary eye on Poly and me, but Rosalind's tone of voice and her obvious distress made them unwilling to question her instructions. They sat close to Rosalind on a long, brown, ubercow-leather sofa.

"He knows?" said Cornell to Rosalind.

"He does now," she replied. "Once he saw Max it was hard to hide the relationship."

"Can we play hide and seek, Daddy?" asked Max.

Cornell gave me a look of disgust and started to protest.

"I told you we shouldn't…"

"Stop," said Sally in a She-Who-Must-Be-Obeyed tone.

Cornell stopped.

"Soon," I told my son.

"Jack's phone," said Rosalind peremptorily. "Tell them what you told us."

My phone obeyed without asking my permission to respond.

"A Chapultepec & Castle executive jet carrying Scott Winfield and Josephine Johnson crash-landed at Hartsfield Port less than an hour ago. There were no survivors."

Cornell and Sally turned the same color as Rosalind. All the blood had drained from their faces.

"We've got to get out of here," said Sally.

"Off-planet would be good," said Cornell.

"Another dimension would be better," said Rosalind.

"Video of the crash confirms your assessment," said my phone.

"What do you mean?" I asked.

"You can spot the track of a surface-to-air missile hitting the plane as it started its approach," said my phone.

"Oh," said Poly.

The Atlanta branches of Homeland Security and the NTSB must be going nuts. I pulled my attention away from Max again and applied my full brainpower to the situation. Winfield and Johnson had likely been flying to Atlanta to be disciplined by The General after screwing up the plan to capture and brainwash corporate leaders attending the Galactic Technology Expo in Las Vegas. Sally,

Cornell and Rosalind were realizing that The General's approach to discipline was draconian—and they were next in line to face the dragon. I nodded slowly and saw Poly mirror my motion.

Max thought it was a game and began to nod, too.

"What?" asked Rosalind. "Have all three of you turned into bobbleheads?"

"No," I said. "It just took me a while to figure things out and ask."

"Ask what?" said Sally.

"Ask if you wanted our help," said Poly.

"And protection," I added.

"No way," Cornell blurted. "He'll terminate us for sure."

"He's going to do that anyway," said Sally. "This way, we have a chance."

"Like the Daleks?" asked Max.

"That's *ex*terminate, sweetie."

Max nodded again, accepting the correction. He went back to staring at my phone, mentally disassembling it.

"Why should we throw in with *them*?" asked Cornell, waving a hand toward Poly and me.

"Because," said Sally, shaking her head, "despite our best efforts, they've managed to screw up The General's plans every time so far."

"How do we know it wasn't just dumb luck?" posed Cornell.

"How many times have they captured *you*, brother?" asked Rosalind. "Zwilniki's plot? The Compliant Plague? Under Hoover Dam?"

"Look who's talking," Cornell shot back. "I wasn't the one tied up with duct tape and left in the Mulbiri Precious Gem and Bullion Repository."

"I was careless," Rosalind shot back.

"In more ways than one," said Sally, glancing at Max and smiling.

Rosalind's cheeks turned red and she looked away from me.

Sally kept needling. "It's only because you were sweet on Jack…"

Poly and I had been following their exchange as it went back and forth like the moving bundle of pixels shifting sides in a game of Classic Pong. Finally, my partner had enough.

"A-hem," she said, loud enough to distract Max from chasing my phone around the perimeter of the living room.

Everyone stopped talking and looked at Poly.

"First," she said, "The General has eliminated a pair of non-performing assets."

Heads nodded around the room. I was glad she wasn't being more blunt in front of Max.

Sally looked at Cornell, then interrupted Poly's summation.

"They could have staged the whole production to make a clean getaway…"

"Doubtful," said Cornell. "They were too self-confident to think they'd ever need an escape plan."

"Maybe, maybe not," said Sally. She shrugged her shoulders, but I could sense wheels turning in her head.

"As I was saying," Poly continued, staring pointedly at Sally. "Second, the three of you are likely next in line."

The pained expressions on Cornell, Sally and Rosalind's faces confirmed Poly's assessment.

"Third," said Poly, "Running doesn't have a high probability of success—especially if you have to bring along…"

"We get it," said Rosalind. She looked at Max and moved her head slowly from left and right, as if she was in pain. Sally and Cornell offered Rosalind sympathetic glances.

"Fourth and last," said my partner, "if we join forces, we may be able to take down The General permanently and get on with our lives."

Cornell, Sally and Rosalind didn't look completely convinced, but they didn't have a better alternative. *The enemy of my enemy is my friend* and all that. I think having it out in the open that I was Max's father might have made it easier, now that they saw how well my son and I got along. In a strange way, we were all family.

I stood up and held out my hand. Poly joined me and put her hand on top of mine. Slowly, Rosalind, Sally and Cornell added their hands to the grip. Max scooted in underneath and put his hand below mine.

It felt like the comic book origin story of the Fantastic Four after their spaceship crashed.

"We accept your offer of help," said Rosalind.

"And protection," said Sally.

"For all the good it will do us," inserted Cornell.

"Let's put an end to The General," I said, hoping to finish our ritual bonding on an optimistic note.

Poly tried to do the same.

"Confusion to the enemy!" she shouted.

"Fusion!" said Max. "H-bomb. Boom!"

It was going to be general mayhem.

Chapter 4

"Meanwhile, back at the ranch…"
— Silent Movie Transition

"Hey, Jack," said Gus from the butte-edge above. "Is it safe to come down?"

"Sure!" I shouted. I'd forgotten all about my new friend.

"Who's that?" asked Poly.

"Gus. He saved my life. He'll be here in a second."

I was *very* surprised when Gus didn't promptly appear, but Chit did. My oldest friend buzzed through the space where the fortress villa's windows used to be and landed on my shoulder.

"Where's Gus?" I asked.

Then I turned my head and saw where he was. The Gojon had gotten even smaller than a praying mantis. He was flea-sized and riding in a narrow space between Chit's head and thorax. If Chit's wing cases hadn't been painted the dusky red color of sandstone and Gus a contrasting green, I never would have spotted him.

My size-changing saurian friend jumped off Chit and grew to human size before he could hit the floor.

"Gustávish," he said, bowing to Poly and Rosalind. "Pleased to meet you."

His tail lifted as a counterbalance when his upper torso bent forward.

The two women bowed back, respectfully, and Cornell waved one hand in greeting from his self-appointed station near the bar. Max looked up from his anachronistic toys, spotted Gus, and ran toward us. As he passed me, he glanced at me and gave me a perfunctory, "Hi, Daddy," before standing in front of Gus, gazing in awe.

"Are you a *dinosaur?*" he asked.

Gus looked at me, then looked at Poly and Rosalind. We all nodded.

"Close enough," said Gus.

Max hugged his leg and started asking Gus about life in the Cretaceous and begging for piggyback rides. Gus looked overwhelmed, so I stepped in to help him out, unwrapping Max's arms and putting my son on my shoulders for the first time. I began to regret I'd never had a chance to do that when he was younger, and *lighter,* because I didn't think I could support him up there for very long without needing chiropractic care.

"Gus needs to leave soon," I told Max. "He's an actor and has to be back in the city to make his big entrance."

"An *actor?*" he asked. "Are you on television? Or the movies?"

Gus smiled at Max, showing lots of sharp teeth. They didn't seem nearly as threatening when they weren't twelve feet long.

"My client hopes I'll be on the TV news tonight," said Gus. "I can send you a clip if I get any air time. And as for the movies, I have a screen test with Tohokaiju Productions in Atlanta next week for a really big role."

"Wow!" said my son.

He was getting too heavy, so I put Max down, but held on to his shoulders so he wouldn't attach himself to Gus's legs again.

"Why Atlanta?" asked Poly.

"Hollywood of the South," I commented.

Gus traded contact information with my phone, made polite goodbyes, and then jumped out of the space where the windows used to be. As he fell, he increased his size until he was almost as tall as the butte and began striding off toward Las Vegas, making great time. I hoped his gig with Kingsworth Electronics would go well. Max was beside himself over giant Gus and couldn't stop telling Rosalind, Cornell and Poly what he'd seen. He was so excited he ran deeper into the fortress villa to tell Sally, too.

I turned my head so I could see Chit out of the corner of my eye and quietly mouthed, "Thanks!"

"Don't mention it," said my little friend. "I was glad to give 'im a ride. It's not the big guy's fault his species has three internal congruencies. It's just a bit of a shock t' find out Murms aren't the only ones that have 'em."

"Droopy the disembodied brain-in-a-bottle has one," I said, just to tease her.

"Yeah, but his is an implant," responded Chit. "That don't count."

"Right," I replied. "Nice work disarming the mine, by the way."

"Don't rub it in. How was I to know there was a timer?"

I would have come up with a snappy comeback, but Poly provided a pleasant interruption with a hug.

"Sounds like you had some adventures," she said.

"You, too," I said.

I extricated an arm from our hug and waved it to take in the frozen thugs and henchmen against the wall, illustrating my words.

"You first," said Poly.

I explained what had happened from the time I'd stepped out of the powder room back at Cornell, Sally, Rosalind and Max's home until I'd made my grand entrance. Poly and Rosalind were particularly fascinated by Gus's timely intervention when I'd fallen off the cliff. I wondered if Poly would ask her mother to help Gus with his acting career as a way of expressing her gratitude for saving my hide.

"Now your turn," I said, looking at both Poly and Rosalind. Cornell might have had a role in the rescue, but I wasn't betting on it.

"We were in the living room—mostly staring at each other…" said Rosalind.

"Awkwardly," added Poly.

"Then the front door opened and five goons rushed in," said Rosalind.

"They sweetened us before we could react," said Cornell, looking disgusted. He frowned at Poly.

"I know, I know," said Poly. "I had a sweetener and should have used it, but I'd put it in my jacket pocket and was too distracted to pull it out and zap them."

"Aunt Sally says *I'm* a big distraction sometimes," said Max.

I'd have to remember that Max would always be listening when he was within earshot.

"Aunt Sally is right," said Rosalind, throwing Poly a conversational lifeline.

I could just imagine Poly and Rosalind looking at each other, then looking at Max, then looking at each other. I knew *I* would be distracted.

"We were carried aboard an airship like so many sacks of flour," said Poly.

"I like flowers," said Max.

"I know," said Rosalind. "So do I."

"Then we were transported here," said my partner. "Where *is* here, by the way? It looks like we're pretty high up and I can see the Las Vegas skyline in the distance."

"You are in Nicky Stone's fortress villa built into a butte nineteen kilometers north-northwest of Sally and Cornell's home," said my phone authoritatively. "Our present height above sea level, according to internal barometric sensors, is seven hundred and sixty meters and the distance to the desert floor is nearly one hundred and fifty meters."

"That's a five-hundred-foot drop, Daddy," said Max. "I'm glad Mr. Gus was there to save you."

I got another hug from Max and was even more impressed by my son. He could do math and metric to English measurement conversions in his head. I couldn't do that until I was five. I felt another pang of regret for not being around for the first years of his life.

"How old is Max?" I asked Rosalind.

"I thought you were good at math," she replied. "Just add two hundred and eighty days to..."

"I'm nearly five," said Max.

"And the most amazing nearly five-year-old I know," I replied, earning me another hug.

I looked back at Rosalind. "Then what happened?"

"We were unloaded and unceremoniously plopped on the furniture," said Rosalind.

She waved her hands to take in the pieces in the room where we were standing.

"At least the sofas and chairs were well-padded," said Cornell.

"A dozen thugs stayed here to watch us and the funny-looking C&C airship with the wings flew off," said Poly.

"Were you all okay?" I asked.

Poly, Rosalind and Cornell nodded.

"It didn't hurt except for the tingling when the chill wore off," said Max. "That felt like the pins and needles you get when your foot goes to sleep. Have you ever been sweetened, Daddy?"

"Too many times, Max. It's not much fun."

"Once was enough for me, Daddy. I came out of it first," he announced proudly.

That was odd. Usually, sweeteners—mini-sweeteners in particular—have a longer and more intense effect on smaller body masses. Rosalind must have read my mind.

"Max was sitting on the floor behind the ottoman," she said. "It must have absorbed some of the blast."

Now it made sense.

"He was great," said Poly. "We were on the corner sofa facing out so we could see each other. Max waited until all the pins and needles had faded. He pretended he was still frozen until he saw me twitch a finger and his mom nod at him slightly. The guards were keeping a close eye on us, ready to tie us up once we'd thawed."

As I'd learned with Martin at the K Street Bar in the SLN Capital hotel, it wasn't easy to reposition people who'd been frozen.

"What did Max do?" I asked.

"He screamed," said Rosalind.

"Want me to show you how it sounded, Daddy?"

"That's okay," I said.

"He sounded like a banshee trying to overpower the decibels at a heavy metal concert," said Poly. "All the goon guards rushed over to him. I pulled my mini-sweetener out of my jacket and zapped three of them from behind."

"Then Mom pried a mini-sweetener from one of the frozen guard's fingers and chilled two more. Mom and Ms. Poly used the guards they'd already zapped as shields and took out the rest of them before they knew what was happening. Aunt Sally took out two guards with karate chops like Miss Piggy."

"Good work," I said, "and smart thinking, Max."

"Mom says I'm precocious," said my son.

"Your mother's right," said Poly.

Max beamed an angelic smile, with just a hint of a little devil hiding inside. He looked a lot like pictures of me at that age.

"Then what?"

"Then my uncle handled the heavy lifting," said Max.

"I carried the frozen thugs and stacked them by the left-hand wall," said Cornell. "It was the least I could do."

"I'll say," Chit whispered in my ear.

"You said Sally was holding more prisoners in the back?" I asked.

"Uh huh," said Max. "They're special."

"Special prisoners?"

"Uh huh," said Poly. "A few minutes later, we saw the C&C airship returning, so the five of us pretended to still be frozen on the sofa."

"Smart move," I said. "You gave your opponents a false sense of security."

"The 'ship dropped off more people and headed back to Vegas," said Rosalind. "When the newcomers entered the room…"

"Mom and my aunt and uncle and Ms. Poly zapped them!" shouted Max.

He ran around in a circle doing some sort of happy dance.

"What made the newcomers special?" I asked.

"They weren't *all* special," said Rosalind. "Only two of them were."

The look on my face was an unmistakable request to tell me more. Poly grinned and filled me in.

"The new arrivals were Scott Winfield and Josephine Johnson."

Chapter 5

"The report of my death was an exaggeration."
— Samuel L. Clemens

"Say what?"

"Winfield and Johnson, the top execs at Chapultepec & Castle," said Rosalind.

"But they're dead!"

"I told you they could have staged it," said Sally.

"Are they actors?" asked Max. "Is that why they're special?"

"They're actors, alright," said Rosalind. "Just not the kind you see in the movies or on television."

"More like *bad* actors," said Poly.

"Max, would you ask Aunt Sally to bring out the special prisoners?" requested Rosalind. "We need to talk to them."

"Okay, Mommy!"

Max ran out of the grand living room at high speed. Sometimes I'm sure human children must have internal congruencies—how else could they have so much energy?

"Did you have a chance to interrogate them?" I asked.

"Sorry," said Poly. "We froze everyone who entered the room, indiscriminately. I zapped them before I realized who they were."

"Think they're thawed by now?"

"Should be," said Cornell. "We gave the *goons* a second zap, but not Winfield and Johnson."

The two of them proved they were no longer chilled out by walking into the room, led by a triumphant-looking Max and followed by Sally, holding a mini-sweetener. The executives' hands were securely tied in front of them with expensive Hermès scarves.

"You!" said Johnson, giving me an angry glance like I was an incompetent subordinate leading an underperforming division.

"Son of a…" said Winfield.

He stopped himself when he remembered Max was in the room. Even villains have virtues, I suppose.

"How did *you* get here?"

I silently answered Winfield's question by pointing at the broken window and the bits of safety glass on the floor. Max noted my gesture and started to move in that direction.

Winfield and Johnson exchanged a glance, shook their heads in a *WTF* expression, and sat sullenly.

"Have a seat," said Poly, "and start talking."

The two of them sat side by side in the center of a large sectional sofa, looking wary—and a bit nervous. The rest of us were in nearby chairs or on the right-angled portions of the sofa. I perched on the arm of the chair where Poly was sitting.

"Stay away from the edge," said Rosalind, using her maternal radar.

Max dutifully moved away. Chit left me and flew to land on my son's shoulder. I don't know what she whispered to him, but the two of them went to the back wall where the Verne Wells & Company models were located. I think Chit wanted to try operating the toy Martian tripod from the inside.

Cornell brought our prisoners a couple of glasses of a dark amber liquid from the bar. Their bound hands had just enough play to grasp the tumblers.

"Drink up," he said. "I expect you'll need some liquid courage."

"You're with *them* now?" asked Johnson, looking from Poly to me.

"Unlike some people, *they're* not trying to kill me," responded Cornell.

"Why did you kidnap *us?*" asked Rosalind.

I was enjoying this interrogation. The former bad guys were doing all the work.

"It's all a big misunderstanding," said Scott Winfield. "We weren't trying to kidnap you, we were trying to get you out of harm's way."

"What do you mean?" asked Sally.

"After The General shot down our plane, we were afraid you'd be next in line for removal," Winfield replied.

"We need your help," said Johnson, "if we're going to stop him from terminating us…"

"…with extreme prejudice," added Winfield.

"Then why send your goons to sweeten and kidnap us?" asked Rosalind.

"They may have gotten carried away," said Winfield. "We just asked them to bring you here in a hurry."

"*We* were the ones carried away," said Rosalind, "and we didn't appreciate it."

"Sorry about that," said Johnson.

She actually did look sorry. I could understand how it happened. Give a goon a sweetener and he'll want to use it.

"Good help is hard to find," added Cornell, "especially with what you're probably paying."

"Your team didn't do much better," said Winfield.

"That wasn't me," said Cornell. "That was Zwilniki. He was always trying to cut corners and go with the lowest bidder."

I filed that away for future reference. Low-quality mercenaries could have been why Zwilniki's forces were so easy to defeat.

"Let me get this straight…" said Poly.

"Aren't you the person I fought at the power station?" asked Winfield.

"Yes, and I was kicking your butt," said my partner.

"Until Josie and I kicked yours—and your friend's," said Winfield.

"I wouldn't call pulling a gun on me kicking my butt."

"Details," said Winfield.

Poly glared at him and he closed his mouth.

"You said you'd brought your associates here for their own protection—so The General wouldn't try to kill them, too?" asked my partner.

Johnson and Winfield nodded. Winfield drank some of the liquid in his glass and grimaced.

"And you wanted help from Rosalind and Cornell and Sally to help take him down?" Poly continued.

"Correct," said Johnson.

Now *she* took a sip of whatever was in her glass. I guessed it was an expensive single malt scotch. That was Cornell's style, especially when he wasn't paying for it.

Poly looked over at Rosalind and Rosalind picked up her cue.

"We'd agreed to work with Jack and Poly to take down The General before we were abducted."

Cornell and Sally both confirmed Rosalind's statement.

"If we join forces, our odds of winning go up," said Poly.

Cornell coughed—it sounded like he was covering up a rude comment.

"What?" I said.

"For all the good it will do us," Cornell replied. "Increasing our odds of success from five percent to ten percent isn't much."

Sally surprised me by chiming in. "It's doubling our chances."

I was a bit more optimistic, but that was probably because I didn't have all the data.

"What do you two bring to the table?" asked Winfield, looking at Poly and me.

"Can't be much compared to us," said Johnson, reinforcing her colleague's arrogance. "After all, we're executives with an entire corporation's resources behind us."

"And detailed knowledge of our segment of The General's operation," added Winfield.

Rosalind cut them off. "Think again. You're both declared dead. The General has installed a new management team to run C&C."

"And your understanding of your portfolio in The General's operation is growing more out of date by the hour," said Cornell. He crossed back to the bar and poured himself a glass of the same stuff he'd given our prisoners. This time, I got a look at the label: Glenmorangie Pride.

My phone buzzed. I looked down at its screen. "Over four thousand galcreds a bottle," it read. I was impressed, and I don't even drink. Still, it would be coming out of Chapultepec & Castle's budget—or would it? No, Winfield and Johnson were smart enough not to charge renting Nicky Stone's fortress villa using an easily traceable corporate account.

"And you know so much more?" asked Josephine Johnson in her flay-the-underlings voice.

"I do," said Cornell quietly.

Say what? Cornell was higher up in The General's organization than Winfield and Johnson? If those two were part of the Nine, did that make Cornell the Mouth of Sauron?

"The General practices good organizational security," said Cornell. "Chief lieutenants know everything about their own silos, but nothing about the others. Only a few of us have been allowed to work across multiple silos."

"Well aren't *you* special," said Johnson.

"Yes, he is," said Sally.

Every time she spoke it came as a surprise.

Josephine Johnson turned around to stare at Sally.

"And who are you, sweetcakes," she asked, "the flippin' Queen of May?"

Sally trained her mini-sweetener directly at Johnson and gave her a far-from-friendly smile. "Wouldn't you like to know?"

Poly and I could both see this was getting out of hand. We needed to cooperate if we were to have any chance at taking down The General. My phone decided to exercise its initiative and made a loud noise resembling a coach's whistle. It made my ears ring, but it got everybody's attention.

"Are you in or out?" asked Poly. "Our odds of success are higher if we work together. Or you could catch the next starliner to Midgard or Terminus and hope The General doesn't come after you."

Midgard was an Earth colony word somewhat colder than Terra, settled primarily by Scandinavians and Finns. Fifty percent of it was covered by glaciers, but the land near its equator was on a par with Manitoba—in winter. Agriculture there was mostly hydroponics and cabin fever was endemic. It was only a garden spot if you were growing rocks. The residents were working on warming the place up, but it would take a few more generations.

Terminus wasn't much better. It was a distant, resource-poor planet settled by a small colony of human academics five years after first contact. The colonists, inspired by Isaac Asimov's *Foundation* series, were trying to write the definitive Galactic Encyclopedia.

Unfortunately, academic infighting brought their grand project to a standstill. It also turned out that faculty members can't run planets effectively. The government, infrastructure, law enforcement and immigration services were currently controlled by a cabal of political science graduate students evenly split between Marxists and anarcho-capitalists. Broadcasts of their deliberations rated almost as high as ones from the United States Congress.

"Good luck with that," said Cornell.

Winfield and Johnson looked uncomfortable. They whispered to each other. My phone would be able to tell me what they said later, if it mattered. After lots of *sotto voce* discussion and several lemon-sucking faces, they appeared to make up their minds.

"We're in," said Johnson.

She seemed reluctant, but I expect joining us counted as the lesser of two evils.

"There are some ground rules," I said.

Everybody looked at me. This was new.

"First, no killing."

Several faces looked at me like I was a wimp for requiring that condition, but they'd have to lump it. After a few beats our new and newest allies nodded.

"Second, we share what we know."

I didn't expect this requirement to have much impact, but I'd put it on the table so I'd have a good reason to pull information out of the others when it felt like they were holding back. This time the nods came faster. I knew everyone except Poly was lying, but took what I could get.

"Third, no hidden agendas."

Rosalind smiled and Cornell laughed. Sally covered her mouth with the hand that wasn't holding her mini-sweetener. Johnson and Winfield looked serious.

"Okay," I said. "I know we'll all have hidden agendas. There will be important choices to make about who controls what after we take down The General."

Everyone nodded.

"But if we don't put those agendas on the back burner and focus on The General's defeat, our odds of success go way down. Can we work together to accomplish our primary goal first, *then* switch gears to see what we can get out of it individually?"

I looked around the room.

"Rosalind?"

"I can do that."

"Cornell?"

"Yeah, yeah. All for one and all that nonsense."

I stared at him.

"Okay. I'm in," he said. He made a sword thrust gesture, turning his words into a joke and diffusing some of the tension in the room.

"What he said," added Sally.

Chit's deep voice came from the back of the room near Max.

"I'm in," she said. "Gotta stick together so I can keep you out o' trouble."

"Thanks," I said.

My phone buzzed and showed a thumbs-up symbol on its luminous screen.

Johnson and Winfield just looked at me unhappily.

"Untie them, please."

My phone crossed the distance to our prisoners on a dozen tiny legs and used an extruded blade to cut their bonds. It was a shame to destroy a pair of expensive scarves, but I wasn't particularly worried about destruction of property at the moment.

Johnson rubbed her wrists and Winfield stretched his limbs to encourage his circulation. Sally took a step back to keep her mini-sweetener out of range of Winfield's arms. I'd have to emulate her and boost my paranoia level to deal with our new allies.

Poly spoke up. "Well?"

"I think you're naïve," said Johnson, "but I'm on board."

"Me too," said Winfield. "Let's get to it."

"An excellent idea," said Poly. "Cornell, you seem to be closest to The General. What can you tell us?"

"Not as much as you might think. The General never meets anyone face to face. It's always by phone or screen with his face disguised."

I sighed. This was going to be harder than I'd hoped.

"I don't know The General's age or gender or even species, for that matter," Cornell continued.

"The General might not be *human*?" asked Johnson.

She must be a Terran chauvinist, given the intensity behind her question. Since EUA was behind the Earth First Militant organization, that made sense.

"That's the problem, Josephine," said Cornell. "I don't *know*. Have you and Scott learned anything more from your interactions?"

"No," said Johnson, slowly shaking her head from side to side.

"The General *has* to be human," said Winfield. "He's all about Earth conquering the galaxy."

"You're probably right," said Cornell, "and I'd make a large bet that he's a Terran man, but my point is that we don't have anything to go on."

"You must have tried to figure it out," said Poly.

"I tried," verified Cornell, "but it's not as easy as confirming that Batman is Bruce Wayne."

"What?" said Max from the back of the room.

"Nothin', kid," said Chit. "Just some adults goofin' around…"

"Ixnay on the oilers-spay," said Rosalind to Cornell, making us all smile.

"We confirmed that the majority of his emails originate from servers in and near Atlanta," said Winfield.

"After tracking them back through several layers of redirection," added Johnson.

"From his vocabulary and the idioms he uses, I'd say The General is in his mid-to-late thirties, or learned English from someone that age," said Rosalind.

"I don't think English is his first language," said Sally.

"What makes you say that?" asked Poly.

"Odd turns of phrase here and there," said Sally.

I was surprised again. I wouldn't have expected her to be high enough up in the EUA hierarchy to ever talk to The General directly.

Before I could raise the question, Poly beat me to it.

"Where do all of you fit into EUA?" she asked.

"We run Chapultepec & Castle," said Winfield. "We're part of the Nine."

"Or we *were,*" said Johnson.

Poly looked at Cornell.

"I'm one of a very small group of troubleshooters reporting directly to The General," he said. "We're his eyes and ears across his organization."

"But you do more than just look and listen," I said.

"Correct," said Cornell.

There was a lot in there he wasn't saying.

"What about you?" asked Poly, turning her head to face Rosalind.

"My role is similar to my brother's," she said, "but more focused on external intelligence gathering."

"So you spy on other companies and Cornell spies on EUA divisions?"

"That's reasonably accurate," said Rosalind.

"How about you?" Poly asked Sally.

"I support Cornell and Rosalind as necessary."

"Like on Mission Impossible when they put a team together?" I asked, jumping in.

"Exactly like that," said Sally.

I couldn't tell if she was mocking me, but the odds were good.

"Whoopie," I said. "The General could be any age, any gender, and any species. He, she or it is probably based in Atlanta, but could be anywhere. He's probably a Terran chauvinist and may not be a native English speaker. Anything else?"

"He's rich," said Cornell.

"Uber rich," said Rosalind.

"Top one thousandth of one percent rich," said Sally.

"Why do you think so?" asked Poly.

"The size of EUA," said Cornell.

"And EUA is just the tip of the iceberg," said Sally.

"We're talking oligarch-level or higher," noted Rosalind.

I posed the question.

"People like… ?"

"Nicky Stone," said Sally.

The owner of this fortress villa.

"Pablo Daniel Figueres," said Cornell.

The man behind the Sirocco Legislative Network and the SLN Capital hotel.

"George Crispos or Janet Yu," continued Cornell.

The CEO and the Chairman of GalCon Systems.

"Cross them off the list," said Poly.

"But…" said Cornell.

"Cross them off."

"Right," said Cornell.

"Roger Joe-Bob Bacon," said Rosalind.

"What?"

Poly and I both said the word at the same time.

"No way," said Poly. "He's too nice."

"It's a stretch," I said.

"The point is," said Rosalind, "we don't know enough to count him out as a candidate."

"I'll concede the point—but what's our next step?" I asked.

For a few seconds, nobody spoke. Then Poly recommended a course of action.

"We need to go back to Atlanta," she asserted.

"Because Atlanta is The General's primary base of operations?" asked Johnson.

That, and because Poly wanted to be with her sister Pomy, who was being sued by EUA for blowing up Factor-E-Flor's headquarters.

"Sounds like a plan," I said.

"How do we get back there without having a close encounter with a surface-to-air missile?" asked Winfield.

I could appreciate why he was sensitive about the question.

I noticed Max had moved away from the back of the room and was again getting dangerously close to the front where the floor-to-ceiling windows had been. He was pointing.

"Mommy, mommy!" he shouted excitedly.

"Yes, Max?" asked Rosalind, moving quickly to intercept our son before he could get closer to the edge.

"We've got visitors," said Chit's deep voice.

I never understood how she produced a resonance like that using only tiny breathing spiracles.

I canceled my fear-flight-fright reaction when I saw the size and color of the approaching dirigible.

It was Queen Sherrhi's giant private airship in all its Dauushan-pink glory. The *Matriarch of the Skies* had arrived.

Chapter 6

"Friends are the best to turn to when
you're having a rough day."
— Justin Bieber

I found the controls that extended the airship docking platform and watched it slide out with a series of clanks. I smiled to realize one of the windows had been a sliding door that would have made my earlier entrance easier, if much less exciting.

Small multi-armed robots working under the direction of the *Matriarch of the Skies'* crew tied lines to the platform's mooring mast. When the airship was secured, Martin, Shepherd, Terrhi and Spike joined us in Nicky Stone's fortress villa. Terrhi's parents, Tomáso and Queen Sherrhiliandarianne, stayed on board. Since adult Dauushans are the size of full-grown African elephants, there wasn't really room for them inside and I wasn't confident the slender docking platform could handle an adult Dauushan's weight.

I made awkward introductions all around, ending with, "And this is Rosalind, the mother of my son Max. We met when I was in graduate school back on Orish."

I was on the receiving end of several raised eyebrows, but Terrhi took it in stride, beamed at me, and trumpeted her delight with three sub-trunks. After giving me a hug, she and Spike bustled off with Max. The three of them played happily together in the back of the living room while the grownups talked.

The new arrivals were surprised to discover that we'd joined forces with our former adversaries and would be working together to identify and defeat The General. As our mutual information exchange continued, Poly and I learned that the royal Dauushan dirigible had picked up Martin and his vehicle and had stored the latter in its capacious hold.

Shepherd told us that Tomáso and Queen Sherrhi were making great progress recovering from being drugged and brainwashed by Winfield and Johnson. We agreed that it was just as well that the Dauushan monarch and her consort could be briefed on the C&C executives' new status before seeing them face-to-face.

Martin kept a distrustful eye on Cornell and Rosalind, but paid special attention to Sally. She had been the one to trip him back in the K Street Bar, causing Martin to accidentally trigger his mini-sweetener and freeze places a man emphatically does *not* want to be frozen.

Shepherd was more concerned about Winfield and Johnson. He was almost salivating over the possibility of interrogating them. I'd have to talk to him privately about that. For them to be useful, they'd need to be treated like allies, not prisoners.

The Pâkk seemed quiet and thoughtful when he found out about Max. He nodded to acknowledge the news, nothing more. I could sense gears turning in Shepherd's head as he fit Max's existence into his complex model of the galaxy. Then again, with Shepherd, gears were always turning.

Martin, on the other hand, couldn't let it go. He slapped me on the back, told me about the joys of fatherhood, and congratulated me on missing out on changing diapers, late night feedings, and croup. It was hard to take, since I deeply regretted missing out on seeing Max go through those stages. I wasn't there to hear his first word, help him learn to walk, or teach him how to play catch. I didn't let on how I was feeling and was glad when Poly changed the subject.

"…so that's why we need to get to Atlanta fast, without getting shot down in the process. Any ideas?"

Terrhi spoke up from the back of the room where Max was rubbing Spike's belly.

"I know how you can do it, Aunt Poly."

"You do?" replied my partner. "How?"

"You can go in the *Charalindhri*. It's got plenty of room and will get you there in minutes. Mom needs to get back to Atlanta soon for a big meeting, so they're headed there anyway."

The *Charalindhri* is an asteroid mining ship twenty kilometers in diameter that the Dauushan monarchy had repurposed as a warship. It was currently floating in synchronous orbit above Las Vegas—and my mom was on board, working in the engineering department.

I wasn't looking forward to telling my mother she had an almost five-year-old grandson. I'd been too embarrassed to let her know about Rosalind, so it would hit her out of the blue.

Maybe Gus could *carry* me back to Atlanta?

"Thanks, Terrhi," said Poly. "The *Charalindhri* is a great idea."

Terrhi waved her sub-trunks with pleasure and Max did a series of moves that resembled modern dance crossed with acrobatics and involved jumping and tumbling over Spike several times. The tri-sabertooth cat took it in stride, but managed to lick Max from his sternum to the top of his forehead with a raspy tongue when he strayed too close to Spike's mouth. Max just giggled.

"I will contact Lohrri and Naddéo on the *Matriarch of the Skies* and have them make arrangements for a shuttle to transport you up to the *Charalindhri,*" said Shepherd.

"They can land on top of the butte to reduce the time we're at risk from missiles," said Josephine Johnson.

"The top of the butte is mined," Scott Winfield reminded her.

"Who cares?" said Johnson. "Melt the surface with a heat beam and the mines won't be a factor. They'll melt, too."

"I don't think Nicky Stone would approve of us eliminating part of his security system," I said.

Johnson continued her dismissive attitude. "So what?"

"So you're already going to lose your security deposit and then some over the windows," I said.

The former C&C executive laughed. "No way," she said. "We rented the place through a shell company so that The General wouldn't trace it back to us. Even if Nicky Stone's property managers *did* trace it back to us, as far as the world is concerned, we're dead. And if they somehow discover we're alive…"

Like from the fortress villa's security cameras…

"…we'll blame the damage on *you.*"

"Thanks for that," I said, in my most insincere voice.

Martin had been following our conversation and joined in. "Once we're all out of here, I'll send an anonymous message to the Clark County Sheriff's office, letting them know about the broken glass. They'll send an official county dirigible out to inspect the place and can contact the property management company. Once they evaluate the damage, they'll see to the repairs."

"Great," I said. "Thanks for your help."

I just didn't feel right about leaving the place open to the elements and anyone light-fingered with lighter than air transportation.

"Don't worry about anything getting wet," said Sally. "It never rains in Vegas at this time of year."

I ruefully shook my head from side to side, remembering the brief rainstorm that had caused me to lose my hold when I was climbing the side of the butte. Climate is what you expect—weather is what you get.

It would probably also be a good idea for us to delete the fortress villa's security videos to cover our own tracks. I was sure Poly and Rosalind incapacitating more than a dozen goons would play well on YouTube and would quickly come to The General's attention. I reached for my phone to start the process, but it wasn't there. I checked the room and spotted it crawling down the near wall just under a beautifully jeweled sconce light that would make a perfect hiding place for a miniature camera. I moved closer and my phone hopped over to my shoulder.

"Did you get everything?"

"From the local server and local backups," said my phone. "A custom-tailored virus took out the cloud copies."

"Thanks! Nice use of initiative."

I didn't know it was possible for a phone to glow with pleasure, not just internal LEDs.

"You *did* save me a copy of Poly and Rosalind kicking butt, didn't you?"

"Of course," said my phone. "Max was impressive, too."

"For an almost five-year-old?"

"For anybody."

Now it was my turn to glow—with paternal pride.

"What do we do with all these goons?" asked Rosalind, pointing at the frozen henchmen piled up against the far wall.

"We'll take care of them," said Shepherd. "We'll put them in a cargo hold and guard them for a few days to give you a running start before The General learns what happened."

"You could just drop them in the middle of the desert," Scott Winfield suggested.

I realized I'd have to work with the man, but I didn't have to like him. I caught his eye and gave him a disapproving look.

"Hey," said Winfield. "We'd give them food and water."

Maybe Winfield wasn't a *complete* ogre?

"I've got a better idea," said Poly. "Let me have your phone."

I gave her a quick hug and my phone switched from my shoulder to hers. The two of them conferred for a few seconds and Poly smiled.

"There are only two telecommunications links for this complex," she said.

"Simple redundancy," I replied.

"Right," said Poly. "One is a congruent connection to Nicky Stone's corporate network facility in Houston and the other is a fiber-optic cable tied to the Las Vegas grid. If we go to the server room two floors down and disable the hard-wired phones, then take the goons' cell phones, they won't be able to communicate with the outside world. I'm sure they'd be happier waiting here in comfort instead of trying to survive on their own in the desert."

Cornell, Rosalind and Sally understood our plan and started searching the goons' clothing for phones and other communications devices. Poly and I followed my phone's instructions and headed downstairs for the server room. We held hands as we walked.

"Jack," said Poly. "We need to talk."

Boy, did we. For hours—but we didn't have that long right now.

"Let's do what we came for, *then* talk," I said.

She squeezed my hand extra-hard in confirmation. It only took a few minutes to erase any incriminating evidence.

My phone figured out how to throw the deadbolt on the inside of the server room, then crawl back out to us through the plenum overhead. We paused outside the room's now-secured door with me looking tenderly at my partner.

"I'm sorry."

"For what?" said Poly.

She sounded like she did when she'd told me about her relationship with her sister Pomy—all raw nerves with her fears close to the surface.

"For getting you stuck in a relationship with a guy who's got a child."

"Why? You didn't know. It was just as big a surprise for you. I can see how much it hurts you not to have known about Max from the beginning."

"But it changes everything…"

"Not really," said Poly. "Max may make things more complicated, but his existence doesn't change the way we feel about each other, right?"

"Uh… right."

"Good answer," said Poly. She sounded rational, but still was really concerned about *something*. I kept listening. "Max is a cool kid. Seeing him helps me imagine what *you* were like at his age. I'm not thrilled by the circumstances or having Rosalind a permanent part of your life—*our* lives—but now that he's here I'm glad *Max* will be part of our lives."

This conversation wasn't going the way I expected. Poly wasn't angry, though she'd made it clear that Max was welcome but Rosalind was not. Poly's body language was projecting something more like anxiety than anger.

"So you're okay with the situation?" I asked.

"Okay is too strong a word—accepting and appreciating are probably better ones."

"I can see that," I said, now puzzled. "If Max and Rosalind aren't the problem, what is?"

"I'm scared," said Poly.

I gave her a long hug, then released her and moved a step back, keeping my hands on her shoulders.

"You just took down more than a dozen goons. What do *you* have to be scared about?"

"When we get to the *Charalindhri,* I'm going to meet your *mother!*"

Chapter 7

"The Shuttle is to space flight what Lindbergh
was to commercial aviation."
— Arthur C. Clarke

Rosalind and Cornell zapped the goons one last time to give us more time to make a clean getaway. My understanding was that sweetening someone three times in one day was the maximum recommended dosage of chilling out. More than that was tied to cumulative physiological problems akin to football players getting too many whacks on their helmets. It felt odd to be more concerned for the goons than Winfield and Johnson, though. That pair were blasé about their henchmen's fate, even though they'd been, you know, *their* underlings.

I hoped I'd never turn into the kind of corporate leader who considered the people who worked for him to be mere cogs in a corporate machine, replaceable components who could be abandoned at a moment's notice. I was confident I wasn't the kind of CEO who scored high on tests to identify psychopaths and sociopaths, but realized that belief could be a sign that I was one. In the far from likely event I ever strayed in that direction, I knew I could count on Poly to keep me from embracing the Dark Side.

The *Sky Mama* ferried our not-so-merry band of Atlanta-bound travelers down to a flat stretch of empty desert near the butte. Eighteen of us were waiting for the shuttle to the *Charalindhri*. We ranged in size from Chit to Queen Sherrhi, including Spike and three of the Queen's royal body guards— my friends Diágo, Lohrri, and Naddéo. I'd hoped the shuttle wouldn't be too crowded, but soon learned that wouldn't be an issue. A boxy, not particularly aerodynamically-shaped Dauushan-pink craft descended toward us, making a low-pitched *whoosh* as displaced air moved out of its way. Its intense, highly saturated color made it stand out in distinct contrast to the blue sky overhead. The rain clouds that had plagued me earlier must have retreated over the eastern horizon—or, given the relative humidity, simply evaporated.

The shuttle pilot angled the vessel's congruency-powered thrusters away from us so we didn't have to endure a sandstorm when it touched down. Human skin is far more delicate than a Dauushan's hide, which meant my epidermis was particularly grateful for the consideration.

The ground-to-orbit transport looked like a Borg cube or a toy block for a Godzilla-sized Gojon. It was only slightly smaller than a basketball court, so there was plenty of room aboard for five elephant-sized aliens and the rest of us. The shuttle's hold was huge and the floor below us was resilient, made from a mutable meta-material I recognized from my graduate school days back on Orish.

We'd just gotten ourselves sorted out. Our suitcases from Martin's Jeep Land Rover were stowed and whatever the Queen and her entourage used for luggage—something the size of a fifty-two-foot shipping container—was bolted to the outside of the hull.

We organized ourselves into small clumps. Poly and I were standing together holding hands. Sally, Cornell. Rosalind, Max, Terrhi and Spike were in a group, with Terrhi playing a reflex-testing hand-slapping game with Max using two of her sub-trunks. Shepherd and Martin were next to each other, but they most definitely were *not* holding hands. Winfield and Johnson stood in a corner apart from the rest of us with a shared wary expression on their faces. The adult Dauushans were on the far side of the compartment. Tomáso and Queen Sherrhi were looking particularly tender towards each other, their sub-trunks entwined. Diágo, Lohrri, and Naddéo formed a protective perimeter around their monarch and her consort.

Where was Chit?

I spotted my little friend perched on Rosalind's shoulder and wondered what the two of them might be talking about. I didn't have much time to reflect on that, however, because our pilot started to deliver an announcement from the cockpit as soon as the loading ramp had closed.

"Good afternoon, ladies and gentlebeings, and thank you for flying with Royal Dauushan. Our flight time from ground to docking with the *Charalindhri* in orbit will be fourteen minutes, twenty-seven seconds, and our maximum acceleration will be one point five Terran gravities. At this time, please make sure your seat backs and tray tables are in their full upright position and that your personal restraint systems are correctly fastened. Your flight crew will be circulating around the cabin if you have any questions. Weather at our destination will be perfect, as it is every day, since the *Chara* is fully climate-controlled and maintained at Dauushan planetary optimum. Have a nice flight and enjoy the ride."

Poly and I laughed.

Terrhi let out a girlish squeal of delight. "Cousin Pattéo is so funny," she exclaimed. "I've missed hearing his voice. Did you know he makes the most amazing furniture?"

The Shetland pony-sized princess turned to Max and winked her upper eye. "He's been giving announcements like that ever since he finished Terran atmosphere pilot's training with Southwest-Air New Zealand last year."

Max didn't know what his new friend was talking about, so he made a goofy face at Terrhi and pulled Spike's tail—*gently.* I was glad to see my son had at least *some* instinct for self-preservation. The big cat didn't react at first. I think he indulged Max initially, treating him like some sort of clueless kitten. When he didn't *stop* pulling, Spike turned his massive head, looked directly at Max, and yawned, showing off incisors that would make a Pleistocene-era *Smilodon* jealous. Max dropped Spike's tail like it was an angry rattlesnake and moved closer to his mother.

Poly and I looked away so Max wouldn't see us grinning. I leaned in close to my business partner and paramour.

"Pattéo?" I whispered. "Real cousin or honorary cousin, do you think?"

"Real," she said quietly. "Relatives of the royal family seem to get preferential treatment in Dauushan culture."

"I wonder if there are any species where rank does *not* have its privileges?" I asked.

"In all the years I spent visiting planets with my mother, I never found one," said Poly.

She gave me a quick hug, then the two of us had fun making sure the restraint system would allow us to cuddle together. As I'd suspected when I'd recognized the material forming the hold's surface, the shuttle used the latest Orishen technology to keep us from bouncing around in flight. Parts of the floor below us became selectively concave—small dips for humans, deep depressions for Dauushans.

When we sat down, spider-like webbing automatically extruded itself around us, leaving our limbs and manipulating trunks free. I'd read about this stuff on Orish and knew that if the pilot turned off the equivalent of the Fasten Seat Belts sign, which would be unlikely on such a short hop, the webbing would be reabsorbed by the smart floor and ready for future deployment. It was a very efficient system, especially when you didn't know how many individuals of what different species you were transporting.

Poly and I were enjoying our restraint system cocoon, though I could sense her elevated pulse rate through her hand.

"There's nothing to worry about. My mom's nice. You heard her voice on the phone when I called her. She told me to give you and Pomy hugs."

"I remember," said Poly, "and your mom *did* sound nice. But I'm still nervous. Weren't you worried when you met *my* mother and father?"

"That was different," I said. "After all the buildup you'd given me about them being ogres…"

"…which turned out to be an understatement…"

"…how could you expect me *not* to be nervous about meeting them?" I asked.

"Yes, but it's different when you bring a girl home to meet your mother for the first time."

I protested. "You're not a girl, you're…"

Poly moved my hand strategically.

"I am too a girl," she said, proving her point.

We both giggled, but nobody looked our way. We were covered in webbing, so we weren't being indiscreet.

"As I was saying," I continued, "You're a highly competent, well-educated woman and my business partner, not just my girlfriend. My mom knows about you and even seems to know *your* mother…"

Poly's eyes widened. "I hope they haven't been comparing notes!"

"I doubt it," I said. "Mom doesn't have much time for gossip. She's an engineer—a power systems engineer at that. If it's not relevant to congruent electric generator couplings, she's not interested."

"What's she like?" asked Poly.

"She'll like *you*," I said.

"No," said Poly, poking me in the ribs with a finger, then regretting it because she'd forgotten about my Kevlar-like Orishen pupa silk shirt. She nipped my earlobe instead. "That's not what I meant. Describe her, please."

"Mom's tall, like me. She's got Welsh-auburn hair almost the same shade as yours…"

"You only love me because I remind you of your mother?" teased Poly.

"That, and other reasons."

"Keep talking."

"She's smart. Smarter than I am."

Poly shook her head when I said that. I appreciated the vote of confidence in my brainpower.

"She's no nonsense on the job, but has a great sense of humor when she's one on one with you."

"Is that where you got yours?"

"Mostly," I said. "Though my step-dad has a dry wit that I learned to appreciate when I got older. Mom's the sort of person who would laugh at a pratfall—so long as she knew it was staged and not a real accident. I think she had too many years of workplace safety training drilled into her to see it any other way."

"What *doesn't* she like?" asked Poly.

"That's easy," I said. "Phony people. Just be your wonderful self and she'll love you."

"Uh huh," said Poly.

That earned my earlobe another nip.

"How does she feel about children?"

Now it was my turn to feel my pulse racing. I'd been suppressing the fact that I'd soon be introducing my mom to Max. I had no idea how she'd react. I knew she loved me, but also appreciated that she'd liked me a lot more when I was older and could talk about serious engineering matters with her, not cartoons and coloring books. She was particularly pleased when I learned how to put things back together, not just take them apart.

I was optimistic that she'd embrace Max with open arms, but finding out Max existed would be almost as big a shock to Mom as it was to me. I suspected I'd also get the third degree about how it happened, and saying, "in the usual way," wouldn't cut it. I felt a bit like a kid being sent to the principal's office, an analogy that was even more apt because I'd been home schooled by my mother.

"Ch-children?" I stuttered. "In favor, I think?"

Poly shook her head back and forth in a *what am I going to do with this guy* way.

"Did you at least send her a text to let her know we were headed up to the *Charalindhri?*"

I tapped my phone. Maybe it had exercised initiative. It stayed silent—coward.

"No…"

I must have sounded younger than Max.

"Then do it now," said Poly. "You don't want to just show up in Engineering and surprise her."

Now that I thought of it, that idea didn't sound so bad. I could take Max and Poly down to Mom's domain and introduce her to both of them with all her colleagues around, so she couldn't overreact.

Before I could share my plan with Poly I was interrupted by a clank from the airlock and another cheery announcement from Cousin Pattéo.

"Ladies and gentlebeings, I am pleased to announce that we have successfully docked with the *Charalindhri*. You may now disengage your restraint system and feel free to move about the cabin. Thank you for traveling with Royal Dauushan!"

Chapter 8

"Mothers are inscrutable beings to their sons, always."
— A. E. Coppard

I'd hoped to have ten or fifteen minutes to prepare myself, but my mother was waiting for me in the docking bay. I walked off the shuttle holding Poly's hand, with Max and Rosalind right behind us. Poly saw Mom—a tall, auburn-haired woman in grease-stained engineers' coveralls—and correctly assessed her identity. She dropped my hand and stepped away from me, her face turning red like the two of us were teenagers who'd just been caught necking on the living room sofa.

"Jack!" shouted my mom, her arms outstretched.

We came together and she gave me a maternal hug, using muscles powerful enough to lift massive congruent power couplings without mechanical assistance. Having the breath squeezed out of me by her strong arms made me feel like I was *home.* Nobody gave hugs with more solidity and enthusiasm than my mom. I hugged her back and realized I should have made time to get up to the *Chara* to see her sooner. The pressure of Mom's embrace squeezed parts of my body that had been damaged earlier in the week. I tried not to wince, but Mom noticed anyway, ending her hug to hold me at arms' length and giving me a *What have you been up to young man?* expression that I knew quite well. I'd have to give her a complete rundown on my injuries later. Then, following family tradition, Mom gave me a not entirely unexpected compliment.

"You're looking great, son!"

"Thanks," I said. "You, too."

Mom made a wry smile and turned her palms up in a silent *"Who, me?"* gesture. Then she saw Poly and her eyes got big. Mom seemed so happy, the corners of her mouth turned up and kept climbing. She pulled Poly in and gave her a hug with every bit as much enthusiasm as she'd given me. Poly was so surprised she squeaked—a sound I'd never heard her make before. I didn't need to worry. After a few seconds, Poly started to hug her back. I could see Mom smiling and looking relieved.

"Nice to meet you, Ms. Buckston," said Poly when the hug ended.

"It's wonderful to finally meet you, Poly," said Mom. "Call me Nory. I've heard so much about you."

"Who's Poly?" asked Poly with a grin. "My name is Julia."

"Oh, *you!*" said Mom, giving her another tight hug and prompting a second squeak.

"I give, I give! I'm Poly!" said my partner when she could draw a breath again.

"I knew it!" said Mom.

She extended her hand to Poly and the two women shook, smiling all the while. After the hugs they'd just exchanged, the handshake was a mere formality.

"Talented, smart, *and* beautiful," said my mom, appraising Poly. "Don't let this one get away, Jack."

"We're together as long as she'll have me," I said.

Poly smiled. This was going better than I'd expected. Then I remembered Max. And Rosalind.

I looked around the docking bay. There weren't any chairs, just empty space. Mom couldn't sit down if she wanted to.

Max was keeping close to Rosalind. I waved him up beside me. He moved hesitantly, his eyes big and curious as he stared at the woman I'd just hugged.

"Mom," I said, figuring I'd just have to plow forward. "This is Max. He's your grandson."

My mother spared a beat to look at me, her eyes as big and curious as Max's. Something in her expression told me that my chance to explain could wait. She made me proud by kneeling next to Max and giving him a grandmotherly hug that looked as enthusiastic as the hug she'd given me, with the intensity of the squeezing recalibrated for the frame of an almost five-year-old.

"Great to meet you, Max," she said when she released the boy. "I'm your Grandma Nory."

"Like the fish?" asked Max.

Mom looked puzzled, so Rosalind interrupted with a clarification.

"No, Max, the fish is *Dory.*"

I had vague memories of seeing bits of *Finding Nemo* and *Finding Dory* on television when I'd flipped through channels, but had considered myself far too old to watch a *children's* movie when Disney and Pixar had released the second installment in the series.

"I knew *that*," said Max, enjoying the attention. "I just meant Nory *sounds* like Dory. I'd never confuse a blue tang fish with my grandmother."

He spoke so earnestly Mom and Poly and Rosalind and I laughed. Mom gave him another hug and Max sniffed, inhaling deeply.

"You smell funny!" he said.

I jumped in to do my part for civilizing the next generation.

"Max! It's not polite to say things like that."

Rosalind looked at me and raised an imaginary flask to her lips with a questioning expression. I shook my head. Mom didn't drink.

"That's my special perfume," said Mom. "Do you like it?"

"Uh huh," said Max. "What is it?"

"Machine oil," said Mom.

"Cool," said Max.

I made a mental note to pick up an extra tin of mechanics' hand cleaner when we got back to Atlanta. I had a feeling my son would be needing it.

Mom stood up and faced Rosalind.

"Who's this?" she asked. I think she'd already put the cube root of eight and the first even integer together to get four.

"Rosalind," I said. "Max's mom."

My mother was better at dealing with heavy machinery than human body language, but even her limited interpersonal radar could sense that Rosalind got a handshake, not a hug. She extended her hand and Rosalind shook it.

"A pleasure to meet you," said Rosalind.

"Likewise," said my mom, keeping her guard up.

The adults exchanged looks worth a hundred thousand words, laden with subtext. Max stood between his mother and his grandmother, smiling.

All of us were walking on eggshells, trying to avoid the elephant in the docking bay, when Terrhi and Spike charged in to say hello. The little Dauushan girl stopped in front of my mom and hugged her around the waist with her outer trunks.

"Miss Nory, it's so good to see you again!" she said. "Isn't Poly pretty? And smart? And fun—just like I told you? Her sister Pomy is like that too, but Jack only has eyes for Poly. Spike thinks they're great together—don't you Spike?"

Terrhi was on a roll, words bubbling like cheese on a pizza hot out of the oven. Which reminded me—I'd skipped lunch.

I was also pleased to clear up a mystery. I now knew who'd told my mother about my romance with Poly and the injuries I'd sustained back in Atlanta when Poly's family was in town. It wasn't a little birdie—it was a little girl.

Mom started backing away from the shuttle entrance and heading for the far side of the docking bay while she listened to Terrhi bring her up to date on our adventures over the past week. Spike graciously allowed Max to ride—or attempt to ride—his broad back and even permitted a few undignified ear-tugs before gently shaking him off and pinning him down with one plate-sized forepaw. Max giggled as the tri-sabertooth licked his face.

Then I realized what Mom had been doing—getting us out of the way. Cornell and Sally and Winfield and Johnson followed her lead and moved with us off to the side. Shepherd and Martin soon joined them.

A fanfare of deep Dauushan brass instruments played over the ship's speakers and Queen Sherrhi and Tomáso stepped off the shuttle. With the queen and her consort, plus three members of her royal guard close behind, the docking bay was getting crowded. I hoped Chit was smart enough not to get underfoot, then remembered she was with Rosalind the last time I'd seen her.

Soon there was even *less* room in the docking bay when yet another adult Dauushan entered through the door to the ship and joined us. She had a pattern of five interlocking dark pink circles painted on her shoulders. They looked like rank insignia of some kind.

"Captain Auntie!" shouted Terrhi.

The girl wrapped her trunks around the new arrival's front legs and made gleeful noises like preteens gushing over the leader of a boy band.

"Welcome, Your Matriarchal Majesty," said the newcomer.

"Hi, Sis," said Queen Sherrhi. "How's the *Charalindhri* checking out on its shakedown cruise?"

Sis? I didn't know the queen had a sister—but it made sense. Royal houses always needed an heir and a spare.

"It's performing quite well," said the newcomer a bit coldly.

Poly leaned close and whispered to me.

"The five circles on her shoulders mean she's the ship's captain."

"And apparently Terrhi's *real* aunt," I replied, softly.

"Except for that fortuitous heat beam failure last Sunday," said Sherrhi, smiling.

"Except for that," said the newcomer, glancing at my mother, but not returning the queen's smile.

Tomáso nudged his regal mate.

"Where are my manners?" said Queen Sherrhi. "Everyone, this is my sister Lüzhiulterianne, next in line in the royal succession after Terrhi and the best starship captain in my family. Lüzhi, this is everybody."

I nodded. Max waved and the rest of our party made various gestures of acknowledgment. From Lüzhi's reaction, I had the sense she'd been fully briefed on our identities.

Terrhi released her aunt and looked up at her mother.

"I thought you said Aunt Lüzhi was the best starship captain in Dauushan-controlled space?"

Queen Sherrhi smiled at her daughter indulgently.

"Whatever may or may not have been said about my sister Lüzhi's ship-handling skills, a princess must learn discretion.

You shouldn't repeat everything you hear, even if it *is* meant as a compliment."

"Sorry, Mom. I know—think before I talk," said Terrhi, hanging her head in mock contrition then popping it back up to smile at Lüzhi. "But *I* think you're the best pilot in the galaxy, Aunt Lüzhi!"

"Can your ship make the Kessel Run in less than twelve parsecs?" asked Max.

That's my boy!

I looked over at Rosalind and made a thumbs-up sign to thank her for raising Max right. An education in the classics is important.

"The *Charalindhri* can make it in nine and a half, young man," said Captain Lüzhi. All three of her large eyes danced with amusement. Then her expression turned serious and she addressed us all.

"I know you need to get to Atlanta in a hurry, but do you have time for lunch and a tour of the ship?"

Lunch sounded great to me, but Poly squeezed my hand anxiously.

"I'm sorry, Captain," said my partner, "but we really need to get home as fast as we can. I'm concerned about my sister."

"And we need to get on with identifying and neutralizing The General," said Cornell.

His tone had a note of bloodthirsty determination.

"The sooner he's no longer a threat, the sooner we can get on with our lives," added Sally.

"Or get off planet," whispered Johnson to Winfield.

I wished I was a Dauushan, so I'd have *three* eyes to keep watch on that pair.

"Some sort of food would be nice, though," I said. "Maybe sandwiches?"

"It will take the ship fifteen or twenty minutes to reposition itself over Atlanta," said Lüzhi. "You *do* want us overhead, don't you, Your Majesty?"

"Yes," said Queen Sherrhi. "Having you closer would be a good idea."

For some reason, I was reminded of the old maxim about keeping your friends close and your enemies closer, but decided I was imagining things.

"I'll have the galley team make you something to eat while we reposition," said Captain Lüzhi. "They can pack it to go and you can eat it on the trip down."

Tomáso rumbled. "I'd like a pan of cook's *strata* if he has some on hand."

"I'll let him know," responded the Captain.

"Want to see the engine room, Max?" asked my mom.

"Sure," said Max, taking her hand and eagerly starting to follow her down the corridor outside the docking bay.

"Can Spike and I come, too, Miss Nory?" asked Terrhi.

"The more the merrier!"

"Don't get grease all over your clean hide," shouted Queen Sherrhi as the door closed.

Poly stepped close to the Queen and whispered something. Her Matriarchal Majesty nodded her huge head and used three sub-trunks to gently lift Poly up close to her ear. The two of them conferred in relative privacy while I focused on our thick-furred companion.

Shepherd cleared his throat, making a deep, grating sound like a pair of mating Tōdons rubbing chitin. I knew that Shepherd was a Pâkk of few words, so when he did speak, it made sense to listen.

"Here's our plan," he said.

I focused on my grizzled bear-like, wolf-like friend's raspy blues-singer voice, ignoring competing rumbles from my empty stomach.

This ought to be good.

Chapter 9

"…a scientific refuge will be established on Terminus."
— Isaac Asimov, *Foundation*

The cooks on the *Charalindhri* made us delicious sandwiches to eat before and during our shuttle ride down to Atlanta. They were the equivalent of tiny dainties for Dauushans, but were substantial meals for humans. The "bread" part of the sandwiches came from a bamboo-like starchy plant where the foot-long segments were slightly inflated instead of straight. They looked a lot like submarine sandwich rolls but were a bit more dense and a lot more chewy. My sandwich was filled with sweet-glazed spiral-cut HoneyBaked ham. The Dauushan's had fallen in love with the stuff after First Contact—so much so that a Dauushan comestibles conglomerate had purchased the company ten years back. My bet was that both the taste and the color of HoneyBaked Ham's primary product prompted the acquisition.

Along with the ham, my sandwich's fillings included a large pale-pink leaf of Dauushan lettuce and half a dozen reddish-pink tomato-like slices the diameter of a cantaloupe. My ever-reliable phone showed me a photo of the vegetable the slices came from. It grew on vines and looked like a four-foot fuchsia zucchini. A pickled pink vegetable resembling daikon added a tang and crunch I particularly enjoyed.

In addition, my sandwich had something roughly equivalent to cheese that I knew came from a "cow" even bigger than an adult Dauushan. The "cow" looked something like a six-legged hippopotamus the size of an eighteen-wheeler. I'd been told it was quite a chore getting the raw materials for making the cheese because the giant hippocows had to be milked underwater. My taste buds confirmed it was worth the trouble, however. The melded flavors in my sandwich were spectacular. I made a mental note to talk to one of my entrepreneurial restaurateur-clients about starting a chain to sell them.

Cousin Pattéo, the pilot of our shuttle, had arranged to have a real-time video feed broadcast on one wall of our vessel's hold. All my companions, except Terrhi, Spike, Queen Sherrhi, Tomáso, and the queen's bodyguards, were secured into familiar small depressions in the hold's floor. The Royal Family would be staying in orbit until things settled down and their bodyguards considered it safe for them to return to the consulate.

Nine humans—and one Pâkk—were in the same small clusters we'd been in earlier. Max was webbed in tightly next to Rosalind. I'd tried to talk Rosalind into leaving Max with my mother, where he'd probably be in less danger, but she wouldn't hear of it. Now was not the time for me to try to assert my parental rights.

We watched the video screen.

"Shuttle launch in five... four... three... two... one..." announced Pattéo.

Our shuttle remained stationary, but the screen showed another shuttle leaving the *Charalindhri's* docking bay. Remote drone cameras followed the second shuttle as it descended. The right hand third of the screen showed a graphic tracking the shuttle's altitude. The other shuttle went slow enough that it's lower hull didn't glow from the heat of reentry. When it was two miles above Hartsfield spaceport, a pair of surface-to-air missiles rocketed toward it from the west. They struck together and turned the second shuttle into a fiery ball of debris. Then all the scattered pieces fell in on themselves and disappeared through a hole in the sky. One of the missiles must have had a congruency vacuum bomb to eliminate the evidence.

I wasn't really surprised that The General had learned that we were on the *Charalindhri.* He must have spies everywhere. Still, I was impressed by the quality of his intelligence and the scale of his response. One moment the shuttle was there—another moment, it wasn't.

"Launch site identified," said my phone. "It's a derelict warehouse near Carrollton."

I wondered if it was the old Walmart distribution center, made obsolete by low-cost teleportation?

"Great," I said. "Martin?"

"Law enforcement cameras and sensors confirm no one present within a quarter-mile radius."

"Light 'em up," I said.

Shepherd relayed my words to the bridge and a narrow beam of heat energy lashed out from the *Charalindhri,* turning the warehouse into a lava-filled crater. A slow-motion version of the destruction played back on the split screen. We watched the roof of the warehouse melt, revealing missile launching bays beneath. I spotted motors powering the retractable roof before they vaporized. The remaining missiles puddled into slag—no longer a threat.

I let out a sigh of relief that we hadn't seen any personnel in the facility. I didn't want their lives on my conscience.

"Nicely done," I confirmed for the *Chara's* weapons' officers.

"The fake shuttle was really convincing, thanks," said Martin to Shepherd.

"Don't thank me, thank the fabricating technicians on the *Charalindhri,*" said the grizzled Pâkk. "It took them less than an hour to build a full-sized shuttle body around a pair of remote-controlled life boats."

"Exactly what I'd expect from the best species of fabricators in the Galactic Free Trade Association," said Poly.

"Do we need to send another decoy?" asked Winfield, sounding nervous.

I don't think he trusted The General to have only one missile installation. Neither did I.

"I think another decoy would be a great idea," I said.

"Launch the mock Royal Yacht," said Shepherd.

His voice went out across the *Chara's* command net. I knew Shepherd and Tomáso were friends, but I was surprised that Tomáso would give Shepherd *that* much control over the operation of the *Charalindhri* instead of entrusting Captain Lüzhi. Whatever Tomáso's reasons, it was a wise move. He couldn't have picked a better being to lead the effort.

We watched a much smaller vessel float out of the docking bay. This ship was shiny—like rose-tinted chrome—and only a quarter of the size of a shuttle. It had a curved, streamlined shape like a submarine sandwich or a segment of the bamboo-like starch substituting for bread I'd had for lunch. However you slice it, the decoy was a fairly good physical copy of Queen Sherrhi's personal space yacht. I'd seen a framed photograph of the royal yacht, the *Fast Mother,* hanging in Tomáso's study.

I had my doubts about whether The General's forces would fire on it. If anything happened to Her Matriarchal Majesty, it would likely ruin Earth's economy and could force Dauush to take drastic measures—like invading the planet—in retribution. Still, The General and EUA Corporation might *benefit* from an interstellar incident. We'd have to see.

We didn't have a long wait. Another pair of missiles rose from a location to the east this time, heading for the mock yacht when it was five miles up, not two. The extra distance gave the *Chara's* weapons team time to use a smaller heat beam to incinerate them before they could strike. The ship's astrogators traced the missiles' trajectories back to an abandoned cereal plant near Covington.

Martin's official police surveillance sources used advanced thermal imaging to confirm the plant was empty, then the *Charalindhri's* primary heat beam lashed out again, melting the plant's steel roof and transforming the missiles and launchers below into their constituent atoms.

"Time for Operation Shell Game," said Poly. Her tone proved she knew things could still get dicey.

Shepherd gave the word and seven shuttles left the *Charalindhri's* docking bay, heading for Hartsfield Port. Well, six of them did, anyway. The first six were heavily armed and packed with Dauushan Drop Marines. We were in the seventh.

I'd hacked our transponder code, so we were now broadcasting that our shuttle was a scientific research vessel called the *Ramblin' Rex* owned by Georgia Tech. The Dauushan fabricators had done an excellent rush job to ensure our radar profile matched our new identity. They'd even painted a *Jurassic World* tyrannosaur's picture on the side.

Masked by the Drop Marines' shuttles, Cousin Pattéo took us behind the bulk of the *Charalindhri* and over to the Georgia Tech space research station orbiting nearby.

"Do you think this will work?" asked Poly quietly.

"If it doesn't, we'll never know."

"There is that," she said.

The Drop Marines' shuttles were well-armed and armored. They had a chance to defend themselves if more missiles headed their way. Our shuttle's safety relied on misdirection and stealth—and the reflexes of the weapons' officers on the *Chara*.

I could hear Max and Rosalind talking from their webbed cocoon a few feet away. Max sounded earnest, like only a bright almost five-year-old can sound, as he explained what his Grandma Nory had shown him in the engine room. The kid understood a lot more about congruent power systems than I expected, though on a very basic level. I made a note to have "the talk" with him about treating congruencies with respect if he didn't want all the molecules in his body spread out between here and Andromeda. Rosalind's responses to Max convinced me she was a good mother—though I think I'd already known that from observing Max's behavior.

Sally and Cornell kept their heads close together. They were whispering so softly I couldn't hear them, but I could catch the tone of their conversation. My guess was they were trying to figure out what they wanted to do next if by some chance they managed to survive the next few days and take down The General. I liked Sally and her smart-ass ways, though it would take a long time for me to warm to Cornell. He'd done too many things to me and people I care about for me to trust him anytime soon, to say nothing of ever *liking* him.

Winfield and Scott were in the same Orishen restraint webbing but seemed to be two of the same magnetic poles. There was a distance between them that it would take a lot of force to reduce.

Their expressions said they'd be much happier if they were almost anywhere else in the universe but here.

Martin and Shepherd were focused on their jobs. Martin connected down to terrestrial law enforcement systems and Shepherd had a direct line to the Dauushan officers commanding the *Charalindhri*.

We stared at the video screen and watched the military shuttles descend, their interweaving paths in an intricate semi-scripted dance designed to confuse anyone trying to follow their motions. The military shuttles were primarily a distraction, giving Pattéo cover to get behind the Georgia Tech scientific research station and begin our own descent as an erstwhile science vessel. The other shuttles would be returning to the *Charalindhri* after they'd landed at Hartsfield Port. We would not. We couldn't go home—it wasn't safe and would just put our friends and employees at risk.

We considered several options, but Poly was the one to find us a safe haven. She'd called Professor Bartolomeww Urrrson from orbit to get his advice. Her Tigrammath former mentor at Georgia Tech reminded her that Georgia Tech had a new, highly secure research facility west of campus that would be a perfect temporary sanctuary. It included space for the EEL— the Extreme Environments Lab—investigating ultra-hot and ultra-cold temperature physics, and the MDL, the Multiple Dimensions Laboratory exploring the possibility that parallel universes might be accessible through properly tuned congruencies. Given the potentially dangerous nature of both labs' research, the university and the city of Atlanta had insisted the facilities be built below ground.

Pablo Daniel Figueres, the owner of the Sirocco Legislative Network, offered to fund the labs' construction if Georgia Tech and the city allowed him to put an SLN Capital hotel and casino on top. Georgia Tech jumped at their frequent benefactor's offer and the city gladly went along for their cut of the expected revenues in taxes and campaign contributions.

Since it would be at least a year before the Atlanta SLN Capital complex was finished, the underground labs had several small residential suites intended for visiting researchers. The secure labs were so new most of their research and support staff still remained to be hired. They wouldn't be running at full capacity until fall. The research facility would work well as a short-term refuge—so long as The General didn't know we were there.

We watched the video screen carefully and clapped our hands when the fake royal yacht and all six of the military shuttles landed at Hartsfield Port without another missile attack. Cousin Pattéo brought our disguised shuttle in for a perfect feather-light touch-down at Georgia Tech's small dedicated landing zone, much to the disappointment of the *Chara's* weapons officers. We were only a few blocks from the new labs, so we could exit below the shuttle and make our way out of sight through underground tunnels.

Max thought it was all a grand adventure—the rest of us, not so much.

Nobody was around when we arrived, but there were envelopes waiting for us at the labs' reception desk clearly labeled with our room assignments and key cards. Professor Urrrson knew how to get things done fast. I made some quick adjustments to ensure Poly and I were closest to the elevator in case any of our reluctant associates decided to make a break for it. I'd rig an alarm to notify me if anyone tried to pass our room.

We were back in Atlanta, and we were safe, but how long would we stay that way?

Chapter 10

"Divide et impera. Divide and conquer"
— Guiding Principle of the Roman Senate

Poly and I were lucky when we settled into our suite. We had luggage and didn't have to worry about clean underwear. Martin had brought his suitcase and Shepherd's along in his Jeep Land Rover, so they were also covered. Unfortunately, Rosalind, Max, Sally, Cornell, Winfield and Johnson didn't have any luggage. My phone made arrangements to have a modest collection of clothing, toiletries, and other essentials delivered to the receptionist's desk in an hour using funds from an untraceable bank account I kept around for a rainy day. Don't ask.

Before I unpacked I called Mike and gave him a heads-up that Poly and I were in town but wouldn't be back in the office for a few days. I didn't elaborate on why, just noted heightened threat levels. He said he'd tell everybody to be extra-careful. Poly called her sister and gave Pomy details about all the high-powered resources we'd lined up to help defend her against the lawsuit from Factor-E-Flor and EUA Corporation. Pomy was glad to hear the good news and promised to meet us in person as soon as circumstances allowed. We didn't tell Mike or Pomy where we were, for their safety and for ours.

Those tasks accomplished, I looked around our suite. The rooms were comparable to a mid-priced hotel, but with science-themed art, not traditional landscapes. Our room's wall screen was flipping through a slide show of colorful fractal patterns. One of the framed prints hanging on a conventional wall was a cartoon-like etching of Galileo dropping an apple off the top of the Leaning Tower of Pisa and landing on Isaac Newton's head. I had my phone make a note of the artist in case I wanted to commission something for Xenotech Support's future corporate headquarters.

Like a cruise ship cabin, our suite's bedroom had two twin beds that could easily be turned into a king. Poly and I moved the nightstands from the center to the sides and slid the twin beds together. I found the piece of foam to cover the gap between the beds along with the king-sized sheets in the closet. We had fun getting our bed recombobulated and properly tested, if you get my drift. Nothing adds more spice to your love life than not being reduced to a cloud of particles by a surface-to-air missile.

"Now what?" asked Poly, leaning up on one elbow after we'd finished our bed testing.

"Get everyone back together, figure out who knows what, determine our next steps…"

"And set about doing them. Right."

I had to pull my brain away from admiring the curve of her shoulder and the way her wavy auburn hair bounced when she turned her head. Poly smiled when she saw my distraction.

"Do you think we can trust them?" she asked, turning her head from side to side just to tease me.

"Who?"

"Winfield and Johnson. Cornell and Sally."

My eyebrows went up and I shook my head slowly from side to side to indicate "No." I raised my shoulders in a supplemental shrug, which is less effective when you're horizontal than it would have been if I'd been vertical.

Poly paused to observe my response, then added, "Not to forget Rosalind."

Rosalind's name made me grimace. I could be objective about the others, but not about her. Why hadn't I been smarter when I'd met her back on Orish? Why hadn't she told me about Max? Why did I still find Rosalind turning up in my thoughts when I was *so* in love with Poly? For that matter, why hadn't I asked Rosalind if she was using birth control, not that I could have trusted her answer? OMG! *What about Poly?*

"Ground control to Major Tom," said Poly.

"What?" I could have just as easily said, "Huh?"

"Where did you go just then?"

"I was thinking," I said, "about Rosalind and Max and birth control."

Poly's face contorted as she tried—and failed—to suppress a laugh.

"You really *are* an innocent, aren't you," she said, stroking my hair affectionately and kissing the tip of my nose.

"Ummm…." I said. "Guilty as charged. Are you…"

"Of course," she said. "I'm on the new pill."

Galactic Free Trade Association medicine could do more than cure cancer. Nicósn pharmacology had solutions for controlling human fertility that were more effective than traditional Terran birth control pills, with fewer side effects. My friend Mistress Marigold's company, Marigold Flowers & Pharmaceuticals, sold a pill called *Choyse*® that was quite popular. Other Nicósn firms offered competitive and complementary variations, like shots and implants.

"I'm sorry," I said.

"For what?" answered Poly.

"For not discussing it ahead of time, like a responsible adult."

"I forgive you," she said. "See that it doesn't happen again."

"What?" I exclaimed, jolted fully out of my distracted reverie. "Every time?"

"No," said Poly. "Consider the topic covered where you and I are concerned. It's your other bed partners I'm concerned with. I don't want Max to have any half-siblings unless *I'm* their mother."

My eyes went wide and my jaw dropped.

"Not anytime soon, mind you."

"That's okay, then," I said, recomposing myself. "What if I'm not in a *bed* with one of these hypothetical other partners?"

"Don't go looking for loopholes on me, buster," said Poly, lowering the pitch of her voice to imitate Chit.

"I won't," I promised, putting my hand over my heart. "I'll stick to enjoying your delightfully infinite diversity."

That made Poly smile and earned me a real kiss.

"Though how do you feel about options that don't include beds?" I said.

"Like the shower?" said Poly.

She grinned, threw off the sheet and headed in that direction to start the water running.

I told my phone to let everyone know we'd be meeting in one of the facility's small conference rooms in an hour and followed. With luck, we might even have time to remake the bed.

* * * * *

We sat at a round table. I hoped we'd have more success than King Arthur and would avoid ill-advised romantic triangles. The table was big enough for twelve, but there were only eleven of us. More like nine, really, because Chit didn't need a chair and Max didn't stay in his. He'd hopped down and was drawing pictures on the room's smart wall with his fingers, softly singing a song I didn't recognize.

Chit's wing cases were painted in Georgia Tech navy blue and gold. She was sitting in front of me on top of a tall stack of wooden university logo coasters. The stack wasn't quite stable, but would be fine if Chit didn't make any sudden moves.

Poly was directly to my right, with Martin and Shepherd on my left. Our reluctant new allies were opposite. Winfield and Scott sat with empty chairs between them and the rest.

Rosalind, Sally and Cornell sat where they could keep an eye on Max while we kept an eye on them.

My phone had extruded limbs and a head and something that resembled a captain's chair from the original *Star Trek*. It sat like it was ready to say, "Warp factor six, Mr. Sulu." I hoped that meant it was taking our current situation seriously. At least it didn't try to make its featureless stick-figure head look like William Shatner. My phone was more Spock than Kirk, anyway.

"I suppose you're wondering why I've called you here today," I said, invoking an appropriate trope.

"Get to the bottom line, Miss Marple," interjected Josephine Johnson. "What do you want us to do?"

I decided to meet her rudeness with my own.

"I want the two of you to tell us everything you know about The General. The more we know, the faster we'll find him."

Poly, Martin and Shepherd all nodded. Max drew a picture of Spike. I turned to Rosalind, Cornell and Sally.

"The same goes for you."

"We'll cooperate," said Rosalind.

"We said we would," added Sally.

"For all the good it will do us," moped Cornell.

Sally affectionately poked him in the ribs and he sat up straighter.

"Where do we start?" she asked.

"Tell us about your interactions with The General," said Martin. "How does he contact you or vice-versa?"

"Mostly he contacts us," said Scott Winfield.

"By text message," said Josephine Johnson.

"From an intermediary," said Winfield.

Martin nodded.

"We get text messages or flash drives delivered by messengers," contributed Cornell.

"Your mission, should you decide to accept it," I joked.

"There's no 'should you decide' about it," said Sally. "You saw how The General reacts when missions don't go well."

"That's right," said Rosalind. "When The General says jump, you'd better hit geosynchronous orbit."

"How do you report back?" asked Poly.

"We contact Manny," said Cornell.

Finally! A name—something we could work with.

"Who's Manny?" asked Chit.

She looked sideways at my phone. It was kicking at her precarious stack of coasters with one of its extended pseudopod legs—whether from boredom or malice, I couldn't tell.

Cornell answered. "Manny is an A.I., I think. The General once joked about using him to coordinate the revolution that would help Earth conquer the galaxy."

"Probably just another chump," said Chit.

"I don't think so," said Poly. "I think the A.I.'s name is short for Manuel Garcia O'Kelly-Davis."

"Brilliant," I said. "The General is stealing Heinlein's idea from *The Moon Is a Harsh Mistress.*"

"I don't get it," said Martin.

"Of course! How did I miss it?" asked Rosalind.

"There's a famous science fiction novel from the sixties where a computer named Adam Selene helps Luna win its independence from Earth," I explained to Martin. "Using an A.I. is an excellent way to coordinate any sort of covert operation. Manny was a human, his best friend, and the book's narrator. "

"I can see that," said Martin, rubbing his chin. "One of the private law enforcement news sites had an article about an A.I. rigging bids on eBay that made several hundred million galcreds last year."

"Did you say *Manuel?*" asked Winfield.

"Garcia O'Kelly-Davis," said Sally. "Open your ears."

"Put a sock in it, sweetheart," said Winfield. "Manuel is the name of the person *we* contact to get our reports to The General."

"Could your contact also be an A.I.?" I asked, then mentally kicked myself. Of course it could. Any Turing-test certified A.I. could pass for a human.

Winfield and Johnson gave me dirty looks. I ignored them.

"Okay," I said. "This approach is a dead end, except for trying to track down the A.I. angle."

"Ahem," said my phone, clearing its non-existent throat. "There's also the oligarch angle."

"Good point," said Poly. "Show us."

My phone leaned a bit forward in its Federation-standard captain's chair.

"Here's a list of the top one hundred wealthiest Americans," it said.

The top part of the smart wall shimmered, then showed the list. I was grateful that my phone didn't interfere with Max's drawings.

"Why only Americans?" asked Martin.

"I know," said Sally. "It's because of the company names. A lot of them are taken from American history."

"The James K. Polk group," I said.

"Maine Havana Insurance," said Poly.

"Chapultepec & Castle," said Winfield and Johnson in unison.

"Huh?" said Chit.

"It's from the Mexican-American War," said Johnson.

"The Battle of Chapultepec in eighteen forty-seven," added Winfield.

Martin started singing in a pleasant baritone, *"From the halls of Montezuma…"*

"Exactly," said Johnson. "That's where the first line in the *Marines' Hymn* came from."

Who knew?

"Okay, I get it," said Martin. "We start with American oligarchs—which lets Nicky Stone off the hook."

"And Roger Joe-Bob Bacon," I added.

"Correct," said my phone. "Now let's focus on Atlanta-based individuals."

The list contracted from one hundred down to five.

"My mother told me Ted Turner is living in Montana full-time these days," said Poly.

"Yeah. He's ninety-two and fully occupied raising buffalo and cavorting with his twenty-three-year-old nurse," added Sally.

One of the names on the smart wall disappeared.

"The heiress to the Coca-Cola fortune is having a grand time with a gold-digging Pyr in the north of Spain," said Sally. "They're in all the gossip magazines."

Living with a Pyr in the Pyrenees?

Rosalind shook her head. "All those tentacles," she said in a breathy whisper.

My brain didn't want to go there.

Another name disappeared.

"What about Alban White?" asked my phone.

White had come out of nowhere to buy Home Depot from Arthur Blank and Bernie Marcus ten years ago. He'd renamed the chain as White House & Home and used the façade of the presidential mansion in all his advertising. That sounded like someone obsessed with American history. Alban White could easily be our man.

"I'll check him out," said Martin. "I've got friends who work for him."

"Be careful," said Poly.

Martin stared at her and narrowed one eye.

"All right, all right, you can take care of yourself," said Poly. "I'll take Pablo Daniel Figueres."

"Do you know him?" I asked.

"No, but Professor Urrrson does, and he can introduce me."

"Great," I said. "Take Cornell with you."

Cornell and Poly were both startled for a moment, then it sunk in. It wouldn't do to have our our new allies operating without supervision. The two of them nodded, without enthusiasm.

"What about the fifth name?" asked Johnson. "Who names their daughter *Bavarian?*"

"Someone a touch sadistic," answered Poly. "When Casper Kreem consolidated Dunkin' Donuts, Winchell's, Tim Horton's and Krispy Kreme to become the continent's Donut King, something snapped in his brain. Thank goodness he only had one child."

"Casper was a nutcase," said Winfield. "I met him once at a conference and can understand why his ex-NBA bodyguards drowned him in a vat of coffee."

"The ultimate dunk," said Poly in a stage whisper.

I couldn't help myself and chuckled.

"Go ahead and laugh," said Winfield. "It *is* funny—but who's going to check out Bavarian Kreem?"

"Nobody," I said. "She's nine."

"Oh," said Johnson.

"I'm going to follow up possible leads to Manny the A.I.," I said.

"Good luck to you," said Rosalind.

"Good luck to *us,* you mean," I said.

Poly raised an eyebrow.

I shrugged and smiled sheepishly.

"That leaves me to watch Max," said Sally. "I'm glad to do whatever I can to support you from here."

"Thanks," said Rosalind, nodding at Sally.

"No worries," Sally responded.

"What are you two going to do?" asked Martin, his eyes on Winfield and Johnson.

"We're going to find out everything we can learn from our connections at Factor-E-Flor, O'Sullivan Engineering, VIGorish Labs and Chapultepec & Castle," said Johnson.

"Can you order us a car?" asked Winfield.

"You're not leaving this building," said Martin. They tried to protest but received one of Martin's full-on cop glares and thought better of it.

Shepherd spoke for the first time during the meeting.

"I will stay with them," he said. "I have my own avenues of investigation that I can perform with a computer and a phone." The Pâkk nodded at the former C&C executives. "I will see that they're able to do their research remotely."

"Thanks," I said. "I owe you one."

Shepherd inclined his head to acknowledge the fact.

"Where do you want *me*, bucko?" asked Chit, buzzing in front of my nose. She'd had to fly off the top of her stack of coasters because my phone had finally managed to topple them with an errant pseudopod foot.

"Why don't you keep an eye on Jack and Rosalind?" Poly said encouragingly.

"Great idea," said Chit. "Somebody has to keep 'em out of trouble."

"Exactly," said Poly.

Chapter 11

"Enjoy yourself, it's later than you think."
— Guy Lombardo

"Let's get started," I said. "There's no time to waste. We can meet back here at seven to trade notes."

"Uh, Jack," said my phone.

"What?"

"It's almost seven o'clock now."

The heel of my palm smacked my forehead as I realized my error. I'd forgotten about the three-hour time difference between Las Vegas and Atlanta. In the few short, but hectic days I'd been in Vegas my body had adapted to Pacific time and our quick hop up to orbit and back hadn't provided my brain with enough cues for it to reset.

"Ouch!" I said. "Sorry about that. Let's rendezvous back here at nine-thirty local time. I should be able to get back in a couple of hours."

"That works for me," said Poly. "I'll see if Professor Urrrson is still on campus. Maybe he can meet me here."

"Make sure he uses the underground utility corridors," I said.

Poly gave me a look just short of exasperation and I realized my mistake immediately. *Don't try to teach your grandmother— or your significant other—how to suck eggs,* I reminded myself. I gave her a half bow and mouthed the words, "Mea culpa." She forgave me, I think, because she kissed me on the cheek. Either that or she was treating me like the village idiot who wasn't very quick on the uptake. I remembered she'd made the same mistake by cautioning Martin earlier and smiled.

"Be careful," I said.

It was fun watching Poly's face as she remembered the last time she'd said those words. We both grinned, then hugged, wiser for the experience.

Martin found our exchange amusing. The corners of his mouth turned up, but he didn't laugh. He'd been married a long time and I'm sure he'd been through a similar relationship equilibrium-setting process.

"I'll call my friends who work for White House & Home later, when they get home," he said. "Most of them work long hours. Right now, I'm going back to my room to talk to my family."

"Give Apollonia—I mean *Apple*—and the boys our best," said Poly as Martin left the room.

"Now is a good time to confirm you have what you need to begin your research," said Shepherd to Winfield and Johnson.

The Pâkk moved to stand behind the pair and the two of them rose in unison, as if being controlled by invisible marionette strings. He escorted the former executives out of the conference room. I don't know how Shepherd pulls that stuff off, but he does.

Sally got up. Max noticed, glanced at Rosalind, and ran over to where I was sitting. He hopped in my lap and gave me an enthusiastic hug, then jumped down and did the same to his mother.

"Time to go, big guy," said Sally, motioning to Max. "I can order something delivered for dinner. What do you recommend?"

"Not the Varsity," said Poly. "I'd like something that at least pretends to be healthy."

"Pizza and salads from Fellini's?" I said.

Poly's expression was neutral.

"How about Ginsberg & Wong's?"

My partner's face lit up.

"I've always wanted to try them. One of my classmates raved about their corned beef and cabbage egg rolls."

"I thought you wanted something healthy," I teased.

"Hey, it has cabbage," said Poly.

"Do you eat those with mustard or duck sauce?" asked Rosalind.

"Definitely mustard, according to my classmate," said Poly.

"Sounds like a plan," I said. "Want a Kosher Pu Pu Platter, Max?"

Max's expression made me wonder if I'd turned into a praying mantis-like Orishen nymph in front of his eyes.

"It's not made from what it sounds like," I added quickly.

"Okay," said my son. "I'll eat anything that doesn't eat me first."

I wondered where he'd picked up that phrase. My mother used to say it on our rare camping trips when I was little.

"Ginsberg & Wong menus have been sent to everyone," said my phone. "A consolidated order will be placed at nine."

"Max and I will be at the street level entrance to pick it up when the drones deliver it," said Sally.

"Drones!" said Max.

He rubbed his lower lip up and down rapidly, to imitate the sound of spinning rotors.

"Don't worry, I'll pick up dinner," said Poly. "I have to be near the entrance anyway."

"Okay," said Sally.

Max was disappointed but was quickly distracted by Chit circling his nose. He managed a fair imitation of the higher-pitched whine of Chit's wings.

Poly typed a message into her phone and seemed pleased to get a quick response.

"Bart can meet us in twenty minutes," she told Cornell. "Please don't be a jerk when he gets here."

"I will be a consummate professional," said Cornell.

Poly removed a mini-sweetener from her pocket and held it up just above the surface of the table.

"I'm counting on it," she said. "Let's meet him at this end of the utility corridor."

"As you wish," said Cornell.

Poly stared at Cornell as if he'd sprouted a second head. I didn't think she liked seeing the man's geek side.

I shrugged. If Cornell was a *Princess Bride* fan, perhaps he wasn't all bad.

My partner and Cornell stood up and headed out the door. Poly blew me a kiss just before she turned out of sight. My cheeks turned a bit red as I realized Rosalind was looking at me with ironic amusement.

"What's so funny?"

"You are," she said. "You're still a puppy."

"And you're still a b—" Chit began. She stopped when she saw the storm clouds cross my face and spun in a slow spiral down to my shoulder.

"Where are we going?" asked Rosalind.

"Not far," I said. "We're headed for a data center just south of here. I just need to make a call to confirm it's okay."

Rosalind leaned back in her chair and stared at me, like I was a chromosome she wanted to modify by inserting a new gene sequence.

"Hello, Ram," I said.

Ram Patel was the president of the North American-Caribbean Cricket League. The league played its games in North American cities in the summer and in the Caribbean in the winter, but made most of its money selling stylish cricket-related clothing to preppies and their alien equivalents on more than fifty planets.

"What can I do for you, Jack?" asked Ram. His voice had an odd amalgam of Brooklyn and New Delhi accents.

"I need to talk to Droopy."

"No problem," said Ram. "Things have calmed down after the graduation-season rush. He should have plenty of cycles available to talk. Just give him a call."

"I'd like to see him in person, if you don't mind. We're not far from your data center."

"We?" asked Ram. "Are you bringing your new girlfriend along? I'd like to meet her."

Did everybody know about me dating Poly?

"No," I said. "This is someone else. A business associate."

Rosalind made a face at me. I made a mostly mock grumpy-frown face back.

"Whatever," said Ram. "I'm sure it will be fine if you vouch for your guest. I'll be here for another hour and will alert building security—just text me when you get here. Droopy will be glad to see you."

"Thanks," I said. "See you in a few."

My phone ended the call.

"Droopy?" asked Rosalind.

"A friend of mine," I said, "and a specialist in artificial intelligence, because a large part of him is artificial."

"Tell me more," said Rosalind as we stood up to go.

She positioned herself close to me as we walked to the exit. Too close, really. It felt like she was playing with my head.

"I will if you give me more personal space."

"Do I make you uncomfortable, Jack?"

"Yes," I said, faster than I'd intended. "It's like you're pushing buttons in my brain I didn't even know I had."

"That's your libido talking," she said. "You ought to listen to it from time to time. I'll back off, for now."

"You'd better," said Chit in her low, gruff voice. "Don't think you can mess with *my* head, babe. Give Jack some space or you'll answer to me."

"I will take your objections into account when planning my future actions, bug," said Rosalind. She theatrically batted her eyes at me just to antagonize Chit, then got back to business.

"Who's Droopy?" she asked.

I found myself relaxing slightly when she increased the distance between us from a few inches to a few feet.

"Droopy is my nickname for Hadramordarupé, a Khaloenian cyber-organic server. He links to all the other remaining Khaloenians and helps provide secure digital commerce services for my friend Ram's mail order clothing business."

"I've read about the Khaloenians, of course," said Rosalind. "Most of them sealed themselves up in a planetoid, right?"

"Correct," I said. "They transferred their thought processes to digital form and are living fully virtual lives inside an artificial planetoid circling a stable brown dwarf star—except for the ones who stuck around, like Droopy."

My phone disguised its identity to Galnet and summoned an autocab. When it arrived, Rosalind got in first and sat on the far left. I put my mini-sweetener in my pocket and sat on the far right. Our separation still didn't feel like enough.

"I thought Khaloenians were only partially artificial," said Rosalind. "If Droopy is still largely organic, how would he know about fully digital artificial intelligences?"

"Khaloenians have built-in congruencies," I said.

"Like Murms," said Chit, "but ours are innate."

"So far as you know," said Rosalind.

"Waddya mean, toots?" asked Chit. "I was hatched this way."

"I think Murms' internal congruencies could have been genetically engineered in place, just like the Khaloenians," asserted Rosalind. "Your whole species could have been designed for espionage."

"Watch your mouth parts, lady," said Chit. "You're gettin' too personal."

"Sorry, bug," said Rosalind.

I stepped in before things got even more out of hand.

"We know that internal congruencies can occur naturally," I said. "Gus has three."

"Come on, Jack, don't be a fool," said Rosalind. "If bugs can be genetically engineered as spies, size-changing saurians can be, too. They'd make great warriors."

"Or in the case of Gus," I said, "whole armies."

"One way or another, Khaloenians have congruencies in their heads," said Rosalind. "I get it. Why do you think that means Droopy can help us locate The General's artificial intelligence?"

"The million-or-so remaining Khaloenians are all linked together through their congruencies," I said. "Almost every commercial transaction in the galaxy goes through at least one of them. I don't expect Manny to have any need for cricket whites, but one of Droopy's friends might know something about an A.I that goes by that name. They could also search for patterns in transactions made by EUA Corporation."

"Accessing those transactions is an e-commerce security violation," said Rosalind. "It's against the law."

"Look who's talkin'," said Chit.

That shut Rosalind down for a few minutes and caused her to look at me with more respect. Her puppy was now a big dog, if not yet a wolf.

"I'm gonna lay low an' be your ace in the hole if anything goes wrong," said Chit, hiding on the back of my neck.

"Nothing will," I said.

"Don't snore, bug," said Rosalind.

Those two were going to be a challenge—not like I didn't have enough problems already.

In the quiet before the autocab got to our destination I thought about the Nicósn bio-engineers who'd created the Compliant Plague during the Pàkk-Tigrammath War. Could they have created Murms and Gojons, or were those two species the result of even more ancient genetic tampering?

I didn't have much time to ponder. It was seven-thirty and we'd arrived at our destination.

Chapter 12

"If I only had a brain."
— Edgar Yipsel Harburg

Ram Patel met us at the entrance to his combined warehouse, office and data center. It was a long, narrow, converted nineteenth-century, red-brick cotton mill with thick walls and high ceilings. My client was very proud of the place. He'd restored it inside and out—I'd seen the architectural awards it had won on the walls of Ram's office. A giant, two-story banner hung from the roof above the front doors announcing that this was the galaxy-wide headquarters of the North American-Caribbean Cricket League. The colorful banner also included logos for the league's sixteen teams. Selling trendy team-logo clothing and merchandise made Ram more money than operating the league, though off-planet revenues for broadcasts were growing rapidly.

Thanks to televised NACCL matches, cricket had become quite popular on Orish, especially for nymphs. White silhouettes of tall, praying mantis-shaped Orishen nymphs holding cricket bats at the ready were affixed to plate-glass windows flanking the entrance—part of a new marketing campaign that had already boosted Ram's sales by fifty-five percent. I wondered if that was why Ram was smiling?

"Jack!" said Ram. "It's great to see you."

He was not quite a foot shorter than my six foot one, but his personality made him seem taller. Ram shook my hand, then looked at Rosalind and waited for me to introduce her.

"Great to see you, too," I said. "This is my associate, Rosalind. She's working with me on a confidential project."

I put my finger to my lips and he mirrored my actions, then took Rosalind's hand and gave her a polite bow.

"Any associate of Jack's is welcome here," he said. "Without him, I would have been out of business."

"That's not true," I protested. "You would have found a way to keep going. Your other e-commerce servers could have picked up the slack."

"Maybe," said Ram, "but I'm glad I didn't have to. Khaloenians expect triple-time for working more than twelve hours a day. They say they need time for contemplating philosophy and quantum physics and…"

"…debating the merits of Rogers and Hammerstein versus Lerner and Lowe?" finished Rosalind.

Wait! How did Rosalind know what I'd done to cure Droopy's depression?

"Exactly," said Ram, still holding Rosalind's hand. "Jack is a genius with cyber-organic server psychology. No one can keep them up and running like he can. Hadramordarupé's productivity has tripled since Jack introduced him to Broadway musicals at the end of March. Droopy hasn't mentioned Kierkegaard, Sartre or Nietzsche in weeks."

"Thanks for the kind words," I said, "but we're on a tight deadline and I need to talk to Hadramordarupé as soon as possible. Is he off-shift?"

"He is," said Ram, "but I'd pay the overtime to get another Khaloenian to cover for him if he wasn't. Follow me and I'll walk you through security."

"Thanks."

"You are most gracious, Mr. Patel," said Rosalind.

"Call me Ram."

Rosalind was working her magic on my client, but I hoped they wouldn't be in contact long enough for it to matter.

Security was first rate at the end of the NACCL headquarters that had been repurposed as a data center. It had better be—I'd designed it. Guests had to sign in, show identification, and be vouched for by a senior-level I.T. or management employee before they could enter. Their bodies and bags, purses and packages were scanned. Rosalind and I both had to leave our mini-sweeteners at the guards' station. Ram's eyes got big when he saw them, but I put my finger to my lips again and he didn't comment.

Visitors and employees had to wear ID badges with embedded tracking chips at all times. Taking off a badge would set off alarm bells and flashing lights throughout the complex. Access to the raised floor area of the data center was through a "man trap" two-stage revolving door that would capture any humanoid trying to enter or leave without authorization. Ram got us through it with a minimum of hassle and led us down the long corridor between racks of conventional servers that led to the Khaloenian's "office."

It was cold in the data center. It was *always* cold in data centers, but the quality of the cold had changed a lot over the past fifteen years as they'd switched from conventional refrigeration to congruency-based chillers using Pluto's atmosphere. I wished I'd remembered to bring a sweater. Rosalind was still wearing the same sneakers, jeans and t-shirt she'd been wearing when I'd knocked on her door in Las Vegas this morning. It was obvious she was feeling the cold more than I was. Ram offered to get her a sweatshirt. He said they kept a few around for times when I.T. employees forgot their jackets, but she demurred.

"Thanks so much for all your help, Ram," I said. "I really appreciate it. If my badge will open Hadramordarupé's office door, I can take it from here."

"It's no trouble," said Ram. "I'll be glad to keep you company and walk you out when you're done."

"You've done so much already," said Rosalind in a husky, sensual voice. "We don't want to take up more of your time. You're a very important CEO, after all."

She leaned down and kissed Ram on the cheek.

"We really appreciate it, but we'll be fine," she said. "Please give our best to your wife and family."

I hadn't told Rosalind about Ram's wife and three boys, though he did wear a wedding ring and she was probably just playing the odds. Ram brightened up from the peck on his cheek, but saw my resolute expression—I didn't want him with me when I talked to Droopy—and made his goodbyes.

"I hope you find out what you need," said Ram, just before he turned to leave. "When you can, let me know how it turns out."

"I will," I said. "I promise."

Ram walked down the corridor between the server cages humming something that sounded like a Bollywood variation on *Singing in the Rain*. Droopy's new passion for musicals must have rubbed off on him. I waved my badge in front of the door's sensor and it slid open with a *whoosh* like doors on *Star Trek*.

"After you," I said.

Rosalind entered and I followed.

Droopy's office was a dimly lit twelve-foot cube of fabric-padded metal. A large flat-screen hung on the left-hand wall. In the center of the room floated Droopy's disembodied brain and associated hardware. Both gently bobbed in a clear nutrient bath inside a glowing glass cylinder that ran from raised floor to dropped ceiling. Tubes and cables entered the cylinder through gasketed access ports connecting Droopy's hardware to the outside world. Small lights flickered inside and outside the tube.

A hazy image appeared in the flat-screen. As it sharpened, I saw that it was a handsome face that seemed like a composite of half a dozen of Hollywood's top leading men. It was also somewhat disquieting because the face had a slight blue tint. We didn't know much about Khaloenians' physical appearance before they'd put their bodies aside, but perhaps this image came close to their original form. Droopy had never used video when I'd visited his office in the past—just voice.

"It's great to see you, Jack!" said the image on the flat-screen. "Who's the doll?"

"This is Rosalind," I said, "and she's a woman, not a doll. It's the twenty-first century, not Damon Runyon's New York."

"I get it," said Droopy. "A secretary is not a toy."

"Rosalind's not my secretary, either, but that's better," I said. "Were you listening to Frank Loesser musicals? *Guys & Dolls* and *How To Succeed in Business Without Really Trying?*"

"That is correct. How did you know?"

"Just a guess," I said.

"Very pleased to make your acquaintance, I'm *shu-ah*," said Rosalind, in an excellent imitation of Miss Adelaide's Brooklyn accent from *Guys & Dolls*. "You seem like a *poifect* gentleman."

Droopy's simulated face beamed and turned a slightly darker blue.

I smiled. I didn't think I'd have to worry about this particular server being down again, even if he did have the blues.

"We need your help," I said.

"It's important," added Rosalind. "Someone is trying to kill us and we have to stop them."

I wouldn't have told Droopy that, but Rosalind usually had good instincts. This time, they proved on target.

"I don't want you to die," said Droopy. "Jack is my best friend. I would do *anything* to help him—and you seem nice, too, Miss Rosalind. How can I help?"

"You can start by telling us everything you and any of your fellow Khaloenian e-commerce servers know about an artificial intelligence system named Manny or Manuel," I said.

"Or HOLMES IV or *Dinkum Thinkum*, or anything that cross-references with computer names used in the works of Robert A. Heinlein," added Rosalind.

I would have covered Rosalind's mouth before she said the last half of her sentence if I'd been fast enough. Given how obsessed Droopy had become with Broadway musicals, exposing him to Heinlein's stories about sentient computers like Dora, Minerva and Pallas Athene could cause problems. I held out hope that Droopy's preference for philosophy and music would prevent him from being distracted by Heinlein's creations.

"This is highly irregular and outside the bounds of Terran law, but I will consult with the other members of my species and initiate a search for the information you have requested," said Droopy pleasantly. "If Jack's life is threatened, violations of local cultural mores are no impediment. Is there anything else I can do?"

"Yes," said Rosalind.

I stepped closer in case I needed to stop her from saying something else that might affect Droopy's psyche.

"Please search for anomalous transactions initiated by EUA Corporation and its subsidiaries. Do the same for any companies associated with Alban White and Pablo Daniel Figueres, as well as for those persons individually."

I stared at Rosalind and shook my head slowly from side to side. She didn't do things by halves. Her request would produce a *huge* data set, with high criminal penalties associated with every gigabyte. Then again, my own request for information about an A.I. named Manny would likely land me in the next cell if our digging was discovered. I hoped it wouldn't come to that. Orange wasn't my color.

I couldn't help but think Rosalind had an ulterior motive for asking for so much data. Did she hope to use it to take over EUA Corporation once we'd dealt with The General—then swallow up White and Figueres' companies? I resolved to call Droopy for a private discussion later to warn him not to give a full data dump of his findings to Rosalind.

"What do you mean by anomalous?" asked Droopy.

I jumped in before Rosalind could.

"Focus on transactions that don't fit with the normal course of legitimate business activities," I said. "Unusually high payments to new suppliers, large transfers of funds to small subsidiaries, purchases with military uses, and so on."

"We're trying to determine the identity of The General," said Rosalind. "The person behind EUA Corporation."

"He's the one who wants to kill us," I added.

"One moment," said Droopy's simulated face on the flat-screen. The lights around his brain in the glass cylinder danced rapidly.

Rosalind and I exchanged glances. It couldn't be this easy, could it?

"Both Alban White and Pablo Daniel Figueres could refer to themselves as a general," said Droopy, after a minute. "Mr. White was made a Georgia General by the state legislature in 2028 and

Pablo Daniel Figueres was given the honorary rank of general in Puerto Rico's state guard in 2025."

"Georgia General?" asked Rosalind.

"It's like being a Kentucky Colonel, but the legislators wanted the people they honored to outrank dignitaries from the Bluegrass State," I said. "They also liked the alliteration."

"It's much the same in Puerto Rico," said Rosalind. "And somewhat like cardinals originally being bishops responsible for individual churches in Rome. Lawmakers in Puerto Rico made Figueres an honorary general for his help buying off—that is, *convincing* Congress and other state legislatures to make the island the fifty-first state. He's nominally in charge of a brigade, but it's purely honorary. A colonel is the real person in charge."

"How do you know so much about Pablo Daniel Figueres?" I asked.

"I refuse to answer on the grounds…"

"I get it. Once upon a time you were assigned to gather covert intelligence from a PDF company."

"I do my homework," said Rosalind, "but the honorary title was more of a joke than anything serious, so it didn't register until I was reminded."

"Was my information helpful?" asked Droopy. His onscreen visage looked like a puppy who wanted to be petted.

"It was," I said immediately.

"You've been *very* helpful," purred Rosalind, using her smooth, sexy voice.

Lights started blinking quickly in Droopy's nutrient tube again. Rosalind has that effect on males—with and without bodies.

"Thanks so much," I said.

I turned to leave, then turned back.

"One more question, please."

"How may I be of service?" said Droopy.

"Could you also research anything related to the Earth First Militant organization? I'm almost positive The General is behind them and *that* may be the organization where he holds rank."

"Certainly, youth," said Droopy.

Anybody less than seventeen thousand years old was a youth by Droopy's standards. He might even know if Murms and Gojons are natural or engineered species. I didn't want to ask that question with Rosalind—or Chit—in the room, for that matter.

"It will take several hours to collect and structure the data you have requested," continued Droopy. "I will transfer it to…"

"Me," I said. "Transfer it to me and I can review your results."

I had no idea what Rosalind would do with that much sensitive data and didn't want to know. Now it wasn't an issue—but the downside was that I'd be the only one on the hook for violating transactional security regulations.

"It shall be as you wish," said Droopy. "Safe travels."

"Felicitous contemplation," I said. Then inspiration struck.

"Before we leave," I said, "have you ever listened to a symphony?"

"I have enjoyed musicals' overtures performed by orchestras," said Droopy, "but not symphonies."

"Try Beethoven's Fifth or Mozart's *Jupiter* symphonies," I offered. "They don't have words, but I think you'll find the underlying mathematics fascinating."

"I shall do so," said Droopy. "Your suggestions have always been excellent."

He was humming Beethoven's opening *bum bum bum BUM* as we left his office. That should not only keep Droopy happy, it should distract him from reading Heinlein.

"That was interesting," said Rosalind after we reclaimed our mini-sweeteners and left the data center.

"It certainly was," I said.

While Rosalind was busy ordering an autocab, Chit perked up and whispered in my ear.

"Hey. Do ya think that guy might be able to tell me where Gojons got three built-in congruencies?"

"Maybe," I said, "but do you really want to know?"

Chapter 13

*"Whoever wishes to keep a secret must hide
the fact that he possesses one."*
— Johann Wolfgang von Goethe

We'd just settled into the autocab for the ride back and I realized now would be a good time to deal with unfinished business with Rosalind.

"Hey Chit, do you have anything with you resembling headphones?"

"Waddya mean?" said my little friend. "Ya think I'm totin' around a backpack tool bag or sumptin'?"

"No, I'm just hoping for a little privacy for a conversation with the other lady in the vehicle."

"If ya call her a lady," muttered Chit.

"Watch it, Peanut," said Rosalind, "or I'll squash you like a…"

"Bug out," I said to the mother of my newly discovered child. "This is between me and Chit."

"I get it," said Chit. "I've got sumptin' *better* than headphones. Havin' a built-in congruency is like havin' a home-grown MP3 player. I can flip down chitin covers on my external ears 'n give ya all the privacy ya want."

Rosalind stared at Chit like she'd grown a second head.

"You have external ears?"

"Ya gotta look close. I usually only need the chitin covers when I'm goin' swimming. Murms were once semi-aquatic, ya know. At least some of our science mugs think so…"

"Great," I said, cutting her off before she could continue. "Thanks for giving me a few minutes to talk to Rosalind in private."

"Don't mention it," said Chit.

I could hear the opening march music from the beginning of *Hamilton* before noticing a tiny click—then the music cut off. Droopy must not be the only one of my friends interested in Broadway musicals.

I was lost in my own thoughts when Rosalind slid toward me.

"Alone at last," she said.

Say what?

I squeezed tighter against my side of the autocab. "Don't start. When were you going to tell me?"

"Tell you what?"

I let out a sigh like an anemic teakettle just taken off the stove. "You know what! When were you going to tell me about Max?"

It was Rosalind's turn to sigh.

"Never," she said. "I'd never planned to tell you."

I could feel my face turning red as my anger rose. I squeezed my fists so tight I almost lost circulation in my hands. Rosalind smiled at me like nothing was wrong and gently put her palm on top of my right fist.

"Don't touch me!" I pulled my fist away at close to light speed. "What do you mean, *never?*"

"Is there an altercation?" asked the none-too-bright autocab A.I. "Does either passenger feel unsafe or threatened? Would one of you like this vehicle to proceed to the nearest police station? Estimated time of arrival is approximately six minutes."

"No," I said, releasing some of my anger in the syllable.

"That should not be necessary," said Rosalind in a honey-sweet voice.

I was ready to strangle her.

"Thank you," said the autocab. "Please note this vehicle is equipped with a safeword. If either passenger uses the word *aardvark* in conversation this autocab will proceed directly to the nearest law enforcement center."

"I appreciate the information," said Rosalind. "Jack, did you know there's a small, non-sentient animal on Dauush called a *daushli* with the same relationship to Dauushans that earth pigs have to African elephants?

I did know. Aardvarks, African elephants, dugongs and manatees are all cousins. Dauushans had several relatives on their branch of the evolutionary tree. *Daushli* had even been an answer on Day Seven during my run on *Jeopardy*, but that's a tale for another day.

"Stop trying to change the subject," I said with a bit more self-control. "Why weren't you going to tell me about my son?"

"Because I didn't want *my* mistake to ruin your life," said Rosalind. "I screwed up and forgot my implant was due to expire."

"But…" I sputtered.

"If you hadn't come to Vegas for GALTEX, you'd never have seen me and would have never known Max existed," continued Rosalind. "You and Poly could advance your awkward courtship, grow your company, and make your mother proud without the complication of having an almost five-year-old son."

"You don't understand. I'm his father."

"And I'm his mother. You left me tied up in the repository on Orish. What was I supposed to think—we had a love that would last through the ages?"

Her words slowed me down for a moment. Rosalind was being matter-of-fact. Her reply seemed unemotional, but like Mr. Spock there were Terran passions underneath. I didn't stop to overthink.

"My father wasn't there for me when I was growing up. He left my mom before I was born."

My head slumped as painful memories overwhelmed me and I fought for self-control. Rosalind's hand slid back on top of mine. I didn't pull away and my fists unclenched.

"I'm sorry," said Rosalind, "I didn't know, but it wouldn't have made a difference. I kept an eye on your career, Jack. I was proud of you for starting Xenotech Support, building a client-base and growing your consulting practice. You're on your way. I didn't want to derail your life."

"I wanted to be there," I said. "I wanted to cut the cord when Max was born. I wanted to watch him speak his first word and take his first step. I wanted to read him bedtime stories, take him to the zoo, go camping—all the things I didn't get to do with *my* dad."

"I thought you said your dad took you camping?"

"My *step*-dad. He married my mom when I was eight."

"You'll be three years ahead of him, then," said Rosalind, trying to soothe me. It had the opposite effect. My hands made fists again.

"I'm his father. I needed to be there. You should have told me!" I kept my volume under the decibels that would trigger a response from the autocab, but just barely. "It's not like you didn't know where to find me."

"Of course I knew where to find you," said Rosalind. "You're in all the on-line directories. But there are other reasons I didn't contact you."

"Like what?" I asked.

"Like my work," she replied. "You're a Boy Scout—a straight arrow. I'm an industrial espionage specialist for an organization that thinks Ethics is an English county east of London."

"That's Essex," I said, then tried to swallow my words.

Rosalind looked at me like I was losing it. I probably was.

"I didn't want to drag you into my orbit. When I met you, you were an idealist, out to change the world. If I'd told you about Max, you would have been tied to me. It would have been like letting a puppy fall in a barrel of tar. I didn't want to mess up your life."

"Ha!" I said. "When you met me, I was running an illegal casino on the campus of Mulbiri Tech. I wasn't a Boy Scout—*or* a puppy."

Rosalind moved close and shifted so her arm was around me. It felt affectionate, not amorous, so I didn't shrug it off.

"I do care for you, Jack," she said. "I wasn't supposed to, but from the first night we met, I realized what kind of man you were and how good you would be for the right woman."

"Huh?"

"You're a good man, Jack. Poly's a lucky woman. I envy her. You don't know how much I envy her."

I still couldn't find my tongue. Then I could.

"He needed his father in his life!"

"He had my brother, and Sally. Cornell couldn't have treated him better if Max was his own son, and Sally might as well be his second mother."

"Cornell," I said, almost spitting. "That son of a…"

"He's not a bad guy, really," said Rosalind. "He could have killed you several times and didn't, because he knew you were important to me."

"Cornell knew about me and Max before I met him?"

"I have a picture of you on my dresser—so Max will know who his daddy is. Cornell's seen it, and he's heard me talk about you for over five years," said Rosalind. "He still teases me about how you threw a spanner into my plans on Orish. You've impressed him."

"I've impressed the chief lackey of a megalomaniac who wants to conquer the galaxy—and kill us, by the way. Big whoop."

"These days you're not exactly Dudley Do-Right of the R.C.M.P.," said Rosalind. "You've been playing fast and loose with the law yourself lately. Want me to give you a list?"

I thought of all the corners I'd cut since I'd first met Cornell in the sub-sub-basement of the Georgia capitol building. Laws didn't mean quite what they'd meant before First Contact turned our legislatures into reality television, but the truth was they'd been headed that way for a long time. I'd always tried to stick to the Golden Rule in my personal and professional life. I believed in treating clients the way I'd like them to treat me. My ethical guidelines were phrases like do your best, treat clients fairly, give them good advice, and deliver value for the galcred. I treated my friends the same way. If stopping EUA and its subsidiaries from taking over the galaxy meant I had to let the ends justify the means from time to time, so be it.

"I don't need a list," I said. "I know what I've done and I know what you and Cornell and Sally have done, too."

"You don't know ten percent of it."

"Then I'll extrapolate and round up. That's not the point. What's done is done," I said.

"Water over the dam?" asked Rosalind.

I remembered the merry chase she'd led me through Hoover Dam earlier in the week.

"Don't go there," I said, but Rosalind could see I was smiling. *Damn, could she manipulate me.*

"The most important thing," I continued, "is figuring out what we're going to do now. We have to do what's best for Max."

"That's something we can both agree on," said Rosalind.

"We'll have to figure out parental rights, shared custody, child support…"

"Child support's not necessary. I've got plenty of money."

"I'm his father," I said. "Child support, living arrangements, vacations when he starts school, holidays…"

"Why don't we see about surviving through the next week or so and try to identify The General first?" asked Rosalind.

"Speaking of surviving," I said, "who's in line to care for Max if something happens to you and Sally and Cornell?"

"You are."

She patted my hand. I squeezed hers and let it go. This was all so confusing.

"If anything happens to all of us, Max—and a sizable trust fund—will be your mother's responsibility."

"My *mother!* Does *she* know?"

"No," said Rosalind, "but now that she's met Max I'll certainly tell her."

"Is there an altercation?" asked the autocab's A.I. "If you wish, this vehicle can transport you to a law enforcement facility. Also, you have arrived at your destination."

"Just let us out," I said.

"Thanks for the ride," said Rosalind. "It's been most enlightening."

The cab's doors opened and we walked toward the research facility. It was late in the day and there was a spectacular sunset behind the girders for the first few floors of the SLN Capital hotel. I heard a small click in my ear, then more music from *Hamilton* before it stopped.

"Well," said Chit. "What did I miss? Did you two lovebirds have a nice talk?"

"Shut up," said Rosalind.

My sentiments exactly.

Chapter 14

*"Tom Friedman says China is so awesome
they make kosher pigs."*
— Jonah Goldberg

We met Poly and Cornell at the entrance to the laboratory complex. She was authorizing delivery of our dinner with a quartet of drones from Ginsberg & Wong, the famed kosher Chinese eatery a mile south of us on Marietta Street. Rosalind and I helped them carry the bags inside.

"Did you use an untraceable account to pay for the…"

The exasperated look on Poly's face when she turned her head made me shut up. Of course she had. I'd probably pay for my words later. I decided to talk to my phone instead.

"I forgot to order anything."

"No problem," said my phone. "Your previous preferences and selections from Asian restaurants and delicatessens compose a sufficiently large universe of choices for in-depth analysis. You should be pleased with what was ordered on your behalf."

"Thanks," I said.

I was looking forward to trying what my phone had picked out.

"I didn't order anything, either," said Rosalind.

"Dishes were ordered for you as well," said my phone, "though without the benefit of detailed analytics. There will be a collection of best-selling items for you. Do you like tempura dill pickles?"

"I don't know," Rosalind answered, "but I'm curious to find out."

The smells coming from the bags were heavenly—a melange of Middle Kingdom and middle European scents made me forget the Dauushan ham and cheese sandwich I'd enjoyed on the orbital shuttle a few hours ago. Bed testing earlier had also helped me build a substantial appetite.

I hoped the food would be filling and remembered the old joke about the problem with eating *German*-Chinese food— half an hour later you're hungry for power.

We returned to the below-ground conference room where we'd met earlier and started to organize the containers and lay out the chopsticks, forks, knives and condiments on a credenza as the others arrived. My phone must have notified them and clanged a virtual dinner bell. Everyone seemed to be hungry, but not all the new arrivals seemed happy. Winfield and Johnson looked like they'd been sucking on lemons dipped in alum. Martin appeared pleased, but Shepherd's stoic face made it hard to tell what he was thinking.

Max didn't so much enter the room as bounce into it with Sally trailing behind. The two of them were hopping as if they were skipping invisible jump ropes and reciting, "Gik-lo, I-o, Rik-o, Gis-so," in high singsong voices. Poly, Rosalind and I laughed. We recognized the rhyme from an old Fritz Lieber story where super-intelligent children used four equations from Einstein's generalized theory of gravitation to help keep the beat. I smiled at Sally appreciatively, continuing to be pleased she and Cornell and Rosalind were bringing my son up right.

Speaking of right, Max ran right at me once he saw me and nearly caused me to drop an open container of hot and sour matzo ball soup when he collided with my leg at high speed.

"Hey, buddy," I said, putting the soup down and picking up my son. "Did you and Sally have fun while your mom and I were away?"

"Uh huh," said Max.

From his higher vantage point he could see everything we'd ordered for dinner. Suddenly he had more important priorities than talking to his father.

"When do we eat?" he asked.

"Now," I said. "I'll unpack your Kosher Pu Pu Platter."

Max made another face at me and squirmed down to hug Rosalind and Cornell. Even Poly got a quick hug as something of an afterthought before the boy found a chair at the round conference table and waited for me to deliver his food. Rosalind got him a bottle of galberry juice and Sally put a plastic knife, fork, soup spoon and wooden chopsticks in front of him. Cornell delivered a stack of napkins and a straw while Poly brought a handful of condiment packets. It takes a village.

I used tongs provided by the restaurant to artfully arrange the items from the Kosher Pu Pu Platter on an edible, recyclable plate and served my son. It made me happy to see Max's frown turn into a smile when he saw the grilled paprika chicken skewers topped with bright yellow pineapple wedges and red maraschino cherries I'd placed on top. He must have been really hungry, because his usual running commentary on the universe stopped while he ate. Max switched from chicken skewers to Vienna sausage egg rolls with spicy Chinese mustard and smiled even more. Sally sat next to him with a plate of her own, so I returned to the credenza, confident he was in good hands.

Shepherd had taken all the Asian barbecued brisket and I certainly wasn't going to fight him for any of it. He was at the table slicing it into strips with a long, hooked blade that wasn't plastic and certainly hadn't been provided by Ginsburg & Wong.

Next to him, I noticed Winfield and Johnson had only taken small portions of a few dishes. Their appetites must be off— they were only picking at their food.

Martin was at the far side of the credenza, balancing a second steamed rye bun filled with chicken livers on top of a mound of Szechuan pickled herring. I hoped he'd make it to the table without losing one of them.

Cornell was next to Martin with a cup of hot and sour matzo ball soup and a Mongolian Beef on 'weck sandwich on his plate. The sight of his sandwich's fist-sized *kummelweck* roll topped with salt and caraway seeds made my mouth water. Chit was sitting on an overturned paper soup cup on the table nibbling on small piece of deviled daikon.

Rosalind and Poly were dishing each other helpings of Moo Shu Sour Cream Blintzes and Pan Fried Gefilte Fish Dumplings. It was surprising to see them cooperating—I hoped they wouldn't end up comparing notes on yours truly.

Rosalind already had half a dozen tempura dill pickles on her plate, but I gave them a pass. I opted for the same items Cornell had selected, plus some Udon Noodle Kugel with Sweet Plum Sauce and a large glass of iced Imperial Gunpowder black tea.

Poly saved me a seat between her and Max. Sally had moved over so Rosalind was to Max's left with Sally just beyond her. I spotted several crispy fried wontons on Sally's plate. They looked interesting and I motioned toward them with my chopsticks.

"What are they filled with?" I asked.

"Spiced prunes," Sally replied.

"Forget I asked."

"Have you ever had Dirty Diapers?" asked Sally between tastes of sticky rice.

"You'd have to ask my mother," I said. "At the time your question was relevant I was too young to remember."

"No," said Sally. "Dirty Diapers are sweets for baby showers. Fold a Hershey's Kiss in a wonton wrapper like it's a diaper around a baby's butt, then bake or deep fry and top with powdered sugar."

"You can do the same with frozen lemon curd or lemon gummy bears," added Rosalind. "For Number One to go with Number Two."

"I think I'll pass," I said.

"So will I," said Poly.

We both stared at our plates for a few minutes before our appetites returned. Thanks, Sally.

Everyone seemed to be more interested in eating than talking, so I took a bite of my sandwich, swallowed, and summarized the results of the expedition to see Droopy.

"...so both Pablo Figueres and Alban White can claim the title of General. I'll be getting detailed information about any anomalous transactions by EUA Corporation and Figueres' and White's companies soon. The Khaloenian e-commerce server network will also keep me posted about any interactions with an A.I. named Manny, Manuel, Adam Selene or other sentient computer names from the works of Robert Heinlein."

I took another bite of Mongolian Beef on 'weck to make it clear I'd finished talking and waited for someone else to report. Shepherd turned to stare at Winfield and Johnson. They fidgeted in their chairs, then Johnson spoke.

"Our sources told us The General is aware we weren't on the plane his people shot down."

"I could have told you that," said Cornell. "I was asked to arrange your deaths an hour ago."

"What?" asked Winfield.

"How?" asked Martin.

"How was I going to have you killed?" said Cornell.

"No," said Martin. "How did you get word from The General?"

"Through a text message on my phone," replied Cornell. "I thought it would be wise not to let him know I'd changed sides."

"I got a text from HQ a few minutes ago ordering me to report on my status and whereabouts," said Rosalind.

"What?" I said, echoing Scott Winfield. "When were you going to tell us about it?"

"Now seemed like a good time," answered Rosalind, calmly. "It came in while you were getting food for Max."

I felt a bit better. She hadn't been holding out on us and omitting important information—this time.

"Did you reply?" asked Poly.

"Not yet," said Rosalind. "I thought we might want to talk about it first."

"Thank you," I said.

Poly gave Rosalind a thumbs-up to show her agreement. I heard a low buzzing sound beyond Rosalind.

"Hey," said Sally. "I just got a text from HQ, too. Report on status and whereabouts immediately. What should I do?"

Martin wiped sauce off his mouth with a napkin and cleared his throat.

"Let's review the situation," he said. "First, Winfield and Johnson's plane was destroyed by a surface-to-air missile."

Heads nodded.

"Then a squad of rent-a-goons kidnapped Cornell, Sally, Rosalind, Max and Poly."

"Check," I said. More nods.

"We hired the retrieval specialists to bring everyone at Cornell's place to a secure location," said Johnson. "I guess they got carried away."

"Yeah, yeah," said Rosalind, still not seeming very happy about the abduction.

"You could have contacted us," said Sally. "We would have been glad to join forces."

"They were afraid of communications leaks," said Cornell.

"Bingo," said Winfield.

The word set Max off and he started waving his arms, shouting "Bingo!" repeatedly.

"If you hadn't chilled us, we would have explained," said Johnson. "Our apologies."

"Water over the dam," said Rosalind.

Rosalind kept using that idiom just to tweak me.

"So The General doesn't necessarily know the two of you are still alive," I said, speaking to Johnson and Winfield.

"He does if he got satellite footage of us boarding the shuttle from the base of the butte to the *Charalindhri,*" said Johnson.

"And he knows we're all in this together," said Winfield.

Cornell put his two cents in.

"I think it's safe to assume The General knew we were on board, since he tried to shoot down shuttles from the *Chara* to Hartsfield Port. And since I got a text instructing me to arrange Winfield and Johnson's deaths, we can be *sure* he knows they're both still alive."

"Not to forget there's been plenty of time for the goons you'd hired to sing their hearts out," said Rosalind.

"Yeah, not to forget," said Winfield. He grimaced.

"Besides," said Sally, "they probably searched the plane's wreckage and tested the DNA on the bodies."

"Great point," I said.

"Thanks," said Sally.

"We can use the team who tested the DNA to help us learn who hired them," I said. I put my phone on the table and asked it to "Make it so."

"Searching," it said.

A chime sounded and a holographic projection of an incandescent bulb appeared above my phone.

"The testing team and the aviation forensics people who investigated the crash site all work for EUA subsidiaries."

"Nice to know they're keeping it in the family," said Poly.

"Big family," I said.

"You have no idea," said Cornell.

"But it doesn't really help us," said Martin.

"True," said Sally. "Now what? How do Rosalind and I respond to our texts?"

"Maybe finding out what everyone else has learned will help us decide," I said. "How did things go with Professor Urrrson, Poly?"

"Great," she said. "He arranged for me to meet Pablo Daniel Figueres at the SLN Tower in Midtown at ten tomorrow morning."

"Excellent. What's your cover story?"

"Trying to sell him on using Xenotech Support to troubleshoot particularly challenging issues with their telecom equipment," she said. "Jeanette Obi-Yu also recommended us to him."

"Us?" I said. "I can come along?"

"I sure hope so," said Poly. "Between the two of us…"

"Three of us, doll," said Chit.

"Three of us," said Poly, "we should be able to get a read on his character and figure out whether or not he could be The General."

I was game, but ten o'clock Eastern time was seven o'clock in the morning by my body's clock. I'd need to get some rest tonight.

"How did things go digging into Alban White's operations?" Poly asked Martin.

"Not as good as they did for you," Martin replied. "I'm meeting an executive vice president at eleven tomorrow. Apparently, no one gets in to see Mr. White. He's a professional recluse at the center of a web of intrigue, if what my friends have been telling me is true."

"What have you heard?" asked Cornell.

"Rumors of secret books, silent partners, hush-hush dealings, things like that," Martin replied.

"It's sad," said Poly. "His company's public image is squeaky clean, but it sounds like it's a swamp underneath."

"Yep," said Martin. "It reminds me of EUA Corporation's convoluted structure, or at least the part of it I can investigate. We'll see if I can get past Alban White's executive vice president-level gatekeeper."

"Best of luck," I said. "Do you want someone to go with you?"

"I will accompany Martin," said Shepherd. It was the first time he'd spoken during our meal.

"Thanks," said Martin. "Your help should up our odds of getting to meet Alban White face to face."

I looked over at Winfield and Johnson and wondered who'd keep an eye on them if Shepherd and Martin were both out. *Maybe I could get Mike or Ray Ray to come over in the morning?*

"I'm glad you're happy the Pâkk is going to keep you company," said Sally, "but how do we respond to these text messages? The General doesn't like to be kept waiting."

"I just told them I was undercover in Atlanta tracking Buckston and Jones," said Rosalind. I noticed her fingers had been tapping on her phone.

"I thought we were going to talk about it first?"

Rosalind looked at me over Max who was painting a picture of Terrhi on his plate with excess mustard.

"If I'd waited for you people to decide, I'd hit menopause first," said Rosalind.

"Who are Buckston and Jones?" asked Johnson.

"Jack and Poly," said Cornell.

"I'll tell them I'm in Atlanta with Cornell trying to locate Winfield and Johnson," said Sally.

"That works," said Cornell.

"None of this is a sure bet to help us find The General," said Poly, echoing my thoughts.

"Yeah, but we should know a lot more tomorrow," I said, starting to stand.

"Hey," said Chit. "I wanna get my fortune."

I walked over and grabbed a plastic wrapped cookie from a stack of them on the credenza, unwrapped it, and put it next to Chit's overturned soup bowl.

"Don't be a wiseass," said Chit. "Break the cookie for me."

"I'll do it," said Max.

He half-climbed onto the table and held Chit's fortune cookie in both hands, snapping it like a wishbone. Small bits of crispy cookie landed on the bowl and a narrow strip of white paper fluttered down. Chit intercepted it.

"What does it say?" asked Poly.

"You learn from your mistakes. You will learn a lot tomorrow," said Chit.

Just what I wanted to hear.

"On that note," I said, "I'm going to bed."

"Goodnight, Daddy!"

"Goodnight, Max."

Chapter 15

"...the accused shall enjoy the right to a speedy and public trial..."
— Sixth Amendment to the U.S. Constitution

"I'm beat," I said as I closed the door to our suite.

"How beat?" asked Poly, patting the bed and leering theatrically.

"Not *that* beat," I said, trying to return her leer and failing.

I sat on the bed and started to take off my shoes. Poly positioned herself behind me and began rubbing my shoulders.

"You know you'll sleep better if you're more relaxed," she said.

"True, and so will you," I offered.

Then Poly and I were startled by a deep voice bellowing close to my ears.

"Watch it with the hands, sister," said Chit.

We'd both forgotten my little friend had hitched a ride on the back of my neck after dinner.

"Sorry," said Poly.

She'd stopped rubbing and I missed her touch.

"I'd appreciate it if you'd get my bottle out of your backpack tool bag, bub," said Chit. "If the two of you are going to get mushy, I'm going to make myself scarce and catch up on my shows."

"Great idea," said Poly.

Chit grunted. I limped over to the low table where I'd stowed my gear with an awkward one shoe on, one shoe off gait. Then I removed Chit's bottle from my backpack and put it in the middle of the small circular table sitting in the far corner of our room.

"Thanks," I whispered, as Chit disappeared inside. "Enjoy watching the exploits of the Congressional Merchant Marine Subcommittee."

"Don't mention it," said Chit. Her voice echoed from inside her bottle. "The new representative from Iowa is *hot!*"

"Speaking of hot," said Poly, "it feels a bit warm in here."

Poly was wearing a cute black bolero jacket, a pretty white blouse with a big red bow, and gray slacks she'd put on after we'd finished bed testing. I felt decidedly underdressed, wearing only khakis, a company polo shirt, and my left shoe. My entire focus was on Poly as I watched her remove her jacket. She was so much better at this seduction stuff than I was. I couldn't keep my eyes off her and stared as she kicked off her pumps and put them neatly in the closet. She hung her jacket above them. Poly returned to the bed and patted a space next to her. I must not have moved fast enough, because I had to dodge out of the way of my flying right shoe.

"Get a move on, buster," she said, imitating Chit's tone. "I don't wanna do *all* the work myself."

"I'm moving, I'm moving," I said, quickly limping over to Poly.

She tugged my elbow as I was standing on one foot trying to remove my other shoe and I toppled over to lay beside her.

"Help me with the bow on this blouse," she requested.

I reached out to pull the bow but didn't quite make it.

"Your aim's a little off, but I can live with it," said Poly.

The tempo of her breathing changed—in a nice way.

"Is this good?"

"Yeah," she said, sounding like her brain was switching to autopilot. "It's getting even hotter in here."

She pulled the bow on her blouse herself, turned, and kissed me. All my concerns about The General pulled a Scarlett O'Hara and were gone with the wind.

"How are you feeling?" asked Poly after we broke our latest clinch.

"Mmmmm…" I said, kissing my way down her neck. "How do *you* feel?"

"Like you can stop any time you want in the next six or eight hours."

"Your wish is my…" I said.

Then a phone rang. It wasn't mine.

"What?" she said, trying to reengage her brain.

"Phone," I said.

It rang again, from somewhere a dozen feet away.

"The closet is ringing."

"Drat," said Poly. "Hold that thought."

She jumped up, managing to look artfully disheveled, and ran to the closet. Her phone kept ringing as she checked the pockets of her suit jacket.

"Hello?" She'd finally found it.

I could hear an urgent female voice coming through the phone's speaker, but couldn't make out any words. I asked a question with my eyebrows but didn't get an answer.

"Okay," said Poly. "Come over right away. I'll order you an autocab. See you in thirty."

Poly clicked off, then typed for a few seconds—ordering the autocab, I assumed. Her eyes were full of concern when she put her phone on the desk and returned to join me on the bed. I tried the *asking a question with my eyebrows* bit again and this time got an answer.

"It's Pomy," said Poly, naming her younger sister. "She sounded frantic. I told her to come over and tell us the details face to face."

"Got it," I said. "I hope it's not too serious."

I sat up, bent down, located my left shoe and began to put it on.

"What are you doing?" asked Poly.

"Getting dressed."

"Didn't you hear me?" asked Poly. "We've got thirty minutes."

* * * * *

Poly and I met Pomy as she got out of her autocab. Pomy's face was white and she had a panic-stricken *about to give a speech naked* look. We exchanged hugs and escorted Pomy down to the subterranean conference room. It still smelled like Hunan Pastrami. I pulled three chairs together and we sat. Poly held her sister's hands to help her feel grounded. Pomy was clearly trying to regain some self-control so she could explain.

"Just tell us, Sis," said Poly. "Use your words."

Poly's last phrase must have been some sort of family code because Pomy's mood switched from panicked to pissed off.

"Don't patronize me," grumbled Pomy. "You'd react the same way."

I was smart enough to keep my mouth shut. My phone decided to hop over to the nearby table so it could follow the discussion.

"Just tell us what happened," said Poly.

Pomy jerked her hands away and opened her purse.

"*This* happened!"

She removed a manila envelope from her purse and pulled out a letter on EUA Corporation Legal Department stationery, holding it up for us to read.

"Please be advised…" said Poly.

"…your trial in the matter of the Factor-E-Flor, an EUA Corporation company, versus Ms. Melpomene Keen-Jones…" I continued.

"…has been scheduled for 2:00 p.m. *tomorrow!*" shouted Pomy, speaking from memory. "How can they *do* that?"

"The Sixth Amendment *does* guarantee the right to a speedy trial," I interjected.

"For criminal, not civil trials," said Poly.

"Sorry."

I made a mental note to keep my mouth shut.

"I thought the wheels of justice turn slowly," complained Pomy. "Now they're moving at light speed. I'm not ready!"

"I don't understand it, either," said Poly. "There's been no time to prepare."

I ignored my mental note and pushed forward, against my own better judgment.

"It shouldn't be a surprise to either of you," I said. "Ever since Earth joined GaFTA, corporations have used arbitration for almost all litigation."

"Right," said Poly, raising her palm to her forehead and silently mouthing, "Doh."

"Which means traditional court dockets are open…"

"…without the typical delays previously forcing cases out two or three years into the future," said Poly. "I'm remembering details from my business law class at Emory's b-school. But even then, two days from suit to trial seems to be pushing it."

Then I noticed the tag line below the embossed EUA corporate name on the letter. *The best justice money can buy.*

"Crap," I said. "Now it's my turn to remember. Ever since the volume of cases shrank to a trickle, the courts have allowed plaintiffs and defendants to buy specific slots on their dockets as a way of funding their operations. Nobody cared because arbitration handled all the heavy lifting."

"Let me guess," said Poly. "All of the competent judges left to become arbitrators, right? We're left with the dregs?"

"It's a national disgrace, that's what it is," said Pomy.

"Traditional courtroom trials *are* broadcast to the stars," I added.

"Like Judge Judy?" asked Pomy.

"Those are reruns," said Poly.

"Most GaFTA member species prefer watching legislators over judges," I said. "Which helps explain why our traditional court system is starved for revenue."

"And why EUA can buy a date two days after they've served the suit," said Poly. "Do we have any recourse?"

"Let me check," I said.

I spoke to my phone and it came back with a quick answer.

"It's all a matter of relative payoffs," said my phone.

"Politics in Boston worked the same way," said Pomy. "You had to pay off somebody's relative to get anything approved."

"No," said my phone. "EUA put up a bid for a given date and you didn't counter it with a larger sum."

"I didn't even know there was a bidding process," said Pomy.

"Ignorance of the law is no excuse," said my phone.

I had to grab it quickly before Pomy threw my phone in the trash with the leftover duck sauce.

"Hey!" I said.

"Please don't shoot the messenger," said my phone. "Court records indicate you were contacted about the bidding this afternoon but didn't reply."

"I had my phone off. I was restoring a mummy and didn't get things wrapped up until after five," said Pomy.

Pomy worked at Emory's Carlos Museum—they had a marvelous collection of artifacts from ancient Egypt.

"Is there anything we can do to change it?" I asked.

"Not after the bidding is complete," said my phone.

"What am I going to *do?*" asked Pomy. "I don't want to go to jail."

"This is a civil trial," said Poly. "The worst that can happen is being assessed for massive damages."

"But I'm a poor grad student," said Pomy. "I can't afford to pay!"

"Then the worst that could happen would be massive damages and personal bankruptcy," said my phone.

Pomy tried to grab my phone and throw it against a wall but it danced out of reach.

"You could contact Jeanette Obi-Yu and seek her wise counsel," said my phone from the middle of the table.

"Her advice *would* be helpful," said Poly.

"You misunderstand," said my phone. "You should get in touch with GalCon Systems general counsel—the head of their legal department—and get that being's advice."

"Smart," I said. "It makes sense."

Poly made a call.

"Hello? Nettie? Mayday!" she said.

It only took three sentences for Poly to explain the situation to her old roommate at Harvard.

"Uh huh. Really? You'd already checked? Who is it? Tonight?"

I surprised myself by being mostly able to decode Poly's side of the conversation. Nettie was a step ahead and had already identified a great lawyer here in Atlanta to help Pomy after we'd told Nettie and her brother and sister about the lawsuit back in Las Vegas. Finally, something was going right.

"Still in Vegas? Pittsburgh?" said Poly. "Thanks! Text me his number and I'll send him the location. Catch you later."

Poly ended the call and typed a quick message. The Obi-Yu siblings must be back in Pittsburgh, where GalCon Systems had its headquarters.

"Good news?" I asked.

"Nettie's got a lawyer here in Atlanta who can help us," Poly answered. "He comes highly recommended by her legal team and will be here in twenty minutes."

"Great," said Pomy. "I need all the help I can get. What's his name?"

"Atticus Finch," Poly replied.

Wow, I thought. *With a name like that he had to be a Pyr. This was going to be interesting.*

Chapter 16

*"Simply because we were licked a hundred years before
we started is no reason for us not to try to win."*
— Atticus Finch

Sometimes timing is perfect. If Earth hadn't been invited to join the Galactic Free Trade Association in 2015 and gained the benefit of advanced alien congruency technology, the Yellowstone supervolcano would have blown within a decade and taken half the United States economy with it. Large congruencies—wormholes connecting points in space—bled the building Yellowstone magma off into the L5 Lagrange point of the Earth-Moon system where the resulting small satellite is currently being terraformed into a luxury resort.

I loved *BOOM!,* the 2022 movie about what might have happened if the supervolcano had exploded. It was considered the best special effects movie of the 2020s and was made by masters of disaster Roland Emmerich, Michael Bay, and the then up-and-coming Pyr director, Cecil B. DeMille.

I hoped Atticus Finch would prove as talented as his Hollywood counterpart.

All three of us went upstairs to the entrance of the complex to wait for Pomy's lawyer to arrive. It was close to midnight and there weren't any cars on the road until we spotted the headlights of an autocab coming up Northside Drive. The cab pulled under the cantilevered concrete slab protecting the main doors of the scientific facility and disgorged a decidedly odd-looking Pyr.

Atticus Finch was wearing a light-colored suit with a matching vest, a white shirt and a dark tie, much like Gregory Peck wore in the cinematic version of *To Kill a Mockingbird*—the original, not the atrocious 2023 remake with Matthew McConaughey.

What made Finch look particularly odd was the way his suit was trilaterally symmetric, with three ties and three rows of vest buttons, one under each eye. No matter which one of his three sides you looked at, he seemed to be the perfect model of a 1930s southern lawyer.

His glasses were even more odd. He wore dark-framed ones like Gregory Peck wore on screen. Pyrs don't have external noses, so wearing glasses poses a quite a challenge. The little lawyer had cleverly rigged up a small, rigid headband of the same material as his glasses frames to solve the problem. It sat a few inches down from the apex of his body and anchored the temple pieces. To continue the incongruency, his glasses had two lenses for each side of his triangular body, even though he only had one eye per side. It probably didn't matter, though. Most Pyrs have perfect vision and the lenses in his unusual eyewear were sure to be clear glass.

Three tentacles extended from the angles of each vertex of the alien's pyramidal body. They stuck out through small openings in the seams of his suit coat. One of the flexible appendages held an old-fashioned leather briefcase and the other two were waving a cordial greeting to our informal welcoming committee.

"Howdy good gentles," said the alien.

He sounded more like Andy Griffith than Gregory Peck.

"Howdy," the three of us replied in unrehearsed unison.

"Which one of you fine people is my client, Melpomene Keen-Jones?" he asked.

"That would be me," said Pomy, moving into a spontaneous curtsy. "And this is my sister, Poly, and her boyfriend and business partner, Jack."

I gave the Pyr a small bow and Poly copied her sister's more elaborate acknowledgment.

"Very pleased to meet you all," said the lawyer. "Let's get busy. There's a lot to do before the trial tomorrow afternoon."

"Yes, sir," I said, holding the main door open for him.

We led Mr. Atticus Finch, Esquire, inside the complex and down to our familiar conference room.

"Thanks for coming out so late," I said as we found seats around the table. I lowered the alien's chair so he could stand on it and we'd all be at the same height.

"Think nothing of it. It's part of the job," said the lawyer. "Why does it smell like corned beef and cabbage egg rolls in here?"

"We ordered dinner from Ginsberg & Wong," answered Poly.

"Ah, I see," said Finch, "or perhaps, I smell. No, that's not right either." The little Pyr tilted slightly from side to side as if it was considering alternatives. "No matter," Finch continued. "Their food's delicious but can't hold a candle to the Nicósn-Pyr fusion at Jade Triangle Garden."

"The new place in Buckhead?" I asked.

"That's the one," said Finch.

He seemed ready to continue discussing the relative merits of local restaurants, then caught himself and pulled his attention back to the matter at hand. He took a yellow legal pad and a sharpened pencil from his briefcase and held the pencil above the pad, poised to write. The end of his tentacle indented slightly, surrounding the pencil to give him better control. With another tentacle, he removed a small recording unit from his briefcase and turned it on. Then he spoke to Pomy in a reassuring southern Mississippi drawl. He didn't have to turn to face her—one of his eyes was always looking in her direction.

"Please tell me what happened on the day in question," said Atticus, "when you were visiting the offices of Factor-E-Flor."

"I was at their offices to ask Agnes Spelman about Poly and Jack. They were missing," said Pomy.

"No," said Finch, "please tell me the *truth* about what happened. We're all covered under attorney-client privilege."

"But *we're* not your clients," said Poly, waving her hand to take in me as well.

"Where is my brain?" asked the lawyer.

I held my tongue and didn't say, "Nine inches below your body's apex."

He pulled three documents out of his briefcase and used all three tentacles to hand one to each of us. He repeated the process with three pens.

"Sign these," said Atticus, using two of his mouths for emphasis.

"Shouldn't we read them first?" asked Pomy.

"My fees and expenses are being covered by the Obi-Yu Family Trust," said the Pyr.

"In that case, just sign," said Poly, following her own instructions. Pomy and I did the same.

"Now that we're all covered under attorney-client privilege," said Finch, "please provide the full details."

"Yes, sir," said Pomy. "Jack and Poly and Chit were breaking into Agnes Spelman's office—she was the CEO of Factor-E-Flor—and I was supposed to provide a diversion to get Ms. Spelman out of there, so they'd have a few minutes to look around."

"Chit?" asked the lawyer.

"A friend of mine. A Murm," I replied. "She's an insect-like being shaped like an oversized ladybug who's great at surveillance."

"I see," said Atticus. "I'm familiar with the species. Were you aware that Ms. Spelman is listed as the lead Factor-E-Flor plaintiff in this suit?"

I rubbed my chin. "No," I said. "I thought Martin had her in custody. She was in jail on Sunday."

"EUA's legal team must have gotten her released," said Poly.

"Why didn't he tell us in Vegas?" I asked.

"Maybe it happened while he was out of town?" suggested Poly.

"Martin?" asked Atticus.

"Capital Police Lieutenant Martin Lee," I said.

"I know him by reputation," said the lawyer. "Is he another friend of yours, Jack?"

"He's a friend of *ours*," clarified Poly.

"Guys," said Pomy. "Let me tell my story."

"Please do," said Atticus.

"I entered the building and told the receptionist I wanted to speak with Ms. Spelman."

"That's not exactly what you said," my phone piped up. "Here's a recording of your entrance."

My phone started to project security camera footage showing Pomy entering the Factor-E-Flor building's lobby onto the upper section of the conference room's smart wall.

"Freeze," I shouted.

My phone stopped the playback.

"Are smartphones covered under attorney-client privilege?" I asked.

"The Supreme Court ruled in 2027 that privilege extends to individuals' artificially intelligent devices," said Atticus, "but it's a moot point in this case. Factor-E-Flor should have a copy of their own security footage."

"Ummm, right," I mumbled. "Never mind."

"Continue," the lawyer instructed my phone.

The video played. Pomy entered and confronted the receptionist, giving an excellent performance as a frantically overwrought, highly concerned family member.

"You tell Ms. Agnes 'Fancy Pants' Spelman that she needs to teleport down here instantaneously and tell me what she's done with my sister and her boyfriend," said Pomy. "My mother and father are distraught and I'm disturbed enough to stand here and annoy you until I get some answers."

"I'm sorry, but no one sees Ms. Spelman without an appointment," said the receptionist. He was a little man with a precisely trimmed Van Dyke beard. "I'm sure I could find an opening on her schedule for you sometime next week. There's no one to speak with you today. Everyone is at a big off-site meeting to prepare for GALTEX."

Pomy wasn't taking it. She raised her voice. "Don't try to put me off, buster. I'm here to see Agnes Spelman and I want to see her right *now*."

A trim black woman of medium height in a gray power suit entered the lobby. She was Spelman's administrative assistant, Ms. Smith.

"What seems to be the problem, Hans?" she asked.

"I'm the problem!" said Pomy. "Where's. My. Sister?"

"I don't know, and I don't care," said Ms. Smith. "Please leave."

"I'm not leaving until I find out about…" began Pomy, playing her part to the hilt.

Ms. Smith crowded close to Pomy, overlapping her personal space and pressing Pomy back toward the entrance as if she had a high-strength personal force field.

"Take the rest of the afternoon off, Hans," said Ms. Smith, "after you lock the doors behind this young lady."

Pomy tried to drag things out, but Ms. Smith wasn't having any of it. The no-nonsense woman took Pomy's arm and pushed her out onto the front steps. Hans locked the doors and disappeared off camera—I assumed to a parking lot in the back of the building. Ms. Smith also went out of camera range.

"That was quite a distraction," said the Pyr attorney.

"You ain't seen nothin' yet," said my phone, sounding like Chit.

"There's additional footage?" asked Atticus.

"Yes, counselor," said my phone.

It switched to a view from another security camera aimed at the front of Factor-E-Flor's headquarters. Pomy removed a salami-sized metal cylinder from her purse, twisted a dial, and tossed it into a row of bushes flanking the entrance. Then she ran out into the parking lot and was off-camera. My phone shifted to yet another view and followed Pomy as she made tracks to the far side of the lot, seventy-five yards away. Then there was a huge *boom* and the feed stopped abruptly.

"What was that long, round object?" asked Atticus.

"A Macerator power pack cylinder," said Pomy.

"And what, perchance, is a Macerator?"

"It's a nickname for Mobile Armored Combat and Emergency Rescue units," answered Poly.

"They were developed by the United States Army before First Contact and are three generations obsolete now," I added.

"Ah, old-fashioned powered infantry suits," said Atticus. "Like in *Starship Troopers.*"

"Exactly," I agreed.

"Which leads to…" said Atticus.

"…how I ended up with a Macerator power pack cylinder," concluded Pomy.

"It's a long story," I said, then started in on the tale of Queen Sherrhi's *Star Wars*-themed banquet in our honor at the Atlanta Teleport Inn last week. Poly picked things up from when the Macerators attacked and my phone displayed a highlight reel showing how the various guests had taken down Macerators and their operators using everything from chairs to tablecloths to serving dishes.

"Impressive," said the Pyr. "You wouldn't happen to have any *more* of these power pack cylinders, would you?"

"There might be another one in my backpack tool bag," I said. "I can check."

"You can do that later and let me know," said Atticus. "I'm primarily interested in the firm that manufactured the cylinders."

"That's easy," said my phone. It projected a hologram of a cylinder in the air above us and rotated it until we could see the relevant details stamped on one side.

"Made by Factor-E-Flor Corporation," said Poly.

"Bingo," said Atticus.

"Will that help my case?" asked Pomy.

"It won't hurt," said the Pyr. "I can show that Factor-E-Flor bears some of the responsibility for the damage themselves."

Pomy started to smile—something she hadn't done since she'd arrived.

My phone returned to projecting video. "This is overhead footage from fire department drones that reached the scene a few minutes after the explosion," it said.

We saw pictures of the front of the building completely crashed in on itself. The second floor, where Agnes Spelman's office was located, tilted at a severe angle. Smoke and dust filled the air and made the scene look hazy.

"Had it been your intent to cause this level of destruction, Ms. Keen-Jones?" asked Atticus.

"Of course not," said Pomy. "I was just trying to create a small distraction. How was I to know there was a live gas main entering the building right under those bushes?"

"How indeed," said the Pyr.

Poly whispered to me. "She could have checked the building's plans before pulling that stunt."

"Give her a break. We were all making it up as we went along," I replied, *sotto voce.*

"To the best of your knowledge, did Factor-E-Flor have any use for a live gas feed?" asked Atticus.

"Reports from the fire department indicate that the company did not," said my phone. "The building was cited by the fire marshal on July 3rd, 2029, for not capping and evacuating the line."

"That's good news indeed," said Atticus. He regarded my phone with increased respect. "Well done," he said. "Would you be interested in a job as my paralegal?"

"Let's discuss that later," I said. "You can't have *my* phone, but I could give you one with similar basic programming you could train to your own specifications."

"Excellent," said the Pyr. "Something for another day."

"Is all that enough?" asked Pomy. "Will you be able to get me off without having to pay massive damages?"

"Nothing is one hundred percent sure," said Atticus, "but from what I've heard so far this evening, I would say the odds are good I can win a substantial reduction in damages, if not an outright acquittal. There's contributory negligence, product liability issues, and more in your favor."

"To say nothing of the fact that EUA orchestrated the whole Macerators' attack at the Teleport Inn and tried to kill us on several occasions," said Poly.

"And there's the booby-trapped elevator with the nova bomb at Zwilniki's hangar that EUA rigged," I said.

"I have more than enough information to represent you well tomorrow, Ms. Keen-Jones," said Atticus. "And I'm afraid that if your associates continue to talk I will overhear something I will be compelled to report as an officer of the court."

Poly and I looked at each other and pulled virtual zippers from one side of our lips to the other.

"Thank you for your help," said Pomy.

"You're quite welcome," said Atticus, "but now I must be going. I have to return to my office to work on my contribution."

"To the case?" asked Poly.

"To the judge," said Atticus. "But don't worry. The Obi-Yu family trust will match whatever EUA puts up to ensure an unbiased verdict."

"Did something change about the American legal system while I was on Orish?" I asked.

"Yes," said the Pyr attorney. "There's an app for buying judges."

"You mean justice," said Pomy, hopefully.

"Don't inquire too closely about sausage making," said Atticus. "The American system is famed galaxy-wide for providing the best judges money can buy."

"If you say so," said Pomy.

"And if we've got enough money on our side to ensure a level playing field," said Poly.

"Of course," said the Pyr. "Not to mention they take PayPal."

Chapter 17

"It's nice finding that place where you can just go and relax."
— Moises Arias

Poly walked Atticus out when he left to go back to his office and work on Pomy's case. I realized I didn't know much about Pyrs' sleep requirements. My phone assured me that they could go for a week without rest when necessary, saying something about evolutionary stresses early in their development as a sentient species that required long periods of hypervigilance. That made me wonder what predators looked like on the Pyr homeworld. They certainly didn't need to be built for speed, given that Pyrs' mobility cilia's top speed maxed out at the pace of a leisurely human stroll.

I posed the Pyr predators question to my phone and it showed us a video of a Pyr armed with six heavy clubs in his tentacles beset by a dozen attackers that I can best describe as trilaterally symmetric shark heads with three mouths. The Pyr in the video was rotating rapidly and bashing away, keeping his opponents at bay. When the sharp-toothed predators hopped up to bite him, the Pyr landed heavy blows that knocked them unconscious. The clubs made a definitive *twack* when they hit and the angry, angular landsharks weren't getting up in a hurry. I didn't worry about Atticus burning the midnight oil after that.

When Poly returned, she decided that it was too late for Pomy to go home. We got Pomy set up in an empty suite and Poly lent her an oversized t-shirt to sleep in. It had originally been mine and was white with the original green Starbucks logo. I'd bought it back before the company had been purchased by a Nicósn financial services company that offered loans and retail banking services along with even better coffee, thanks to Nicósn bioengineering. On the company's new logo, the mermaid had beard tentacles and a galcred symbol instead of a star on her crown. I liked the old one better.

We were in Pomy's room ready to head back to our own. Pomy had changed into the Starbucks shirt so she could go right to bed. Unfortunately, she was quivering like a string on an electric bass that had just been strummed, though she tried to put up a brave front.

"Good night, Sis," said Poly, hugging Pomy tight enough to dampen most of the quivering.

"Good night," Pomy replied. "And *thank* you. I'd never survive this without you."

"You'll do fine," I said, collecting my own hug and sensing Pomy's trembling directly. "Get some rest and try not to worry."

"You might as well tell me not to think of pink elephants with blue polka dots," said Pomy.

Poly and I laughed.

"Don't make fun of me," said Pomy. "I'm so wound up, I don't know if I'll be able to get to sleep."

"We're not making fun of you," I said. "We're thinking of Terrhi."

That won us a quick, nervous smile from Pomy.

"Would you like a drink?" asked Poly. "We can order a booze delivery with some mixers."

"No, I need a clear head tomorrow. Any other ideas?"

"You could hum the *Tallis Canon* when your head hits the pillow and see if that helps," suggested Poly.

"That doesn't work for me," said Pomy. "My mind keeps free-associating and turns it into the *1812 Overture*."

It made sense. She substituted cannons for canons.

"I have a never-fail way to help you relax," I said.

"You do?" asked Pomy. "*Please* tell me."

"Yes, Jack," said Poly. "Tell us."

From her tone, I was afraid Poly thought this was something I'd learned from Rosalind.

"I learned this from my step-father," I said to reassure. "It always works for me."

"What do I do?" asked Pomy.

"Pull back the bedclothes so you can just fall back into bed when we're done," I said. "Poly can tuck you in."

Pomy stuck her tongue out at me to show she wasn't five and didn't need to be tucked in, thereby demonstrating that she did. She pulled back the coverlet, blanket and top sheet.

"Now what?"

"Sit on the edge of the bed. Close your eyes. Put your feet flat on the floor. Keep your back straight and your shoulders square."

Pomy complied. I could still see a slight tremble, but her posture was good.

"Breathe in through your nose—use an eight count—and let the air out slowly through your mouth."

Poly sat down in one of the armchairs to one side and also followed my instructions.

"This feels good," said Pomy.

"Don't talk, breathe," I said, "and listen."

I heard Pomy *and* Poly breathing together, keeping the same rhythm. It was time for the next phase. I modulated my voice to produce a soothing tone.

"Imagine that your skull is filled with warm water. There's an imaginary axle that runs from just in front of one ear to just in front of the other."

I paused to give them time to visualize.

"Now imagine there's an old fashioned wooden water wheel, the kind with big wide buckets, rotating around that axle. It moves from your chin to your forehead to the crown of your head, then over the top and back again in time to your breathing. It goes up when you inhale, collecting warm water, then releases that water when you exhale, sending it down your spine."

Both sisters were relaxing. The muscles on Pomy's face were no longer tense and she wasn't quivering. Poly's face had a beatific smile. The exercise was working.

"Feel the water flowing down your spine as you exhale. Sense the warm liquid moving down your back to your hips, then out along your legs, past your knees and along to your ankles and your feet. Feel the warmth flowing as you breathe and let the water carry waves of relaxation all the way out to the tips of your toes. Breathe. Let the water flow."

Pomy and Poly's breathing was slowing. Their eyes were closed and they were focused on my words.

"Now let the water flow along your shoulders and down your arms," I said. "Let the warm water move down your arms, past your elbows and wrists to your hands."

I'd used this technique on myself several times—it was my favorite way to get to sleep when I was too keyed up. I also used it to calm myself before important client meetings when I needed to be centered and at my best. I wondered if it was a form of hypnosis—self-hypnosis in my case—and decided I wasn't going to try issuing any hypnotic suggestions. I was sure that wouldn't end well.

"Sense the movement of the water down your arms," I said. "Feel the warmth flowing out to the ends of your fingers. Feel the warmth flowing down your back, along the channels of your body. Your neck is relaxed. Your shoulders are relaxed. Your trunk is relaxed. Your arms are relaxed. Your legs are relaxed. Let the water flow and know you're at peace."

That did it. Pomy was in some sort of self-induced trance. She wasn't quivering and her body had lost all the tension that was making it impossible for her to sleep. I crossed to her and gently guided her body down to the mattress, putting her head on a pillow and covering her with the sheet, blanket and coverlet. Her breathing was easy and rhythmic and her face looked like an angel's from a Renaissance painting. She should get a good night's sleep.

I walked over to Poly and helped her stand. She wasn't really awake, but she let me guide her back to our room on autopilot. She took off her clothes without engaging the conscious part of her brain and I tucked her in much the same way I had for her sister, except Poly got a kiss on her forehead. Then I took off my own clothes, put my phone on the nightstand and climbed in with her, sliding to the center so I could feel her warmth beside me.

"Thank you," murmured Poly.

"Sleep, my love," I said.

My own breathing became slow and regular and I was only momentarily distracted by an unfamiliar sound.

My phone was snoring.

Chapter 18

"Puerto Rico is one of those places you can be
as quiet or as crazy as you want..."
— Bruce Forsyth

I ordered two dozen Dauushan-hummingbird-egg-and-sausage-filled steamed buns from Take a Bao, the well-reviewed Chinese specialty restaurant on 10th Street across from Georgia Tech's Paper Museum. I'd learned to love filled steamed buns when my mom took an assignment in Jakarta to advise the Indonesian government on the most effective way to convert their existing oil, gas and coal power plants to modern, non-polluting congruency-based systems.

The Chinese enclaves in the multi-island nation's capital made wonderful bao. I was just a kid and ran wild exploring the city's nooks and crannies. There were days when I ate bao for breakfast, lunch and dinner. I loved getting them fresh out of the steamer when they were too hot to hold in your bare hands. Did I mention I learned to juggle that summer?

Poly complimented me on the relaxation technique I'd shown her last night. She said it really helped her sleep, though I thought our other exercise earlier in the day might have made some small contribution to her peaceful slumber. Pomy slept well, too, without—I assumed—Poly's additional exercise, so perhaps my relaxation technique *was* the primary factor. She didn't seem consumed by worry the way she'd been last night. Now Pomy was confident, if not optimistic, about what the day would bring. We got her off early, after she'd had a bao and a cup of tea, so she could go back to her place and prepare. Poly and I promised we'd meet her at the courthouse an hour before the trial.

The rest of our somewhat merry band were on Las Vegas time physiologically and still asleep. I sent emails letting them know about Pomy's trial this afternoon and said we'd meet and exchange notes at dinner at seven. I was trying to get us closer to dining at normal hours for Atlanta, not Sin City, and thought that time was a reasonable compromise.

Poly and I had cleaned up the business outfits we'd worn to meet Rosalind, Cornell and Sally the morning before. Our appointment with Pablo Daniel Figueres was in just over an hour and it was important for us to look professional. Her gray business suit only needed to be brushed off to be presentable and my blue pinstripe was fine after I gave it five minutes with a hot iron to get the wrinkles out. I was glad I hadn't had to climb the side of the butte in a suit or my ensemble would have been a total loss. We inspected each other, looking for stray bits of lint or other imperfections. I removed an auburn hair from Poly's shoulder by flicking it with the bottom edge of my hand.

"That should do it," I said. "You're perfect."

Poly straightened my tie and kissed my cheek.

"There. You are, too," she said.

Chit popped out of her bottle to join us.

"Watch it, sister," said my little friend. "You'll give 'im a big head and it's big enough already."

"I love you, too," I replied. "Coming with us?"

"Wouldn't miss it," said Chit.

She buzzed over to land on my shoulder. Her paint scheme matched the color of my hair and she found a spot to hang out where my hair just covered her body at the nape of my neck.

"Careful," I said. "That tickles!"

"Be glad I don't bite," said Chit.

"I'll bet you say that to all the boys," teased Poly.

"Wouldn't cha like t'know?"

"If I could interrupt your badinage for a moment," I said.

Poly laughed. So did Chit.

"Whadda ya want, bucko?"

"Are you okay with hanging around in Fiqueres' office after we leave to see what you can find out?" I asked.

"I figured as much," said Chit. "Ya only want me for my ears."

"And your charming disposition," added Poly.

"That, too," I said. "Will you do it?"

"Of course I'll do it. I gotta help you apes figure out who The General is, don't I?"

"We'd appreciate it," said Poly, sweetly.

"Now she's tryin' t' butter me up," said Chit. I could hear a smile in her voice.

"Let's get going," I said. "Traffic is a bear at this time of day."

"You must have heard about that grisly ten-car pileup on I-85," said Chit.

"Ursus arctos horribilus," said Poly.

She opened the door to our suite and held it for me and Chit as we left.

My phone summoned an autocab and we were soon on our way down Marietta Street for our ten o'clock audience with Pablo Daniel Figueres.

Figueres' penthouse was at the top of the SLN Tower, across from the CNN Center and Royal Dutch Philips Arena, not far from the hulking black bulk of EUA's corporate headquarters. SLN Tower was the first skyscraper built in Atlanta to incorporate galactic materials and technologies. Even before counting its dirigible mooring mast and broadcast antennae, the building came in at five thousand, two hundred and eight-one feet, so Figueres' marketing team could brag it was over a mile tall.

The oligarch's personal living quarters were on three of the upper-most floors beneath the dirigible depot, but we weren't going that high. SLN Enterprises' executive offices were on the one hundred twenty-seventh through one hundred and thirtieth floors.

"You should do the talking," I said. "You're the recent Georgia Tech grad. That should give you an in."

"Right," said Poly, "but feel free to jump in. Figueres is supposed to have a soft spot for entrepreneurs. After all, he started SLN in his dorm room."

I nodded. Pablo Daniel Figueres was a self-made billionaire— in galcreds, not just dollars—and was the top philanthropist and number one business celebrity in the metro-Atlanta region.

I'd been surprised and pleased that he will willing to meet with us, especially on short notice.

"Do you think PDF is The General?" I asked.

"I don't know what to think," said Poly. "That's why we're meeting him. Some of Figueres' rhetoric when he was promoting Puerto Rican statehood sounds a lot like Earth First Militant language on a smaller scale."

"Really?"

My phone took that as its cue to play an excerpt. I heard Pablo Daniel Figueres' highly recognizable voice. It was the same voice that blared constantly from video ads at the SLN Capital Hotel in Las Vegas.

"It is time for the people of Puerto Rico to take their place on the American stage, and more, on the *world* stage and the *galactic* stage. It is time for her people to *lead,* not just be small cogs in a large, uncaring machine. It is time for the citizens of Puerto Rico to show that they are not just extras entertaining tourists in a tropical island paradise, but a people of destiny."

"I see what you mean," I said. "Sounds like there's enough megalomania there for him to be The General."

"I agree," said Poly, "but we'll know more soon."

"Why does he sound like such a wack-a-doodle in that speech, but have such a good rep as a businessman?" asked Chit.

"He got lucky," I said, "and made a Dauushan long ton of money by locking up Terran legislative broadcast rights early."

"Then he was smart enough to spread his wealth around to get everyone on his side," added Poly.

"Yeah, yeah, I get it," said Chit. "He can point to all the jobs he's created with the Sirocco Legislature Network, plus his hotels and casinos, along with donating money for buildings at Georgia Tech…" said Chit.

"And SLN Stadium for the Falcons," I continued.

"Not to forget all the charity work funded by the PDF Foundation," said Pomy.

"So he's a saint?" asked Chit.

"Hardly," I said. "I've heard stories about how he's kept competitors out of lucrative contracts."

"That's better," said Chit. "Saints are hard to be around—not that I've ever had to worry about that with *you,* bucko."

"I've never claimed a halo," I said.

"Couldn't prove it by her," said Chit. She must have meant Poly.

"Oh," said Poly. "You mean when I was trying to get him into bed? He wasn't a saint, just skittish."

"Hey!" I said. I didn't know how I felt about them discussing me when I was with them in the autocab. "Let's get back to talking about Figueres."

"Is he really a Puerto Rican chauvinist?" asked Chit. "Does that make him a racist?"

"More of a P. T. Barnum-style promoter, I'd say," Poly replied. "He's not trying to drag anybody else down, just lift up Puerto Ricans specifically and Hispanics in general."

"Isn't he the one who talked Marvel Comics into replacing Captain America with a skinny kid from the streets of San Juan who took super soldier serum?" I asked.

"I read that," said Chit. "They made him Captain Puerto Rico for a year."

"And they didn't even have to change Cap's costume," I said. "The fans got a kick out of that."

"If we can get back on topic, please," said Poly.

"I thought we *were* on topic," said Chit. "He's not a racist, but how does Figueres feel about galactics?"

"I assumed he'd love them," I said. "They've made him a multi-billionaire."

"He hires lots of GaFTA member species to do play-by-play for his legislative broadcasts," said Poly.

"Most are drawn from the relevant species for each receiving planet," I said. "Except for Pâkk planets. They want announcers who do more than grunt."

"Prey species are better at holding Pâkks' attention," said Chit. *That made sense.*

"While SLN does hire non-Terrans for some roles, over ninety-two percent of their employees are from Earth or one of her colonies," said my phone.

"That's the smoking gun," I said. "With those kind of numbers, Figueres must be The General and behind EUA Corporation. Earth Über Alles."

"What percentage of SLN's operations are based on Terra?" asked Poly.

"Ninety-five percent," said my phone.

"Ummm…" I said, trying to figure out how to walk back my previous assertion.

I was saved from having to reply by an announcement from the autocab.

"SLN Tower," said its synthesized voice, optimized for maximum appeal across ages, genders, species, and cultures.

"Great timing," I said. We were fifteen minutes early.

Poly and I looked up but couldn't see the top of the building a mile above us. I understood the top third of the tower had its own weather patterns, but was glad it wasn't raining where we were at ground level. We pushed through the revolving doors to enter the expansive five-story lobby. The walls were polished purple and green Nicósn marble shot through with sparkling veins of gold and silver. The sea life that formed limestone and later marble on Nicós was quite colorful. The floor was also marble—black this time—with lots of tiny copper flecks. I didn't know what planet it was from and made a mental note to look it up later.

Banks of elevators surrounded the lobby, and a large circular reception desk in the center was staffed with dozens of SLN employees assisting visitors. We stood in line for an open customer service rep and didn't have to wait long.

"Mr. Figueres' office? Do you have an appointment?"

We gave him our names and he consulted a screen only he could see.

"Very good, Ms. Keen-Jones, Mr. Buckston. That's the one hundred and thirtieth floor. I'll escort you to your elevator."

Poly and I murmured our thanks.

The young man—he was a Sikh with beard, turban and dagger—walked toward the back of the lobby with us following like ducklings behind. We didn't stop at any of the lobby's large banks of elevators, but were delivered to a lift marked *Private* that was thirty paces down an arched corridor. Our guide pushed the button and waited with us until we were aboard.

"Have a productive meeting," said the Sikh as the doors closed.

Chit started to clear her throat, about to speak, but Poly coughed to cover the sound.

"Jack," she said, "don't say a thing. I don't want to hear any of your Sikh jokes. You don't know who might be listening."

"Right," I said, getting her meaning. The elevator was probably bugged—and not just by Chit. My little friend also got the message and kept quiet.

The lift rose rapidly, but I didn't have to worry about my ears adjusting. The entire building was pressurized to nine hundred and eighty-three feet above sea level, the pressure at the ground floor. I'd read about that in an engineering magazine while waiting to see a prospective client a few years ago and was fascinated by how they'd pulled it off. Pressure doors also served as fire doors and building management could evacuate all the oxygen from a floor and replace it in less than six seconds. That allowed them to put out any potential conflagration before it could get established, without injuring any sentients located on that floor.

Poly squeezed my hand quickly just before the doors opened, then let go and returned to her consummate business professional mode.

"Welcome to SLN Enterprises," said a young woman with a peaches and cream complexion, blonde hair, and a pronounced south-Georgia accent. She wasn't a dumb blonde, however. There was intelligence in her eyes and I expected she had an M.B.A. from a respected university's business school to her credit. This magnolia had a steel core.

"Thank you," I said.

"It's good of Mr. Figueres to see us," said Poly.

"Yes," said the blonde. "It is."

That was surprising. I'd expected better manners. Perhaps the young woman was more steel than magnolia. Alternatively, perhaps she didn't know why her boss was willing to meet with us on short notice. She struck me as the sort of person who needed to know all the details.

"I'm Camilla Moultrie, Mr. Figueres' personal assistant," she said. "He's still in a meeting but you can wait in a conference room until he's free."

Poly and I nodded.

"That's fine," said Poly. "Thanks."

Camilla took us to a spacious conference room with seats for twenty around a long, polished, dark-wood oval. Poly and I didn't sit.

"Would you like anything to drink? Water? Juice?" She paused for a moment before adding the generic term for soft drinks in metro-Atlanta. "Coke?"

"I'm fine, thank you," I said.

"So am I," said Poly.

Camilla left, but we couldn't talk privately. This room was probably bugged, just like the elevator. It didn't matter, though. The outer wall of the conference room was floor-to-ceiling windows.

Poly and I were pulled toward the windows as if in the grip of a tractor beam from the *Enterprise.* We were facing north-east and could see the skyscrapers of Midtown, Buckhead, and the Perimeter to the north and the tall granite egg of Stone Mountain to the east. There were plenty of fluffy white clouds scudding by below us that gave the view a heightened sense of three-dimensionality.

I looked for the Ad Astra complex and could spot the upper stories, but not my garden apartment. The football stadium at Georgia Tech was easy to spot. So was the old Mercedes Benz stadium slightly to the west. Figueres had mothballed it so he could build a new sports palace for the Atlanta Falcons in

Gwinnett county, northeast of town. I could make out SLN Stadium just east of I-85 about twenty miles north. Poly was equally caught up in the view.

"There's my apartment," she said.

"Where?" I asked.

"See that big yellow church on Emory's campus?"

"Glenn Memorial?"

"Uh huh," said Poly. "It's just around the corner from there on Oxford Road."

"If you say so," I replied.

Was it weird that I'd never been to Poly's apartment? She always came to my place.

"It's almost hypnotic, isn't it?" said a mellow baritone voice behind us. "You should see it from my penthouse."

Poly and I turned around. She extended her hand.

"Mr. Figueres," she said. "It's a pleasure to meet you."

They shook hands, then it was my turn.

"Thanks for seeing us," I said. "We expected Ms. Moultrie to come back and retrieve us."

We shook. He had a firm, friendly grip and the relaxed manner of a man who didn't have to prove anything. My first impression was that he was the sort of guy I'd *like* to have as a client.

"Call it an idiosyncrasy," said Figueres, "but I like to see how people I'm going to meet for the first time handle the view."

"Did we pass?" asked Poly.

"Oh, yes," said Figueres. "You couldn't turn away. Small-minded people get bored and look at their cell phones after only a few minutes."

"I could look at that view for hours, Mr. Figueres," I said.

"Call me Danny," said Figueres. "May I call you Jack?"

"Of course," I said. "Not Pablo?"

"Pablo was my father. My friends call me Danny or Danny-El."

Danny was of medium height with a compact, muscular build and a face on its way to being craggy in another couple of decades or so when he hit his fifties. His dark black hair was thick and lustrous and his smile seemed genuine. He looked like he did in his ads, but came off as more authentic in person than when he was on-screen in sales mode.

"And you must be Poly?" asked Danny. He pronounced it, tentatively, as *Poe-Lee*.

"It's Poly as in *Poly*technic," said Poly.

"Or *poly*math," said Danny. "*Poly.* I remember now. That's what Dr. Urrrson called you. He thinks you're the best student he's had in a decade and you've got quite an impressive resume. Dual master's degrees from Georgia Tech *and* Emory."

Poly looked embarrassed.

"That was very nice of him to say," she said.

"Don't be afraid to blow your own horn," said Danny. "You've earned it."

Poly smiled and asked, "How did you get my resume?"

"I called my human resources department," said Danny. "We recruited you at both Emory *and* Tech. Why didn't you accept our offer? If money was the issue, I'll double it, and bump you up two levels in the org chart."

"That's very generous," said Poly, "but Jack's made me a partner and we're going to build Xenotech Support Corporation together."

She smiled at me and I smiled back, my affection for her obvious in my eyes.

"So *that's* how it is," said Danny. "I can't compete with that."

Now both of us blushed.

"I checked *you* out, too," said Danny, addressing me this time. "A doctorate in Mutatechnology from Mulbiri State on Orish at twenty-one. Fluency in ten Terran and seventeen galactic languages. Built a successful technical support company in three years. Friends in high places, like the Dauushan royal family. You're pretty impressive yourself, Jack. I'd ask you if you wanted a job, but I know your answer will be the same as hers."

Danny waved toward Poly.

"But the two of you didn't come here for the view. Let's move over to my office where we'll have some privacy."

We trailed along behind Danny, returning to duckling mode, and found ourselves in his business office. It was what you'd expect a powerful CEO's office to be, with a brag wall filled with photographs of Danny with celebrities and important people, dark wainscoting, and understated elegance just the right side of opulence. A large Puerto Rican flag hung from the top of the wall opposite his desk chair so it was always in easy view. Our interest in the flag was obvious.

"I keep it there so I'm always reminded of where I came from," he said.

"You were the skinny kid from the streets of San Juan who took the super soldier serum," said Poly.

"Sort of," said Danny, "if getting into Georgia Tech was super soldier serum. I was just a kid trying to get by. I tried to pull a street hustle on a lawyer from Atlanta and got caught at it. He and his wife were in Old San Juan on vacation. Instead of turning me over to the police, he changed my life. I don't know why, but I guess he saw something in me. He was the one who paid my way into a good prep school here in town and got me accepted at Tech."

"That's quite a story," I said. "Why isn't it in your autobiography? I loved *From San Juan to the Stars,* by the way."

"Thanks," said Danny. "I'll tell my ghost writer. It's not in there because my benefactor asked me not to mention it. He didn't want it getting out that he had a soft side."

"I can understand that," said Poly, "with him being a lawyer and all."

Danny took a phone out of his suit pocket and tapped a few keys.

"That should do it," he said. "I turned on a portable privacy field. Camilla thinks she needs to know everything I know to help her do my job for me."

Poly and I laughed, nervously. We'd had the same feeling about Camilla spying on *us*.

"Have a seat," said Danny. He invited us to take seats on a couch behind a coffee table in a corner of his office and sat in a comfortable armchair close by.

"Spill it," he said. "What did you come here to talk about?"

As we'd discussed, Poly took the lead.

"We came here to find out if you're The General—the evil mastermind behind EUA Corporation and the Earth First Militant movement."

Wow! No beating around the bush for my partner.

Maybe it would have been better if *I'd* taken the lead in this particular conversation.

Chapter 19

"A small leak will sink a big ship."
— Benjamin Franklin

"Excuse me," said Danny. "I think I was just insulted, but what you said makes so little sense I'm not sure."

His posture shifted from open to defensive as he crossed his arms over his chest.

"No," said Poly. "Now that we've met you we don't think you're The General, but we did think it was a high probability earlier. This visit was to scope out whether you were friend or foe."

"I take it you've decided to put me in the *friend* category?" said Danny. "What about Aragorn?"

"Huh?" I said.

Then it hit me. I recited a line I'd memorized from *The Lord of the Rings*. The hobbits had just met Strider and aren't sure whether to trust him.

"... a servant of the enemy would look fair and feel foul," I quoted.

"I look fair, I hope," said Danny, "and I hope I feel fair, too, not foul. At least I try to treat my employees, customers, and other stakeholders fairly."

"That was my read," said Poly. "I think I'm a good judge of character, and while you clearly *are* a character..."

Danny uncrossed his arms and smiled.

"... I don't think you're a Terran chauvinist hell-bent on conquering the galaxy for the glory of Mother Gaia, even though you *are* a general."

"You mean that honorary title in the Puerto Rican state guard?" asked Danny. He started chuckling. "That was the governor's way of showing her appreciation for not running against her."

It was my turn to laugh. "I knew you were too smart to run for public office."

"Thank you for that vote of confidence," said Danny. "In that case, I'll hold off deciding which side of the boundary between sense and madness you and your partner are on until we've gotten to know each other better."

"Much obliged," I said. "That's the most we can expect under the circumstances." I paused, then changed direction. "We're trying to learn as much as we can about EUA Corporation. Have you had any dealings with their executive leadership team?"

"We've got a dozen or so joint ventures with EUA," said Danny. "They've partnered with half the Terran 500, but I haven't been down in the trenches negotiating our deals with them. I usually just come in and shake hands with one of EUA's EVPs when it's time to sign contracts. It's a photo op thing for the business press."

"Do you remember any of the EUA executives' names?" I pressed.

"No, sorry," said Danny. "Camilla would, I'm sure. I can ask her."

"Maybe later," I said. "Give yourself a few more seconds to think."

Danny rubbed his chin like it was a genie's lamp.

"Got it," he said. "The folks at that company with the weird name."

"Chapultepec & Castle?" suggested Poly.

"That's the one. Scott Winfield and Josephine Johnson."

"We know about them. Anybody else?" I asked.

"Some Ivy League guy and a tall woman who comes on like a blonde Jessica Rabbit," said Danny. "My apologies, Poly."

"Don't worry about it," said Poly. "I know who you mean and you're right on target."

She stared at me for a long moment. I wasn't looking forward to our next private discussion about Rosalind.

"Are there more?" I asked, hoping to coax something actionable out of our conversation.

"Just their top legal people," said Danny. "EUA's got a crack legal team—real deal makers. They're not the usual gaggle of unimaginative gray suits that tell you what you can't do all the time. Their corporate counsel folks have *vision*. That's why they're so good at hammering out joint ventures and acquisitions."

"Fascinating," I said.

I didn't mention that Poly's sister would be in court against one of EUA's corporate sharks in a few hours. I also didn't tell Danny that people high up inside EUA were trying to kill us. That would probably make it a lot easier for him to categorize us as crackpots.

"What's this about The General and the Earth First Militant organization?" asked Danny.

"Remember when the Princess of Dauush was kidnapped on First Contact Day?" I asked.

"Of course," answered Danny. "Everyone was watching the news instead of my legislative broadcasts."

"That was an Earth First Militant operation orchestrated by Anthony Zwilniki at VIGorish Labs."

"And EUA had recently acquired his company," said Poly.

"That doesn't prove EUA was behind it," challenged Danny.

"Winfield and Johnson confirmed it," I said.

"How do you know all this?" asked Danny.

"Jack and I handled the rescue," said Poly. She smiled at me and squeezed my hand.

"That was *you?* I'm impressed."

I smiled back and replayed my favorite memories of saving Terrhi, which did *not* include getting shot.

"Thank you," said Poly.

"The rescue was one thing," said Danny, "but keeping your involvement out of the media was a real coup. Believe me, I know."

That was more a matter of keeping ourselves out of the spotlight to try to preserve some semblance of normal lives. The twenty-four-hour news cycle can be brutal.

"I'm glad you were impressed. That makes a perfect segue into the *other* reason we're here," said Poly. "We're looking for consulting opportunities. Could we be useful to SLN in some capacity? You wanted to hire both of us—why not *rent* us? Is there any way Xenotech Support Corporation can be of service to you or one of your companies?"

I saw what she was doing. Poly was putting the conversation back on a more traditional business footing, instead of sliding toward having Danny label us as paranoid conspiracy theorists.

Danny rubbed his chin again.

"There *is* something I could use your help with," he said.

"Name it," said Poly.

"We're leaking," said Danny, "and I want to find out who's responsible."

"Leaking?" I asked.

"Leaking money. Leaking information. Leaking top people," said Danny. "My auditors uncovered some of it. A million here, a million there, and pretty soon you're talking real money."

I asked a leading question. "You said information and people as well?"

"Right," said Danny. "I.T. and H.R. uncovered patterns that didn't make sense. Details about key bids leaking to competitors. Senior sales people and software developers leaving without telling us where they were going, that sort of thing."

Poly and I nodded.

"It's never been so much that the VPs running any single division of SLN would get suspicious," said Danny, "but from where I sit it tells me we're being targeted."

"From what you've said, I'd agree," I contributed.

"I'd usually have my own security people investigate, but I don't know if any of them are part of the problem," said Danny.

"Bringing in outsiders makes a lot of sense," said Poly. "It's hard to know who you can trust on the inside."

"Uh huh," said Danny. "But this sort of investigation's not really in your wheelhouse, is it? You specialize in alien tech support, right?"

"Technical support is only one of our core competencies," answered Poly. "We're also quite skilled in industrial espionage and covert assignments. You can ask Jeanette Obi-Yu at GalCon Systems, if you'd like a reference."

"I already did," said Danny. "Bart Urrrson dropped her name yesterday. I called Nettie right after he asked for this meeting."

"Then why did you say we didn't handle investigations?" asked Poly.

"I wanted to see if you'd tell me about the job you just did for her," said Danny.

"I'd never mention the specifics of client assignments without prior approval," said Poly.

"Jeanette said you'd say that," said Danny "She told me all about what you did for GalCon Systems in Las Vegas."

Poly didn't say anything. Her expression remained neutral. Danny laughed.

"Congratulations. You passed again," he said. "You can keep a secret. Jeanette told me about one of her people turning out to be a mole, and how you and Jack uncovered her."

I started to squirm—on the inside, anyway. I was feeling uncomfortable about the idea of uncovering Rosalind. Pictures from our brief time together on Orish fleshed, I mean flashed in front of my eyes. *Get your brain in focus, Jack!* I hoped Danny never realized that the Jessica Rabbit woman from EUA was also the person who'd stolen the plans for GalCon Systems' new router. I was glad Poly was carrying the conversation.

"In the interest of full disclosure," said Poly, "Nettie and I were roommates at Harvard."

"Full marks for honesty," said Danny, "and something I already knew. Janet Yu, your mother, and I all served together on an advisory board for the Smithsonian back when you and Nettie were in college. I was just a kid and they helped show me the ropes."

He and Poly exchanged smiles.

"Mom told me about that," said Poly. "She wanted you to ask me out."

"Back then, I was too young and full of myself to ask you or Nettie out," said Danny.

"You only had time for models and starlets," said Poly.

"I was going through my Tony Stark phase," said Danny.

"And you've outgrown that stage now?" asked Poly.

"Maybe," hedged Danny.

Both of them shrugged, then laughed.

It made sense that Pablo Daniel Figueres would know Barbara Keen, Poly's mother and the highly successful publisher of *Keen's Guides* to the various planets of the galaxy. Perhaps it wasn't so surprising that we'd managed to get an appointment with Danny at short notice after all. I was getting impatient with all the chit-chat. When would he cut to the chase and tell us the specifics of what he needed?

"Now that the preliminary fencing is over," said Danny, "let's cut to the chase."

I wondered if I was unconsciously developing skills as a projective telepath.

"I need you to look into my leaks from multiple directions," he said. "Forensic accounting, digging into server access logs, reviewing personnel records, whatever it takes to get to the bottom of things and find out who or what is siphoning off money, information, and my best employees."

"We'd be glad to handle the investigation," said Poly.

She named a fee. I made sure I didn't react to the number—I was used to dealing with small and mid-sized clients, but Poly must have learned how to play in the big leagues at business school or her mother's knee. Danny didn't react either. He just nodded.

"Send me a contract and I'll sign it," said Danny, "after I've had a chance to run it by my legal department."

That was another test. Poly didn't fall for it.

"I don't think it would be wise to have this agreement in writing," she said. "We don't know who in your organization might be involved and the fewer the number of people who know about our investigation, the better."

"I couldn't fool you," said Danny. "You're Barbara Keen's daughter, all right. That reminds me, I need to get in touch with your mother. We're negotiating a full-package legislative broadcast deal with the Fthtipth and Babs always had amazing insights into their psychology."

Babs?

The Fthtipth were a galactic species that looked like Mylar balloons and floated about in the atmosphere. They had a special appreciation for the nuances of hot air, and therefore a special love for the deliberations of Terran legislative bodies.

"I think she's making the rounds of the Pyr pleasure planets with my father right now," said Poly. "Her last message said something about 'making up for lost time.'"

"Maybe I'd better not interrupt her," said Danny.

"I wouldn't advise it," said Poly. "We can all shake on the deal. I know your word is your bond."

"And my phone can capture it on video for a permanent record," I said.

Poly gave me a *don't-screw-up-the-deal* look, but I had a method to my madness. My phone hopped off my belt, extruded arms, legs, and a head. It walked across the coffee table to stand by Danny.

"Capturing video is a specialty," said my phone. "You can be confident it will remain fully confidential."

"How does it *do* that?" asked Danny. He waved at my oddly *mobile* phone.

"It's an Orishen mutacase," I said. "I can hook you up with my supplier."

"That would be great," he said. Then his own phone made the *ding* of an incoming text message.

"That should be a link to a site where you can purchase a mutacase," said my phone. "Any color you want so long as it's black."

"You've programmed it with *initiative,* too?" chuckled Danny.

I nodded, though I didn't know how much I wanted to encourage him. A lot of his people's jobs might be up for review if he got his hands on my custom artificial intelligence mods. It was time to change the subject, even if it might blindside Poly.

"In the interest of full disclosure," I said, "it's my turn to share more information. We traced the Galcon Systems' industrial espionage back to an EUA company."

"Chapultepec & Castle," said Poly.

She realized what I was doing. We'd established a relationship based on trust with Danny and now was the best time to tell him the rest of the story. I didn't think he'd write us off as crackpots now.

"And uncovered a plot to steal intellectual property from hundreds of companies at GALTEX engineered by EUA Corporation," I continued.

"That failed, thanks to us," said Poly.

"Which led to EUA shooting down Winfield and Johnson's plane," I said.

"I saw that," said Danny.

"On the news?" asked Poly.

"No. Out my window yesterday morning. I literally saw it," said Danny. "It was a huge fireball. The talking heads on-line said it was either swamp gas coming up from the Okefenokee or a private dirigible explosion. Too bad about Winfield and Johnson."

"They're fine," I said. "They were afraid The General might not be happy they screwed up his plot to steal intellectual property, so they weren't on board."

"Maybe those two are smarter than they seemed," said Danny. He shook his head. "It was also a stretch to use an old flying saucer excuse like swamp gas to explain the explosion."

"EUA has people in high places in news organizations," I said. "And no one ever went broke overestimating the gullibility of the average Terran viewer."

"I know," said Danny. "In my line, that applies to galactics as well. I'm glad EUA isn't coming after *me.*"

"Not yet, anyway," said Poly.

"No," said Danny. "I don't think they will."

He looked thoughtful. There was something he wasn't telling us, but now was not the time to dig deeper.

"There's more," I said. "EUA tried to shoot *us* down yesterday, too."

"The other two explosions?" asked Danny.

"Uh huh," I said. "We sent down decoy shuttles."

"From the *Charalindhri?*" he asked. "So the heat beam that slagged those two warehouses was you, too?"

"Well, it was technically based on orders from Queen Sherrhilian-darianne of Dauush, but yeah," I confirmed.

"How do you know any of this was connected to EUA?" asked Danny.

"We were there when The General was planting hypnotic suggestions in the minds of the tech company executives at GALTEX," said Poly.

"But nobody's ever seen him," said Danny. "That's part of his mystique. Somebody could have been pretending to be him."

"Winfield and Scott report to The General," I said. "At least they *did* report to him. They got their instructions for the Vegas plot through their normal channels and had no reason to believe it wasn't their boss."

"Plus," said Poly, "we're in contact with other senior people inside EUA. They've told us there's a contract out on our lives, so we're keeping a very low profile."

"That doesn't sound like the EUA Corporation I know," said Danny. "They play rough, but not *that* rough."

"Surface-to-air missiles are pretty rough as far as I'm concerned."

"Okay," said Danny. "I *do* have a back channel to a guy fairly high up at EUA. I could check with him and find out what he knows."

"We'd really rather you didn't do that," said Poly. "We don't trust anyone at EUA."

"I can appreciate that," said Danny.

"I can assure you that our need to stay mostly out of sight won't interfere with our ability to find out who's responsible for your leaks," said Poly.

"Though I'd caution you to prepare for *more* trouble if EUA turns out to be behind your problems," I said.

Poly gave me a why-did-you-have-to-say-that look. Danny frowned.

"We're not starting your project with preconceptions," said Poly. "We're going to explore all possibilities. We just want you to understand that based on our experience, EUA Corporation will be one of the options we'll explore."

"Right," said Danny unenthusiastically.

Clearly it was time for us to go. Poly stood. Danny and I did, too.

"Let's shake on our arrangement," she said.

We shook. Danny had a firm grip. My phone got it all on video, including Danny restating his agreement to our fee. He kept looking at my phone, with the same mentally-taking-it-apart expression that Max had used. My phone seemed glad to jump back on my belt before our host dissected it.

Danny pushed buttons on his phone, turning off his portable privacy field.

"Thank you again for seeing us," said Poly as Danny opened his office door. We stepped out and moved into the area where Camilla Moultrie had her desk and played gatekeeper for her boss.

"We really appreciate your donation," I said, "and you'll make such a big difference in children's lives."

Danny gave me a wry smile, acknowledging my misdirection. I felt Chit crawling down my back then creeping her way along my left leg toward my ankle. She tickled.

"Have a great day," he said.

"You, too," said Poly.

I was distracted, so I just nodded. I couldn't feel Chit anymore.

Poly and I didn't speak until we'd left the building and were in an autocab heading back to the Georgia Tech underground research complex. My phone sat across from Poly and me in the vehicle.

"How are you doing, little buddy?" I asked.

My phone relayed my question to Chit and translated it into silent Pyr pulse-codes. It also translated back, turning Chit's message into something that mimicked her voice.

"Doin' fine, bucko," said Chit. "It made more sense to check out the executive assistant, not the big honcho. Somethin' about her didn't smell right."

I'd had the same feeling.

"Smart move," I said.

"You bet it's smart, chump," said Chit. "I think she works for EUA."

Chapter 20

"…the race is not to the swift, nor the battle to the strong…"
— Ecclesiastes 9:11

We were still downtown and our autocab had just turned up Marietta Street when Chit's excited voice came through my phone's speaker.

"Wait a second," she said. "Bad news. The Flower is deploying mobile assets after your autocab to capture you."

"What?" asked Poly.

"Who?" I added.

"Chit is referring to Camilla Moultrie," said my phone.

"You bet your sweet assembler code I am," said Chit. "She's sending seekers, buzzlers and orcas to track you down."

That wasn't good. Seekers were remote-controlled four-wheeled pursuit and capture vehicles much like oversized autocabs, but with magnetic grapples, light armor, and non-lethal weapons. They looked like streamlined SUVs and had the semi-melted appearance so common in vehicles inspired by Orishen designs. Buzzlers were powerful, riderless motorcycles with high-pitched engines sounding like angry soprano didgeridoos. The autonomous two-wheeled vehicles had pairs of harpoon guns—and sophisticated artificial intelligence systems. They were fast and could maneuver through traffic more effectively than the larger seekers.

Orcas were tanks with tires, not treads. They were big, round, and the last gasp of militarized policing before police departments returned to sanity. Their name came from their shape and their typical black and white paint scheme. Orcas had thick armor, heavy weapons, and carried a squad of SWAT-style assault troops inside. The city of Atlanta had unloaded all of its orcas years ago, but rumor had it that several corporations and oligarchs had snapped them up to transport bodyguards and augment their own security details.

"Autocab. New destination. Lenox Square Mall. Execute," said Poly.

"New destination: Lenox Square Mall. Confirmed," intoned the autocab's A.I.

Our vehicle turned right on Ivan Allen, Jr. Boulevard, just north of the original Georgia Aquarium building and south of the new, even larger buildings added to exhibit galactic aquatic species. Ichthyosaurs need *lots* of space. I was glad Poly was thinking fast. We didn't want to lead our pursuers to the underground laboratory complex where we were staying. Lenox Square Mall was seven or eight miles away, which should give us time to think of something.

"Can't this thing go any faster?" I asked.

Our autocab was piddling along, moving at or below the speed limit on streets that weren't crowded and wouldn't be until the afternoon rush hour.

"Autonomous vehicles are required to scrupulously observe all traffic regulations," said my phone.

I spotted a seeker and a couple of buzzlers turning off Marietta Street to follow us. They weren't dawdling.

"How can we take control of this thing?" I asked.

Substituting actions for words, my phone jumped onto the dashboard of our autocab and extruded something that looked like the connector R2-D2 used to stop the trash compactors on the Death Star. It plugged what it had extruded into a circular receptacle on the autocab's dash and turned it left and right, like opening a safe. I heard a cheerful *chirp* and the words *Manual override accepted* from the autocab's A.I. Soon, our vehicle's speed doubled and we were opening up some space between us and our pursuers.

Buzzlers were created to minimize the need for police officers to engage in high-speed chases. Their intended mission was to catch and hold felons trying to escape the scene of a crime. It was unusual for them to be in private hands, but unusual didn't mean impossible. The two buzzlers pursuing us were unmarked and definitely dangerous.

One of the low-slung, riderless black cycles fell in behind us and fired its harpoon weapon. My phone jerked our autocab sharply to one side and the barbed head of the buzzler's harpoon missed us and caught in the back bumper of a delivery van. Thirty feet of titanium-alloy cable unspooled behind the missile's head. A massive steel anchor at the other end of the cable popped off the buzzler, flipped out its arms, and dug into the asphalt of the boulevard. The buzzler's A.I. software must not have been updated recently because it crashed into the taut cable and fell on its side, only to be crushed by the delivery truck when it rebounded after making an abrupt stop.

One down.

The second buzzler was holding back—I assumed to analyze what the other buzzler had done wrong and correct for it. I could hear the rumble of its congruency-powered motor revving, making a sound like an angry eight-hundred-pound mosquito. I wanted to swat the blasted thing or zap it with the technological equivalent of DEET. Unfortunately, I didn't have anything I could use as a weapon—or did I?

I examined the interior of the autocab to see if there was anything I could throw. Poly figured out what I was doing and started her own search. There were small flat screen panels on the backs of the seats in front of us. They tilted to optimize their viewing angle—enough so we could get our fingers around one edge and pull.

With a splintering rip of plastic, the screen on my side came loose. A few seconds later, so did Poly's. The buzzler may have been holding back but the seeker wasn't. It was gaining on us and would soon be in range to fire its magnetic grapples. Standard seekers were mostly used by law enforcement to capture joy-riding kids who'd hacked autonomous vehicles. They normally had strict do-no-harm protocols. I didn't think the vehicle tailing us was standard issue, however. I glanced through our cab's back window and saw ominous-looking gun ports opening just above its front bumper.

I pushed a button on my arm rest and the window on my side of the autocab went down. My phone had us moving at a pretty good clip and took a left turn onto Williams Street on two wheels. Air blasted into my face, but I loosened my seat belt and stuck my upper body out the window. It didn't make sense to throw the screen at the seeker's windshield—the seeker-drone's driver was probably sitting in an air-conditioned pod in one of the nearby skyscrapers. My target was the sensor array, a transparent bubble the size of a softball where a hood ornament would have been a couple of generations ago.

I held my breath, took careful aim, and launched my screen in a high arc. It not only landed *on* the sensor array, it embedded itself in the hood. The seeker slowed and fell back.

That was two.

The remaining buzzler kept pace with us but didn't try to close or fire its harpoon. I think it was biding its time until more assets could join the hunt. It didn't need to track our position—Camilla Moultrie surely had our autocab's transponder code by now.

"Nice shot," said Poly.

We roared down the Williams Street on-ramp to the Connector, moving so fast I expected to hear a sonic boom when we neared the bottom. We shot out into light midday traffic on the stretch of road where two interstate highways came together, bisecting downtown Atlanta. My phone made me wish our autocab had an inertial dampening field as it cut across four lanes of traffic to get to the section that would soon become I-85 North and take us to Lenox Square Mall. Traffic wasn't at rush hour migraine levels—it was barely the equivalent of a slight headache.

I'd hoped we were done with vehicles trying to stop us, but we weren't that lucky. Three more seekers and four buzzlers were coming up fast on multiple lanes. All of them were painted a lustrous, metallic black with a sheen like scarab beetles. I hoped they wouldn't mob us and consume us like the beetles in the *Mummy* movies. One of the seekers stayed in our lane, while the other two pulled alongside of our autocab to flank us, left and right.

Two buzzlers pulled in front of us and two more filled in the corners behind us.

"Too bad we don't have a Golden Snitch," said Poly. She was trying to keep up a brave front.

"What do you mean?" I asked. "What's Quidditch got to do with a high-speed chase?"

"If we had a Golden Snitch, the seekers would have to chase it or risk losing the game," answered Poly.

"There's more at stake now than the House Cup," I replied, "and we don't have a Golden Snitch."

"Not necessarily true," said my phone.

I'm glad it was good at multitasking, able to talk and drive at the same time.

"Do tell," I said, "and make it snappy."

"Yes, please," added Poly. "It won't be long before we're forced off the road."

"You understand how the seekers know where we are, right?" asked my phone.

"They're following the autocab's transponder code," I said.

"Correct," said my phone.

"Aren't the remote pilots getting a direct camera feed?" asked Poly.

"They used to before evaders began using congruency-powered solar corona bombs," said my phone. "The light blasts from the bombs ruined the pilots' vision, so they switched over to just tracking transponders."

"How does that help us?" I asked.

"The cab's transponder will be easy to disable," said my phone, "and the vehicle's operation can be handled manually."

"You want one of us to drive, without an A.I. assist?" asked Poly.

"In a word, yes," said my phone.

"I'll be glad to do it," I said, "though getting into the front seat will be a challenge."

"Don't sell yourself short, Sweetheart," said Poly. "I know you're good at complex athletic positions."

"Please leave our love life out of it," I replied with a grin as I started to climb over the center armrest. "What will *you* be doing?" I asked my phone.

"Simulating this 'cab's transponder and leading the seekers away."

It was a better plan than anything I'd come up with.

I awkwardly fell or slid or somehow contorted myself into the driver's seat and took the wheel, keeping the throttle pushed to the floor and weaving a bit so the seeker operators wouldn't think I was completely at their mercy.

The seeker behind us had opened the panel masking its magnetic grapple and would soon be trying to capture us, so my phone moved quickly. Once it knew I was ready, my phone disengaged from the autocab and hopped nimbly into the front passenger seat to begin its reconfiguration. Its mutacase lengthened and became more rounded at the ends until it looked like a thick business card between two soft-drink cup lids, turning itself into a dual-fan drone.

I pushed a button in my armrest and the autocab's right front window rolled down. My phone rose from its seat, hovered momentarily, and zipped out. The blades of its rotating fans made a high-pitched noise that seemed like a whining piccolo compared to the buzzlers' thrumming outback roar.

Go go go! I silently encouraged, then closed the window.

I watched with delight as my phone zoomed off sharply to the right, heading up I-75 at the point where the interstates split while our now-anonymous autocab stayed on I-85. The three seekers followed my phone and were soon out of sight as the highways diverged. It may have been just a trick of the light or my phone playing games with its refractory index, but I thought I saw a glint of gold just before it vanished.

Now we only had four buzzlers to worry about—two ahead, two behind. The buzzlers' A.I. units were not fooled by my phone's maneuver, but they hadn't deployed themselves well. The two in front were not positioned to use their harpoons. Unfortunately, the same could not be said for the pair on our tail.

I was too busy weaving from side to side, trying to avoid other traffic, to do anything about the buzzler cycles on our rear bumper. Poly, however, was Ms. Resourceful. Still holding the flat screen from her side of the autocab, she turned around facing backwards and climbed on top of the armrest between the two front seats. She used her free hand to trigger our vehicle's sunroof and pecked me on the cheek while waiting for it to retract. Then she stood on the arm rest and stuck the upper half of her body through the opening.

More air came rushing in and Poly's body acted like a small sail, requiring me to focus even more attention on driving, not what she was doing. I did see the results of her actions in my rearview mirror, however. The flat screen caught the inside front wheel of one of the buzzlers, flipping it over and sending it careening into its companion, which had just been about to fire its harpoon. The force of the impact caused the second buzzler's harpoon to launch and the barbed missile embedded itself into the road behind us. The two interlocked buzzlers were left spinning around a ten-foot arc on the harpoon's cable like a pair of flies tied up with a long human hair by a sadistic schoolboy.

I didn't wait for the two lead buzzlers to fall back and redeploy. Instead, I accelerated, crossed the short distance separating us, and smacked into them. Their front wheels rose off the ground, like rearing stallions, but they didn't spin out or tip over. Poly pulled herself back into the autocab.

"Excuse me," she said.

She reached behind my head and removed the detachable headrest. It was heavy and well-padded with two long, thin steel rods to secure it in place. I could see her do the same thing to the headrest on the other front seat. Then half her body disappeared again. I laughed out loud when the rods on one of the headrests caught in the spokes of the rear wheel of the right-hand buzzler and it tumbled to the right, out of control.

Poly's next shot wasn't as effective. The padded part of the other headrest smacked into the rear wheel of the remaining buzzler, knocking it off balance, but not fully destabilized. I rammed it on an angle with the autocab, finishing the job and sending it crashing against a Jersey barrier two lanes to the left. Luckily, all the other self-driving vehicles on the road had given us a wide berth.

"Nice shooting," I said, resting my palm on the back of one of Poly's legs.

"Thanks," said Poly, lowering her body all the way back inside and slipping into the front passenger seat. "Nice assist."

Our exit was coming up on my right so I took it and headed east toward Lenox Square Mall. Its huge, multistory parking lot would be a good place to lose potential tails. I couldn't see any vehicles chasing us in the rearview mirror, which I imagined would be the next item to be turned into an improvised thrown weapon if it came to that. Breaking the mirror would mean seven years of bad luck, but I hoped the ill-fortune would fall on our enemies, not on us.

"The mall's ahead on the right," said Poly, confirming what we both already knew. She scanned in every direction, making sure we were in the clear.

I accelerated up Lenox Road and was speeding toward the retail complex, making good time, when our luck ran out. A black and white orca half the size of a city bus ponderously pulled into the intersection directly ahead. It blocked most of Peachtree Road and I was going too fast to avoid it. I stood on the autocab's brakes and only tapped the side of the orca instead of slamming into it full speed. The huge cannon on the orca's turret swung our way. It tilted down to point directly at our vehicle. Poly and I flung our doors wide and dove out. The first shell split the autocab in half like an eggshell and knocked me over. The blast didn't do much for my hearing, either.

When I got to my feet, I looked across the burning remains of our autocab to check on Poly. She was standing, if a bit unsteady on her feet, and seemed okay. Her face was dirty and her suit was beyond repair, but she smiled at me and waved. I ran to join her, avoiding chunks of flaming wreckage, and saw the orca's main ramp-door was swinging down. Well-equipped hostile forces would soon emerge to capture us, since Poly and I were in no condition to escape.

I'd nearly lost hope when I heard screeching tires. A white van—*my* white van—hopped the median on Peachtree Road in front of the mall and pulled up next to us. The driver's window rolled down and the sliding door near us opened. I was expecting to find Mike at the wheel, but it wasn't him. It was someone I didn't know, though he seemed vaguely familiar—maybe from Las Vegas. I couldn't tell what he looked like because he was wearing a programmable disguise like a welder's mask, but made from flat screen film. The mask was currently displaying thirty-six-year-old Arnold Schwarzenegger's face. He was saying something I couldn't understand.

"What?" I said, cupping my hand around my ear.

"Arnold" looked impatient. He fiddled with the mask's controls to up the volume.

"Come with me if you want to live," he said in an electronically distorted Austrian accent.

Poly and I got in and buckled our seat belts. Arnold peeled out.

Chapter 21

"Who was that masked man…?"
— The Lone Ranger TV Show (1949-1957)

"THANK YOU!" I said to our rescuer.

"You don't need to shout," he replied.

"I'M SHOUTING?" I asked.

"I THINK SO," said Poly.

"Cut your decibels in half and you'll both be fine," said the man in the Schwarzenegger mask.

Even with my damaged eardrums I still heard gunshots coming from behind us. A squad of armored attackers on heavy-duty Segway-like personal transports were rolling our way, firing in our direction. So far, it seemed like they'd been trained at the Imperial Stormtrooper Marksmanship Academy. Then a bullet pinged off my van's left side door column and I revised my assessment of our pursuers' abilities. I was also grateful I'd let the van dealer talk me into the bulletproof glass package. Poly squeezed my hand and leaned so her mouth was close to my ear.

"Good thing we're wearing our Orishen pupa-silk shirts," she said, ducking to reduce her target profile.

"Yep," I said, squeezing back and speaking into *her* ear. "But you don't need to crouch. Bulletproof glass."

"Smart," said Poly. "This way I can sit up and see what's going on."

We observed as the driver navigated into the mall's surface parking lot and swiftly sought the relative safety of a lower level of the extensive six-level parking deck. Arnold steered back and forth around redwood-sized support pillars like he was going down a slalom course until we reached the far back corner of the structure near the entrance to the MARTA terminal.

Arnold mumbled something.

"WHAT?" I asked.

"Get out!" he said. Arnold's face looked like he was shouting but he didn't sound that loud.

I wondered how long it would take my ears to return to normal.

He opened his door and followed his own instruction. The van's sliding door opened, so we unbuckled and did the same. Then we trotted along behind him to the stairs down to the station. I looked over my shoulder and saw my van charging at a clump of attackers. They scattered like bowling pins and a few of them fell off their transports. If luck was with us, we'd have a few unobserved minutes to catch a MARTA train and escape.

Our guide and rescuer didn't stop at the station, however. Instead, he raced to the far end and led us down yet another flight of stairs into a long, dimly lit tunnel heading back the way we'd come. It had old-style florescent fixtures at intervals along the ceiling, flanked by conduits for obsolete cabling.

"WHERE ARE WE GOING?" I asked.

The two of us were close to the same height, so I knew I'd be able to hear his answer if he spoke up. Arnold didn't choose to reply, so we kept following. It was odd not to be able to hear my own footsteps, since I expected there'd be quite an echo. When I was little I'd always tried to hold my breath when going through the tunnels on the Pennsylvania Turnpike. I'd talk my mom into beeping our car's horn just to hear the sound reverberate. Beeping a horn didn't seem like such a good idea in our current situation, however.

No matter how my ears were damaged, I could still hear gunshots and see a fusillade of bullets bouncing off the tunnel's walls. I turned and saw half a dozen armored figures on Segway-like scooters speeding up the tunnel. They were firing fat-barreled shotguns that echoed like giants stomping their feet—boom, *boom*, BOOM! My hearing was coming back.

"Stay low," said our guide. "Their weapons pull high. I've got this."

Poly and I crouched and moved in random patterns, trying to make ourselves more challenging targets. Our guide found his phone and was typing rapidly. Unfortunately, the scooter squad was also *shooting* rapidly. One of the bullets bounced off a wall and hit Poly on the shoulder. She winced.

"They're rubber!" shouted Poly.

"That doesn't mean they can't hurt us."

I looked back to see if the shooters were gaining on us. They were, so I faced front and sped up my pace. Our guide stabbed his phone and three beats later the gunfire stopped. I heard sounds of chaotic collisions behind me and turned around again. So did Poly. We were delighted to see that all of the Segway squad were caught in a large net that must have been hidden in the ceiling. I hugged Poly and gave our guide a thumbs-up, then we continued making tracks down the tunnel.

My ears felt funny. I yawned and felt something pop—I didn't think we were *that* far underground. Instead, it was just my inner ear telling me my hearing was coming back online. I could now make out my own footsteps on concrete. I looked over at Poly. She was yawning, too. Maybe we were both recovering?

"Is your hearing back to normal?" I asked using moderate decibel levels.

Poly moved her lips, but I couldn't hear anything. I looked puzzled, then she smiled.

"Just messing with you," she said. "My ears are okay now, too."

I stuck out my tongue at her, then blew her an air kiss and accelerated to catch up to our guide. He was a dozen paces ahead of us. Poly stayed with me.

"Sorry about the shouting," I said when we caught up.

"Apology accepted," said our guide.

It was odd. His tone managed to be both businesslike and affectionate, like Shepherd training Pâkk pup-cubs how to hunt.

"Thank you for rescuing us," said Poly softly.

"You're welcome," said our masked rescuer.

"Now WHO THE HELL ARE YOU?" said my partner.

I nearly said, "*Shush,*" but thought better of it.

"Later," said our guide, sounding more and more like Shepherd. The Pâkk wouldn't use two words when one would do.

We moved back a few steps to give Arnold his own space, since he didn't seem open to conversation. I spoke softly to Poly, just to hear my own voice, and hers.

"This tunnel would be a great place to play D&D," I said. "It has lots of cool doors and branches."

"I think they use it for live action role playing once or twice a month," said Poly.

That made sense. It would also explain the net trap in the ceiling. Was our unidentified benefactor a gamer? Where did he get the code to release the net?

"How did you hear about LARPing down here?" I asked Poly.

"Mike told me about it."

I considered Xenotech Support Corporation's first employee. Mike was both a nerd and an Army vet. I could see how the hobby would appeal to him.

"Did Mike mention where the tunnel comes out?"

"He didn't say anything about that, but I'll bet he talks CiCi into joining him next time he goes LARPing," said Poly.

"I won't take that bet," I said. "Half the company will probably come along."

"Only half?" asked Poly.

"Ray Ray won't come if Pomy's not coming," I said.

"Oh, crap," said Poly. "What time is it? We have to be at the courthouse downtown for Pomy's trial!"

"It's not even noon yet," I reassured. "If we get out of here soon, we'll make it by one o'clock like we promised."

"We'd better," said Poly, loud enough so Arnold could hear her.

The universe must have been listening, because the tunnel stopped at a freight elevator a hundred feet farther along. A wide industrial stairway went up to our right and steel double doors labeled *Freight Elevator: Authorized Personnel Only* were on our left. Our guide pushed the button to summon the elevator. The doors slid open without making a sound anything like the whoosh of a turbolift. I got in, following Poly and "Arnold," but didn't feel too comfortable. The last time I'd been in a freight elevator I'd had Ray Ray and a nova bomb for company.

As we ascended, our guide fiddled with his mask. Instead of being away from his face like a welder's mask, the thin screen's film now hugged his features. I watched as it transformed from Arnold Schwarzenegger into the less universally recognizable face of David Tennant, the tenth Doctor Who. I looked puzzled and our guide responded.

"It only has so many presets," he said, as if that explained everything.

Poly didn't seem to recognize our guide's new face and I smiled, looking forward to long marathons of watching the classic science fiction series with her.

The elevator stopped with a slight bump and wobble—or should I say wibble wobble—and opened on a utilitarian cinder block corridor with a linoleum floor. The walls were painted a cheerful creamy yellow and the doors in front of us had a sign reading *To the Mall*. We were obviously in a service area. The Doctor led us through the doors and I knew where we were— right next to the security station by the food court. We took an escalator up to the mall's main level and found a comfortable area to sit near a Starbucks.

"Meet me here in half an hour," said our guide. "The restrooms are one floor up and there are plenty of places to buy new clothes. Make yourselves presentable—you have to be in court soon."

Poly and I had seen our reflections in store windows, so we knew we wouldn't make a good impression on any judge of character or fashion.

"I don't have my phone. I can't buy anything," I said.

I pulled out my wallet and showed them it was empty. I'd used my last bill to buy breath mints before meeting Sally at her ballroom dance club in Vegas. Things had been so hectic since I hadn't had time to hit a cash machine.

"If we shop together you can use *my* phone," said Poly.

"But that would take too long," I lamented.

Our guide stood up, pulled out his wallet, and handed me ten hundred-galcred notes.

"Cash still works," he said. "You can pay me back."

"Whenever you tell me who you are," I said.

"Or not," he replied. "Now get moving. We're on a really tight schedule."

Poly and I took another nearby escalator up to the restrooms and emerged with freshly scrubbed faces and fewer clothes, since our suit jackets weren't remotely salvageable. We hugged and sped off in different directions. I went to Neiman Macy's, where I knew they'd have off-the-rack suits in my size made from Orishen mutaphabrics for a perfect custom fit. Twenty minutes later I was wearing a conservative white shirt, red tie, and blue pinstripe much like the ones I'd trashed earlier—a perfect ensemble to project gravitas in a courtroom. I knew Neiman Macy's would have what I was looking for, since that's where I'd bought my original suit a year earlier. Everything was on sale, too. I still had half of our guide's galcreds in my wallet.

When we met back up at Starbucks our guide was holding a white paper bag and tapping his foot impatiently. We were only five minutes late. Poly and I had literally bumped into each other at the bottom of an escalator as we'd hurried to meet our deadline. She was coming down from the second floor wearing a suit much like the one she'd totaled. It looked a lot like something I'd seen on a poster at Neiman Macy's and Poly confirmed that she'd purchased her ensemble there, too. That's why we were both traveling in the same direction, though we'd been shopping on different floors.

"Why did you leave the restrooms going the other way?" I asked.

"Victoria's Secret first," she replied.

I just nodded and smiled. Some things are unmentionable.

"You'll both do," said our guide, looking us up and down. "Straighten his tie, then follow me."

Poly did as he requested, adding a quick kiss after her adjustment. We trailed after our guide as he walked out of the mall and stood by the vehicle pickup area. An impressive white car pulled in front of us and opened its doors. I didn't recognize the make or model, which in these days of large-scale 3D printing isn't *that* unusual, but still.

You know how certain high-end black cars have a finish that makes you think you could fall into it and never hit bottom? This car was like that, only white. It was so lustrous, nuanced and layered that it seemed like someone had carved a car out of a giant pearl. It had rounded corners and the typical Orishen-inspired melted look, but on this car it didn't look average—it looked exceptional.

Oh, yeah, the front and rear doors were gull wings, but they folded as they rose so you didn't need lots of lateral clearance. If I didn't have to run a business, I'd consider trading in my van to own a car like that. Not really, but I might spring for a second parking place at my building to get one. Poly climbed into the back and I slid in after her.

The interior was a deep tan leather—not the stuff made from cows, the modern stuff made from Nicósn synthetics that wears better and doesn't stain. The seat felt better than the one time I'd ridden in a Rolls Royce Silver Cloud. I wasn't sure I wanted our trip to the courthouse to be a speedy one.

"Nice car," said Poly.

What an understatement. That was like saying that Poly was a "nice girl." Wait, that didn't come out quite right. Like Poly, this car was so much more than just "nice."

"Thanks," said our guide. "To the courthouse and step on it."

"As you wish," said the car.

I was in love.

Chapter 22

"Take me for a ride in your car-car."
— Peter, Paul & Mary

Medium-heavy noon-hour traffic heading south seemed to melt away ahead of us like the Greenland icecap before Earth implemented advanced Tigrammath climate engineering. The big white car purred its way from Buckhead to Downtown Atlanta, adding a subliminal hum of power to its congruent motor's near-silent operation. I opened my window a crack to hear the instrument assigned to this model by the Vehicle Grand Harmony Standard committee—it was a Vulcan lute. Whoever designed this vehicle had a sense of humor as well as a sense of style.

"Why are you acting weird?" asked Poly after I'd closed my window.

"Weird?" I replied.

"You've been all spaced out for the past ten minutes."

"I just like this car," I said. "A lot."

"Is that all?" replied Poly with a smile. "I thought you might have figured something out about The General." She lowered her voice. "Or about our mysterious rescuer."

"I can hear you," said the man wearing David Tennant's face. "And I think you should be focused more on Pomy's case than my identity."

"You *would* say that," I said. "It's a self-serving prescription, right Doctor?"

I watched him in the rear-view mirror. He nodded, then tilted his head and turned his shoulders slightly. I finally remembered where I'd seen him before—I recognized the way he held himself as he sat.

"You were in the lobby of the Grand Pyridian in Las Vegas," I said. "You were reading the *Galactic Times-Journal.*"

"Guilty as charged," said the man. "You're very observant, Jack."

"How long have you been following us?" asked Poly.

"I refuse to answer on the grounds that it may incriminate me."

"That long," said Poly. The corner of her mouth turned up and she raised one eyebrow.

"Whose side are you on?" I asked.

"That should be obvious," said our rescuer. "I have been—and always shall be—your friend."

"Yeah, right," said Poly. She made a face at me and gave me a Vulcan "live long and prosper" one-handed salute.

"I can also see what's happening in the back seat," said the enigmatic man.

Poly's eyes lit up. "You can? Well watch this."

She slid over and climbed into my lap, then began seriously kissing me with the heat and intensity of a blue-white star. The mnemonic for stellar spectral classes involuntarily popped into my head. *Oh, Be A Fine Girl, Kiss Me Right Now Sweetie.* Poly was definitely following the recommendation of the mnemonic. I did my best to kiss her back, despite my surprise. She began kissing my neck and put her mouth against my ear.

"Can we trust him?" she whispered.

I kissed her neck and nodded, then worked my mouth up to her ear.

"I think so," I said, "for now."

Poly gave me another half dozen or seven kisses then broke our clinch and resumed her seat, smoothing her skirt to look prim and proper. My head was spinning—in a nice way for once.

"I hope you enjoyed that," said our rescuer. "I'm glad I have at least your temporary approval."

This guy knew too much. He reminded me of Shepherd.

"You've got to admit, it's smart to be careful," I said. "You could be working for The General."

"Like Cornell and Sally and Rosalind?" he asked.

"They're on our side now," I asserted.

"We hope," said Poly and the man simultaneously. They looked at each other in the rear-view mirror, a bit surprised to be in sync.

"I get it," I said. "We're temporary allies, and they're looking out for their own self-interest, but for now their interests and ours are aligned."

"For now," said the man.

"Hey," said Poly. "If we're going to work together, we need something better than *The Doctor* or *Arnold* to call you."

Our rescuer didn't reply for a few moments. I knew that meant he was trying to come up with some appropriate bit of misdirection.

"Call me Chilly," he said.

"Like peppers?" asked Poly.

"No," said the man. "Like cold."

I thought I liked this guy but I still shivered.

"Speaking of peppers," said Chilly, "I forgot to give you these."

He tossed the white bag he'd been carrying when we'd rejoined him at Starbucks toward the back seat. I caught it and looked inside. There were two stuffed Nicósn banana peppers the size of large plantains nestled in napkins. They were filled with a savory protein paste that came from the Nicósn equivalent of aphids and had been grilled to perfection. I didn't think too much about it, since I'd had them before and knew they were delicious despite their six-legged provenance.

I handed Poly a stuffed pepper and a handful of napkins and bit into the end of my own pepper with gusto. Escaping capture and possible death really increases my appetite and it had been a long time since the Dauushan-hummingbird-egg-and-sausage-filled steamed buns at breakfast. Poly munched on her pepper enthusiastically. We both warmed to Chilly.

"Don't get any filling on the carpet or upholstery," I said to Poly between bites. I was being very protective towards our vehicle.

"Careful yourself, lover," she said, dabbing a dot of white stuff off the corner of my mouth. It tasted like ricotta cheese laced with oregano, parsley, and a hint of curry. Now I was thirsty.

"You wouldn't happen to have any…" I began.

Chilly pressed a button on the dashboard and a small bar was revealed across from us.

I reached for a Diet Starbuzz.

"I'll take a Coke Minus," said Poly.

I passed her one. The Coca-Cola Company had recently perfected soft drinks that resulted in net negative calories by tweaking drinkers' metabolisms. They were proving so popular that the company was now making Sprite Minus, Fanta Minus, and more. I couldn't wait until they cross-licensed the technology to the Starbuzz people.

While we cheerfully chomped and guzzled, I took a few minutes to learn more about Chilly.

"Do you know my friend Shepherd?" I asked.

"I refuse to answer on the grounds that..." said Chilly.

"Got it," I said. "Nothing consequential. Where are you from?"

"Not from a long time ago or another galaxy," said Chilly, "but far, far away."

"Are you an alien?" asked Poly. "A galactic?"

"No to the first—I'm as human as you and Jack," said Chilly, "and yes to the second."

"You're a Galactic but not an alien?" she asked. Her forehead scrunched as she tried to figure it out.

"Are you from one of the Terran colony worlds?" Poly asked.

"In a way," he said.

I could see a twinkle in his eye in the rear-view mirror. He was playing with us.

"Where do you live now?" I asked.

"Here in Atlanta."

Crap. He wouldn't tell me more than that.

"Have you been spying on us?" asked Poly

Chilly just laughed. Given recent events, the question was asked and answered. Of *course* he'd been spying on us. I wondered if he'd been one of the people bugging my apartment at Ad Astra?

"*Why* are you spying on us?" I asked, trying a different approach.

"I've been following your exploits for a long time," said Chilly.

"Meaning Jack and me, or just me, or just Jack?" asked Poly.

"Uh huh," said Chilly.

He was lucky Poly and I didn't start throwing empty soft drink cans at him. The man was frustrating, but he seemed so full of glee as he obfuscated that I couldn't hate him for it. I saw his face soften and he threw me a bone of information.

"If you go back far enough I'm here because of a natural disaster, Jack," said Chilly. "That's all I'm saying for now, but I hope we'll have a chance to talk more after you identify and take down The General."

"Great," I said, meaning, "Crap."

"Approaching destination," said the luxurious white car.

We were downtown and coming up on the Fulton County Superior Court building. Bright lights on our left invited us to visit Underground Atlanta—restored and turned into a shopping and entertainment venue run by subterranean species like Knōmz and Sporlocks. Its enticements beckoned, but we didn't have time to dally. I could see the courthouse down the block across an intersection.

The place was a classical revival palace that looked like a turn of the twentieth century bank headquarters crossed with New York's Metropolitan Museum of Art. It was built from granite and stood eight or ten stories tall with giant pillars extending over most of its height. I rolled down my window so I could stick my head out and see more of the magnificent structure. Then I heard buzzing and my phone flew through the open window to land on the seat between Poly and me. I pulled my head in and rolled up the window.

"Where *were* you?" asked my phone.

"It's a long story," I replied. "At least you knew you could find us here. Thanks for your quick thinking."

"Glad to help," said my phone.

It retracted its rotors and reconfigured itself into its usual cell phone-shaped form, then hopped on my belt. Its weight felt reassuring. I reminded myself to check and see if it wanted a reward for all the help it had provided—but now was not the time. The car dropped us off in front of the courthouse and Chilly stuck his head out the driver's side window.

"I hope everything goes well for Pomy," he said.

"Thanks," said Poly.

"We can hope," I added, staring longingly at the white car.

"See you later," said Chilly as he—and his amazing vehicle—pulled away.

Somehow I was sure we would.

Chapter 23

"Before anything else, preparation is the key to success."
— Alexander Graham Bell

The courthouse lobby was a soaring, turn-of-the-twentieth-century Beaux Arts delight, with lots of dark wood and marble. I'd read the original 1914 lobby had been a boring box with low ceilings until a special grant from the PDF Foundation in the 2020s had funded substantial renovations and carved the current impressive lobby out of the center of the building. I loved the new design.

They'd managed to integrate the security checkpoint with the overall architecture by crafting a pair of tasteful Nicósn bogwood arches that mimicked the shape of the ceiling. Dozens of sensors inside each arch checked us out as Poly and I walked through them.

One of the security guards tracking readouts on a flat screen turned to stare at me.

"Empty your pockets, please," she said, smiling.

"Is something the matter?" I asked.

She didn't reply, but kept smiling and handed me a sturdy plastic bowl with a rubber base. I dumped what I was carrying into the bowl with a clatter. The guard took the bowl and Poly and I followed her to a table against a side wall.

"Wow!" exclaimed the guard, placing the bowl reverently on the table. "A Wenger Supertalent!"

Wenger was one of the two companies that had made Swiss Army knives. They'd been acquired by Victorinox twenty-five years ago.

The guard was a tall woman with dark eyes and beautifully braided black hair. I didn't know what to make of the way she was staring at my Swiss Army knife. My multifunctioned pride and joy was over three inches wide and took up a lot of room in the bowl.

"That's right," I said. "You've got a good eye to spot one with a basic scanner."

"Thanks," she said. "I didn't know they still made Supertalents."

"They don't. My stepfather gave it to me—and he got it from *his* father."

The guard's expression was rapturous. "It's got *everything,*" she gushed.

"Not quite," I said. "No Allen wrenches."

"You can fake them with the awl," she said.

She was correct. I'd done that several times to help disassemble fire door mechanisms when I needed to get into places before I'd made my mutakey.

The otherwise-dignified uniformed woman looked like a small child gazing longingly at a hot fudge sundae. "May I touch it?"

"Sure," I said. "But just for a minute. We have to get to court."

"Thanks so much," said the woman. "I won't keep you long."

She picked up my knife and held it, staring at all the options. She pulled out the metal saw *and* the wood saw, to appreciate the difference between them, then folded them up and handed my knife back to me with two hands.

"I don't suppose you'd be interested in selling it?"

"No," I said, "but watch the on-line auctions. They show up at intervals."

"Rare intervals," said Poly.

I didn't know she was into classic Swiss Army knives. I had a lot to learn about the woman I loved.

"Here's your mini-sweetener," said our guard, handing it back to me. "Please keep all weapons securely on your person," she continued, shifting back to her rote-memorized standard speech.

Our delay was unusual. I'd heard that security checks were a lot easier since sweetener drones became standard equipment in courtrooms. The right to bear arms was not infringed, but if anyone tried to start something, a silently hovering sweetener-equipped drone would chill them out in a hurry. Still, I was frequently stopped going through checkpoints by weapons enthusiasts wanting to check out my knife. Thank goodness my phone wasn't trying anything fancy and still looked like a phone.

"Jack?" asked Poly when we'd move a dozen steps farther on.

"Yes?"

"If they're not scanning for weapons, what *are* they scanning for?" I laughed.

"Mostly they're trying to identify high explosives, poison gas, compact congruent energy bombs, and other large-scale bad stuff," I replied. "But they also continue security scanning to ensure patronage jobs for judges' friends and relations."

For some reason, my answer made my *phone* laugh. It had a unique perspective on the absurdity of the human condition.

"Which way to Pomy's courtroom?" asked Poly.

"Take the main stairs up a floor and then turn right," my phone answered.

It must have taken initiative and downloaded plans for the courthouse. I was pleased to see that the lobby improvements had included faux signs of age for the main staircase. When they built it, they simulated over a century of footfalls wearing low spots into the marble treads. I fit my soles into the dips and climbed behind Poly. It was a few minutes before one o'clock—we would be on time.

We spotted Pomy and Atticus Finch from the top of the stairs and headed in their direction. Seconds later, Poly and Pomy embraced. After the sisters' hug, I squeezed Pomy's hand and murmured something supportive. Pomy was trembling and appreciated our physical contact.

Poly's sister was wearing a white blouse, a long navy skirt, and a matching embroidered navy vest that made her look much younger than her age. To my eyes, Pomy could pass for a high school girl ready to dance at Atlanta's Greek Festival. If I was on the jury I'd declare her innocent without waiting for any evidence to be presented.

"Nice ensemble," I said, softly.

"Thanks," Pomy whispered. "I picked it up last year on a trip to Athens. Atticus suggested it when I described what I had in my closet."

Then something long and flexible tugged my sleeve.

"This way," said our little Pyr lawyer. "There's a conference room we can use before the trial."

Finch scooted off along a perpendicular corridor, carrying his old-fashioned leather briefcase in one of his tentacles. He used a second tentacle to open the conference room door and third to wave the rest of us inside. The room had a table, chairs, and a credenza with bottles of water. There was enough room for eight around the table, but Atticus had us gather near him at one end. He lowered his chair, then hopped onto it somehow and fiddled with his phone while Pomy, Poly and I took seats close to him.

Poly sat next to Pomy so she could hold her sister's hand and offer reassurance. Finch's phone must have had a Cone of Silence app, because I soon sensed the sound-dampening effect of a Cone.

"Now we can talk in private," said Atticus. "Thank you for coming, Jack and Poly. Your presence will be quite helpful."

"Glad to be here," I said.

Pomy looked nervous and so did Poly, though she was trying hard not to show it.

"First," said Finch, "Pomy will sit next to me at the defense table."

He nodded at Pomy and she nodded back, understanding, but still uncertain.

"I'd like the two of you to sit in the first row of seats behind the bar," continued Atticus.

"I'll be right behind you, sis," said Poly.

"I'm counting on it," said Pomy.

That would put me behind Atticus, which should at least give me a good view of the proceedings, since Pyrs are only four feet tall.

"I don't expect to call you to the stand," said Atticus with his mouth that faced Pomy, "and hope it won't even get that far."

"Th-that's good," stuttered Pomy. "I'm so nervous, I'm not sure I'd make a good impression."

"Please remain calm," said Atticus. "You must project an image of blameless rectitude."

"Isn't that illegal in Georgia," I joked.

Poly rolled her eyes at me and focused on Finch. Pomy laughed, but it was short and just this side of panic.

Atticus was wise enough to ignore me.

"Keep in mind that you'll be very close to the jury box," said the little lawyer. "They'll be watching you and you must remain centered, serene and assured. Make them love you and they'll never convict you."

"Ummm… okay," said Pomy.

It was clearly going to take a lot of work for her to practice what her counsel advised.

"Remember the waterwheel," I said. "Feel the warm water inside your head."

"Is this some sort of Terran religious ritual?" asked Atticus. "If so, I don't mean to interfere, but time is precious and I have a lot of details to cover."

"Go ahead," said Pomy.

I watched Pomy's breathing change as she went through the steps of the relaxation exercise I'd taught her last night. Her breaths were slowing and becoming more measured.

"It's not a religious ritual, Mr. Finch," said Poly. "Jack's just trying to help Pomy get control of herself."

"An admirable goal," said Atticus, "and one that I see is effective."

Pomy had lost her previous expression of panic. She was no longer a rabbit facing a wolf—she was a rabbit contemplating a field of fresh clover, contentedly chewing her latest mouthful. I hoped my exercise hadn't been *too* effective.

"Don't worry, Jack," said Pomy quietly. "I can hold it together."

"I know you can," said Poly with more force than necessary.

All of inhaled deeply and exhaled slowly, except Atticus, and some of the oppressive fear hanging over us evaporated.

"Please go on," said Pomy. "I understand I need to get the jury on my side."

"Correct," said Atticus, "especially since there is video evidence of Pomy committing the act that resulted in the damage specified in the complaint."

"Indisputable video evidence?" asked Poly.

"I'm an attorney," stated Atticus. "For attorneys in a court of law, *nothing* is indisputable."

"Got it," said Poly. I even detected a hint of a smile in her expression.

Atticus didn't waste time bringing us back to reality. "Opposing counsel is a bulldog. She's a local litigator who used to be an assistant Fulton county district attorney."

Pomy nodded.

"How do you fight a bulldog?" asked Poly. "Once they latch on to something they never let go."

"By not fighting it head on," answered Atticus. "By throwing enough things at the beast fast enough that it starts spinning around trying to bite its own tail." He spun around on his chair to illustrate his planned approach.

"Keeping her off-balance makes sense," I said. "How?"

"I have video evidence of my own that Agnes Spelman, Factor-E-Flor, and EUA might not be happy to see made public," said Atticus. "If I show it to them before the trial officially starts, we may not have to go through the rest of the formalities."

"That would be great!" said Pomy.

I mentally translated her statement into, *"Whatever it takes to get me out of this—fast."*

"What if your video evidence isn't persuasive?" asked Poly. "This trial is as much a matter of punishing me and Jack and Xenotech Support for getting in EUA's way as it is an attack on Pomy."

"Right," I added. "And what if EUA's increased their bid for the judge, trying to buy a favorable verdict?"

"You don't have to worry about that," said Atticus. "I've know Judge Jordan for more than a decade. Once the bidding has stopped and both sides have matched their contributions, he stays impartial, without wheedling for more money from one party or the other."

"That's reassuring," I said, wishing I knew less about modern methods of jurisprudence and feeling about as innocent in my understanding of the current legal system as Pomy looked in her long skirt and vest.

"Will you be playing the contributory negligence angle?" asked Poly.

"And the ignorance angle?" added Pomy. "I didn't mean to blow up the building and I had no idea there was a gas main by the front entrance."

"If I need to," said Atticus. "Just remember, your intent was to create a distraction, not destroy property."

"That will be easy to remember," said Pomy, "since it's the truth."

"Telling the truth is always the best way to lie," said Poly.

"Are you sure you haven't gone to law school?" asked Atticus.

We all laughed and more nervous tension dispelled.

Atticus reached into his briefcase and removed a thick envelope. He pulled out twenty-five or thirty eight-by-ten heavily annotated color glossy photographs from the envelope and fanned them in front of us with a pair of tentacles.

"These still photos will supplement the video evidence I plan to present and will give each juror something more immediate and tangible to hold," said the Pyr. "Each one is a reminder of who was where, when and why."

"I hope one of them isn't a picture of Pomy arming her Macerator power pack cylinder," said Poly.

"Have no fear of that, young lady," said Atticus. "However, there *is* a close-up photo showing who manufactured the cylinder."

"Factor-E-Flor," I contributed.

"Correct," said Atticus, grinning back with two mouths. He put the photos back in the envelope and returned them to his briefcase.

"Can we get back to my question?" said Poly.

"What question was that?" asked Atticus.

"There have been so many," said Pomy.

"What if your video evidence isn't persuasive?" responded Poly.

"It will be," said the Pyr.

"But what if it isn't?" persisted Poly.

"In that case, dear lady," said Atticus, "opposing counsel, Factor-E-Flor, and EUA Corporation are in for a very *big* surprise."

Chapter 24

"This is a court of law, young man, not a court of justice."
— Oliver Wendell Holmes

I was impressed when I stepped into the courtroom. It was huge, with thirty-foot ceilings and dark-stained oak wainscoting extending six feet up from the floor. At the far end of the room the entire wall was made of the same wood, expertly carved into borders and panels. Four tall dark-wood Doric columns stood like sentinels of justice on either side of the regal and impressively ornamented judge's bench. The flags of Georgia and the United States stood in opposite corners of the far wall. Marble busts of Solon and Moses near the flags frowned out from atop plinths crafted as smaller versions of the Doric columns.

We all moved a few more feet inside the room. The dozen rows of spectators' benches on either side reminded me of church pews. I had my jaw open and was rubbernecking like a first-time tourist in New York City, taking in the portraits of famous jurists on the walls and the ceremonial blank spot reserved, I'd heard, for an incised marble version of the Ten Commandments, should the Constitution's freedom of religion clause ever be repealed. I turned my head and looked up. There was a balcony above us, with five or six more rows of benches for overflow crowds.

Tables for the prosecution on the left, the defense on the right, and the jury box beyond that completed the furnishings except for a wooden lectern between the tables where the attorneys could put their notes if they used them.

The only thing that didn't match my mental picture of an American courtroom, after watching years of Law & Order reruns, was the carpet. A beautiful Persian rug the size of my living room rested on the floor in front of the lawyers' tables. It was woven from faded red, black and cream threads in a medallion pattern with an understated repeating border. It looked old—and expensive. I figured the judge must be a collector.

Once I'd taken in the physical details of the space I noticed the people. There were a lot more of them than I'd expected. A disheveled man with an aisle seat in the second row behind the defense table was wearing a monocle camera that made him look like a bargain basement version of Deadshot. He had a cloud of gnat-sized audio-visual drones circling his head, marking him as a reporter.

"Who's that?" I asked Atticus.

"That's *Hot Rod* Rodney Random," said the Pyr. "He's a freelancer with connections to the big news outfits."

"How did you get him to show up?" asked Poly. "This trial isn't worth a slot on the nightly news."

Atticus chuckled. If he didn't seem to be such a nice guy, I would have said it was an evil chortle.

"You'd be surprised what shows up on the nightly news," said the Pyr. "I did what I needed to do to get him in the proper spirit." The two of his mouths I could see smiled.

"You appealed to his better nature?" I asked.

"I slipped him a bottle of Jack Daniels."

"I guess that's one sort of proper spirit," said Poly.

I wished I could roll my eyes like she does. I didn't see what value some random reporter provided, but this wasn't my rodeo.

Pomy was standing close to Atticus, treating him like a security blanket. She wasn't saying much and was turning her head this way and that in nervous paranoia, trying to figure out where future attacks would be coming from. There wasn't much I could do to reassure her. I wasn't feeling too comfortable myself.

When *Hot Rod* shifted, I saw Martin sitting in the row ahead of him. He was turned partway around watching the entrance and spotted us. I wasn't sure why my friend was here, but my confidence rose because of his presence. I smiled and Poly waved. Martin nodded in acknowledgment.

I glanced to the left and spotted Ms. Smith, Agnes Spelman's executive assistant, sitting in the first row behind the prosecutor's table. Spelman herself was at the table, standing next to a short, almost tiny woman with her back to us.

"Is that the bulldog?" asked Poly, indicating the tiny woman with her gaze.

"Yes," said Atticus. "Don't underestimate her."

I didn't understand what the little lawyer meant until she turned around. The woman was truly petite, not quite five feet tall, and wore a light blue pinstripe power-suit with a short skirt. The suit's attempt to convey an I'm-in-charge attitude was countered, however, by a white-on-white patterned button-up blouse with an oversized bow at the neck that flopped and bounced as she moved.

Her hair was medium brown with blonde and hot pink high-lights, styled in a pixie cut. I think she had five earrings in her left ear and two in her right, but couldn't be sure at this distance. The overall effect of her ensemble made her come across as somewhere between a sophomore in high school and a freshman in college.

Now I understood the Pyr's warning. Her look had to be part of a calculated strategy.

When she noticed us, her mouth turned up in a perky smile. I immediately wanted to like her and protect her. My reflexive reaction proved the rationale behind her image. I stifled a compulsion to smile back and wave.

"When you said she was a bulldog, you meant she graduated from the University of Georgia, right?" asked Poly. "They're the Bulldogs. She doesn't look old enough to vote, let alone old enough to have graduated from law school."

"Hey," I protested, "I had a B.S. before most people graduate from high school. It's possible."

"I know all about your B.S.," teased Poly. "I didn't say it was impossible, I was just surprised."

"Ms. Brunhilde Dagomar Kone *is* a graduate of the University of Georgia," noted my phone. "At least for her undergraduate studies."

"Her law degree is from Harvard," said Atticus.

"Brunhilde?" I asked.

"Dagomar?" asked Poly in the same, incredulous tone.

"Traditional names in her family, I believe," said Atticus. "That's why she goes by Bulldog."

"Got it," I said.

With names like that, I'd opt for a nickname, too. Come to think of it, given that my name is Ajax, I had.

"Harvard?" mused Poly. "Maybe *that's* why she looks familiar."

I'd felt that I'd seen Ms. Kone somewhere before, too, but I didn't have Poly's Harvard connection. I'd figure it out later.

As we proceeded up the aisle to our seats, a short older man with thinning hair wearing a scowl and a charcoal gray suit worth more than my van brushed by me and sat next to Ms. Smith. He made her move in instead of stepping past her.

"Who's Mr. Congeniality?" I asked Atticus before we sat down.

"The head of EUA's legal department," said the Pyr. "He's Adolphus T. Kone, the Bulldog's boss—and her father."

"Ouch," I said. "Boss Kone."

Poly poked me in the ribs. I was spared further abuse over my comment echoing the name of a famous Boston-area science fiction convention, *Boskone,* by Martin giving Poly a hug. He slid in and Poly and I assumed our seats behind Pomy and Atticus. To my surprise, Pomy was looking calm and controlled. I wondered if Poly or Atticus had given her some sort of tranquilizer, but knew neither of them would. Like a university president, Pomy needed to be in complete control of her faculties.

It was two minutes until two, so we didn't have long to wait until things got started. I noticed the court reporter, a gray-haired woman in her sixties with perfect posture. She was sitting in her own wooden enclosure in front of the prosecutor's table. The court reporter cracked her knuckles, making me wince, then started typing on an odd, toy-sized typewriter with funny looking keys. Her fingers moved so quickly they seemed to blur. I expected she was putting in the date, time, judge's name, courtroom, and other preliminaries.

With one minute remaining, a pair of guards escorted the jury into the jury box. There were six women and six men, with a range of ages, apparent socio-economic statuses, and races that accurately reflected Atlanta in 2030. I was impressed by the person, persons, or A.I. who had handled the selection process.

At the stroke of two an older man with close-cropped gray hair and a protruding belly stepped onto the carpeted area at the front. He took a deep breath and bellowed a string of rolling phrases.

"All rise! The Superior Court of Fulton county—in the great state of Georgia—is now in session. The Honorable Henry S. Jordan, presiding."

I got to my feet, along with everyone else, but my mind was spinning. The judge's name was Henry *Hal* Jordan? Green Lantern would be handling Pomy's case? Then I remembered—Atticus had called him Jordy, not Hal. I soon saw why. A door opened behind the judge's bench and a tall, broad-shouldered man in his seventies with a thick head of white hair entered. He was wearing long black robes and looked like someone you might hire from central casting to play a judge on television. I was shocked to see him wearing sunglasses and carrying a red and white collapsible cane.

Musical memories of Arlo Guthrie's *Alice's Restaurant* flooded my brain. I thought of the annotated photographs with circles and arrows on each one in our lawyer's briefcase. I also considered the importance of video evidence for the trial and shook my head. This could be bad. *Very* bad. It could be another case of American blind justice and Pomy would be doomed.

Then the judge sat down, folded his cane, took off his sunglasses and snapped a louvered, gold-colored metallic visor over his eyes. I abruptly switched contexts—not Hal Jordan; Jordy or Geordi LaForge. The judge looked out at the courtroom and nodded at the the older man. Some obscure part of my brain dredged up the name of the older man's office. He was the bailiff, the clerk of the court, and he issued a brief, two-word command.

"Be seated."

We sat.

The bailiff continued. "In the matter of Factor-E-Flor, an EUA Corporation company, versus Ms. Melpomene Keen-Jones, all pray heed and attend."

He stepped back and stood near the court reporter's station. The judge swatted away something that looked like a mosquito and glared at me. Then I realized he wasn't focused on me, but on *Hot Rod* Rodney Random, seated immediately behind me.

"No one can say I am not a supporter of a free and independent press," said the judge. His voice matched his looks, inspiring respect and confidence in his judgment and impartiality. "But if you can't keep your microdrones under control, Mr. Random, I will have you ejected from my courtroom."

"Yes, your honor," said *Hot Rod* Rodney contritely. "It won't happen again."

"See that it doesn't."

I'd felt as paranoid as Pomy when the judge had seemed to stare at me. Poly held my hand until my pulse rate returned to normal. I didn't like being in situations where I didn't know what to expect. My prior knowledge of the judicial system was limited to watching the second half of episodes of *Law & Order: Luna City* and *Law & Order: Atlantis Dome* when I felt homesick on Orish. It was odd that the ultimate punishment in both those locations involved airlocks.

"Will counsel please approach the bench," said Judge Jordan. It wasn't a question. Atticus and the Bulldog stepped in front of the judge—or glided on mobility cilia in the Pyr's case. A Cone of Silence field snapped into place and not only restricted sound, it distorted sight enough so I couldn't read the judge's lips. A few seconds later, the private conference was over and the lawyers returned to their tables.

"It was just routine," Atticus whispered to Pomy. "He asked if we'd made every effort to settle things without the court's intervention."

Pomy nodded, still maintaining her iron control and keeping a pleasant, neutral expression on her face. I saw two jury members smile at her, which I took as a good sign. The judge looked at the Bulldog.

"Are you ready to present your opening argument, Counselor?" he asked.

"I am, Your Honor," she said.

She stood and approached the jury, giving a slight bow to the judge and turning her head to look at Pomy and frown as she made her way from the prosecutor's table.

"Gentlebeings of the jury," the Bulldog began, "today I will present incontrovertible video evidence of Ms. Keen-Jones' willful destruction of Factor-E-Flor's headquarters using an improvised explosive device. Her act cost my client hundreds of thousands of galcreds in property damage and weeks of business disruption. It's only pure luck that her actions didn't result in the deaths of any Factor-E-Flor employees."

The tiny litigator paced in front of the jury box, trying to catch each juror in turn. Every few steps she would smile at one of them, then turn and frown at Pomy, as if to emphasize what a terrible person Poly's sister was. Her tactics were working. Several jurors also frowned at Pomy and smiled back at Brunhilde Dagomar.

"Once you have seen the video evidence," the Bulldog continued, "your own eyes will compel you to render a unanimous verdict of guilty. Thank you."

The Bulldog returned to the prosecutor's table, the back of her short skirt waggling as she moved. She returned to her chair and sat with perfect posture, her upright demeanor reflecting the merits of her position. Now it was our turn.

Atticus hopped down from his chair and glided in front of the judge's bench. The top of his pyramidal form bent a little, as if he was bowing slightly, and two of his eye stalks extended and dipped to acknowledge the judge. Then he spun sixty degrees, as if on an axle, and moved over to the jury box. Several jurors were smiling. One, who must not be very familiar with Pyrs and their methods of locomotion, tried to hide a laugh.

"Good gentles," said the Pyr, "you will see several videos today. Factor-E-Flor's counsel will show you what *they* want you to see, but I intend to show you the *rest* of the story, demonstrating that Factor-E-Flor's own negligence is responsible for the damage to their headquarters."

The little lawyer removed a white handkerchief from inside his suit coat and paused to rub his glasses with it. I wondered if he was imitating someone he'd seen in a movie or on television. The gesture did serve to focus the jury's attention on him.

"I will also show you that Factor-E-Flor and their parent company, EUA Corporation, are culpable for improper actions far beyond mere negligence related to their own headquarters," said Atticus. "When you've seen and heard all the facts, I am confident that you will return a verdict for my client of not guilty."

The Pyr made a slightly tilting bow to the jury, spun around a hundred and eighty degrees on his base like someone rotating in a office chair, and glided back to his seat at the defense table. When he hopped up to sit there, more members of the jury smiled. Atticus was the perfect defense attorney to counter the coiled steel cuteness of the Bulldog. The person recommending him to Nettie Obi-Yu had given good advice.

As expected, the Bulldog opened her presentation with the videos of Pomy arguing with the receptionist and Ms. Smith in the lobby of Factor-E-Flor's headquarters and Pomy setting off the Macerator power pack cylinder near the entrance. Two large wooden panels on either side of the judge retracted, revealing flat screens, so jurors, counsel, and spectators could see the videos. I couldn't tell if Judge Jordy was getting a video feed directly to his visor or looking at a screen embedded in his judicial desk, but he seemed to be following what was happening well enough.

After seeing the power pack cylinder explode and bring the front of the building crashing down, things didn't look good for our side. Eight out of twelve jurors were giving Pomy a stink eye.

Then it was time for Atticus to present his case. It was three thirty, according to the analog clock my phone had decided to display on its home screen. The judge gave us a fifteen-minute break to take care of biological necessities. I was glad he wasn't the sort of guy to knock off work early on a Friday afternoon. Atticus turned around and tugged on my sleeve with a tentacle.

"Please ask Ms. Kone and her father to join me," he said.

I was interested in handling my own biological necessities, but followed his instructions. The two lawyers followed me back to the defense table. Agnes Spelman and her assistant trailed behind.

Adolphus Kone's face grew pinched and his nose lifted as he got closer to our table. The Bulldog's father kept his distance from Atticus as if he could barely tolerate being near the little alien. When he stood across the table from Atticus he was ill-mannered and sniffed, as if the Pyr smelled bad. I'd always thought the three and four-sided species had a pleasant, minty scent myself.

While I'd stepped away, Atticus had removed a large tablet computer from his briefcase and had queued up a series of videos. When the EUA and Factor-E-Flor lawyers arrived, he positioned the tablet where they both could see it. Agnes Spelman and Ms. Smith crowded in as well. Then Atticus started the first video. Smith was talking to Spelman in Spelman's office.

"We've restored enough Macerator units for an effective attack, but have had some trouble finding enough trained operators," said Ms. Smith.

"How many is enough?" asked Spelman.

"Two dozen," said Smith.

"That should do it," said her boss. "Make it so."

Atticus paused the playback.

"Where did you get that?" barked the Bulldog.

"Creative use of the discovery process," said Atticus. "I also have a video of Spelman and Smith discussing planting a nova bomb at a starship hanger near Hartsfield Port."

The Bulldog's father was staring daggers at Smith and Spelman. His daughter didn't seem too happy either.

"If you could give us a moment," said EUA's top legal honcho.

Poly, Pomy, Atticus, Martin and I headed out of the court-room to give them space. *Hot Rod* Rodney Random followed us after a Cone of Silence surrounded the pairs of lawyers and clients. He went one way while the rest of us went the other. I was urgently looking for the *necessarium*, but overheard Poly's question for Atticus.

"Were the videos the big surprise you had planned?"

The Pyr's eyes twinkled. I didn't know they could do that, but perhaps there was some sort of physiological system for back lighting.

"By no means," said Atticus. "The *big* surprise is still to come."

So long as we were winning, I was starting to like this court-room stuff.

Chapter 25

"Always mystify, mislead and surprise the enemy if possible."
— Stonewall Jackson

We returned to the courtroom with five minutes to spare. Both Adolphus and Brunhilde Dagomar Kone were waiting for Atticus at the defense table.

"Your videos aren't admissible," said the Bulldog. "They're not relevant to the current case and their authenticity is suspect."

"We're not cutting a deal," said her father. His face looked as long, sombre and serious as an Easter Island statue.

"Then you won't mind if I share them with *Hot Rod* Rodney," said Atticus.

"If suing you for libel is not minding," said Boss Kone. "We'll slap an injunction on you so fast the top of your pointy little head will spin off."

I didn't know if that was anatomically possible for Pyrs, but the mental picture was entertaining, even if I wasn't pleased with Kone's threats.

"None the less," said Atticus, "the public—and more than one level of law enforcement—would find conspiracy to commit murder and destroy property by one of your corporate executives quite interesting."

He waved toward Agnes Spelman at the prosecution's table.

Boss Kone looked mad enough to spit lightning bolts. He was clearly someone used to getting his own way.

"Publish and be damned!" Adolphus thundered. He tried to swat a gnat hovering around his forehead but missed. His hand made an impressive splat when his palm collided with bare skin.

"Did you get that Rodney?" asked Atticus.

The reporter, tracking his bugs from the back of the courtroom, gave the little Pyr a thumbs-up.

"Excellent," said our lawyer. "Make sure you give me a chance to review the final cut before you post it."

I could see metaphorical steam coming off the top of Boss Kone's head. So could his daughter.

"If you post these videos—made without consent—I can't be responsible for the consequences," said the Bulldog.

"Should I construe that as a threat?" asked Atticus.

"Take it as you will," said Brunhilde Dagomar.

"All rise," said the bailiff.

We resumed our seats with only a minimum of milling and confusion just before the judge returned. He adjusted his visor, scanned the room, and sat down.

"Mr. Finch," he said. "You're up."

"Yes, your honor," said the Pyr. "The defense calls Cumulocirrus Jordan."

As the bailiff called our first witness, Atticus turned to the judge.

"No relation, your honor."

Atticus, the judge, and the witness laughed. 'Lo Jordan was a black man in his early fifties, built like a fireplug. He wasn't fat—he was solid and not much taller than he was wide. He looked strong enough to arm press an anvil. The man was shorter than the Bulldog, but must be three times her weight. He was wearing a custom-tailored suit—not as expensive these days as it was before mutable morphabrics—and looked centered and dependable.

"Mr. Jordan," said the Pyr, "would you please tell us your occupation?"

"I am the chief building inspector for the city of Atlanta," Jordan replied.

"Would you summarize your experience in that role?" asked Atticus.

"The prosecution accepts Mr. Jordan as an expert witness," said the Bulldog. "His many years of service as a building inspector are well known."

This was a smart tactic on the Bulldog's part. I knew all about 'Lo Jordan from my work at Ad Astra. The Bulldog seemed to be doing Atticus a favor, but was really trying to minimize the weight of Jordan's testimony by not allowing a recitation of his credentials. Atticus didn't fight it, however.

"Did you personally inspect Factor-E-Flor's premises in July of 2028?"

"I did," said 'Lo Jordan.

"Were they fully compliant with Atlanta's building codes?" asked the Pyr.

"They were not," said Jordan.

He kept as sentences as short as his stature.

"What was Factor-E-Flor's most significant violation?"

"They did not remove the live gas main buried eight inches below the surface near their front entrance," said Jordan, waxing loquacious.

"Why was this a violation?" asked Atticus.

"Because it might blow up the building," said Jordan.

It looked like the Bulldog was going to object to his statement, but she reconsidered and kept silent.

"Did Factor-E-Flor's management respond to your report noting this violation?"

"They did not."

"Do you know *why* they didn't respond?" asked the little lawyer.

"No," said Jordan, "but many companies would rather pay the fines for non-compliance instead of incurring the large one-time cost required to remediate the problem."

"Objection," said the Bulldog. "Speculation."

"Sustained," said the judge.

"Withdrawn," said Atticus.

At least a seed had been planted in the jury's mind.

"Have you studied the reports of the damage to Factor-E-Flor's headquarters?" asked Atticus.

"I have."

"Is the level of damage what you'd expect from the gas main exploding?"

"It is."

"Would an exploding Macerator power pack cylinder be enough to account for the damage you reviewed?"

"No."

"What would account for that level of damage?"

"The gas main exploding."

"Would an overloaded Macerator power pack cylinder be the minimum necessary force necessary to trigger a gas main explosion?"

"A lit match would be enough," said Jordan, "if the integrity of the pipe was compromised."

"In your experience," said Atticus, "are gas main pipes the age of Factor-E-Flor's often compromised?"

"They are."

The Bulldog rose to her feet. "Objection!"

"Overruled," said the judge. "And sit down."

Brunhilde Dagomar sat.

"Your witness," said Atticus, waving a cheery tentacle at the Bulldog. She didn't smile back but popped back up out of her chair like the weasel in the old nursery rhyme. It was fascinating to watch the way Atticus manipulated the jury's perception of the Bulldog by having her stand, sit, and stand in rapid succession. The big bow on her blouse had bounced comically in response to her vertical motions.

"Mr. Jordan," said the Bulldog from the lectern. "How many office buildings in Atlanta the age of Factor-E-Flor's have been damaged due to gas main explosions over your career."

"Two," said Jordan.

"Two?" asked the Bulldog.

Her eyes went wide. That wasn't the answer she'd been expecting. She recovered enough to ask another question.

"Factor-E-Flor and...?"

"Widget Technology and Fabrication's headquarters next door," said Jordan. "It's a near-identical structure."

The Bulldog stopped him before he could do more damage.

"No further questions."

Jordan stepped down and took a seat a few rows behind me on the defense side.

"Next witness," said the judge.

"The defense calls Jean-Jacques Bonhomme," said Atticus.

I did a double-take, since I hadn't noticed J-J in the court-room. My one-time client took the stand and made the usual affirmations. Atticus led Jean-Jacques through a few questions to establish his role as president of WT&F and confirm that his corporate headquarters was only a stone's throw—or perhaps a bomb's throw—away from Factor-E-Flor's building. A satellite view flashed on the screens to either side of the judge's bench, showing the only thing separating the two companies was a screen of mature pine trees on a ten-foot patch of bare ground between their respective parking lots.

"Mr. Bonhomme, please tell the court about the phone call you received on the Sunday evening before your building was destroyed," said Atticus.

J-J looked uncomfortable, but he spoke—haltingly—as if trying to avoid stepping into pools of quicksand.

"I was in New York City, visiting my mother, when the call came in around seven o'clock in the evening," said Jean-Jacques. "The caller didn't give her name, but said WT&F needed to fabricate something right away, based on specs she'd provide."

"Did you do what she asked?" Atticus probed.

"Yes, but the giant robot flew away."

"Giant robot?" said Atticus incredulously. "She wanted you to build a giant robot?"

"A giant *combat* robot two hundred and fifty feet tall," continued J-J. "But it disappeared before I could arrange for delivery."

"I see," said Atticus. He paused and cleaned one of his pairs of glasses with a pocket handkerchief. "Is this the only time you heard from this woman?"

"No. She called again."

"There was a second call? Please tell us about that one."

"It wasn't a request this time," said Jean-Jacques. "It was a threat."

Atticus approached the judge and removed a Darth Vader thumb drive from one of the pockets of his three-sided suit.

"Your Honor, this drive contains an authenticated recording of the second call my witness referenced. Independent vocal identification experts have confirmed that the voice talking to Mr. Bonhomme belongs to Ms. Agnes Spelman, CEO of Factor-E-Flor," said Atticus. "May I play the recording for the jury?"

The judge leaned down to review something that must have just appeared on his smart desk. He nodded.

"Proceed," the judge instructed.

Atticus handed the thumb drive to the bailiff. A few seconds later, the recorded phone conversation began to play. Waveforms flowed across the flat screens on either side of the judge's bench while scrolling text below reminded everyone of the speaker's identity.

A cold, hard woman's voice was speaking. It had a hint of a Caribbean accent. "Mr. Bonhomme, if you don't produce my order on time, you'll be very, very sorry." The voice paused to let her message sink in, then continued. "I advise you to seriously consider the consequences of failure to comply with my instructions. If you don't produce my order on schedule, you and your company won't be producing orders for *anyone* in the future. Do you understand?"

"Yes," said Jean-Jacques's petrified voice on the recording. On the stand, the here-and-now J-J was trembling from the memory.

The recording abruptly switched to a dial tone, then ended. I glanced over at Agnes Spelman She was the sister of Columbia Brown, the woman who had shot me in a VIGorish Labs' hangar near Hartsfield Port almost two months ago. In profile, her face looked like it had just received a massive injection of botox. She didn't react at all. I hoped the jury would draw the proper conclusion from her lack of expression.

"What did you do after you received Ms. Spelman's call?" Atticus asked J-J.

"I left town and flew to Las Vegas," said WT&F's CEO. "I had some business there and wanted to get out of town as fast as possible."

"Were you afraid you might be killed?" asked Atticus.

"Wouldn't you be?" returned Jean-Jacques.

"Please answer the question," instructed the judge. He leaned down to follow the interrogation more closely.

"Yes," said J-J. "I was afraid Ms. Spelman would kill me, or arrange for me to be killed."

"Thank you," said Atticus. The Pyr waved a tentacle at the judge to appreciate his intervention and continued his examination of the witness.

"What happened to WT&F's corporate headquarters shortly after your conversation with Ms. Spelman?"

"It was blown up," said Jean-Jacques.

"Did you witness the explosion firsthand?"

"No, I got a call from the fire department, informing me of the damage."

"Your Honor," said Atticus, "I would like to question an officer from the Atlanta Fire Department to share her direct knowledge of subsequent events."

"That's fine," said Judge Jordan. "Mr. Bonhomme, you may step down temporarily. Remember, you are still under oath."

"Yes, Your Honor," said J-J.

He took a seat at the far end of the row where Martin and Poly and I were sitting. I took advantage of the interlude as a new witness was sworn in to ask Martin a question, *sotto voce.*

"What ever happened to all the disassembled two hundred and fifty foot robots?" I asked.

"They were reassembled in a police impound warehouse near the airport," said Martin. "Factions from three law enforcement agencies *and* the military are fighting over who gets to control them."

"Nice to know," I said, quietly. I could think of several circumstances where a few giant robots might come in handy.

A familiar-looking woman in an official City of Atlanta Fire Department dress uniform was taking the stand. It was Clarisse Beatty, the woman in charge at WT&F after the explosion. I started to wave, then realized where I was and sat on my hand. Atticus established her *bona fides* and skipped right to the most essential part of her testimony.

"Did you investigate the cause of the explosion that severely damaged Widget Technology and Fabrication's headquarters?" asked the intense little Pyr.

"I did," said Clarisse in a no-nonsense, just-the-facts tone.

"Can you tell us your findings?" asked Atticus.

"I can do better than that," said the firefighter. "I've got video of the act of sabotage being committed."

"Objection!" shouted the Bulldog. "Any such video was not provided during discovery and its provenance has not been established. It could be a fake and showing it to the jury would be prejudicial."

"Please sit down, Counselor," said the judge in a kindly tone. "I'll take your objection under advisement."

He theatrically pulled a handkerchief from somewhere and wiped his forehead to buy himself time to think, I assumed. Then he spoke to Atticus.

"Mr. Finch, would you mind if I asked Officer Beatty a few questions directly?"

"Go right ahead, Your Honor."

"Thank you," said the judge. His visor made it impossible to read his eyes, but he seemed to be amused by the way the trial was going. Judge Jordan smiled at Clarisse and spoke almost casually.

"Did you verify the authenticity of the recording?" he asked.

"I did," said Clarisse. "The official position of the Atlanta Fire Department is that the video is an authentic recording of the events immediately prior to the explosion, taken by WT&F's external security cameras."

"Was the perpetrator of the sabotage aware of the cameras?" asked the judge.

"Objection! Speculation," said the Bulldog.

The judge and half the courtroom laughed.

"Withdrawn," said Judge Jordan, smiling. "Let me rephrase. Were the external security cameras easy to identify?"

"They were not," said Clarisse. "They were integrated with the exterior lights. No separate units identifiable as cameras were visible."

Poly nudged me with an elbow. I looked at her and grinned. The hidden cameras had been part of my program of improved physical security for WT&F.

"Thank you," said the judge. "At least we can be confident the perpetrator of the sabotage wasn't completely stupid."

"Objection," said Atticus. "Assumes facts not in evidence."

Now three-quarters of the courtroom laughed.

"Very true, Counselor," said the judge. "But I'm convinced of it's authenticity. I'll allow the video to be shown."

"Exception," said the Bulldog.

"Noted," said the judge. "You wanted a speedy trial, Ms. Kone. You can't have that without a few discovery items falling through the cracks."

The Bulldog looked like she'd just bitten into a Scotch bonnet pepper. Agnes Spelman turned and stared daggers at me. I smiled back, glad that the jury had a clear view of her expression. The video began to play on the pair of screens above the judge's bench.

The scene was clear. It was a wide-angle view of the front entrance to WT&F's familiar headquarters. Nothing seemed to be happening, then everything happened all at once. A cylinder that looked a lot like a Macerator's power pack appeared out of thin air a few inches above the ground and rolled over to a bush near the stairs and ramp leading to the HQ's main door. We could hear the sound of feet running on concrete, then asphalt, then nothing. The screen went blank as my hidden cameras were vaporized by the explosion that severely damaged the near side of the building.

Around the courtroom, everyone was making puzzled noises. Nobody could tell what had happened. Before the hubbub could grow louder, Atticus asked another question.

"Could you rewind and show us a close up of the bomb?"

"Certainly," said Clarisse.

The video ran in reverse until the Macerator power pack cylinder started to fall. Then Officer Beatty zoomed in on the device.

"Can you identify any details about the manufacturer?" asked Atticus.

The focus of the video shifted and framed a small metal plate on one side of the cylinder.

"Please tell the court the name of the company that made the bomb?" Atticus requested.

"Factor-E-Flor," said Clarisse.

"Thank you," said Atticus. "It's very hard to identify the individual delivering the explosive device. Do you have anything further to add about the person who planted it?"

"I do," said Officer Beatty. "We couldn't make a solid ID using visible light, but then we watched it again in infra-red."

I was glad I'd spent more of J-J's money to get top of the line cameras. It was time for the rest of the story. The video ran again, but now we could see a dim red image of a human form approach the front of the building, drop a Macerator power pack cylinder, and run. Factor-E-Flor's minions must have managed to get some Blend Into The Scenery cloth—or maybe they still had some left over from when they'd stolen bolts of the stuff from Morphicouture last March.

"Once we realized the saboteur was using light-bending fabric as a disguise, we used image-enhancement algorithms on the perpetrator's face," said Clarisse.

The video ran yet again. This time, the fuzzy infra-red image of the person with the cylinder became distinct. Poly gasped, and I may have, too. It was Ms. Smith, Agnes Spelman's executive assistant. I looked over and saw Ms. Smith was standing up and trying to crawl over Adolphus Kone in order to leave the courtroom.

"Stay where you are," commanded Judge Jordan. "I expect Mr. Finch will want to ask *you* some questions shortly."

Ms. Smith didn't say anything. She just returned to her seat and tried to look invisible, without benefit of B.I.T.S. cloth.

"Thank you, Officer Beatty," said the judge. He turned to Atticus. "Do you have any further questions for this witness?"

"Not at present, Your Honor," said the Pyr.

Clarisse stepped down and slid into the far end of the row occupied by *Hot Rod* Rodney Random. The Bulldog stood up.

"Your Honor," she said, "this is most irregular."

Her father made a loud *hrrrumph* sound.

"Counselors, approach the bench," said Judge Jordan. Aldophus *hrrrumphed* again. "You, too, Mr. Kone, if you're going to continue making that noise."

The white-haired judge made a point of *not* turning on his Cone of Silence field.

"Don't you think this farce has gone on long enough?" asked the judge. "It's clear Factor-E-Flor and WT&F are having some sort of Hatfields and McCoy's feud and you're using the legal system as well as high explosives to harass each other. It makes me wish dueling was still legal in Georgia."

"Your Honor!" objected the Bulldog.

"HRRRRUMPH!" said her father.

"My feelings exactly," said Atticus. His eye facing our way winked at us.

Boss Kone exploded like a Macerator power pack cylinder going off over half a dozen gas mains.

"I won't *stand* for this," he ranted. "I'll have this declared a mistrial and have you removed from the bench for judicial misconduct! I'll sue the Fire Department of the City of Atlanta and WT&F and any party associated with this gross miscarriage of justice."

The Bulldog's father took a deep breath but didn't seem to be winding down.

"This is not a schoolyard. You can't get out of a lawsuit by asserting the other party did the same thing to the defendant. I'm going to speak to the district attorney and have him initiate *criminal* charges against Ms. Keen-Jones. WT&F, and Xenotech Support Corporation. I'll keep them all so tied up in litigation that they'll be spending the rest of their lives in depositions, courtrooms and jail!"

I thought he'd finished, but Boss Kone still had one more horse to flog. He turned to Atticus.

"And you, you pusillanimous little ball of alien dough and slimy tentacles," he exclaimed, "I'll see you disbarred. Your kind don't belong on Earth in the first place, let alone in the legal profession."

"That's *quite* enough," said Judge Jordan in an icy tone. Lights on the side of his visor were pulsing an angry red.

"And my tentacles are *not* slimy," said the little Pyr, smiling. He waved to *Hot Rod* Rodney with one of the referenced tentacles. "Did you get all that?"

Rodney flashed him a thumbs up.

Boss Kone's face turned redder than a Nicósn's. I thought he was going to try to strangle Atticus, which would have been a challenge, since Pyrs don't have necks. The Bulldog was easing away from her father, trying to put some distance between them. Boss Kone rushed Atticus, arms outstretched to capture and crush the Pyr, if strangling proved impractical.

"I'll get you, you alien scum, you!" shouted the Bulldog's father as he charged.

Then things went even *more* crazy. With a faint whiff of ozone and a sharp crack from the hardwood floor below the large carpet in front of the judge's bench, Queen Sherrhiliandarianne the Second, Matriarchal Majesty of Dauush and all the Dauushan worlds, teleported into the courtroom. She snatched up Boss Kone in three sub-trunks before he could reach Atticus and held him over her head where she could stare at him eye to eye.

"You're the top lawyer for EUA Corporation," the queen bellowed. "You can get me The General. He kidnapped my daughter. He poisoned my people with grajja, he ruined an important state dinner party, he tried to infect us with the Compliant Plague, and he had the effrontery to try and kidnap *me!*" she shouted. "He even shot down my shuttles with surface to air missiles. The General must answer for his crimes against my realm. Bring him to me in twenty-four hours or *you* will face my wrath and the might of all Dauush."

Kone wasn't in a position to throw his weight around any longer. Queen Sherrhi out-massed him by several tons. He stared at the spectators, then the judge, his eyes imploring anyone to help him.

"Don't look at me," said Judge Jordan. "This is above my pay grade."

"Please put my father down, Your Majesty," said the Bulldog calmly, "Or I'll be forced to sue you for assault."

Queen Sherrhi squeezed Boss Kone with her sub-trunks until he squeaked. It sounded better than his *hrrrumphs.*

"Would you prefer to charge me with murder?" intoned the queen.

"We'll drop the suit against Ms. Keen-Jones as a sign of good faith," said the Bulldog. "And I will encourage my father to set up a meeting for you with the head of EUA Corporation tomorrow."

"Very good," said Queen Sherrhi. She put Boss Kone down— none too gently—and he collapsed on the floor. "Have The General appear at the Dauushan consulate by five."

"We'll do our best," said Brunhilde Dagomar.

It was fascinating to watch a woman less than five feet tall stand up to an angry adult Dauushan.

"See that you do," said Queen Sherrhi.

She recentered herself the carpet and disappeared with a boom-crack of in-rushing air as she teleported away. The courtroom was buzzing.

"Case dismissed," said the judge. He banged his gavel, but the noise it made was only a faint echo of the sound of Queen Sherrhi's departure.

Atticus gave him a friendly wave with one tentacle, then glided back to the defense table on his mobility cilia and shook Pomy's hand with another.

"Looks like you're in the clear," he told her.

Pomy gave the little Pyr a hug, then sat down like a marionette with cut strings. Poly winked at me and gave me an enigmatic smile. I remembered her one-on-one conversation with Queen Sherrhi on the *Charalindhri* and considered that she'd had time for a private talk with Atticus when she'd walked him out after our initial meeting. Had she set this all up?

I was glad I had such a wise—and sneaky partner. Maybe direct action would help us find The General sooner, rather than later.

I still needed to congratulate our lawyer for a job well done.

"Hey, Atticus," I said. "When you told us you had a big surprise, you weren't kidding."

"You weren't the only one surprised," said Atticus. "I was expecting Tomáso."

Chapter 26

"Think not I am what I appear."
— Lord Byron

"Where are you headed next?" asked Martin as the courtroom began to clear.

"I'm taking Pomy home," answered Poly.

"Do you think that's a good idea?" I asked.

"Then I'm bringing her over to our underground research facility," Poly continued. "I'll help her pack first." She stuck her tongue out at me while Martin was looking elsewhere.

"That means a long commute for her back to the Carlos Museum on Monday," I noted.

"She said Dr. Liddell-Scott and Dr. Urradu told her to take next week off," said Poly. "They saw how upset she was about the lawsuit."

"Great," I said. "Want company?"

Poly looked over at Pomy. Her sister looked ready to be poured into bed and allowed to sleep though the weekend.

"I've got this," said Poly. "It will be easier on Pomy if she only has to cope with me, not both of us."

"That makes sense," I said. "What's on your plate, Martin?"

"I'm going to the Alban White Foundation's offices to see if I can talk to the man himself."

"Want company?" I repeated. This time I got a different answer.

"That would be great," said Martin. "With my badge and your b.s. we'll be sure to see him."

"Hey, I resemble that remark!" I protested.

"It was meant as a compliment," said Martin dryly.

"I thought Shepherd was going with you?" I remembered.

"He was," said Martin, "until I learned Alban White is a xenophobe."

"I hope he's not as bad as Adolphus Kone," said Poly.

"From what I've heard, White and Kone are cut from the same cloth," said Martin.

"A sheet with holes in it?" I suggested.

"You had to go there," said Martin, his dark brown eyes twinkling.

I shrugged. Poly gave Martin a hug and me a hug and a peck on the cheek. Then she helped Pomy up and guided her toward the exit.

"Bye, guys," said Pomy in a low-affect sleep-deprived voice.

"Take good care of yourself," I said.

"Right now, that's Poly's job," said Pomy, momentarily sounding more coherent.

The two sisters walked away and I marveled how much I loved both of them—albeit in different ways.

"Did you drive?" I asked Martin.

"My cruiser can be out front in five minutes," he replied.

"I call shotgun!"

"Not a good thing to say around a police officer," teased Martin.

"The Alban White Foundation closes at five," said my phone. "All due haste is recommended."

"Tally-ho!" I said.

"And Mr. White is the fox," said Martin.

"Walk, don't talk," said my phone.

So we did.

* * * * *

The Alban White Foundation offices were north on I-75, near the Cobb Galleria. White had purchased the Atlanta Braves shortly after taking over and renaming Home Depot, so he wanted his foundation to be close to the Braves' stadium in Cobb county. Martin parked his police cruiser in a parking structure adjacent to the Foundation and we took an elevator up two floors to the courtyard level.

Ordinary mortals couldn't approach the Foundation's offices without going through the courtyard, though I suspected White and his senior executives had a way to access their space without going outside. Once I saw the exterior of the Foundation, I understood why supplicants had to approach from outside— the exterior was truly impressive. It was clearly designed to intimidate and looked like a cross between a French chateau and a rococo castle along the lines of the one built by Mad King Ludwig.

The place was tall and assembled from massive granite blocks, with crenelations for archers, should they be needed to hold off hordes of angry peasants. Windows in the upper stories were fitted into heavy metal frames and looked like they actually opened—a rare feature in these days of climate-controlled buildings. Maybe they were designed that way so occupants could poor boiling oil down on attackers more easily? The overall impression conveyed was that the lord of this castle wanted the *hoi polloi* to respect his power and keep their distance. We approached anyway.

"What did you tell your friend at White House & Home?" I asked Martin. "And will he use his connections with Alban White? What makes you think we won't be turned away by the first dragon guarding the great man's sanctum?"

In my experience, people like Alban White's toadies had toadies, restricting access through multiple levels of functionaries.

"I told him enough to get the great man interested," Martin answered, "and my friend gave me some magic words that should get us in the door."

"Like *open sesame?*"

"No, like *law enforcement consideration.*"

"You're willing to come across like a cop on the take to further this investigation?" I asked.

"If it isn't true and it gets us in to see him," said Martin. "A man like Alban White can appreciate the benefit of having friends in high places."

"Uh huh," I said. "Police lieutenants are really up there."

"I may have also intimated that I'm an intermediary for my boss's boss."

I slapped my friend on the back.

"That's more like it," I said. "Don't just put your own neck on the line, get the high command involved."

"It seemed like a good idea at the time."

"I admire your chutzpah," I said.

"Keep my parents out of this," said Martin, a smile crossing his usually serious face.

"I didn't think I'd brought them up," I responded.

"Don't you know the classic definition of chutzpah?" asked Martin. "It's the sheer gall of a man who kills his parents, then begs the court for mercy on the grounds that he's an orphan."

"Right," I said. "I'm sure your parents are wonderful people who deserve full lives. I'll admire your moxie, instead."

"Thank you," said Martin, his face back to its usual deadpan.

We had arrived at the foot of the grand staircase leading up to the chateau-castle's huge main doors. Climbing them was an effort and most people would be winded by the time they reached the top. Martin, of course, was in great shape, but I had to lump myself in with *most people* and needed to pause to catch my breath at the summit. There was a thick rope descending from a hole in the door frame on the left. I'd seen *The Wizard of Oz*. Once my breathing had returned to normal, I pulled on the rope. A bell rang.

"Go away," said a voice from a hidden speaker. "We're closed."

"Stated business hours for the Alban White Foundation say you're open until five o'clock," said my phone authoritatively.

"Not on Friday afternoons," said the voice.

"Mr. White will want to hear what I have to say," asserted Martin.

"You and every other person who shows up here with their hand out," said the voice.

I'd been looking around and had spotted the camouflaged speaker and several hidden cameras. Not only that, I'd identified a small door to the left of the large main wooden doors. It's outline blended in with the mortar patterns of the massive stone blocks, but it was clearly visible once you knew where to look. I could see both a keyhole and a small indentation where it could be opened from this side. I picked up my phone and whispered to it. It jumped down and followed my suggestion.

"Come back on Monday," the voice continued. "Better yet, don't come back at all."

While the voice was talking, my phone had opened the small stone door, revealing a young man in an alcove. He was seated in a chair watching us on a flat screen. The man was dressed in all white livery, with bits of off-white piping on the shoulders and shirt cuffs. I stepped close and did my best to loom over him. Martin would have done it better.

"Excuse me," I said, loud enough to make the man jump. "We're not going anywhere and you're going to let us in. I've spotted eight security holes in your defensive perimeter already and they'll be on Galnet in three minutes if you don't."

Martin joined me next to the young man, looming professionally.

"And you'll be a hero for letting us in," said my friend. "Mr. White will be very interested in my proposition."

"I am under strict orders not to let anyone in without an appointment," said the young man.

"You didn't ask if we had an appointment," I said.

"I figured you'd lead with that if you had one," said the man.

"Send them up," interrupted a harsh voice from a speaker on the young man's desk. "They intrigue me."

The young man gulped and stammered. "Y-yes, Mr. White. Immediately, Mr. White."

He clicked a button on his screen and the large main wooden doors opened.

"You can go right in," said the young man.

We stepped away from his alcove and he slammed the small stone door behind us. The first dragon had been a pussycat.

* * * * *

A tall, expressionless woman in a similar all white uniform met us inside the main doors. It took a lot of chutzpah to require your retainers to wear white livery—the stuff must be a real pain to keep clean. Our escort was my height and wearing white faux leather boots that probably cost as much as the monthly retainer I charge most of my clients. Fauxs are small, goat-like alien quadrupeds and prey animals for the feline Tigrammaths. Their hides are usually mottled with browns and tans. Finding pure white ones is a challenge. The woman had blue eyes, a pale Nordic complexion and long ash-blonde hair in a single braid that extended down to the small of her back. She looked more like a Brunhilde than the Bulldog and seemed like the reason the phrase Ice Maiden was invented. Her movements were precise and perfect.

We followed the Valkyrie through echoing corridors of polished Italian marble with walls covered in impressive and somewhat disconcerting works of art. A large painting of a division of the U.S. Cavalry defeating a band of Sioux warriors in the late nineteenth century was followed by a huge fresco of *The Rape of the Sabine Women*. A niche further on featured a statue of Perseus holding the head of Medusa aloft by its snakes. I was sensing a theme—brutal conquest with a heavy dose of misogyny. Alban White was looking like a very good candidate for being The General.

As we proceeded, heavy doors swung or slid open just as we reached them. I had a sense of *deja vu,* then remembered where I'd seen something similar. The doors' movements reminded me of the opening credits from a spy spoof television show from more than half a century ago that I'd seen on the *Ancient Gems* channel. It took me a few seconds to remember the show's name—*Get Smart.* I thought that name was good advice for Martin and myself as we moved forward for our meeting with Alban White. We'd need all our wits about us for that encounter. Then I remembered that the title was meant ironically. Maxwell Smart was anything but intelligent. He relied on dumb luck more than wisdom for success. I'd take that option too, if it worked.

We finally reached a pair white marble doors so ornate I knew they must lead to Alban White's private office. They were covered in carvings that recapitulated themes from the art on the walls we'd passed earlier. Bundles of sticks around axes were prominently featured and so were angry armored angels carrying fiery swords, their flames accented with copper and gold foil. Howard Hughes had fewer screws loose than Alban White, I was sure.

For all that the man's choice in decorating motifs was off-putting, in person Alban White tried to charm.

"Welcome, gentleman," he said, waving us to comfortable armchairs in a sitting area in one corner of his palatial office.

He was as pale as the Ice Maiden, but his eyes were an even more intense blue, like a pair of deep glacial lakes.

"Contact lenses?" I whispered.

"Shhh," said Martin.

The rest of White's coloring made me think he might be an albino. His eyebrows were white and his short hair was a shade lighter than the Valkyrie's. Even from a distance, I could see blue veins and red arteries in his neck as if his skin was translucent. He didn't offer to shake hands and I was fine with that. Something about the man gave me the creeps.

"Thank you for seeing us," said Martin.

The three of us sat down. Our host took the largest, most imposing chair.

"An executive at White House & Home spoke highly of you," said White. "I hope he was correct in his assessment."

"I'm sure you'll find our conversation valuable," said Martin. "This is my friend, Jack Buckston, with Xenotech Support Corporation."

"Ah, yes," said White. "Your fame precedes you. I loved the video of your dirigible chase down the Strip in Las Vegas."

I nodded and offered a tight-lipped smile. I wasn't thrilled that video had gone viral.

"That will be all, Andy," said White to the Valkyrie.

Andy? I thought. I would have expected Ingrid or something else more Scandinavian.

The Ice Maiden left through the marble doors, leaving the three of us alone.

"Tell me, Lieutenant Lee," said Alban White, "what could a respected member of the Georgia Capitol Police need from me?"

Before Martin could tarnish his reputation, I jumped in, doing to Martin what Poly had done to me in Pablo Daniel Figueres' office.

"My friend doesn't need anything from you," I said. "I do. He pulled strings so that I could pitch you on using Xenotech Support Corporation for your companies' toughest technical challenges."

White didn't look at me—he looked at Martin.

"I must say, Mr. Lee, I'm disappointed," he said. "I expected better from someone with your reputation."

Martin didn't reply, maintaining his default police officer's no-nonsense face. I knew I'd hear a few choice words from him later.

"Don't blame Martin," I continued. "He had a contact at White House & Home and I begged him to help me get in to see you."

"I'll have a few choice words to share with the executive who recommended Lieutenant Lee," said White, "but you're here and White House & Home does have a difficult technical challenge. Let's see how you'd solve it."

I'd been prepared to give my standard sales pitch, but this might be easier. If I could prove my technical skill, I could gain more insight into White's business operations and redeem Martin in the process.

"I'm glad to try," I said. "Tell me about the challenge."

"It's all about productivity," said White. "It's going down and I don't know what to do about it."

"How does that tie to information technology?" I asked.

"I don't think it does," said White, "but my people insist it's an IT issue, not a fault in their management."

Martin looked at White then looked at me hopefully. I could see that he thought White was setting me up with a no-win proposition.

"How does this lack of productivity manifest?" I asked. "Are people screwing around on web sites where they shouldn't go?"

"No, it's nothing like that," said White. "Our systems are locked so tight and supervisors get copies of employees daily browsing history, so there's no risk of anybody wasting time that way."

I was getting a better idea of White's personality and management style. He was a control freak and reluctant to extend trust or give autonomy to the people who worked for him. He probably considered them minions, not intelligent contributors to the success of his business.

"What do your executives say the problem is?" I asked.

"They keep complaining about system upgrades taking too long," said White. "They sit down at the start of the day, turn on their computers, and tell me it takes them more than an hour for everything to update. I think that's nonsense. It never happens to me."

Of course it doesn't, I thought. Your people on the night shift make sure you never have to go through that kind of pain.

"Then they tell me there are software updates following the operating system updates, and that can take another hour."

I believed Alban White. I was sure White House & Home had a complex IT environment and every package must have its own patch requirements.

"There's an easy solution for that," I said. "Have all your employees leave their computers on overnight so that updates to systems and software can happen then, not first thing in the morning."

"Wouldn't that cost me a lot more money for power?" asked White.

I now understood that he didn't fully comprehend the business implications of the galactic technology revolution.

"Have you seen any power bills lately?" I asked.

I was sure he studied department budgets line by line.

"I know there was something about power costs mentioned under Miscellaneous Items," said White.

"Exactly," I said. "With modern galtech you could cover ten times your current power use under petty cash."

"Hrrrrmph," said White, sounding just like Adolphus Kone. "But wouldn't leaving our computers on all the time be a security risk?"

"Not if you use Orishen mutable paranoid A.I. software," I said. "It's great at preventing improper access to corporate computers."

"No alien technology!" thundered White. "We're a one hundred percent Terran operation."

"Uh huh," I said.

There was a lot his I.T. people weren't telling him and I wasn't going to spill the beans on them, especially given White's obvious xenophobia.

"There's a Terran company that makes comparable software," I said.

I didn't mention that they were simply marketing an Orishen company's product under their own label.

"Splendid," said White. "I'm always glad to support innovative Terran companies. I'll introduce you to my Chief Information Officer and the two of you can implement your recommendations. You can talk to my legal department about a contract and a retainer for Xenotech Support Corporation."

"Thank you, Mr. White," I said with feigned enthusiasm. I was sure that working for his company would be soul-destroying.

"And you," said White, turning to Martin. "Thank *you* for bringing Mr. Buckston's talents to my attention. I'll have to promote your friend to show my appreciation."

While he talked to Martin I watched Alban White's ear twitch in a way I didn't know ears could move. It was like he had a tiny bug in his personal operating system, and I wasn't talking about an entity like Chit. Martin looked pleased that his friend wouldn't suffer for his assistance. White stood up, so we did too. Andy entered as silently as she'd left.

"Andy will see you out," said Mr. White. "Terra Triumphant!"

His final comment sealed the deal. Alban White *must* be The General. We followed Andy back to the main doors and the staircase. Martin and I didn't say a word until we were in his cruiser and driving south on I-75 back to the research lab near Georgia Tech.

"We've found him!" I exulted.

"Probably," said Martin.

For anyone else, that would have meant, "Certainly."

"Just one problem," said my phone. "Alban White isn't a human being."

"What!" I said.

Martin echoed with "What?"

"And neither is the chilly Ice Maiden," my phone continued. "Why do you think her name is Andy?"

Chapter 27

"Conversation is food for the soul."
— Mexican Proverb

Martin and I picked up some Pâkk-Mex for dinner at El Taco Lobo-Oso on Northside Drive heading south from I-75. I love their ubercow fajitas. I got one huge zoomin' uber-onion for the table—they're big enough to serve twelve. We also selected a range of other dishes that most people found delicious and even people not typically fond of Pâkk-Mex would eat. Pâkk-planet rice grains are the size of the last two joints on my little finger. They're bland, but far more nutritious than grains of *Oryza sativa,* the most common rice on Terra. I didn't order any Pâkk-style refried beans, though. I didn't want to stress the ventilation system in the research complex. Martin insisted that we should pick up a small container of uber-hot Pâkk peppers. I only agreed because it gave me an excuse to add a large, creamy ubercow-milk flan—the one dish that's sure to put out the fire caused by the peppers.

Thus fortified with enough tasty food for a small army, Martin drove us back to the complex. When we got out of my friend's official state bubble-top, the two of us were carrying enough sacks to play Santa Claus. Martin told his police cruiser to park a few blocks away, where it could return quickly if necessary. Shepherd or one of the other people inside must have been watching for us. The door to the research facility opened and Martin and I, our arms straining—well, *my* arms straining—carried our precious dinner down to the conference room. Everyone except Poly and Pomy was waiting for us there. Max rushed me before I could put anything down.

"Daddy! Daddy! Daddy!" he shouted.

I grunted from the impact of his body with my lower torso and swung my bags of food onto the table before one or both of us ended up wearing *mole poblano* sauce.

"Hiya, Sport!" I said. "Did you stay out of trouble today?"

"Mom and Aunt Sally said I had to study my Tig-ram-math gra-phol-ogy," piped Max. "They write everything using little pictures."

"Not exactly," I said. "Only their *formal* writing system uses pictograms. For everyday communication, they use something like cuneiform, made with their claws."

"Like the Mes-o-po-tamians?" asked Max. "I love saying that word."

"Isn't Max awfully young to be teaching him how to read and write Tigrammath?" asked Scott Winfield.

"He's almost five," said Rosalind. "I was reading six languages by the time I was his age."

"How many can Max read?" I asked.

"Seven," said Sally proudly.

"We saw cuneiform tablets at the British Museum," said Rosalind.

"Max loved the idea of forming words with sticks. He called it reeding and writing," added Sally.

Winfield groaned.

"Smart kid," said Poly, bustling in the door to the conference room with Pomy in tow.

"I'm not just smart," said Max, beaming. "My mom says I'm ingenious."

"You certainly are," I said.

Then it hit me.

Rosalind took Max to the British Museum and I wasn't there with them!

I sighed on the inside so I didn't worry Max, then picked him up and swung him three hundred and sixty degrees around before returning him to his feet.

"Wheee!" shouted Max. "Again!"

"Later," I said. "It's dinner time."

Shepherd moved bags of food from the table to the nearby counter and took out assorted containers to make it easier for everyone to select what they wanted.

"We got you an ubercow rib," I told the primarily carnivorous Pâkk.

Shepherd gave me an ironic Mr. Spock smirk as he held up a wrapped package twice as long and half-again as wide as a baseball bat.

"Thank you," said Shepherd, curling back his lips to reveal extra-long incisors.

I hoped that meant he was smiling. Martin and I looked at each other and the lieutenant winked. Ordering the rib had been his idea.

I fixed Max a plate with some Tōdonese paralettuce salad and an ubergoat-cheese quesadilla. Rosalind saw what I was doing and nodded her approval. Kids need healthy dinners.

"Here you go, big guy," I said, delivering the plate to Max. He was kneeling on his chair with his elbows on the table, holding a plastic knife and fork like he couldn't wait to tear into his meal.

"Thank you, Daddy!"

My son was polite, at least, though his table manners resembled a juvenile Pâkk's once he started eating.

I waited while the others got their food. Poly put together plates for Pomy and herself and brought them both back to the table. Pomy was slumped in her chair like someone had removed her spine. I watched Pomy perk up a little when she tasted the uberostrich steaks with chocolate-coffee mole sauce. That dish had been *my* idea.

Scott Winfield and Josephine Johnson were still off their feed—or maybe they didn't like Pâkk-Mex. They both took a little salad and some ubercow taco meat in giant tortillas made from pressed single kernels of ubercorn.

Cornell and Sally actually smiled at me when I'd gotten into line behind them. They looked like they were in a good mood and I wondered if they'd found a particularly pleasant way to occupy *their* time this afternoon like Poly and I had done last night.

When it was my turn at last, I selected a generous serving of ubercow fajitas, a few pieces of zoomin' uber-onion, and some of the uberostrich steak with mole, plus tortilla chips and a large helping of guacamole.

To botanists' surprise, avocados readily took to the climate on Påkk planets like Neuva Påkkjuk and grew to enormous sizes. Martin and I had picked one of the big green fruits the dimensions of a honeydew melon off the counter display at El Taco Lobo-Oso. The crew there cut it in half, removed the interior, and filled both sides with tasty guacamole. I was sure we'd have some leftover, but you can never have enough guacamole.

I took my plate and a bottle of Diet Starbuzz to the table and sat between Poly and Martin. For a few minutes we were all too busy eating, then Max hopped down and moved over to draw on the smart wall.

"You can have some flan," said Rosalind.

"Thank you, Mommy," said Max.

He wasn't really listening to her. I got up and brought some bowls and a box the size of a large pizza over from the counter to the table.

"Hey, big guy," I said to get Max's attention.

My son looked up. I opened the box, revealing a huge custard in caramel syrup. I opened and closed the lid as if it was a puppet's mouth, using a high-pitched voice to say, "Hi Max! I'm one of your biggest flans."

Max rolled his eyes and said, "Daddy!"

Several of the adults at the table looked away and covered their mouths. Winfield and Johnson scowled at me. Rosalind decided to wait before serving Max any flan.

"On that note," said Poly looking past me to get Martin's attention, "what happened when you went to see Alban White?"

"We were almost certain he was The General," said Martin.

I swallowed a bite of taco. "But it turns out he isn't human."

"Huh?" said Sally.

"Analysis determines that Alban White and his associate named Andy are both androids," said my phone. It had jumped onto the center of the flan box on two legs. Its weight was depressing the lid far enough I was afraid it would damage the custard.

I signaled to it to move closer to me. My phone realized where it was and seemed to notice what was happening. It extruded eight legs, distributed its weight, and carefully scuttled off the box and over to my bottle of Diet Starbuzz. Then it switched back to a form with two arms, two legs, and something vaguely resembling a head and leaned against the bottle nonchalantly.

"Sorry about that," it said.

"No problemo," I replied.

"Who has the technology to build androids that perfectly duplicate human beings?" asked Scott Winfield.

Poly jumped in. "EUA Corporation?"

"Not at any of the divisions *we* know about," said Johnson.

Scott and Johnson both looked at Cornell.

"Well…" said Rosalind's brother, "The General kept the fully-organic, human analogue android project under tight wraps…"

"I *knew* it!" said Pomy with more animation than she'd shown all day. "White House & Home is an EUA front company."

I hadn't realized Pomy was that clued in about EUA, but Poly must have updated her on the details of our investigations.

"That means EUA is even bigger than we thought," I said. "They control their own subsidiaries *and* all of Alban White's holdings."

I was momentarily distracted by a buzzing sound overhead. I looked up to see Chit flying down from a ventilation shaft in the ceiling. My little friend circled a few times and landed on top of my phone's pseudo-head.

"It's worse than that, Bucko," said the Murm. "The Sirocco Legislative Network and Pablo Daniel Figueres are part of EUA's corporate empire, too!"

Chapter 28

"I'm a traitor, but I don't consider myself a traitor."
— Aldrich Ames

"No way!" said Poly. "Figueres is a stand-up guy."

"Way," Chit responded. "I heard him on the phone with an EUA bigwig."

To one side, I noticed Shepherd tapping his ear a few times. The grizzled Pâkk then pushed a button on a controller embedded in the table in front of him. Suddenly, the smart wall turned into a flat screen, startling Max and most of the rest of us. The faces of Tomáso, Queen Sherrhi, and my mom appeared for a video-conference. Tomáso had Max's line drawing of a castle guarded by a dragon superimposed on one of his massive front legs. Max recovered quickly and started adding a picture of Spike chasing a squirrel to Tomáso's other leg.

"What's up, Your Matriarchal Majesty?" I asked.

"Tomáso's spies…" said Queen Sherrhi.

"…report something big is in the works from EUA Corporation," continued Tomáso. "There are plans to disrupt the upcoming G70 meetings that start on Monday."

"The what?" asked Pomy.

"A series of meeting of the heads of the seventy largest Galactic economies," said Poly. "It's being held here in Atlanta. It kicks off with some sort of tour on Sunday for the delegates and their mates, including a meet and greet with their favorite legislative stars at the Capitol building. Then they'll visit the Georgia Aquarium, the World of Coke, and the Center for Civil and Human Rights."

Those were the big three attractions at Centennial Olympic Park. I normally tune out any news about politics—the noise to signal ratio is usually too high—but I vaguely recalled reading about the meeting in the context of its impact on traffic in metro-Atlanta. This must be the big to-do Terrhi told us her mother had to attend.

"I'm here to represent Dauush," said Queen Sherrhi. "We're pushing two new models of fabricator and it's a great publicity opportunity."

I nodded, hearing, but not comprehending.

"Haven't you seen the signs at Ad Astra?" asked my mom. "The delegations are staying there and the meeting itself will be held at the Figueres Center at Georgia Tech."

"I haven't been home for a few days," I noted.

"I know," said my mom. "I've been following your exploits from orbit."

"Uh huh," I said, still a bit confused. "Hey! How do you know about signs at Ad Astra?"

My mother's image fidgeted for a moment, then replied. "I may have visited your apartment while you and Poly were in Las Vegas," she said.

I looked back at the screen incredulously.

"Close your mouth, Jack," said Poly.

"Don't worry, I wasn't butting in where I'm not welcome," said my mom. "Mike invited me."

"He never mentioned that to *me*," I said, still shocked. "And he's never met *you*. How could he invite you?"

"He didn't want to bother you while you were on vacation…"

"…and since you were spying on my apartment anyway," I observed.

My mother changed the subject, sort of. "You always were a bright child. A power-related issue had come up…"

"At Pour Me, Limited?" I asked.

The custom metal casting company had only been a Xenotech Support client for six months and their congruency-powered equipment for heating the metal used for casting was prone to glitches.

"That's right," said my mom. "I knew how to solve their issue so I jumped in."

"Thanks for your help, Ms. Buckston," said Poly.

"I was glad to assist," said my mom. "And please, dear, call me Nory."

"Will do, Nory," said Poly.

My partner was simultaneously holding my hand and stroking my arm, trying to settle me down. It was working, though the zoomin' onion I'd eaten was having an interesting and rather loud conversation with the guacamole already in my stomach.

"What was the problem?" I asked.

"Their molds weren't curing properly," answered my mother.

"You mean their fungi," I corrected. Pour Me, Limited, used genetically engineered heat-resistant mushrooms to help their casting. The custom fungi grew around the company's hand-carved sculptures and fit so tightly they picked up every nuance and detail, much like plaster of Paris around lost wax carvings. The firm had a new contract to produce expensive chess sets for Tōdons and the individual pieces were the size of adult humans or larger.

"Don't get too clever with me, son," said my mom. "I know that all molds are fungi…"

"…but not all fungi are molds," I laughed.

"Wait!" Chit exclaimed. "Weren't the fungi molds?"

"Sure," I said. "For casting giant chess pieces. Once they grew all the way around the sculptures, they were cut in half. Then the original sculptures were removed and the two halves were clamped back together."

"But you just said they *weren't* molds," said my little friend.

"Right," said my mom, getting into the spirit of things. "And they weren't yeasts, either."

"I feel like I've just consumed a few ounces of yeast byproducts," mumbled my little friend. "English. What a language."

I ignored Chit's protest and returned to my mother. "How did you solve things?"

"I eliminated leakage," she replied.

"Do I wanna know?" asked Chit.

Poly jumped in. "That's what Danny Figueres wants us to do at SLN."

"Different context," said my mom. "This was leaking photons."

"From the melting furnace?" I asked.

Pour Me's techs heated their casting metals using congruencies connected to the Sun's corona. Without proper tuning and shielding, the furnace could let through a lot of light, not just heat.

"That's right," said my mom. "And fungi…"

"…prefer a dark, moist environment," said Poly, clapping her hands with pleasure at figuring it out.

"Exactly," I said.

"So the client is happy?" I said.

"Ecstatic," said my mom. "They even modified the face of the white queen to look like me."

"I'll have to order a set," I said.

"You'll need a bigger apartment," said Poly.

She was right. My apartment didn't have enough room for sixteen four-foot pawns, let alone the major pieces.

"Maybe just a white queen," I said. "I can use it as a hat rack."

My musing on interior decorating were interrupted by the clearing of a pair of very large throats. I'd somehow forgotten about Queen Sherrhi and Tomáso, which is a lot like forgetting about elephants in the room.

"Sorry," I said.

"We need to ensure that nothing disrupts the G70 meetings," said Tomáso, picking up where he'd left off.

"So we've got the weekend to find and stop The General?" I asked. "No problem."

My sarcastic tone conveyed my frustration.

"The General will show himself to me tomorrow," rumbled Queen Sherrhi.

I wasn't counting on that—The General was proving to be a master of deception.

"Or else," said the queen.

Then again…

"Perhaps Chit can tell us what she's learned," said Shepherd.

His raspy, blues-singer voice grabbed our attention.

"Go ahead, little buddy," I said, motioning to Chit.

My phone located an unused paper cup near my bottle of Diet Starbuzz and turned it upside down. Then it reabsorbed its pseudo-head, forcing Chit to relocate. The Murm moved gracefully and treated the cup like a soapbox. I could hear a whoosh of air drawn up into her spiracles.

"It's like this, see," said Chit. "Camilla Moultrie, Daniel Fiqueres' executive assistant, clearly works for EUA. I traced her calls and confirmed that several of them went to EUA's headquarters."

Max giggled. I hadn't realized he'd been following the adults' conversation.

"You *bugged* her phone," said my son. He started chortling.

"I like you, kid, but don't push it," said Chit.

"I'm sorry, Ms. Chit," said Max. He covered his mouth with his hand to disguise continued giggles.

"Anybody else here five years old?" asked the tiny Murm, her compound eyes flashing dangerously.

I kept a straight face, and so did almost everyone else. Martin and Shepherd never had any problem doing so, but I did hear a girlish laugh and an amused growl off screen from the video-conferencing system's speakers. Terrhi and Spike must be just off-camera.

"Could there be legitimate business reasons for the calls?" asked Poly. "Are you *sure* Moultrie wears a black hat?"

"Sweetheart," replied Chit, "that woman wears a black hat and a ski mask."

"Why?" asked Max. "It's warm out."

"She means Camilla Moultrie is a bad guy, like a bank robber," Rosalind said.

Max nodded once, then turned back to the smart wall and began to draw raccoon masks on his sketches of Spike and Terrhi.

"She was talkin' t'someone at EUA about your trial," Chit told Pomy. "Moultrie said it was a shame you weren't found guilty, by the way."

"I don't think I like this Camilla person," said Pomy.

"I don't either," I added.

"What about Danny Figueres?" asked Poly. "I *like* him. I don't want to think that he played us."

"He played you like fiddles at a hoedown," said Chit. "I heard him talking to some bigwig at EUA for half an hour this afternoon. Danny promised to come to his place for dinner over the weekend."

Fiddles at a hoedown? Then I remembered I'd told Chit about introducing Droopy to *Oklahoma.*

"Figueres could be friends with someone there without being under EUA's thumb," asserted Poly.

"Occam's Razor, girl, Occam's Razor," said Chit.

I didn't want to think Figueres was part of EUA either, but it sounded like he was firmly in their orbit.

"I found some information about SLN and PDF as well," chimed in Rosalind. "Early funding for the Sirocco Legislative Network came from Conch Ventures, an EUA affiliate. Figueres must be in their pocket."

It hurt to admit, but evidence against Danny was building up. Conch sounded like an obvious shell company.

"We'll operate on the assumption that Figueres and his companies are part of EUA until proven different," I stated.

I stood up and my phone saw what I was trying to do and played the Star Trek communicator's signal to get everyone's attention.

"Now what?" I said. "Figueres is EUA. Alban White is EUA and not even human. EUA's corporate structure is a mass of misdirection. How do we find The General?"

"He will show himself to me at the Dauushan consulate by five o'clock tomorrow," rumbled Queen Sherrhi.

Even Tomáso looked skeptical about that, but I didn't argue with Her Majesty and he certainly wasn't going to.

"That can be Plan A," I said, "but we need a Plan B."

Queen Sherrhi lowered and raised her head to acknowledge what I'd recommended. She turned to her consort and the two of them exchanged tender looks, then entwined sub-trunks in a show of affection and mutual support.

"And probably Plans C and D, too," added Martin.

I nodded my agreement.

Terrhi's face inserted itself at the bottom of the videoconferencing screen, followed a second later by Spike's toothy head.

"Can I help? Can I? Can I?" said the cute alien princess.

Spike rolled his eyes and went with the flow.

"Sure," said Poly.

With Terrhi, it was better to give her something to do than to leave her—and Spike—to their own devices.

Cornell caught my eye.

"I may have some thoughts on Plan B," he said.

"Do tell," I encouraged.

"I'm not sure why, but The General still seems to think I'm a loyal part of his organization," said Rosalind's brother. "I don't know if he's sincere or just manipulating me, but I think that may give us a way to find him."

"What are you thinking?" asked Poly.

"If I initiate communications, perhaps your phone could trace the call from congruency to congruency and get a fix on The General's physical location."

"Wouldn't the signal's path be obfuscated?" asked Sally. "That's basic tradecraft."

"Of course," said Cornell. "But I expect Jack's phone is up to the task of identifying all the false hops and tracking the call to its ultimate recipient."

I looked at my phone and could swear it was preening from Cornell's compliment.

"Worth a shot," it said, feigning modesty.

"That's Plan B," I said. "Suggestions for Plan C?"

I watched Poly stare at Scott Winfield and Josephine Johnson, then turned her gaze to Sally.

"Don't look at me," said Sally. "I was watching Max all day while Rosalind was doing research."

"Thank you," said Poly.

She returned to the former Chapultepec & Castle executives.

"What about you two?"

The pair looked at each other uneasily.

"They spent all their time trying to find out who The General had promoted into their old positions," said Shepherd.

"Any luck?" I asked them.

"No, blast it," said Winfield.

"Nobody's talking," said Johnson. "It's like we don't exist."

"For people on The General's team, you probably don't," said Martin. His normally stony face looked like he'd just opened a bottle of hydrogen sulfide.

The two former executives crossed their arms and mirrored Martin's expression. This meeting was a laugh a minute. Then Terrhi lightened the mood.

"What can Spike and I do to help, Uncle Jack?" the little girl piped up from the big screen.

I did some quick thinking.

"There's a nine-year-old little girl named Bavarian Kreem," I said. "I'd like you and Spike to call her from the *Charalindhri*, make friends, and see if she knows anything about EUA Corporation and The General."

"We can do that," said Terrhi. "It will be *fun*, won't it Spike!"

"I'll text you her number," I told the Shetland pony-sized girl.

My phone worked its investigative magic and chimed to tell me it had found Bavarian Kreem's contact info and transmitted it to Terrhi.

Terrhi smiled and Spike showed a lot of teeth.

"That's Plan C," said Poly. "Any thoughts on a Plan D?"

"My only plan is to go to bed and sleep for a week," said Pomy.

"Of course, sis," said Poly. "You've been through a lot already. But we still need a Plan D."

"I've got an idea," I said. "Let's pay a visit to EUA's headquarters tomorrow."

"On a Saturday?" asked Poly.

"There should be people working there in the morning, at least," Martin noted. "I know some of EUA's subsidiaries operate seven days a week so there should be corporate personnel at HQ on duty to support them."

"Remember to be at the consulate tomorrow by four. We need to have everything in place before The General shows up," said Tomáso.

"We'll be there," I said, still not all that confident that Queen Sherrhi's ultimatum would work.

"Good night, Jack," said my mom. "Sleep tight."

I felt my cheeks start to turn red.

"Good night, Mom."

"Good night, Ms. Buckston," said Poly.

"Nory," said my mom with a stern look followed by a grin.

There was lots of waving and good wishes from all assembled— except Winfield and Johnson—then the videoconference ended. Max immediately started drawing pictures higher up on the smart wall.

"Jack," asked Rosalind, "when you said we were going to visit EUA's headquarters, who did you mean by *we?*"

"I was thinking just Poly and me," I replied.

"I've been there several times and know my way around," said Rosalind.

"So do I," said Cornell.

Poly responded to Cornell. "I don't think it's smart for you to go so long as there's a chance The General thinks you may still be on his side."

"You're probably right," said Cornell. He looked at Rosalind. "And the same goes for you."

"Not if I go in disguise," said his sister. "They'll never recognize me."

Poly and I exchanged a meaning-filled glance.

"Okay," said Poly. "We'll meet upstairs in the lobby at nine tomorrow morning."

"Bedtime, sport," said Rosalind.

Max pretended not to hear her.

"One," said Rosalind. "Two."

"Okay," said Max. "Can I have some flan first?"

"Sure," Rosalind answered. "Your father will serve you."

"Anybody else want flan?" I asked.

Several people indicated they wanted some, so I set up an assembly line with Max. I filled small bowls and my son delivered them. When we were the last two remaining to be served, I gave us heaping portions. It was fun to watch my son spoon up the caramel flavored custard. At the speed Max was eating, he finished quickly and went back to the smart wall to finish a drawing.

While Max was distracted I had a private word with Rosalind.

"What happens when you get to three?" I asked.

"You don't want to know, and Max doesn't either," she replied.

I nodded with feigned wisdom. There was a lot I had to learn about being a parent.

I chased the last bits of flan around my plate and reflected on the relative calm of the moment. It was a peaceful end to a hectic and stressful day. Then my phone rang.

"Who is it?" I asked.

"Mr. Gokusátshu," said my phone.

"Put him through."

"Hi Jack," said a familiar voice. "This is Gus from Las Vegas. My screen test in Atlanta is on Sunday. I'm coming into Hartsfield on a red-eye. Is there any chance I could stay with you folks on Saturday night?"

The Gojon had saved my life. What could I say?

"Hi Mr. Gus!" shouted Max.

"Hi Max," said Gustávish through my phone's speaker.

You could tell the big guy was smiling from his tone of voice.

"Of course," I said, ignoring Max's interruption. "I'll send you the address."

"Great," said the size-changing saurian. "See you soon!"

After the call ended Chit spoke up.

"The big green dude with three internal congruencies is headed here?"

"Uh huh," I said. "He's a broke actor and we'll put him up for a night or two."

"Big whoop," said Chit. "By the way, bucko, don't think for a minute that you're going to EUA's HQ without *me* tomorrow."

"Wouldn't dream of it," I said, mentally kicking myself for the oversight.

"Let's call it an early night," said Poly. She squeezed my hand.

"I want to stay up to visit with Max," I protested.

"He's going to bed," said Rosalind, rising. "Give your father a good night kiss, Max."

"Okay," said Max. He left the smart wall, hopped into my lap and pecked me on the cheek. Then he hugged my neck and jumped down to follow his mother out the conference room door.

"Let's call it an *early* night," repeated Poly, squeezing my hand even harder.

Her unsaid message finally percolated through my dense, foot-thick skull.

"Yes, let's," I said. "See you in the morning!"

Chapter 29

"When things go wrong, don't go with them."
— Elvis Presley

Poly closed the door to our room and kissed me. I returned her kisses enthusiastically and managed an awkward duck walk from the entryway to our bed. It was easy to pull off because Poly had placed her shoes on top of mine. Her arms were around my neck and partially supporting her weight until we inelegantly flopped on the bed. It became a game not to breathe or break our clinch until the amount of oxygen reaching our brains was sufficiently reduced that autonomic reflexes took over.

"Whew," I said, inhaling deeply and leaning back to appreciate my partner. "You certainly know how to focus a guy's attention."

"Thank you, good sir," Poly replied. "You're not so bad in that department yourself."

I bowed—or rather, I inclined my head and smiled. Bowing wasn't practical when I was horizontal.

"What do you think we'll find at EUA headquarters tomorrow?" asked Poly between nibbles on my ear.

"That tickles," I said, squirming. "I don't really know. I just want to shove a stick in the hornet's nest and see what happens."

"Speaking of shoving a…"

I kissed Poly before she could complete her sentence, though I certainly shared her sentiment. She kissed me back and my phone decided to leave my belt and scoot over to the nightstand where it wouldn't be an impediment to the two humans in the room getting more comfortable. It was always very considerate that way.

"You're wearing too many clothes," said Poly.

She was right. I hadn't even taken off my suit jacket and neither had she.

"Thirty second time out?" I suggested. "We just bought these outfits and it would be a shame to get them wrinkled."

"Agreed," said Poly.

We extracted ourselves from each other's embrace and stood up. Poly kicked off her shoes and placed them neatly on the floor of the closet. I did the same with *my* shoes, then took off my jacket and carefully hung it on a wooden hanger. I moved closer to Poly, helped her remove her jacket and repeated the process with another hanger. Poly grabbed my tie and pulled me close for more kisses.

"Hey, I thought we were on a time out!"

"You don't always play by the rules," Poly replied.

"True enough," I said, kissing her back and starting to unbutton her blouse.

"Let me do that," she said.

That was fine with me. She could do it faster. I unbuckled my belt and put my pants on a hook without emptying my pockets. I'd be wearing the same outfit in the morning to visit EUA.

Poly had taken off her blouse and skirt while I wasn't watching. She was down to a slip and was leaning against the side of the closet door, standing on one foot while she worked on removing her pantyhose. I made a mental note to talk to one of my suppliers on Orish about developing pantyhose out of a kind of morphabric that would take *itself* off.

"I'm ahead of you," she said.

"It looks like we're even from here," I said.

"You've got six items left and I've got three," said Poly.

I was enjoying the playful look in her eyes and pulled off my tie, dress shirt and undershirt in one quick motion.

"Now we're even," I remarked.

I was using my toes to slide my socks off while Poly was counting. Her slip landed on my head to distract me.

"No fair," I said, "and I'm still ahead, two items to one. When did women start wearing slips again?"

"Since I saw them in a display window at Neiman Macys."

"That's my Poly, always keeping up with the latest fads in fashion," I said, grinning broadly so she knew I was teasing.

"I don't think you understand how this game is played," Poly teased me back.

"Educate me…"

Her bra soon joined the slip on my head. Now enlightened, I tossed both garments over my shoulder.

"I think I like being educated," I responded.

"We're even again," grinning Poly. "And don't worry, you're in good hands for your remedial instruction."

She'd moved back to the bed and reclined, adopting a *come-hither* pose. I took three steps toward her and jumped on her like Tigger pouncing on Pooh. We rolled together like a pair of kittens wrestling, without using claws or teeth. Okay, maybe *some* teeth. Things were just starting to progress from kitten wrestling moves to more interesting interactions when my phone rang.

"Who is it," I said in a tone somewhere between distracted and annoyed.

"Who cares?" said Poly. "Don't answer it."

"It's Mike," said my phone.

"Mike wouldn't call if it wasn't important," I said. "It could be a client emergency."

"Simulate Jack," ordered Poly. She kissed me before I could countermand.

"Hi Mike," said my phone using my voice. "What's up?"

"It's Ellie at Morphicouture," my phone relayed. "I'm really sorry to bother you, but her contact preferentiator is screwed up and I don't know how to fix it. I hope I'm not calling at a bad time."

I reached for my phone to take the call but Poly rolled on top of me and pinned my wrists to the bed. I might have been able to toss her off, but had no particular interest in doing so.

Contact preferentiators are clever examples of highly adaptable Orishen software. For decades, it's been increasingly difficult to figure out and remember individuals' contact preferences. Some people want to be called. Some *never* take calls. Some want text messages. A subset of people want emails or physical letters. Others want to be contacted by Spacebook Messenger, NYTimes-Twitter, or Google SnapCat. Multiply that by a hundred more Terran communications options and tens of thousands of additional ways to connect used by the varied species of the Galactic Free Trade Association and it's physically impossible for companies to efficiently manage contacting their clients or for individuals to figure out the best way to reach their friends. Getting someone's preferences wrong could mean they'd never receive your message.

I'd set Morphicouture up with top rated contact preferentiator software from Mulbiri Client Relationship Management Associates, a firm launched by fellow Mulbiri Tech grads.

"What are the symptoms?" asked my phone, still using my voice.

Poly was still holding me down, but I wasn't fighting back. Her face was next to mine. I could feel her warm breath when she exhaled, but both of us were paying attention to the conversation, not each other.

"Ellie's team just sent out a big announcement about their fall collection…" said Mike.

"It's only May," I said, softly.

"The fashion industry follows its own calendar," Poly whispered.

"Is everything okay there?" asked Mike. "It sounds like someone's with you."

"Everything's fine," said my phone. "Keep going."

"Her marketing people sent out the announcement late this afternoon," Mike continued, "and tonight the client complaints have been coming in non-stop."

Poly rolled off me and sat up. I sat up, too. It's not an easy thing to do when a beautiful, more than half-naked woman is cuddling next to you. I flattered myself to think that Poly might have a similar problem focusing. We both listened closely.

"Why are they complaining?" asked my phone in its Jack voice.

"Because their contact preferences are all screwed up," said Mike. "People who prefer text messages are getting tweets. Clients who want emails are getting engraved golden plates delivered by drones. Spacebook Messenger clients are receiving self-destructing SnapCat messages that fade to random pictures of felines after they're read. It's a mess!"

"Can't Shuvvath figure it out?" asked my phone.

Shuvvath, being the only Orishen currently employed by Xenotech Support Corporation, should have a special affinity for his homeworld's technology.

"He's tried," said Mike, his voice rising in pitch and desperation, "but his last fix only served to change clients' contact preferences to a *different* set of wrong options, not fix them. No matter what we do, the preferentiator stays screwed up. Help us, Obi Jack—you're our only hope!"

Poly leaned close to my ear and said "No, there is another."

I think she meant herself—and she was probably right.

My phone got cute and started playing background music from *Star Wars: Episode IV - A New Hope.*

"Tell your phone to stop being cute," grumbled Mike. "It's not funny. Ellie is frantic and we don't know what to do."

I started to reach for my phone again, but Poly put her arms around me to stop me.

"Sounds like the software may be suffering from synesthesia," she said.

"Hi Poly," said Mike. "I didn't know you were there. From what I've seen, that's an accurate diagnosis."

Synesthesia was the name medical science gave to humans who had their senses crosswired, hearing colors, seeing tastes, and so on. It was a genetic condition present from birth and most synesthetes didn't want to be cured. This was different. Morphicouture's contact preferentiator software had been working correctly for a few years now. I'd installed and tested it myself.

"Have you turned it off and…" my phone started to say.

I reached out and grabbed my phone—this time with no interference from Poly. It wouldn't do for Mike to believe I thought so little of his skills to suggest turning the system off and on again. I was sure he'd done that twenty steps earlier.

"Stop clowning around, Jack," Mike insisted. "This isn't a laughing matter. What do we do?"

My phone displayed Mike's worried face on its screen.

"Can you access the client contact preference database directly and make sure it's not corrupted?" I asked.

"We can try," said Mike. "Shuvvath?"

My phone switched its view to one of my security cams so I could see both Mike and Shuvvath bent over laptops at the dining room table in my apartment.

"The database tables appear to be correct," said the nymph, air rushing through his spiracles. For all that he looked like a killer praying mantis with razor sharp blades on his chitin-covered arms and legs, the Orishen was soft-spoken.

"That means the problem must be with the data access layer or the business objects layer," said Poly.

"Maybe in Terran software," I said, "but Orishen software is more complicated. It has a morphic layer."

"Morphic layer?" asked Mike, echoed by Poly.

"It adapts to match shifting client requirements and new external conditions," I explained. "That saves a lot of development time. Something must have shocked the preferentiator's morphic layer into revising itself."

"I checked the morphic layer," said Shuvvath, his mandibles clicking in exasperation. "It's fine for a few seconds, then the next time I look it's changed again."

That triggered the paranoid sensors in my brain. Poly was a step ahead of me.

"Did anything strange happen recently?" she asked.

"Somebody broke into Morphicouture eight or nine weeks ago," said Mike.

"I think we have different definitions of recent," I said. "Did anything happen in the past week?"

"A new intern started in I.T.," said Shuvvath.

"Have you been staying in touch with Ellie?" I asked.

"With José," answered the Orishen.

José handled production and I.T. for Morphicouture while Ellie took care of marketing and design.

"What's the intern's name?" asked Poly.

"Julie Eastman," said Mike.

"Could Julie be short for Juliard?" I mused.

"Juliard Eastman," said Poly. "Those are two of the top music conservatories in the country. Sounds a lot like Columbia Brown."

"The last person spying on Morphicouture," said Shuvvath. "She almost had me killing children when she forced me into artificially accelerated metamorphosis."

Poly and I exchanged a quick glance, remembering the excitement of our first date.

"You think Julie Eastman is an EUA plant?" asked Mike.

"Odds are good," I said.

My brain segued into what would have happened if Max had been listening to this conversation. He'd want to know what kind of plant Julie Eastman was. I'd tell him poison ivy or maybe deadly nightshade.

"If you lock the new intern out of the system, then have Shuvvath work his magic to reset the morphic layer, you should be fine," I said.

"What do you want us to do about Eastman?" Mike asked. "I just deleted her access."

"I'll have Martin…" I said.

"Lieutenant Lee says he's putting her under surveillance," said my phone. Gotta love its initiative.

"Sounds like a plan," said Mike.

"Morphic layer reset," said Shuvvath. "The contact preferentiator software is now working properly."

"Super," said Poly. "Time to reach out and touch someone."

"That was AT&T's slogan from forty years ago," said my phone, "it is not licensed for use by Mulbiri Client Relationship Management Associates."

"I wasn't referring to a slogan," said Poly. "I was stating my plans for the next hour."

"Have a great evening, Mike… Shuvvath," I said.

"You too," said Mike.

Shuvvath clicked his mandibles in a pattern I knew meant he was laughing.

My phone ended the call.

Chapter 30

"And darest thou then to beard the lion in his den…"
— Sir Walter Scott

Poly and I were smiling as we waited in the lobby of the research facility at five minutes to nine the next morning. Then Poly saw Rosalind and her smile changed to a controlled, neutral expression. I wondered just how smart it was to have them both on this expedition. Despite Poly's obvious reservations, I was glad to have someone familiar with EUA's headquarters on the team.

"Wearing your pupa silk shirt?" I asked Poly.

"Uh huh," she replied. "You'd better be, too."

"Count on it," I said. "You made me promise never to leave home without it. I'm fond of my hide and want to keep it in one piece."

"I'm fond of your hide, too," said Poly.

She put her hand on my chest and caressed me lightly, then punched me in the solar plexus to make sure I really had it on. The shirt went rigid and I barely felt her blow.

"Ow," said Poly, rubbing her knuckles.

"Told you," I said, taking her hand and kissing the damaged digits.

"If you two could focus for a minute," said Rosalind, "we can try to make this happen."

Rosalind was wearing a short, curly brown wig and thick, over-sized Ncyclopedia-brand VR glasses. Her conservative pantsuit ensemble was padded, disguising her figure and making her look ten years older. It was a well-chosen disguise—she looked like she could be some executive's hyper-efficient assistant. Poly nodded at Rosalind, acknowledging and appreciating her look.

I heard a high-pitched buzzing and felt Chit's tiny weight land on my shoulder.

"Who's Grandma?" said my little friend.

"Good to see you, too, bug," said Rosalind.

Chit sniffed.

"Yeah, yeah," said my little friend. "You know the territory, but remember, I've got my eye-facets on you."

"I never doubted it," Rosalind replied.

"Where's Max?" I asked.

"Studying Pyr pulse codes with Cornell and Sally," said Rosalind. "I told him we should be back in time for lunch."

"That would be great, if we can pull it off," said Poly. "I'm less optimistic. If we're going into the lion's den, we ought to be prepared to run into a few lions."

"And the occasional water buffalo," I added.

"Don't *you* start," said Rosalind.

I pulled myself up short, wondering how I'd inserted my foot in my mouth this time, and realized my words could be seen as a commentary on the extra padding Rosalind was wearing. It had never crossed my mind that she'd perceive it as an insult, but perhaps Poly's proximity was increasing her sensitivity. Then I saw Rosalind's grin and figured out she was putting me on. I decided my smartest move was to keep my mouth shut and not dig a deeper hole.

"Ready to go?" asked Poly.

Rosalind and I both nodded. The three of us walked out of the research facility and found the autocab Poly had ordered for us waiting at the curb. Somehow we all ended up in the back seat with me in the middle and Chit on the back of my neck. It wasn't a comfortable ride. The cab drove us south on Marietta Street, heading for EUA's headquarters on the east side of Centennial Olympic Park.

EUA's HQ always gave me the creeps. It wasn't tall, like the SLN tower. It was broad and black and brooding. It reminded me of a gigantic version of Abraham Lincoln seated in his chair in the Lincoln Memorial, if you replaced our sixteenth president with Darth Vader and changed the color scheme to match. Two long wings flanked a central courtyard devoid of life and energy.

In the back, the building rose in tiers, looking like simian shoulders and an ugly, squared-off head with sharply flared sides reminiscent of Vader's helmet. Its windows were black, non-reflective, and did not allow any light from inside to escape. The place looked like a cross between the worst of Bauhaus and Soviet-era brutalist architecture. Just being in its shadow made my stomach uneasy.

That was one reason why I had our autocab drop us off on the far side of the park. Walking along the green-flanked paths and taking in the gondolas of the slowly rotating two hundred foot SkyView ferris wheel calmed me down and strengthened my resolve to get through what was ahead. I was also feeling like a dog who hasn't gotten enough exercise. I hadn't hit the gym in a week and yesterday's adrenaline spike while we were chased didn't help.

"What's the plan?" asked Poly.

"Walk in and ask to talk to The General?" I offered.

Rosalind laughed and tried to disguise it by covering her mouth with her hand and turning it into a cough.

"I wouldn't advise that," she said. "My understanding is that there are extensive dungeons underneath EUA headquarters."

"Dungeons?" said Poly, her eyes widening.

"Okay, call them holding cells or interrogation stations or detainment facilities…" said Rosalind.

"…but they're dungeons," I completed.

"Right," said Rosalind. "And we don't want to risk being thrown into them."

"What do *you* suggest?" asked Poly.

"Once I get in, we're golden," said Rosalind. "We should try to get to an upper floor and speak to a higher-level flunky, though we might learn a lot just from keeping our eyes open."

I looked at Poly. She nodded.

"Let's do it," I said. "Who do we want to talk to?"

"Someone in legal or human resources," said Rosalind. "They're high up, without being too senior."

"Not that slimy Adolphus Kone," said Poly.

She rubbed her mouth with the side of her fist and looked ready to spit, but didn't.

"You've met Boss Kone?" asked Rosalind. "I know him well. Not one of my favorite people."

"Not one of ours, either," I said. "He was at Pomy's trial."

"Why would the head of EUA's legal department be at such a low-level proceeding?" mused Rosalind. "He normally has his junior attorneys handle cases like that."

"He was just there to observe, I think," said Poly. "His daughter, Brunhilde Dagomar, was counsel for the prosecution."

"The Bulldog?" asked Rosalind. "She's a piece of work."

"She's a piece of…" Poly began angrily.

"She is indeed," I broke in, "but Atticus won the case and Pomy's in the clear, so lets focus on our reconnaissance."

"Yes, darling," said Poly.

She was looking at me, but pointedly *not* looking at Rosalind. Poly didn't sound like she was teasing me or being affectionate, so I struggled with why she added the endearment. It confused me, when I needed to concentrate.

Rosalind ignored Poly.

"We just need to get inside and on an elevator," she said. "I can get us hooked into their systems or connect to someone who can help us once we get past whoever is playing guard dog."

"Let's hope Rosalind is as effective as Orpheus in putting Cerberus to sleep," I said optimistically.

"With our luck it will probably be a hydra rather than a dog," lamented Poly.

"Seven heads *would* be more of a challenge than three," said Rosalind.

"Given that we're going into the lion's den, it's probably a chimera, not a hydra," I suggested.

"With double-regenerating heads like a hydra," said Poly.

"And I forgot to bring my sword," said Rosalind.

"You have a sword?" I said, before I could stop myself.

Rosalind looked at me sideways and moved her head slowly from side to side.

"You could borrow Mike's," said Poly.

"Mike has a sword?" I asked.

I was a slow learner today. I could tell my brain was was stalling, trying to come up with a reason *not* to enter EUA HQ. The lack of a rhetorical sword seemed as good a reason as any, given the gyrations my mind was ready to go through.

"Several, actually," said Poly. "A steel broadsword, three rattan swords for SCA combat, and half a dozen boffers for LARPing."

We had crossed the park and were now at the entrance to EUA's unwelcoming courtyard. In front of us was slab of black marble like one of the monoliths from *2001: A Space Odyssey* turned on its side. It had six-foot-tall sans-serif letters carved into it announcing that this was EUA's world headquarters. I didn't want to take another step and would rather enter Mordor. We all stopped, reluctant to pass into the foreboding courtyard. The stalling continued.

"Mike's in the SCA?" I said.

"Uh huh," said Poly. "He joined in Drachenwald."

"Where in the ten thousand planets of the Galactic Free Trade Association is Drachenwald?" asked Rosalind.

"It's the SCA's largest kingdom in Europe," said Poly.

"What's the SCA?" asked Rosalind.

"The Society for Creative Anachronism," said Poly. "It's a historical recreation organization, mostly focused on stuff up to the reign of Elizabeth."

"King William's grandmother?" asked Rosalind.

"No, the first Queen Elizabeth," said Poly.

"Oh," said Rosalind.

I could see she was puzzled by why we were talking about something so inconsequential.

"I went to an SCA event on Orish once," I said. "It was fun. Most of the nymphs painted their chitin to look like samurai armor. It made them look even *more* intimidating."

"You continue to surprise me, lover-boy," said Poly, giving me a peck on the cheek that did a lot to boost my spirits while making me feel like she'd planted a flag on my shore. "We'll have to suggest that to Shuvvath if Mike ever drags him along to an SCA event. Maybe we can all go."

"That would be fun," I said, not particularly minding being claimed by Spain, um, er, Poly.

"Let's get this show on the road, buckos," said Chit. "This ring ain't gonna destroy itself."

"What ring?" asked my phone.

It was out of character for my phone to miss a Tolkien reference. I didn't answer and we stepped into the courtyard, crossing the dark pavement to the main entrance with quick steps, just to get it over with. The front entrance did nothing to reduce my anxiety. The doors were thick, opaque and imposing with no indication of what I needed to do to open them. Rosalind knew the secret, however. She leaned her shoulder into one of the doors and encouraged Poly and me to help her push. Thanks to our joint efforts, the door slowly opened. As it did, I realized it was six inches thick and made of heavy, black-enameled metal. The place felt like a vault, not a corporate headquarters. It made me wonder what they had to hide.

If it took this much effort just to open the door, what would the gatekeeper be like? We soon found out as a trio of uniformed security guards approached. They were the size of NFL offensive linemen crossed with sumo wrestlers and didn't seem pleased to see us.

"State your business," said the one in the lead.

"Marion Ravenwood to see Adolphus Kone," said Rosalind matter-of-factly.

"Check in at reception," said the lead guard, waving toward wide counter that looked like it was carved from a chunk of obsidian. Behind it stood a woman who could have been the inspiration for the phrase *old battle ax.*

"Whaddya want?" she croaked.

Her voice sounded like a cross between a rusty hinge and a strangled cat.

"Don't give me any crap, Mildred. I've got to report in and these two have critical intel."

"Yes, ma'am," said the receptionist, her creaky voice disappearing. "Right away, Rosey."

I was getting a bad feeling about this. So was Poly. We looked at each other, then at Rosalind. We she pulling a fast one on us? How did the woman behind the desk recognize Rosalind, for that matter? I could barely recognize her.

The receptionist made a call and waved us to move beyond her counter, back into the interior of the lobby. Rosalind moved deliberately, like she knew where she was going. Soon we were out of sight of Mildred and the security guards, standing alone in an octagonal chamber surrounded by archways.

"What's going on?" I protested.

"Shut up, you idiot," said Rosalind. "When I want your input I"ll ask for it."

Poly was seething, about to tear into Rosalind. I put my hand on her shoulder to hold her back. My eyes were signaling to go with the flow, at least for now. Maybe Rosalind didn't want us giving away her new allegiance.

"Which way now?" asked Poly, back in control.

Rosalind led us into one of the archways on the left. I hoped there wasn't anything sinister about her choice of direction. We moved through something that felt like an invisible curtain and found ourselves in an elevator compartment. Rosalind pushed a button—I couldn't see the floor she selected, but immediately felt my ears adjusting to a change in atmospheric pressure.

"Where are we…" I began to say.

Rosalind pulled a mini-sweetener out of a jacket pocket and pointed it at my mid-section. I didn't feel too bad about that. I was wearing my Orishen pupa silk shirt and knew that Rosalind knew I was wearing it.

"What part of 'shut up' don't you understand?" barked Rosalind.

I closed my mouth and kept it closed. I also grabbed Poly's hand and held it reassuringly—in part to make sure my partner didn't practice kung fu moves on the mother of my child. Life can be complicated.

A few seconds later, after I'd yawned twice to help equalize the pressure in my ears, the elevator's door opened. We found ourselves on the forty-second floor, according to a sign on the wall in front of us. Forty-two seemed like a perfectly reasonable answer on where to get off.

"This way. March!" ordered Rosalind, poking her sweetener into my back and directing Poly and me to the left and along a dark, deserted corridor. She pushed us through a door on the right and into a darkened space. Rosalind did something with her phone. I soon heard and felt the telltale subliminal lack of external noise of an activated Cone of Silence field.

Poly wound herself up and was about to give Rosalind a piece of her mind. Chit beat her to it.

"Hey Granny, are you turning traitor?" asked my little friend. "If you are, I'm gonna make you wish you was never born."

"You and what army, bug?" asked Rosalind. "Give me a break. We're inside EUA's headquarters and I know how to tap into their secure networks from here."

"I thought you wanted to meet with somebody?" asked Poly.

"I wanted to get inside and take an elevator to an upper floor," said Rosalind. "From here, I can do almost anything, so keep quiet and let me work. Please."

The last word was only added as an afterthought, but I forgave Rosalind for her attitude. She was under a lot of stress. Rosalind took out her phone and started pushing virtual buttons on its screen. My phone hopped up on my shoulder to follow what she was doing.

"She's tapping a secure wireless comm channel," said my phone. "Now she's pattern-matching, looking for any references to The General."

Rosalind's phone chimed. She looked at the screen and her face showed surprise, amusement and concern, in that order.

"What is it?" asked Poly.

"What's wrong?" I asked.

My phone had been looking over Rosalind's shoulder and responded when she didn't.

"The General has a meeting with Bavarian Kreem in his office on the sixty-sixth floor in fifteen minutes to discuss EUA acquiring her company," my phone informed us.

"What's the big deal about that?" asked Poly. "The General seems to have control of every other major Atlanta corporation, why not Consolidated Donuts?"

"Today the doughnuts, tomorrow the sprinkles," I said, trying to lighten the mood.

"It's not funny," said Rosalind. "Bavarian isn't alone."

"She's only a kid," said Poly. "You'd expect her advisers to be along."

"No," said Rosalind. "That's not it. *Terrhi* is with her!"

Chapter 31

"I don't care if he's a bastard…"
— Lyanna Mormont

Rosalind crossed to the door and flipped a switch. The darkened room turned bright and I saw we were in an office—Rosalind's office, from the name plate on the desk reading McBryde. Between Rosalind and her brother, the pair had more names than the Atlanta phone directory.

A large flatscreen hung on the office wall. Rosalind put her phone down on her desk and slaved it to the screen so we could watch the progress of Bavarian and Terrhi and Spike as they walked down a long black corridor. I felt a bit better knowing Terrhi had Spike along to protect her.

I was impressed by Terrhi for acting so promptly on the task I'd set her, but I was concerned that Tomáso and Queen Sherrhi probably didn't know their daring daughter and her trisabertooth pet had left the *Charalindhri* and returned to Atlanta. It would be a major understatement to say her parents would be displeased to learn Terrhi was in EUA's headquarters without an armed escort.

"Could you turn up the audio?" asked Poly. "I want to hear what they're saying."

"What's the magic word?" replied Rosalind.

My partner gritted her teeth and didn't lose her cool. "Pretty please, with powdered sugar and shredded coconut?"

At least Poly hadn't lost her sense of snark. Neither had Rosalind.

"Since you asked so nicely—and I *like* shredded coconut."

A couple of keystrokes on Rosalind's phone activated microphones along the corridor.

Terrhi was talking to Bavarian, a young human girl with short blonde hair wearing a white pinafore and a determined expression. Bavarian was juggling three small amber balls in one hand, tossing them in a simple rolling out pattern. I wondered if they were some new fad for children, like Pokemon when I was a kid.

"What's the plan?" said the Dauushan princess.

"The *plan*," said Bavarian, "is to carve The General a new…"

"As long as we don't provoke him *too* much," said Terrhi. "My mom wants him at the Dauushan consulate at five o'clock today and it wouldn't be wise to start with him in a bad mood."

"Why should *his* mood be any different than *mine?*" asked Bavarian, her face looking like she'd been forced to eat liver.

"Why are they on the wrong floor?" remarked Rosalind, noticing the numbers on the office doors. "The General is on the top floor. They're two floors down, with the heads of legal and human resources."

"Isn't that where you wanted to end up anyway?" I asked.

"Yes," said Rosalind, "but not while trying to rescue two little girls and a hundred-and-fifty-pound cat."

"What makes you think they'll need to be rescued?" asked Poly.

I thought about it for a few seconds, then nodded.

"You may have something there," I said.

"If The General thinks he's going to get *my* company without a fight, he doesn't know me very well," said the nine-year-old girl.

She sounded more like she was thirty-nine, or maybe forty-nine. I made a mental note never to cross her.

"How can you stop him?" asked Terrhi. "EUA has a private army. Several of them, actually, counting their subsidiaries."

Terrhi was more innocent than Bavarian, but also wise beyond her years.

"Consolidated has plenty of dough if I want to hire my own mercenaries," said Bavarian.

Rosalind, Poly, Chit and I all groaned at the pun, which we weren't sure was intentional. Even my phone made a sad chirp. On the screen, Spike kept his four true-feet on the carpet and covered his eyes with one of his forepaws. I still wasn't sure how much the big cat understood.

"You'll need a lot of mercenaries," mused Terrhi.

"Uh huh," said Bavarian. "I'm also making new friends—and *they* have armies."

She started scratching a hard-to-reach spot on the back of Terrhi's head. Terrhi looked thoughtful and wriggled under Bavarian's fingers.

"There is that," said the Shetland pony-sized girl.

Spike's mouth opened, showing off his dagger-like teeth. I wasn't sure if it was a laugh or a yawn.

"How're ya gettin' such great audio 'n' video, Grandma?" asked Chit.

"The whole building is monitored," answered Rosalind. "You just have to know how to tap the relevant feeds."

"Let's hope The General's internal security team isn't following this," I added.

"You can be sure they are," said Rosalind. "But the girls and the cat are the perfect distraction. I can count on them taking most of internal security's attention while I climb an air shaft to the sixty-sixth floor."

"What's up there?" asked Poly.

"The General's private office and apartment," said Rosalind.

"You're climbing twenty-four stories in an air shaft?" I asked.

Rosalind crossed to her desk, opened a drawer, and removed a small drone and a large spool of motorized cable.

"I'll be taking the express route," she said, pointing at her equipment. "This baby made it really easy to break into…"

I coughed.

"This baby will make it much easier," she revised. "The human security people's eyes will be elsewhere."

I could see how things would work. The drone would carry one end of the cable to the sixty-sixth floor and secure the loop at one end to something convenient. Then she'd hook the motorized end to a harness and let the motor lift her up the vertical distance. I stared at the components long enough to memorize their dimensions, since I knew I'd want a similar rig for myself in the future. Something like that could really come in handy for running cables up elevator shafts—and diverse other uses.

"Want some company, Toots?" asked Chit.

"I'm not Grandma anymore?" returned Rosalind.

"Things are lookin' up for ya these days," said Chit, taking in her climbing equipment.

"Come along if you want, bug," said Rosalind. "You don't weigh much."

Chit snorted and Rosalind made a face at her. I think the snort was another unfair comment on Rosalind's extra padding. The Murm buzzed over and landed on the back of Rosalind's neck. After buckling on a harness from another desk drawer, Rosalind moved to pick up her phone from the top of her desk. My phone intercepted her movement and scanned her communications device.

"Taking over tracking and relay functions," said my phone.

The screen shimmered momentarily and responsibility for following and displaying Bavarian, Terrhi and Spike shifted. Rosalind would need her phone to control the drone. She pushed a guest chair over to the corner of her office below a ventilation hatch. Then she looked at me with an expression that demanded instant obedience.

"Give me a boost," she commanded.

I stepped up on the guest chair and cupped my interlaced hands. Rosalind used my body as a ladder and ascended my torso until she stood on my shoulders. I braced my calves against the arms of the chair to stabilize myself, then looked up. I felt her weight shift and watched her arms move as she searched the pockets of her pantsuit for something to use to handle the screws holding the hatch to the ceiling.

"Chill, toots, I got this," said Chit.

My little friend buzzed up to one corner of the hatch, then another and another. Soon the hatch was hanging by one final screw. Rosalind twisted the hatch cover out of the way and tossed the drone and connected cable up the shaft. A couple of minutes later, Rosalind's body rose up the shaft, moving at high speed. I stepped down from the chair, rubbed my shoulders, and gave Poly a hug.

"I hope she finds something useful," I said, looking up the shaft. "How are the girls doing?"

"Terrhi and Spike and Bavarian are about to go into an office," she said. "It says Adolphus Kone on the door in gold letters."

"That's an important clue about who they're going to see," I said.

Poly ignored my intentionally dumb remark and watched the action on the screen. It looked like the girls and Spike were about to tug open Kone's door. Bavarian must have put her amber balls into a pocket, since they weren't in her hand anymore.

"Can we see inside?" I asked my phone.

"Scanning," it said. "Confirming."

The view changed and we saw Bavarian and Terrhi entering a palatial office decorated like one of the more over-the-top rooms in Versailles. It was designed to intimidate, but I didn't expect the decor's effect to work on either of the girls. They'd both grown up with luxury.

Given the angle of the security camera, we could clearly see the back of Adolphus Kone's head. I was surprised to realize he wasn't using any of the alien technologies that were so effective at reenergizing dormant hair follicles. His bald spot reflected light from recessed congruent bulbs in the twenty-foot ceiling.

"Good morning, ladies," said Kone in a patronizing, sing-song tone, as if the girls were still babies. "Please come in and have a seat."

He pointed at a morphurniture sofa to one side of his office that I knew could adapt to both Bavarian and Terrhi's dimensions. A tall, wingback leather swivel chair was also part of the collection of seats arrayed nearby. The girls and Spike opted to remain standing, though they moved toward the sofa. Kone sat in the high, wingback chair and rotated to face Bavarian and Terrhi. His chair reminded me of Jean-Jacques' office furnishings that were designed to help the little man feel bigger. Spike jumped on the back of the sofa and loomed like he was ready to pounce if necessary. Two could play the intimidation game.

My phone switched surveillance cameras to follow the action, providing closeups as necessary.

"Can it, you old creep, and skip the small talk," said Bavarian. "Where's The General?"

"He couldn't make this impromptu appointment," said Kone. "He's meeting with a head of state later this afternoon."

"Told you," said Terrhi, nudging Bavarian with one of her sub-trunks.

"Please don't distract me," whispered Bavarian. "This isn't easy. I need to concentrate."

Terrhi nodded and gave Bavarian a bit more room.

"I'm one of The General's top lieutenants, fully empowered to negotiate on his behalf," said Kone.

"You're just a lieutenant?" scoffed Bavarian. "I don't talk to anyone below a full colonel."

Kone made an unpleasant little sound that might have been what he considered a laugh.

"You're talking to me, or nobody," he said. "And tell that mongrel alien feline to get off the furniture."

Spike yawned again, showing off his long, sharp teeth, and ignored him. Kone didn't press it. Terrhi muttered under her breath.

"Spike is *not* a mongrel. He's a pure-bred tri…"

Bavarian elbowed Terrhi and the Dauushan girl didn't finish her sentence. I was impressed by the quality of the surveillance microphones. They were picking up *everything*.

"Here's the deal," Adolphus Kone pontificated. "Twenty-seven billion galcreds for Consolidated Donuts, payable in EUA and Chapultepec & Castle stock. We'll announce the deal when the markets open on Monday."

"It's worth thirty billion," said Bavarian.

She got up on the sofa near Spike so she could look Kone directly in the eye. The sofa formed a flat, stable base below her.

"And Chapultepec & Castle stock will be worthless as soon as the news of their GalCon Systems industrial espionage stunt comes to light," Bavarian continued. "GalCon Systems will file suit against C&C before you can make your announcement."

"How does Bavarian know about the industrial espionage?" I asked Poly.

She looked back at me and raised one eyebrow.

"Oh, right," I said. "Terrhi."

"Uh huh," said Poly. "Now shush, I'm enjoying this."

We returned our full attention to the screen.

"You forget, child," said Adolphus Kone unctuously. "EUA Corporation and its subsidiaries are privately held."

"Maybe so," said Bavarian, "but the virtual tracking stocks on the galactic markets will take a nose dive."

"Do you think The General cares one iota what the galactic markets think?" barked Kone. "EUA will see Earth put in its rightful place *commanding* the galaxy, with alien species bowing down to *us*. The daily cash flow from Consolidated Donuts is essential to funding Terra's ultimate victory."

The lawyer's face contorted with the zealous intensity of a true believer. He stared at Terrhi and Spike like they were rats or cockroaches. His look made my skin crawl and I was twenty-two floors away.

"He's scaring me," I told Poly. "We've got to find his boss and put a stop to EUA's plans."

"He's scaring me, too," said Poly. "Let's hope Rosalind locates The General!"

Bavarian was back at it. She was jumping up and down, acting closer to nine than thirty-nine.

"I don't care about your insane motivations," she shouted, jumping up and down on the sofa. "I'm not selling my company."

Spike was leaning forward next to the girl, growling and ready to attack if Kone tried anything. Terrhi moved in front of Bavarian, imposing her own body between Bavarian and Kone. The tension in the room was so thick it would take a lightsaber to cut it.

Kone sat up straight and waved his right hand in a circular motion. Three gimbal-mounted sweetener rifles noiselessly descended from the tall ceiling and pointed at Bavarian, Terrhi, and Spike.

"Perhaps you were under the misapprehension that you had a choice in the matter, Miss Kreem?" said Kone.

The sweetener rifles began to whine and waves of color pulsed along their barrels to make it clear they were charged and ready.

"Can you take over control of the rifles?" I asked my phone.

"Negative," it replied. "Rosalind has those passwords."

"Drat," said Poly. "Do you think we can make it up there in time to be useful?"

"Maybe," I said. "If internal building security doesn't stop us."

"Wait a second," said Poly, putting her hand on my phone and rubbing its back cover. "Can you send a recording of what just happened to the Dauushan consulate? We could use a squad of Drop Marines about now."

"Negative," said my phone. "The entire building functions as a Faraday cage."

"Double drat," I grumbled.

Poly and I continued to watch things happening in Adolphus Kone's office. It turned out we didn't need to worry about Bavarian Kreem. The girl removed the three amber balls from a pocket on her pinafore and deftly tossed them at the sweetener rifles. The balls expanded, filling the rifle barrels with a quick-hardening goo that rendered them inoperative.

Bavarian and Terrhi walked toward Kone's office door. Spike followed them, but paused to lean on Kone where he was sitting in his high, wingback chair. The big cat put his paws on the lawyer's shoulders and licked Kone's face with his raspy tongue. Then Spike planted the tips of his three incisors along Kone's collar bones and leaned into him. The trisabertooth didn't break the skin, but his message got through unambiguously.

Poly and I were pleased to see that the girls and cat were not detained as they made their way out of the building.

"That was exciting," I said, giving Poly a release-of-nervous-tension hug.

"I'll say," she said, hugging me back enthusiastically. "Remind me never to cross Bavarian Kreem."

"I'm right there with you," I said, shaking my head from side to side in admiration of the young girl's moxie. "What a performance."

Then our attention was diverted by thumps from overhead, in the ventilation shaft. Rosalind's feet appeared and then the rest of her was gently lowered to stand on the chair.

"What was a performance?" asked Rosalind, while replacing the ventilation shaft cover.

"Bavarian Kreem," said Poly. "We'll show you the video later."

Chit buzzed off Rosalind's neck and landed on my shoulder.

"You're not gonna believe it, bucko," she said.

"Believe what?" I asked.

"We checked out the sixty-sixth floor," said Chit.

"And there's nothing there," said Rosalind. "The General is gone."

Chapter 32

"If you meet the Buddha on the road, kill him."
— Linji Yixuan

To my surprise, we didn't have any problems exiting EUA's headquarters. I guess their security people were used to seeing Rosalind escort interrogation subjects out of the building. Rosalind kept a sweetener discreetly pointed on us to support the illusion that we were her prisoners.

I was glad I was wearing my pupa silk shirt, though. Rosalind seemed to be working out her frustration over not finding The General on the sixty-sixth floor by poking me frequently with the tip of her sweetener. She kept it up even after we moved into the park.

"Hey," I protested. "Cut it out. How would you feel if I poked you?"

"Promises, promises," said Rosalind with a grim smile.

Poly turned around and glared at Rosalind, then at me. I realized what I'd said and felt my face turn red.

"I didn't mean it *that* way," I protested.

"She did," said Poly.

"EUA's surveillance continues a hundred yards into the park," said Rosalind. "I had to keep up the subterfuge."

"I think you just like poking him," teased Poly. At least I hoped it was teasing.

"Skip the territorial displays for now, ladies," said Chit from her perch on my shoulder. "And watch out for escaping squirrels. They'll run you over!"

We caught up to the girls in the middle of Centennial Olympic Park. They were standing together in the center of a wide, paved path, talking animatedly and giving Spike time to have some fun. He was busy chasing the park's well-fed squirrels. These bushy-tailed tree-dwellers hadn't yet learned how fast Dauushan trisabertooth cats could move, unlike the more experienced ones back in the Ad Astra courtyard.

Bavarian and Terrhi waved as we approached, but didn't pause their conversation. From twenty feet away, it came across as two high-pitched birds chirping at each other, accompanied by excited hand and trunk gestures. The two girls were really hitting it off.

I wondered what would happen when Bavarian met Max? He'd probably want to start his *own* company. I promised myself I'd back whatever great idea he came up with, though he'd probably also go to Bavarian and Queen Sherrhi so he'd have leverage to get the best deal on funding.

Poly and I had to step apart quickly as a pair of angrily chittering squirrels ran between us, hoping to increase the distance between them and Spike. One of them nearly collided with Rosalind, but she gracefully stepped out of the way.

"Be careful, you big galoot," she said to the boisterous feline. I hadn't heard the term *galoot* since I'd first met Rosalind when she was playing the part of a nineteen forties' *femme fatale* to seduce me—not that seducing me was much of a challenge at the time. After that, I had my guard up.

Spike strolled over so I could scritch him behind his ears. Poly and Rosalind also rubbed his back and sides until the big cat's purring was as loud as the hum of a giant congruent electric generator from one of my mom's old power plants. The trisabertooth rolled over and enjoyed having six hands scratch his belly. All six of his paws waved joyfully at the ends of his powerful arms and his head arched back. It was an invitation, so I rubbed him under his chin and was rewarded with even louder purring.

The park's squirrels took advantage of Spike's distraction to climb distant trees. Finally, the big cat got back on his feet and nudged us over to where Bavarian and Terrhi were standing.

"Hi Spike," said Bavarian, after Spike rubbed his big head against her pinafore. Then the girl turned to Terrhi. "I *like* your cat," she said.

Terrhi beamed. "Who's a big boy," she said, using nine sub-trunks to rub her pet in more places simultaneously than a mere three humans could manage earlier.

Spike seemed to be in cat heaven from all the attention.

"Could I *buy* a trisabertooth of my own?" asked Bavarian. "They look like they're super pets!"

"I'm sorry," said Terrhi with a serious expression at odds with the one on Spike's face. "That's not possible. Trisabertooth cats like Spike are very rare and have been the ceremonial guardians of members of the Dauushan royal family for countless generations."

Poly covered her mouth, but not before a few giggles escaped. My mouth fell open in unspoken amazement. I hadn't realized Spike was a rare ceremonial guard cat. Rosalind looked puzzled and Bavarian's face was sad, a mask of disappointment.

"Tell her," said Poly to Terrhi. "Don't be mean to your new friend."

"O-kay," said Terrhi, smiling more broadly than Spike had been. "Can you help me out, please, Aunt Poly?"

"Sure," said my partner. "Trisabertooth cats aren't rare. Mom took me back country on one of her trips to Dauush. There are tens of thousands of them in the wild across the Dauushan empire. I saw quite a few myself. There's some question about their degree of sentience, so you can't buy them, but if a cat or a kitten decides it likes you, that's all it takes."

"Sorry for teasing," said Terrhi, tentatively extending a sub-trunk to Bavarian like an olive branch.

The blonde girl grabbed the offered sub-trunk and pulled it to bring the Dauushan girl closer. Bavarian grabbed Terrhi's head and gave it a bear hug.

"Ohhhh, *you!"* she said.

Her free hand gave Terrhi a noogie, making the Dauushan girl squirm. I was pleased to see the tough cookie I'd watched get the better of Adolphus Kone in EUA's headquarters could also behave like a typical nine-year-old girl.

"How did Spike choose you?" Bavarian asked Terrhi.

"We were at one of my mom's back country chalets on a working vacation," Terrhi answered. "I was really little—only three or four."

"About the size of a Saint Bernard," inserted Poly for the benefit of the other humans.

"I liked to play behind the chalet, near the woods," Terrhi continued. "The guards were busy talking about my aunt Lüzhi and weren't paying much attention to me when I noticed a trio of big eyes staring at me from the edge of the forest."

"Spike?" asked Bavarian.

"Shush," said Poly. "Let Terrhi tell it."

Bavarian zipped her lip and nodded contritely.

"I thought it might be a trabbit or a traccoon," said Terrhi, "so I broke off some crunchsticks from a patch by the house and carried them over near the forest."

"Crunchsticks?" asked Rosalind quietly.

"Dauushan celery," Poly replied. "It's pink."

"Doesn't that go without saying on Dauush?" I asked.

"Pretty much," said Poly.

"Then what happened?" asked Bavarian.

"Nothing," said Terrhi.

"Why?" Bavarian asked.

"Because trisabertooth cats *hate* crunchsticks!" said Chit. She was riding on my shoulder so it sounded like she was shouting.

"How do you know?" I asked my little friend.

"I get around, bucko, I get around."

Terrhi acknowledged Chit's comment. "She's right, Uncle Jack. Trisabertooth cats *do* hate crunchsticks."

"How did you get Spike to come out of the forest?" asked Bavarian.

I could hear the wheels spinning in the little girl's brain. Once she knew the secret, she'd be on the next starship to Dauush.

"I wouldn't have, without help from our cook," said Terrhi. "I put the crunchstick stalks down on a bare patch of ground near the forest. Then I moved back to wait and see if the owner of the eyes would come out to eat them. Nothing happened, so after a while I got hungry and unwrapped my lunch."

"What did cook pack for you?" I asked.

"A sandwich like the one you ate on the shuttle heading back to Atlanta from the *Charalindhri*," said Terrhi.

"A sub?" I asked.

"That's just weird," replied Terrhi. "Why is it called *that?*"

"It's short for submarine," said Rosalind.

"And it's called that because the shape of the sandwich resembles a Terran undersea craft," said Poly.

"We don't have submarines on Dauush," said Terrhi.

"Why not?" I asked. "Don't you have oceans?"

"We *have* oceans," said the Shetland pony-sized girl. "They're just not very deep."

"Lots of mud wallows," mused Rosalind.

"Uh huh," said Terrhi. "Anyway, we name them after the part of males they use to get females pregnant."

"Makes sense t'me," said Chit.

I was sure Poly would be teasing me about my submarine the next time we were in bed together. Then I changed mental gears and filed Terrhi's tidbit about shallow oceans on Dauush away in my mental off-planet cartographic trivia database.

"What happened next?" asked Bavarian eagerly.

"Then this kitten smelled the HoneyBaked Ham in my submarine sandwich and came out of the forest to beg for a taste," said Terrhi. "He *loved* HoneyBaked Ham."

"Understandable," said Poly, licking her lips. It was getting close to lunch time.

"I fed him all the ham from my sandwich and he curled up on the grass in front of me and went to sleep while I finished everything else. His tummy was so full it bulged," said Terrhi.

I nodded encouragement—I wanted to hear what happened next as much as Bavarian.

"He was cute and tiny—only the size of a Terran house cat. I watched him sleep for half an hour and rubbed his belly while he slept to hear him purr," she continued.

"Uh huh," said Poly. She made keep-talking motions with her hands.

"Then I heard a noise from the edge of the forest. The kitten was instantly awake, his head scanning back and forth. A long-tailed trabbit was eating the crunchsticks I'd left there."

Terrhi paused, her eyes dancing as the happy memory replayed in her brain. Spike was looking at her fondly.

"The kitten was next to the trabbit so fast I thought he teleported. The trabbit—not much smaller than the kitten—bounced in the air to get away, but the kitten was too fast. He grabbed the trabbit's middle tail and it popped right off. The trabbit bolted for the forest, but the kitten came back to me with the middle tail in its mouth and the remains of the crunchsticks held in its two front paws," said Terrhi. "We've been together ever since."

"That's quite a story," I said.

I leaned over and gave Spike another scritch.

"Why did you name him Spike?" asked Bavarian.

Spike yawned, showing off his three scimitar-like incisors.

"Oh," said Bavarian. "Forget I asked."

"No worries," said Poly. "By the way, I'm Poly. Nice to meet you. This is my boyfriend and business partner, Jack." Poly took a short breath. "And this is Rosalind."

"Nice to meet meet you face to face," said Bavarian. "Terrhi's told me all about you."

"Don't believe half of it," I said, smiling.

"Hey," said Chit from my shoulder. "What am I, chopped liver?"

"And this," I said, shrugging to emphasize my shoulders, "is my very talented friend, Chit."

"Pleased to meet ya," said Chit in her deceptively deep voice. "I'm a Murm."

"Pleased to meet you, Mr. Chit," said Bavarian.

"That's *Miz* Chit," said my little friend.

"Sorry," said Bavarian.

"No problem, ducks," said Chit. "Just don't let it happen again."

"No sir, err, ma'am," Bavarian replied.

She was clearly in child-mode right now, not businesswoman-with-a-killer-instinct mode. I liked both versions of the girl.

We started walking toward the west side of the park, farther away from EUA's headquarters, but kept talking while we walked.

"Nice job handling Adolphus Kone," said Poly.

"How do you know about what happened with *him?*" asked Bavarian.

"The whole negotiation was recorded," said my phone. It had climbed up on my other shoulder and had extended arms, legs, and a cartoon-like head from its mutacase.

"That's Jack's phone," said Rosalind. "Sometimes I think it's smarter than Jack."

"Hey," said my phone. "What do you mean, *sometimes?*"

"Now you're sounding like Chit," I teased.

"It should only learn from the best," said Chit.

"*We* wanted to learn more about The General," said Terrhi. "That's why mom said it was okay for me to come along with Bavarian."

"Your parents know you're here?" I said. I'm sure my eyes were wide.

"Uh huh," said Terrhi. "Mom said it was time for me to spread my wings."

"You have *wings?*" said Bavarian. Clearly the girl had a lot to learn about xenoanatomy.

"It's just a figure of speech for Dauushans," said Terrhi, "though not for Tōdons."

Tōdons were shaped a lot like turtles and even larger than the elephant-sized Dauushans. Several months ago I'd been surprised to learn they were actually more like beetles and had wings hidden beneath their shells.

"I'm glad your mom approved you going along with Bavarian," I said. I'd been dreading the prospect of informing Tomáso and Queen Sherrhi about their daughter's activities.

"Mom wanted to know as much as she could about The General before their meeting this afternoon," said Terrhi.

"That makes sense," said Poly.

"Unfortunately…" said Chit.

"The General is missing," said Rosalind. "His office and luxury suite are both cleared out."

"Mom's not going to be very happy if he blows off her meeting," said Terrhi. "I hope he shows up. It's a nice planet you've got here. It would be a shame if anything happened to it."

I hoped Terrhi wasn't realizing what she was saying. Was the future of Earth really hanging on The General showing up? I knew Earth's standing in the Galactic Free Trade Association was a lot like a nephew who is good at telling funny stories—but no matter how much the galaxy liked our legislative broadcasts, we didn't have a tenth of the power or status of the Queen of All Dauush. There wasn't time to worry about something like *that*.

"We need to get back to where we're staying," I said. "Would you like to come with us? We'll get lunch."

"No, thanks," said Terrhi. "Mom said I had to come right home after the confrontation."

"Okay," I said, taking in Terrhi's phrasing.

"And I'm going over to the consulate with Terrhi," said Bavarian. "Her folks want to meet me."

"I'll bet they do," said Poly, smiling.

Rosalind, Poly and I all exchanged knowing glances. I wouldn't be surprised if Queen Sherrhi and the Dauushan planets weren't soon part of the young Donut Queen's empire. Bavarian pulled out a tiny cell phone and tapped a few keys. My phone beeped.

"Thank you," it said. "The team really appreciates it."

"Appreciates what?" I asked.

"A thousand-galcred virtual gift card good at any Consolidated Donuts-owned company," my phone replied.

"That's very kind of you," I said, already thinking about what I wanted for breakfast tomorrow.

We'd reached Marietta Street on the opposite side of the park.

"Here's our ride," said Bavarian, as a giant donutmobile pulled up nearby. It was the size of a flatbed truck with two huge donuts, one horizontal, one vertical, mounted on it. There was plenty of room for Terrhi, Spike and Bavarian to fit inside, plus a small army of assistants, if Bavarian *had* assistants. That reminded me of something.

"Hey," I said as Bavarian was about to close the donutmobile's door. "How can a nine-year-old get away without having any adult supervision?"

Bavarian didn't bristle or take my question as an affront. She answered me matter-of-factly.

"I fired them all," she said, "and got myself declared an emancipated minor. It only took the judge fifteen minutes to agree to sign the papers."

"And how many galcreds?" asked Poly.

"Two hundred and fifty thousand," said Bavarian.

"I like your style, kid," said Chit.

"I might not have had to fire my guardians and advisers if they'd been as cool as you all," said Bavarian as she closed the hatch.

"What did *that* mean?" I asked rhetorically.

Rosalind chuckled.

"What?" asked Poly.

"This will be amusing, if it plays out the way I think it will," said Rosalind.

"What do you mean?" I persisted.

"Never mind," said Rosalind, shaking her head. "None of us may live through the next few days."

"Hey," I said. "It sure looks like we're ahead on points, at least. EUA's on the ropes."

"You don't know them like I do," said Rosalind. "The General is ruthless."

"Maybe so," said Poly, "but we don't know if he's even still on planet."

"He's still here," said Rosalind. "I'm sure of it. And I'm getting a bad feeling about this."

Unpleasant scenes from the *Star Wars* saga played in my brain, but I pushed them aside. We needed an autocab to get back to the research facility. I scanned the street to see if one was in hailing distance so I wouldn't have to bother ordering one. There were always plenty of autocabs in this part of town.

My eyes stopped when they saw a tall, green, scaly tyrannosaur-like being with his thumb out standing near us on the curb.

"Gus?" I said, raising my voice.

"Jack?" said the Gojon, turning around. He was only between six and seven feet tall at present.

"I thought you were taking the red-eye last night," said Poly.

"I was, but the ticket to Atlanta cleaned me out," said Gus. "Without any money, I had to hide on a MARTA train at bug size. A wind current swept me off the train at the CNN Center Station, so I thought I could hitchhike up to the address you gave me."

"Sorry I didn't realize you were that broke," I said. "I could have sent a car to the airport for you."

"I'm an actor," said Gus. "I'm always broke."

He smiled when he said it, which made it sad, not heartbreaking.

"Anyway," Gus continued, "you're already putting me up. I didn't want to be a burden."

"You're no burden at all," I said.

"Right," said Poly. "You saved Jack's life, after all."

"Yeah, but still…" said Gus.

The big green guy was incredibly sincere and so nice I really hoped he'd make it in the entertainment industry, but I was afraid he lacked the killer instinct required for true stardom.

An autocab pulled up at the curb.

"Hop in, everybody," I said.

The ride back was a lot less stressful for me. Gus sat between Rosalind and Poly, their mutual tension bouncing off his thick hide without causing him damage while Chit and I sat in the front passenger seat. The autocab's algorithms for opening the front doors were one reason why I didn't suggest Gus should shrink down to make more room.

"What time is your screen test?" asked Rosalind.

"Seven o'clock tonight," said Gus. "The address isn't far from where you picked me up."

"Great," said Poly. "There's a bus that runs right down Marietta Street from where you'll be staying to Centennial Olympic Park. It should only take half an hour for you to get there."

"That sounds easy," said Gus. He hung his head. "It would be easier if I had some money."

I tapped a few keys on my phone and got affirmative chirps back.

"I just transferred five hundred galcreds to your account," I said. "It's a loan. An investment in your career. You can pay it back or pay it forward, take your pick."

Gus reached over the front seat and squeezed my shoulder with one of his longer-than-standard tyrannosaur-type arms.

"You're a good sentient being, Jack Buckston," he said.

Poly rescued me from having to reply.

"I'm starving," she noted.

"So am I," said Rosalind.

A deep rumble like the sound of moderately powerful earthquake came from the center of the back seat.

"Sounds like you are too, Gus," I remarked. "You're welcome to join us."

"Thanks!" said the alien would-be actor. "I haven't eaten since noon yesterday. What are you having?"

"I don't know about lunch," I said, "but I know what's for breakfast."

"What?" asked Gus innocently.

"Donuts!" the rest of us shouted.

Chapter 33

"Ask not what you can do for your country. Ask what's for lunch."
— Orson Welles

We got back to the research facility without incident. After all the excitement we'd had leaving Danny Figueres' office and being chased up the Connector, I was fine with having an uneventful trip. I'd polled everyone in the autocab on the way north to find out where they wanted me to order lunch and the consensus was an Indo-Pâkk place not far away on Tenth Avenue called Sacred Ubercow. What with Pâkk-Mex and Indo-Pâkk, various types of Pâkk-fusion cuisine have had a big impact on Terran dining— especially for meat dishes.

I was pleased to see the drones delivering our meal were waiting for us as we pulled up. My phone and I acknowledged receipt and Poly, Rosalind, Gus and I had an easy time carrying the bags and containers inside and downstairs. Chit didn't have the requisite size or muscle-power to be much help, though she did offer to pay. Given how little she'd be eating, I didn't take her up on it.

"Your loss, buddy boy," said my little friend.

I asked my phone to pass the word about lunch to the others' electronic devices, so everyone was waiting when we arrived in the conference room we'd been using for meals. That reminded me—I needed to update Tomáso and Queen Sherrhi.

"Please send a copy of the recording we'd made of Bavarian getting the better of Adolphus Kone, including Spike's contribution on the way out, to Tomáso and Queen Sherrhi."

"Already done," said my phone.

"When did you manage that?" I asked.

"While you were talking to Bavarian and Terrhi," it answered.

I was pleased, actually, and a little surprised—though I knew I shouldn't have been. Initiative is a good thing, if coupled with judgment, and my phone was beginning to put the *pro* in proactive. I think what would have *really* surprised me was if my phone had *not* sent the recording. This way, at least, the details would reach Terrhi's parents *before* Bavarian arrived. I considered it important they immediately understood what to expect from their daughter's new friend. Where Bavarian was concerned, they'd need all the advanced notice they could get.

"What do you have there, Daddy?" asked Max.

He'd wrapped himself around one of my legs so I had to drag him along as I transported various components of our meal to the counter. I was carrying half a dozen meter-long lengths of what looked like eight-inch diameter PVC pipe, colored orange, green and white, like the Indian flag. Some pipes were painted black and red as well, in traditional Pâkk designs.

"Lunch," I said, teasing him.

"No!" shouted Max. "What's *for* lunch?"

"Kablobs," I said.

"Kabobs?" asked Sally.

"No, kablobs," I replied. "They're an Indo-Pâkk thing. They're *like* kabobs, only the chunks on the skewers are big and blobby."

Sally—and Cornell standing next to her—wore puzzled expressions.

"Here, I'll show you," I said. "It's easier than trying to explain."

I ran my finger along a seam on one of the pipes and it split open longitudinally, creating a serving dish for the kablob. I tested the ends of the steel skewer to make sure they weren't too hot, then lifted it up so everyone could see. It was as if someone had threaded four or five knobby spheres slightly smaller than bowling balls onto a metal rod. Some of the spheres looked like meat, while others were clearly vegetable and at least one was of indeterminate origin.

Shepherd's mouth turned up and his nostrils flared. I could tell he was even more interested in the kablobs than he'd been in the huge ubercow rib I'd ordered for him last night.

"What's the gold-colored one in the middle?" asked Cornell, indicating the blob in question with a digit.

He was pointing at the indeterminate blob.

"That's a giant samosa," I said. "The crust wrapped around it is spherical, like a baked apple."

"Yum!" said Max. He flicked his finger like the tip of a wand. "Wingardium Levi-sam-o-*sa!*"

I floated the skewer through the air toward my son. Poly got him a plate and Rosalind made a long knife materialize from somewhere to slice off a chunk of samosa from the gold ball and a piece of tandoori chicken from a red ball at one end. Sally brought him tongs and a much smaller knife and my son started eating with gusto.

Shepherd collected two of the meat kablobs—one chicken tikka baked in a tandoori oven and one made of curried Neuva Pâkkjuk uberlamb prepared *en croute* with the same dough the chef used for his naan. Martin made himself an Indo-Pâkk taco, of sorts, by slicing bits of several kablobs into a round of whole wheat paratha flatbread and slathering them with sweet chutney. Poly opted for slices from an orange-colored ball of ostrich shwarma accompanied by sides of salad, hummus and naan.

Pomy seemed worn, stretched past her limits like too little hummus spread over too much pita. She sat at the table, barely able to hold up her head. I was pleased to see her react when Poly sat next to her, though. Pomy stared at Poly's plate and inhaled deeply, savoring the exotic scent of the shwarma. Then she summoned the strength to speak.

"I'll have what she's having."

Poly got up to assemble a second plate and I considered the main component of the spicy dish. Ostrich had become increasingly popular off-planet ever since ORC, the Ostrich Ranchers Cooperative, had started marketing it as uberchicken, but the Pâkk planets had protested the rebranding and the whole thing was mired in litigation. ORC had initially expanded its production by selling its products to Hindus as a stand-in for beef. Unfortunately, the ranchers' slogan, "Ostrich, the other red meat," was also facing lawsuits from the Worshipful Galactic Consortium of Pork Producers.

I was glad I didn't have to worry about similar litigation. Business to consumer marketing made business to business marketing look easy.

"What's this?" asked Cornell, pointing to a short, wide plastic cylinder. When he picked it up, the contents sloshed.

"Classy lassi," answered Rosalind. She was busy dishing matar paneer—made with peas and cheese—over rice tinted purple with Nicósn royal saffron.

"What makes it classy?" asked Sally. She had just nibbled on a crisp papadum cracker and was still dangling a piece of it in her mouth like a cigar.

"Caviar," said Rosalind. "It's mixed in like the boba in bubble tea."

"Beluga?" I asked. "From sturgeons in the Caspian?"

I made a reminder to double-check the bill. Beluga caviar was still something only oligarchs bought, despite valiant efforts using alien technology to rescue Earth's largest salt-water lake.

"No," said Rosalind, "we're not made of money. It's from Lake Cussler in the Sahara. Ninety percent of the Caspian sturgeons' caviar is crap."

"Worth a try," said Cornell, pouring himself a serving, then sticking a ladle into the cylinder to get some caviar. "Not bad," he said, after a sip. Cornell smacked his lips and filled a glass for Sally.

Martin was being deliberate about making his selections. He had taken about a quarter of one of the bright yellow kablobs, which turned out to be a deep-fried head of cauliflower dipped in a chickpea-flour batter enhanced with lots of turmeric. Then he'd pulled off a small chunk of samosa-kablob with tongs. Now he was adding some chicken tikka and an unusual naan-descript starch. Every move was well thought-out and economical. I studied Martin's movements carefully, in hopes of emulating him. Martin had style.

On the far side of the table I saw Winfield and Johnson sharing a pan of what must be the deceptively plain-looking ubergoat biryani. I hadn't warned them that I'd ordered the rice and meat dish Påkk-standard spicy, which was around twenty-five on an American one-to-ten scale. They weren't trying to put out the heat effectively with lassi or some other milk product—they were using water, and that only fed the flames. It was like trying to use a Type A, water-based fire extinguisher on a grease fire. The two former Chapultepec & Castle executives were sweating and their eyes were watering like they'd been tear gassed.

After a few seconds to appreciate the schadenfreude, I tossed them jumbo single serving cups of mango sherbet to help cut the heat. The sherbet stayed cold thanks to a tiny congruency in its packaging connected to the thick, very cold oxygen-nitrogen atmosphere of Niflheim, a gas giant planet in the Midgard system.

"Didn't you know the Scoville scale had to be recalibrated as exponential to handle Pâkk peppers?" I said, smiling.

Johnson gave me a dirty look and Winfield gave me the finger. Their tongues hadn't recovered enough to talk.

Gus was standing behind me, like a stranger at a wedding, waiting to go last. I waved him ahead of me.

"Dig in," I said. "There's plenty of food and if there's not, I'll order more."

"Thanks, Jack," said the big green alien sincerely. He tried to give me a hug, but his arms, while longer than what you'd expect to find on a tyrannosaur, were still too short to wrap around me. That didn't stop me from giving *him* a hug, though. Gus was like a large friendly dog that wanted to please, but was tripping over himself in the process.

He dug into the food arrayed on the counter like he hadn't eaten in days, filling three separate plates and balanced them precariously on one of his arms. I followed in his wake and assembled a diverse collection of spicy veggies, proteins and starches from the limited selection of comestibles Gus hadn't taken.

I took a deep breath before I sat down. The conference room smelled strongly of curry and probably would for days. Curry was one of those things that stayed around, like guests at the Hotel California. In time, the cleaning robots would probably eliminate it, but it could take a billion years and the sun might go nova before they succeeded.

I found my usual spot between Max and Poly. Gus didn't need a chair. He balanced on his tail like a kangaroo, fitting into an open space at the table near Winfield and Johnson. They fobbed their ubergoat buryani off on him and Gus ate it gleefully, admiring its high-powered capsicum kick. From the opposite side of the table, it appeared that the former C&C executives were now on a diet of naan and water.

The food was delicious. All the nervous energy I'd expended at EUA must have taken a lot out of me. I was starving and ate like a pack of ravenous Pâkk. I nearly got curry sauce on my tie and resolved to change into something more comfortable right after lunch.

Chit was sitting on an upside-down tumbler drinking a thimbleful of classy lassi and munching on a tiny piece of boti roll. She was amusing Max by telling him a tall tale about how another Murm watched a stranded Dauushan explorer stuck on Terra in fourth-century south Asia simultaneously invent pottery and tandoori. I was convinced it *had* to be a tall tale until Chit brought up Ganesha, the pink, elephant-headed god, and then I wasn't so sure.

While we were eating, my phone played the encounter between Bavarian and Adolphus Kone on the wall screen. There were lots of cheers of "You go girl!" and assorted hoots of approval as the video played. Spike got a special round of applause when he licked Boss Kone on his way out. When the video finished and most of us were done eating, I took a last bite of papadum dipped in cool, green raita sauce and tapped on my glass to get everyone's attention.

"That was the good news," I said, pointing to the smart wall where the video had played. "Rosalind has the bad news."

"Chit and I checked out The General's office and living quarters on the top floor of EUA's headquarters and found them deserted, as if he's pulled out completely," Rosalind reported.

"The turkey took a powder," said Chit with her own brand of eloquence.

"Tomáso is very concerned that Queen Sherrhi will not react well if The General doesn't show up at the Dauushan consulate this afternoon," said Shepherd. He paused and repeated, "Very concerned."

After what Terrhi had said earlier about this being a nice planet and it being a shame if anything happened to it, I didn't want to find out what the queen had in mind for The General or for Earth. I loved Terrhi and respected her parents, but Queen Sherrhi ruled an empire and had her own priorities.

"The General is a tricky S.O.B.," said Cornell. "From everything I know, he still needs help from Dauush for his own plan of galactic conquest. I'm worried about Queen Sherrhi's safety when The General *does* show up, which I think he will."

Shepherd was following Cornell intently. I watched him enter and send a text message while everyone else's attention was focused on Cornell.

Martin cut in.

"I have bad news of my own. I'm being pulled off working with you for a new assignment. My superiors want me to focus on protecting the delegations attending the G70 meetings— starting on Sunday. I tried to explain my current investigation was tracking a possible threat to the G70 attendees, but they're not hearing it. The meetings are an all-hands-on-deck thing. I'm stuck handling security for the dignitaries' meet-and-greet at the Capitol building and their tour of the major attractions in Centennial Olympic Park. It's supposed to be part of a GAFTA-wide effort to build stronger connections with one of their newest members, though I think it's mostly about the dignitaries getting a chance to see their favorite Georgia legislative stars face-to-face."

"Is the SkyView ferris wheel on the agenda, too?" I asked.

"Only for the species small enough to fit in the gondolas," said Martin with a strained smile.

He was *not* looking forward to playing nursemaid to off-planet delegations instead of tracking The General.

"At least you're going to be well-positioned if EUA tries anything on Sunday," said Poly.

"Yeah," added Rosalind. "You'll be in sight of EUA's headquarters on the east side of the park all day."

"Not t'mention the mile-high SLN Tower on the south side," chimed in Chit.

She still thought Danny Figueres wore a black hat, and for all Poly and I liked the guy, maybe he did.

"Where do you think The General has gone?" I asked Rosalind, Cornell, and Sally. I didn't bother asking Winfield or Johnson—I knew they'd be useless.

"First," said Cornell, "you have to understand that none of us have ever met him face-to-face. He's always on video or in the shadows."

"I'm sure he uses a voice distorter, too," said Sally, "though I've only seen him on my phone's screen a few times when I've received special assignments."

"Cornell would know best," said Rosalind. "He's the one who's worked most closely with The General. I'm more like the top operative on the old Mission Impossible movies who got recordings that self-destruct, saying, 'Your mission, should you choose to accept it.'"

"Did you ever turn down an assignment?" asked Martin with professional curiosity.

"I suggested revisions to plans fairly often," Rosalind replied, "but I had the impression any assignment I turned down would be my last."

"So did I," said Cornell.

"Me too," echoed Sally.

"Let me phrase things another way," I said. "Does EUA own any properties nearby that would be good places for The General to relocate?"

My phone's screen lit up.

"Droopy's investigations have identified a highly probable location," said my phone.

We all stared at it while it hopped from my belt to the table, grew arms, legs, and a head, and strutted over to stand next to Chit's overturned tumbler.

"Well," said Poly. "Where is it?"

A yellow smiley face appeared on my phone's screen as it answered. "Ad Astra."

Chapter 34

"And in the sixth month the angel Gabriel was sent from God..."
— Luke 1:26 KJV

"Jack! I'm glad you're here!" boomed Tomáso's deep voice as we entered his personal living quarters adjacent to the Dauushan consulate. "Welcome!"

He patted me on the back with a sub-trunk—none too lightly—and waved to Shepherd a few steps behind me.

"Good to see you too, you old scoundrel," he said to the grizzled Long Pâkk operative.

"Tomáso," said Shepherd, inclining his head to his friend with respect.

I can still remember the first time I'd met Shepherd. He'd come to my rescue when I'd really needed help. That's when he'd told me the difference between the Pâkk's two philosophical camps.

"My people consider other species to be sheep," he'd said, "but Long Pâkk see them as wool and Short Pâkk see them as lamb chops."

Back then I was pretty sure Shepherd had been speaking figuratively, not literally. Today, I wasn't quite so sure, but I knew I didn't have any interest in being doused with mint sauce. I was grateful to Shepherd and the other Long Pâkk for keeping the Short Pâkk's more aggressive impulses in check. The General's home-grown Terran terror was enough of a challenge.

Poly, Rosalind, Chit, and Cornell had come with me to meet with Tomáso and Queen Sherrhi. It was four o'clock on Saturday afternoon. We all wanted to be in place prior to The General's arrival at five to obey the queen's imperial summons.

On the autocab ride over to the Ad Astra complex, the humans in the vehicle had placed bets on whether or not The General would show. Rosalind and I thought he would. Poly and Cornell thought he wouldn't. Chit said she didn't care one way or another—her galactic Murm hive mind would locate The General and deal with him in the fullness of time. Shepherd kept his own counsel and didn't offer an opinion. That's why Martin's approach to stoic *cool* is my model. There's no way I could live up to Shepherd's.

Poly stepped forward and bowed to Queen Sherrhi. "You're looking great, Your Majesty," she said. "It's almost like you're glowing."

Terrhi's mother smiled and patted my partner on the back, much like her consort had patted me, but with less force. The Dauushan matriarch winked one of her three eyes at Tomáso, then looked toward where we'd entered. Rosalind was a few steps behind Poly, close to the wide-open roll-up door. She seemed nervous.

Cornell stood just outside Tomáso's spacious apartment with only half of his body visible. He seemed reluctant to enter. I wondered why, then I remembered he had kidnapped Terrhi and had no idea how her parents would react.

"Come in, come in," said Queen Sherrhi, motioning to Cornell with a few sub-trunks. "Don't worry. I have no current plans to crush you under my feet."

Cornell didn't look reassured and remained in the doorway until Shepherd took him by the elbow and pulled him into the huge entry chamber. Perhaps Cornell had been wise to stay back. As soon as he was within six feet of the queen, Sherrhi grabbed him with a pair of sub-trunks and held Cornell up so high his hair almost brushed the ceiling. She stared at him, taking his measure.

In the background, the door to Tomáso's living quarters rolled down into metal security plate with the solid thunk a hammer hitting an anvil.

"So *you're* the one who took my daughter," Queen Sherrhi rumbled, her voice half an octave lower than Tomáso's. "I didn't realize that earlier—all you humans look alike to me."

"I was just following orders," squeaked Cornell, though the queen wasn't squeezing him, yet. I was impressed that he was retaining all his bodily fluids.

"That's not good enough," said Queen Sherrhi. "Save it for the Royal Inquisitor."

She seemed to be really hamming it up.

Cornell turned white. I'm sure his brain was filled with visions of racks and thumbscrews. Sherrhi gave him a final shake and put him down gently. The room filled with a bubbling subsonic hum—Queen Sherrhi was laughing.

"Hey, I was just messing with you," said the queen. She sounded exactly like Tomáso when he'd found me trying to help Spike deal with obnoxious squirrels. "You're on our side now—the enemy of my enemy is my friend and all that." Sherrhi leaned over Cornell and lifted his chin with a sub-trunk. "Now, my new ally—what can you tell me about The General?"

Cornell was unsteady on his feet but regained his composure quickly.

"I'm not sure what you want to know," said Cornell. "But I *can* tell you I have no idea where he is."

"I'm not concerned with *where* he is," said Queen Sherrhi. "I want to know how he *thinks.*"

"He's devious and thinks six moves ahead," offered Rosalind. Her mind was working faster than her brother's at the moment.

"He's also very private," said Cornell. "I'm one of his top people and I've never met him face to face."

"Ditto for me," said Rosalind. "I've never seen him either."

"Ditto?" Tomáso asked me, speaking in what passed as a stage whisper for a Dauushan.

"The same for me," I translated. "From a brand of early Twentieth Century print-reproduction technology called a spirit duplicator."

"We have those on Dauush," said Tomáso quietly, "but they're for mass producing alcoholic beverages."

"Let's talk later," I said, visions of competing with Brown-Forman-Beam dancing in my head.

"Shush!" said Poly. "And it's from a Tuscan dialect going back to the 16th century."

Tomáso and I looked appropriately contrite. Queen Sherrhi continued her interrogation.

"Why do you think he's hiding his true identity?" she asked.

"Because he's a coward," interjected Chit from her perch on my shoulder.

"Why a coward?" asked Rosalind. "Why not a clever strategist, working through misdirection?"

"The General *is* a clever strategist," said Cornell. "Recent reversals notwithstanding."

Everybody looked at Poly and me. I nodded and Poly performed a small curtsy to acknowledge our role.

"He's up to something," Cornell continued. "He doesn't like being put in a corner with no alternatives and he *really* doesn't like losing."

"What do you think he'll do about Queen Sherrhi's ultimatum?" asked Poly.

"Yes," rumbled Tomáso. "Will The General risk an interstellar incident by offending the Dauushan monarchy?"

The big pink alien looked at his spouse and ruler affectionately.

"I don't think so," said Rosalind.

Cornell indicated his agreement with a dip of his head.

"I think he'll find a way to obey the letter, if not the spirit of the summons," said Cornell.

"A weasel, not an eagle?" asked Poly.

Rosalind's eyes sparked in enthusiastic agreement.

"He's the consummate corporate weasel," she said. "And will probably find a way to turn the meeting to his advantage."

"If he tries," said Tomáso, "he'll soon find that running a corporation is not the same as ruling an empire."

Queen Sherri sidled close to Tomáso and tenderly rubbed her massive side against his.

"That's why I keep you around," said the queen, her eyes twinkling. "You always know the right thing to say."

Their sub-trunks entwined briefly, then separated.

"What do you think The General will do?" I asked. "So far, he's failed at every turn."

"Go after Terrhi again?" suggested Rosalind.

"She's very well-guarded," said Tomáso.

"Like she was when she walked into EUA's headquarters this morning with Bavarian Kreem?" Poly asked.

"She was never at risk," said Queen Sherrhi. "There was an attack shuttle filled with Dauushan Drop Marines hovering about the building—and recording equipment in Spike's collar was tracking everything."

The news about Spike was an interesting, though not unexpected nugget of data.

"Besides," said Tomáso, "she's perfectly safe *here*. No one would try to take her from the Dauushan consulate or these apartments. This is imperial Dauushan soil and we have a massive contingent of bodyguards covering the building."

"Uh huh," I said, thinking just one Dauushan guard weighing in at over ten tons would be a heavy contingent. "Our sources indicate The General could be hiding close by—somewhere in the Ad Astra complex."

"Where are Terrhi and Bavarian?" asked Poly, seeming to change the subject.

"They're in Terrhi's room with Spike," said Queen Sherrhi. "We wanted to share some big news without the girls overhearing."

"Overhearing what?" asked Terrhi from the far side of the room near the hall leading deeper into the apartment. Bavarian Kreem was with her and Spike was walking between them.

"How long have you two been listening?" asked Tomáso, adopting a clearly feigned stern-father persona.

"Long enough to be worried," said Bavarian.

"Long enough to want to hear your big news," added Terrhi.

Spike yawned and licked his tongue around his jaw nonchalantly.

"Spike wants to hear the big news, too!" Terrhi insisted.

Tomáso and Queen Sherrhi moved even closer together. Their heads turned so they could lock eyes for a moment. Sherrhi nodded.

"As you wish," said Tomáso. "It's probably better for you to hear our announcement while your friend is visiting."

"Out with it," said Rosalind.

"What's the buzz, Your Queen-ness?" asked Chit.

"I'll bet *I* know what it is," said Chit with a sing-song lilt to her voice. "Tomáso and Sherrhi are…"

"Terrhi," said Queen Sherrhi. "You're going to have a baby sister!"

I didn't know what sort of reaction I expected from Terrhi. My general impression was that she was behaving like a five-year-old who had just finished off half a bag of Halloween candy and a six-pack of Mountain Dew. She was literally bouncing off walls and executing vertical leaps of such height that I wanted to see if the surface gravity of Dauush was substantially higher than Earth-normal.

Her frenetic motion was accompanied by a non-stop, high-pitched, high-volume litany of semi-relevant phrases that seemed to feature the phrase *baby sister* every few syllables. Bavarian had moved to stand next to the human adults to reduce her odds of being hit by Terrhi as she behaved like a pinball on a particularly lively machine. Spike crawled under Tomáso to reduce his risk of a collision.

I saw Rosalind reaching for her mini-sweetener, but put my hand on her arm and pointed to the maxi-sweeteners tracking her from the ceiling. She took her hand out of her pocket and stood closer to me, Poly, and Cornell. Shepherd stepped back against the closed door and watched with what I suspected was a Påkk expression of amusement. The corner of his mouth turned up a millimeter, anyway.

Bavarian finally grew tired of her friend's energetic trajectories and tackled Terrhi, turning Terrhi's head by tugging her sub-trunks and taking her down like a cowboy roping a calf. It was hard to believe the tiny girl could handle someone Terrhi's size so easily. I think Terrhi was sufficiently shocked by Bavarian's actions that her manic antics simply stopped. The two girls stayed on the floor, chattering and giggling together.

I took advantage of the lull in the excitement to ask a question. "When's the baby due?"

"In about two Terran years," answered Tomáso, sounding like a second-time proud papa-to-be.

That gave us plenty of time to plan a shower.

"I'm very happy for you both," said Poly, "but now I'm even more concerned." She spoke directly to Queen Sherrhi. "How well do you get along with your sister?"

The bubbling subsonic hum returned for a few seconds.

"How well did the Plantagenets get along with *their* siblings?" asked the queen.

Memories of the Christmas court at Chinon from *The Lion in Winter* flashed through my brain. All of Henry Plantagenet's children had knives and knew how to use them.

"What if The General has cut a deal with your sister?" Poly continued. "She'd be next in line to rule Dauush if anything happened to you and Terrhi, right? Acting before there's a spare to go with your heir is so much the better."

"That traitorous *rogue!*" bellowed Sherrhi.

I covered my ears to block out the queen's angry trumpeting. I wouldn't want to be Lüzhiulterianne right now.

"What if The General were to eliminate you and your daughter in a way that wouldn't implicate Lüzhi?" said Poly.

"Then she would gain the throne and could put the manufacturing might of all Dauush at The General's disposal," said Cornell.

"And together," I realized, "they could…"

"Conquer the galaxy," shouted Poly, Rosalind and Cornell in unison.

"Did you say something?" asked Terrhi, coming up for air from her conversation with Bavarian.

My phone chose that moment to speak.

"It's five o'clock," it said. "There's someone at the door."

Chapter 35

"There is no substitute for victory."
— Douglas MacArthur

"It's a human in a Remote Hands rig," said Tomáso, checking the screen of his skateboard-sized phone.

I stepped over to him, reached up for the device and pulled it down to take a look. The courtyard outside was empty, save for a young woman.

"Emma Ann?"

Everyone was staring at me—their faces full of unspoken questions. I could tell my jaw had dropped so I closed it. I released Tomáso's huge phone but kept a hand on one of his sub-trunks.

"Please let her in," I said.

Tomáso tapped a few keys and the door to his living quarters began to rise. When it was halfway up a young woman in telepresence operative's gear entered, moving a bit unsteadily. She took a few steps into the entry hall. I knew it was Emma Ann because I'd seen her in mirrors half a dozen times when she was my remote doppelganger, helping me support my clients south and west of the city. I didn't understand why she was here in Atlanta now, though.

Usually the screen covering the Operative's face showed a real-time image of the person working remotely—like me, when I was paired with Emma Ann. This time, instead of showing anything human, the screen was black with a frowny-face emoticon sketched out in white. Five gold stars were displayed in a shallow arc at the top of the screen. I knew better than to try to talk to Emma Ann directly and expected there'd be time for that later. Queen Sherrhi understood Remote Hands protocols as well.

"The General, I presume," said Her Matriarchal Majesty. "Be assured that I am not amused."

The mouth of the frowny-face moved and an electronically distorted voice came from speakers in the Operative's suit.

"I don't care if you're ROTFLMAO," it said.

Instead of saying the individual letters making up the internet abbreviation, the voice pronounced it "ROT-ful-MAO."

"Shouldn't that be ROTFLYAO?" joked Chit, three inches away from my auditory canal. "Rolling On The Floor Laughing *Your* Ass Off?"

"Shush," I said. I needed to focus.

"Close the door," I whispered to Tomáso.

He push a few buttons on his phone and the door began to descend behind Emma Ann. She walked closer to Queen Sherrhi and glanced down to take in Terrhi and Bavarian on the floor. I noticed Spike had moved from his hiding place beneath Tomáso to join the girls—as protector or playmate, I couldn't tell.

I inspected Emma Ann with new eyes, since I'd never been physically in the same room with her before. She was a fit, competent, and professional-looking young woman. I'd always been impressed by her commitment to being the best Operator she could be. Now she moved hesitantly, as if she was resisting her Prime's instructions. Once Emma Ann was farther inside the entry hall I could tell that something seemed odd about the back of her suit. I couldn't quite figure out what, so I filed my observation away for later and watched The General and the queen continue their verbal combat.

"Stop attacking me and members of my family, or face the consequences," said Sherrhi.

"What consequences? There's nothing you can do to me," replied The General.

The frowny-face emoticon shifted to a sneer.

"I can put EUA Corporation out of business—or acquire it. I command the wealth of the Dauushan empire."

"You can't buy what's not for sale, you misshapen alien pachyderm. EUA is privately held."

"Maybe not, but I *can* put you out of business. If I say the word, every company on Terra will shun you, or risk losing access to Dauushan imports and technology."

That was a powerful disincentive. Dauushan 3D printers were essential to Earth's economy and nearly half the products sold on the planet were made on Dauush. It was something about economies of scale.

"You won't be in any position to issue threats if the atmospheres of all the Dauushan planets are flooded with grajja dust," the frowny-face icon intoned.

Poly was tugging on my arm, but I couldn't pull myself away from following the battling titans.

"The top Dauushan botanists and Nicósn pharmacologists are working with the CDC on developing a vaccine to block grajja addiction," said Queen Sherrhi. "In a year, your dust will be useless."

"Unfortunately," said The General, "you don't have a year. I can teleport millions of pounds of grajja dust into your planets' atmospheres tomorrow."

Queen Sherrhi stomped her foot in anger, then held back her consort as Tomáso contemplated an attack. I knew Emma Ann wasn't The General, and so did Sherrhi and Tomáso, but it's hard not to lash out at an immediate and proximate target. I put my fingers around my own mini-sweetener, wondering how much effect it would have on an angry Dauushan. I'd probably have more luck playing King Canute trying to hold back the tide. Thank goodness Tomáso seemed to regain a measure of self-control, despite the way his sub-trunks were lashing.

While everyone watched Tomáso's internal struggle, I spoke to my phone.

"Can you trace the signal coming into Emma Ann's suit?" I asked. "Maybe we can follow it back to The General."

"No can do," said my phone. "Remote Hands' security is too strong to crack."

I was disappointed, but pleased at the same time. It wouldn't be good if Remote Hands' systems were easy to penetrate—too many companies depended on its services.

"Crap," I said.

"Perhaps that expression of frustration is premature," said my phone. "Given your high-level access to Ad Astra's cameras and microphones, it's straightforward to monitor all the feeds across the complex and see if any of them turn up phrases The General has recently spoken."

My phone was right. I had root-level access to Ad Astra's systems because I was trading technical support expertise for reduced rent. What I had, my phone had.

"Any hits yet?" I asked.

"Processing," said my phone.

"Jack," whispered Poly. She was tugging my arm more insistently and pointing at Emma Ann.

"What?" I said, concentrating on my phone's screen as it listened in on hundreds of rooms across the complex.

"Look at her back," said Poly.

A cantaloupe-sized metal sphere was hanging from the bottom of the thick metal box that formed Emma Ann's Remote Hands backpack. I recognized the shape.

"Crap, crap, crap!" I said, not worried that I might be interrupting the queen and The General as they crossed metaphorical swords.

"Your heightened frustration level is premature," said my phone. "There are still several thousand feeds to review."

"Better make it fast, then," I said, not bothering to disguise the tension in my voice. "That's a nova bomb!"

Queen Sherrhi hadn't heard my words. She was saying, "My fabricators can make billions of gas masks overnight to protect my people from your dust."

"But can you convince every single one of your people to wear a gas mask every hour of every day?" asked The General. "Your people are every bit as stubborn as humans—millions will ignore any command that's inconvenient. Do you want to risk turning every independent-minded thinker across your planets into a grajja addict?"

"You don't understand Dauushan solidarity," said the queen. "My people will obey me—I am their Matriarch."

"Maybe your people aren't as united behind you as you think," snarked The General's frowny-face icon.

"He's stalling," said Rosalind.

She'd heard what I'd said about a nova bomb. I nodded at her to confirm I agreed, exchanged a glance with Poly to confirm she knew what I had in mind, and told Chit her part in my plan. Shepherd sidled over to a panel on the far side of the roll-up door. I didn't know why, but I had confidence in Shepherd's response to a crisis.

"Now!" I shouted.

Chit flew off my shoulder and landed on one of Tomáso's giant ears.

"Open the door," my little buddy instructed.

Tomáso took out his phone and started pushing buttons. I took five quick steps toward Emma Ann and tried to twist the nova bomb off the bottom of her RH backpack. It couldn't be that easy—and it wasn't. The bomb was welded to the metal box strapped to her back that held the Remote Hands processors. Time to improvise.

I fumbled in my pocket and found my Wenger Supertalent Swiss Army knife. Its largest blade made short work of the lower straps. As I moved to cut the upper ones I found my phone was already on Emma Ann's neck, cutting her shoulder straps with something like a box-cutter extruded from its mutacase.

"The nova bomb's been remotely triggered," it said. "We have less than ten seconds before it goes off. The odds of success are…"

"Never tell me the odds," I said as I pulled the bomb and backpack off Emma Ann and flung it toward the opening door where Poly was waiting to receive it. The bomb was reciting to itself, counting down. "Seven, six, five…"

My partner caught the awkward assembly and repeated my toss, using her whole body and a hundred and eighty degrees of rotation to send the deadly device flying out into the empty courtyard.

"Close the door!" shouted Rosalind.

"Goodbye, cruel world," said the nova bomb just after the countdown ended.

I never understood the logic behind using voice circuitry or sophisticated A.I. software on one-time use hardware.

Tomáso was already pushing buttons on his phone, but Shepherd was faster. He'd opened the panel on the far side of the door and signaled for Poly to move out of the way. The warning was unnecessary, since Poly was already retreating farther into the entry hall. I was pleased to see what Shepherd had triggered— a foot-thick blast door descending rapidly from the ceiling. It reached the floor at the same time a concussive blast rocked the Dauushan consulate.

The shock wave made me unstable. I lost my balance and fell into Emma Ann. She landed face down, cracking the mask with the frowny-face on her Remote Hands suit and leaving it frozen in a crazed expression. I expected my expression to be fairly crazed at the moment, too, exacerbated by the fact that under other circumstances Emma Ann and I would be in a compromising position. I rolled off and got to my feet as fast as I could, hoping Poly hadn't seen us.

"Are you okay," I asked Emma Ann as I helped her up. She threw off her mask and shrugged out of the front half of her rig, now unsupported by the cut straps. My phone must have been thrown off—it was no longer on her neck. Emma Ann put her arms around me—she only came up to my chin—and squeezed. I hugged her back and spoke soft, reassuring words as her ragged breaths became more regular. After a minute, Emma Ann replied.

"It was awful, Jack," she said when we broke our hug and she stood on her own, without using me for support. "So awful. I *hated* being that terrible man's operative."

"I'm sorry you had to go through that," I said. "Did you know about the nova bomb?"

"No," said Emma Ann. "Someone welded something to the back of my rig while I was under The General's control. I didn't know what it was, but it threw my balance off."

That explained her unsteady movements when she'd entered.

"Why are you here in Atlanta?" I asked. "I thought you lived in Newnan?"

"That's your fault," said the young woman.

"Jack's fault?" Poly asked. She'd made it through the shaking without falling and came over to put her arm around my waist.

"Uh huh," said Emma Ann. "From what Jack told me, everything sounded so much more exciting in Atlanta, so I applied and got into Georgia State for summer term. All my credits from West Georgia Technical College will transfer and Ray Ray said I could stay at his place while I find my own apartment. He's friends with my big brother and now he's working for *you,* which is really cool! I let Remote Hands know I was available for assignments in Atlanta and got one right away. I never thought my first job here would be for such a despicable client."

"You poor thing," said Poly. She gave the younger woman a sympathetic hug. "Did you get enough excitement for the next week or so?"

"I got enough excitement for the next *decade,*" Emma Ann asserted. "Is there still time to change my major from Telepresence to something boring, like Accounting?"

"Chin up," said Poly. "You'll get past this, not that you wouldn't excel at accounting."

"I thought ya used Excel *for* accounting," said Chit, who chose that moment to return to my shoulder.

Emma Ann laughed. If was a half-hearted laugh—the kind you get when you need to release nervous tension—but it made her smile, which meant she'd be okay. A small sub-trunk pulled on Emma Ann's elbow.

"Would you like something to drink?" asked Terrhi. She had a can of Diet Starbuzz in one sub-trunk and a bottle of water in another.

"Diet Starbuzz sounds great," said Emma Ann, popping the can and taking a long swig.

Bavarian brought over a tray of drinks for the rest of us. I grabbed a Diet Starbuzz of my own, while Poly and Shepherd opted for water. Rosalind and Cornell were sipping tumblers of an amber liquid that smelled alcoholic, which was perfectly understandable after our latest close call.

"Are you two okay?" I asked Terrhi's parents.

"How's the baby?" asked Poly.

"We're fine," said Queen Sherrhi, "and no worries--it takes a lot more than a few shock waves to cause problems for a Dauushan fetus at this stage of gestation."

"Good to know," I said.

"Without your fast thinking," said Tomáso, "Dauush would have had a new Matriarch."

"We're rather fond of the current one," said Poly with a smile.

Queen Sherrhi, however, wasn't smiling.

"Now," she said, in a threatening basso, "I shall deal with my treacherous sister!"

"Don't forget," said Tomáso, "you've also got the G70 meetings Monday morning and the delegates' Atlanta tour tomorrow."

"I won't forget *my* duties, like Lüzhiulterianne has forgotten *hers,*" said the queen. "You can be sure I will devise and *execute* the appropriate actions."

If I were Lüzhi, I didn't think I'd like hearing Queen Sherrhi's emphasis on the word *execute.*

"I guess The General knows we're not on his side anymore, Sis," said Cornell.

"Not necessarily," said Rosalind. "We could have been brought here against our will."

"Close the door!" said Cornell, imitating Rosalind's shout.

"You're right," said Rosalind. "I sort of forgot about that."

"Now we're really the pig, not the chicken," said her brother.

Poly looked at me for a second, then got it—bacon and eggs for breakfast. The chicken is involved; the pig is committed.

"I wish we'd actually had a chance to capture The General when he showed up," said Poly.

"Yeah," said Rosalind. "But he outsmarted us."

"He tends to do that," said Cornell, finishing the rest of the amber liquid in his tumbler in one gulp.

"Not necessarily," said my phone.

"Where were you?" I asked.

"Continuing to search the Ad Astra security recordings," it said.

"Even while you were cutting the straps on Emma Ann's backpack?"

"Multitasking is a specialty," it said.

"Thank you for helping to save me," said Emma Ann.

"You're quite welcome," said my phone.

"Well?" I asked. "What did you find?"

"The General," said my phone. "He's upstairs."

Chapter 36

"I have learned to hate all traitors…"
— Aeschylus

"Upstairs?" I asked.

"On the fourteenth floor," said my phone. "Room 1417."

The trivia engine in my brain informed me that was the number of archvillain Sinestro's space sector in the Green Lantern comic books. It was probably just a coincidence, though The General was a comparable representative of evil. My mind tried to spin off on a tangent casting my friends as members of the Green Lantern Corps, but I shut it down hard.

"Are you sure?" I asked.

"That's where Ad Astra's surveillance systems recorded someone saying the words The General said."

"Good enough for me," said Cornell.

"Is he still there?" asked Poly.

"There is still at least one human in the room," said my phone.

"That makes sense," said Rosalind. "The General would need someone else to attach the nova bomb to Emma Ann while he was directing her movements."

"If we move fast, we can catch The General—and his accomplice," said Poly. "Where's the elevator?"

"There isn't one in these apartments," said Tomáso. "Dauushans like living on the ground floor."

"Where's the nearest elevator to the fourteenth floor of this part of the complex?" I asked Shepherd.

I wasn't sure, but I thought he lived in the building.

"Outside, to the left, first doors on the left," said Shepherd in economical Pâkk fashion.

"Don't just stand there, open the blast door, ya big hairy galoot!" Chit ordered.

Shepherd's fingers touched something on the panel beside him and the blast door slowly lifted into the ceiling.

"Tomáso?" asked Poly gently, getting his attention with a wave.

The Dauushan consul looked away from his spouse for a moment. Queen Sherrhi appeared to be ticking off ways to punish Lüzhi and Tomáso stood ready to talk her down if she sounded like she would do something rash. He noticed Poly and pulled out his phone. The roll-up door on the other side of the blast door also rose.

"Where's the queen's security detail?" I asked.

"Deployed around the perimeter, I expect," said Tomáso.

"Anybody in the parking garage?"

"Lohrri and Naddéo."

"Great," I said. "Have everybody on high alert looking for The General in case he tries to leave the building."

Tomáso nodded and pushed more keys.

By this time, both doors were a few feet up. With my phone on my belt and Chit hanging on to my collar, Poly, Rosalind, Cornell and I rolled underneath them, followed by Emma Ann and Spike, once he'd confirmed Terrhi was safe.

I didn't try to stop the trisabertooth from coming with us—cats aren't good at following orders. I did try to dissuade Emma Ann, however.

"Stay inside the consulate," I said to the Remote Hands Operative. "You've been through enough."

"No way," said Emma Ann. "I want to give that creep a piece of my mind."

"But you're not armed," said Poly as we ran through the consulate's private courtyard, dodging holes in the concrete and smoldering ornamental shrubbery. We headed left once we reached the main public courtyard.

"Says who?" asked Emma Ann.

She was holding a nine-inch switchblade in one hand and a mini-sweetener in the other.

"Not me," said Poly, looking over her shoulder at Emma Ann with a smile.

Not counting my phone, Emma Ann was better-armed than I was.

"Why the small arsenal?" I asked as we ran.

"My big brother told me I should always be prepared to defend myself," said Emma Ann.

I think I liked her big brother.

A dozen yards to the left were a set of glass double doors. I tossed my phone ahead and it had them open before we reached them. They led to a lobby with banks of elevators on either side. We wasted ten seconds figuring out that we wanted the elevators on the right. The ones on the left started at the twenty-first floor and above.

Cornell, Rosalind, Poly and I each pushed the up button in frustration to try to speed up a car's arrival. Emma Ann seemed patient, but her expression was hard. I guess Operatives had to learn patience to be good at their jobs.

"If ya keep pushin' it ain't gonna come any faster," observed Chit.

"It makes us feel better to be doing *something*, bug," said Rosalind.

My phone chimed.

"Elevator operating system access obtained," it noted.

The door to the car in front of us opened and we all piled in, looking more like a rugby scrum than a well-ordered team. I was surprised to see an ATM at the back, but figured if there could be banks *of* elevators, there was no reason not to have banks *in* elevators.

My phone's control of the car's systems meant we were spared the cliche of stopping at every floor, encountering an old lady with an umbrella going out to walk her corgis, or a troop of roaming bravos out to rob us. Our vertical trip was uneventful, except for Chit wanting to use the ATM.

"Are you kidding?" I asked.

"Hey, bucko," she said. "I just need some small bills."

"For you, aren't they *all* small bills?" asked Poly.

"Badum-bump," said Rosalind.

I think Chit was just trying to get us to loosen up a bit. We were almost to the fourteenth floor.

"Ready to rock and roll, everybody?" asked Cornell.

He pulled out a mini-sweetener and held it at the ready. Rosalind, Poly, Emma Ann and I all readied our mini-sweeteners. My phone climbed from my belt to my shoulder, opposite Chit. Spike yawned to loosen up his jaw. The elevator doors opened.

A sign pointed to Rooms 1401-1421 on the right. We tiptoed down the carpeted hallway like Elmer Fudd stalking wabbits. When we were outside 1417, Chit flew over to the bottom of the door and listened. She returned and whispered in my ear.

"I hear two humans. They're arguing—and their voices sound familiar."

"Crap," I thought.

My phone hopped from my shoulder to the locking mechanism above the door nob and worked its magic. I nodded at Cornell and Rosalind. They opened the door and stormed into the room, scanning for places to aim their mini-sweeteners. Poly and I were right behind them, with Emma Ann and Spike guarding our rear.

Scott Winfield and Josephine Johnson were standing in an elegant suite, drinking scotch and arguing about which one of them would replace Cornell as The General's chief lieutenant. When we made our entrance, they stopped their debate and froze in place without any need for us to use our sweeteners. The pair didn't look happy to see us and seemed even less so when Spike approached and gave them his predator's *you-could-be-lunch* stare.

We were standing in an apartment designed for human needs and tastes. The living room was luxuriously furnished, with a high-end Terran leather sofa and overstuffed chairs arrayed around a fieldstone fireplace. It had the feel of a sitting room in a British gentleman's club with green wallpaper, red accents, and lots of dark mahogany. A hand-woven Persian rug resembling the one I'd seen in the courthouse covered the hardwood floor. Doors led off to what I assumed would be a kitchen, bathroom and bedroom.

"Check the other rooms," I said to Rosalind and Cornell.

The siblings did a circuit and were back quickly.

"They're clear," said Rosalind.

"We checked all the closets and under the beds," added Cornell.

I looked at the carpet again and confronted Winfield and Johnson. "Did The General teleport out?"

"No way," said Johnson.

"He wouldn't risk *his* brain cells by teleporting," said Winfield, "but he made *us* teleport in."

"At least that wouldn't do you any harm," said Cornell. "You don't have any brain cells to risk."

I don't think he liked hearing the two of them talk about replacing him.

"How did you get out of the research facility?" asked Poly.

"Martin had to leave early, and Pomy stayed in her room," she said, "so only Sally was around to watch us."

"Let me guess," said Rosalind. "Max distracted her…"

"And bingo, we walked right out," smirked Johnson. "We took an autocab to a convenience store and bought a cell phone."

"When we explained things to The General, he said all would be forgiven if we'd help him with a special project," said Winfield.

"He said he'd give us our old jobs back," said Johnson.

"If we would weld a bomb on her backpack," added Winfield, pointing at Emma Ann.

"While The General stayed out of sight in the bedroom," said Johnson.

"We just had to get to EUA's headquarters," said Winfield.

"So our autocab took us to downtown to HQ and we teleported here," said Johnson.

"Why did you teleport instead of taking an autocab directly to Ad Astra?" I asked.

"Great question," said Winfield. "I think The General was punishing us."

"He was, I'm sure of it," said Johnson, rubbing her temples. "I've never teleported before. I think it's giving me a migraine."

"Poor baby," snarled Rosalind, holding her mini-sweetener to the side of Johnson's head. "I'd be glad to cure your headache. And remember, there's only a one in ten thousand chance of permanent brain damage from teleporting."

"Temper temper," said Poly.

My partner was lucky Rosalind's eyes weren't lasers or she would have been vaporized. Rosalind lowered her weapon and stepped away from Johnson. I could hear her counting down from one hundred in Orishen, using mutable emphatic scatological suffixes after each one.

"You were in here with The General?" I asked. "Does that mean you know what he looks like?"

"We know about how tall he is," said Winfield.

"And?" said Poly, stroking her thumb close to the trigger of her mini-sweetener. Winfield got her meaning.

"He's short. About five-foot five."

"Why don't you know what he looks like?" I asked.

"Because he was wearing a full coverage Remote Hands Prime suit," said Emma Ann.

"Maybe," said Johnson. "But we aren't even sure he's a *he*. We had to wait in the other bedroom when The General left."

"Oh, he's male alright," said Emma Ann. "I can tell by the way he made me walk. And he's not young, either."

"If he didn't teleport, how did he leave without any of Tomáso's security-types spotting him?" asked Poly.

"I figured *that* out," I said. "It's my fault. I was only thinking in two dimensions."

I looked up. Poly got it.

"The roof?" she said. "There are cameras on the roof."

She snatched my phone off my shoulder and held it out in both hands.

"Show us the roof cams," she ordered. "We have to find him."

My phone started to display camera views on its own screen, then switched to the smart wall on the far side of the living room where the pictures were nearly life-sized. In the middle of the roof, fifty-nine floors up, two dozen adolescent pterodactyl-like Quirinx fliers were practicing their takeoffs by diving off the side of the building. At the far end, a pair of workers were rolling a wooden box the size of refrigerator onto a cargo dirigible. The view at the near end showed an aged female Pyr wearing a raccoon coat and a broad-brimmed purple hat with a peacock feather gliding on her mobility cilia into the passenger seat of a two-being ornithopter.

"Who's that?" I asked.

"That's Zelda Fitzgerald," said Emma Ann. "She's famous! I've seen her picture all over the gossip pages for her affairs and the news sites for her charity work."

"Thanks," I said, marveling at Emma Ann's capacity for trivia even though it ran in a different direction from own.

"Can you access the cameras' history?" asked Poly. "Maybe The General already left?"

"Yes," said my phone, "and no. The cameras' history is available, but these views show the only activity in the past hour."

"This is real time?" I asked.

"Correct," said my phone.

"How do I get to the roof?" I mused rhetorically, then raced for the door with Poly and Emma Ann at my heels. I looked to my right and saw Spike loping beside me. For The General's sake, I hoped I caught him, not the big trisabertooth.

* * * * *

We raced up the stairs from the top floor elevator lobby to the center of the roof and saw the flock of adolescent Quirinx gathered around a flat box. When we got closer, I saw they were eating a pizza topped with large bugs that were still crawling from slice to slice. Chit buried her head in my hair.

"I can't look," said her muffled voice.

"Give me a break," I said, "Murms and Terran insects have no evolutionary ancestors in common. Just be glad I speak Quirinx."

I started to walk toward the fliers, careful not to frighten them and warning Poly, Emma Ann and Spike to stay back with an upraised hand.

"Can you help me with the higher pitches?" I asked my phone.

"Over six million forms of communication are readily available…"

"Is that a yes?"

"Affirmative."

I tweeted a greeting to the Quirinx pizza-eaters, using my unassisted vocal chords.

None of them paid me any attention. I needed to up the stakes and motioned Spike forward. The trisabertooth understood what I needed, opened his mouth wide enough to swallow a flier in one bite, and roared like the legendary Divine Wind.

That got the fliers attention. We were lucky they froze in fear instead of flying off.

"Who wants to make a thousand galcreds?" I asked in Quirinx.

A flurry of beaks bobbed their interest. In short order, four fliers had their talons embedded in the rigid fabric of my Orishen pupa silk shirt. At least they were only ruining one of my casual polo shirts and not one of my good suits. Poly would have joined me on this stage of the chase, but she didn't speak Quirinx.

"Follow that ornithopter!" I tweeted.

I took a running start—slowed a bit by the wings of the four fliers on my back—and jumped off the side of the building.

Chapter 37

"This flapper is likewise employed diligently to attend his master..."
— Jonathan Swift, *Gulliver's Travels*

Flying is a lot like falling—with style, according to Pixar. After my initial leap and subsequent descent, the quartet of Quirinx on my back started flapping in unison to regain and maintain our initial altitude. The sky was nearly cloudless, so I had no trouble spotting the ornithopter far ahead, flapping its own wings on its way south from Ad Astra. It was cold enough at this height that I wished I'd brought a jacket. The wind had enough bite that I would have been smart to bring goggles as well, but I persevered. It would be worth it if I intercepted The General.

"Hey, bucko," said Chit from her secure perch on my shoulder. "How come you went after the ornithopter, not the cargo dirigible?"

"Instinct," I said. "I just knew."

"Try again," said Chit, "and don't try to snow me—it ain't easy to do. You always have logical reasons for your actions except when you're lovey-dovey with Poly."

I thought about her question for a few seconds, which helped distract me from how high up we were. Our height probably wasn't a problem for Chit—she had her own wings. I had to depend on the kindness of Quirinx strangers.

"It was Zelda Fitzgerald's mobility cilia," I said. "They weren't moving right."

"Waddya mean?" asked Chit.

"The cilia tend to move in unison when they're doing the work of gliding a Pyr's mass along," I said. "Zelda's cilia hung straight down and waved back and forth at random, as if all of them weren't even touching the ground."

"Ya think it was The General in a Pyr suit, with wheels on the bottom?" asked Chit.

"Uh huh," I said. "You can buy suits like that for cosplay at Atlanta Costume. They're really popular at Dragon Con."

"I'll keep that in mind for Labor Day weekend," said Chit. "But I don't get it. The General *hates* aliens. He's a rampant xenophobe."

"That's another reason I went after the ornithopter," I said. "Cornell said The General is devious, and I could see him using our prejudices about *his* prejudices against us."

"If you say so, buddy boy."

Chit clammed up, which gave me time to look around. All in all, I would have rather been distracted by conversation.

We were gaining on the ornithopter. I could tell it was a Terran-made craft, but recognized its underlying Orishen design. The machine's broad wings were flapping in slow, even strokes. The original Orishen version had wings that could morph into a fixed, swept-back configuration and included a high-powered congruent engine for longer flights. Since it hadn't switched modes, I was confident its destination wasn't too far away. My Quirinx assistants would never be able to catch it if it wasn't moving at its current sedate pace.

We were heading generally south. I looked down to find landmarks and saw Peachtree Road below us. I even spotted the corner where my favorite branch of Fellini's Pizza was located. I wondered if The General was hoping to return to EUA headquarters, his own version of Barad-dûr, or had some other destination in mind?

At this point, The General's destination didn't matter. We were gaining on him. The ornithopter was built like a First World War-era biplane, featuring open pilot and passenger compartments. The big difference was that it had giant, flapping batwings affixed to the sides of the fuselage, not a pair of fixed wings above and below. The original Orishen ornithopter design had dragonfly wings, since there aren't any species resembling Terran bats on Orish.

I could see the top of Zelda's head in the back seat of the 'thopter. She was still wearing her absurd, broad-brimmed purple hat with a peacock feather and for some reason it hadn't blown off. That gave me even more confidence we had the correct quarry, because Pyrs don't have external ears. Short of using cyanoacrylate adhesive, there was no way to anchor her hat in place unless it had been sewn on as part of a costume.

I couldn't tell if the pilot was a man or a woman, or even human. Only an upper torso and head were visible. The head wore an aviator's helmet and goggles. A long white scarf was wrapped around the pilot's neck and fluttered back in the wind. I had to figure out a way to convince the pilot to land where I wanted, not where The General wanted. Peachtree-Dekalb Airport, a small general aviation field, was too far away, so it was out.

Then I remembered that ornithopters didn't need long runways. The roof of the huge new parking garage at Atlantic Station, a multi-use development north of Georgia Tech with lots of retail, would be a good spot to try to force them to land. I could see its flat, multi-acre expanse off in the distance along our line of flight.

"Hey Chit," I shouted against the noise of the wind. "Are you awake?"

"I'm a thousand feet up riding on the shoulder of an idiot being carried like a dwarf snatched by an eagle and you're asking me if I'm awake?"

"When you put it that way…" I said, contritely.

"Waddya need?" asked my little friend.

"Do you have any weapons on you?"

"Other than my rapier-sharp wit?"

"Other than that, yeah."

"I got my stinger," said Chit.

"Where do you have room for a cruise missile?" I asked.

"Not that kind of stinger—it's a set of congruency-powered capacitors that can give a high-voltage zap ta anybody tryin' ta get too friendly."

"Why haven't I heard of this before, little buddy?"

"Need ta know, chump. Need ta know."

"Right," I said. "If we get close enough to the ornithopter, do you think you could fly over and threaten to zap the pilot unless the 'thopter lands at Atlantic Station?"

"Yeah," said Chit. "I'll give it a shot. What's the worst that can happen?"

I didn't want to think about that and stuck out the first three fingers on my left hand, making an "M" to appease Murphy.

I shouted up to the Quirinx fliers. They increased their pace and brought us a dozen feet above and behind the ornithopter. Somehow they knew to stay a bit back so the people in the 'thopter couldn't see us. I credit the sneakiness teenagers learn from trying to keep their parents clueless about what they're really up to.

"Time to go, little buddy," I offered.

"Sitting Bull!" shouted Chit as she jumped off my shoulder.

What was wrong with "Geronimo?" I wondered. Then again, given our relationship, Chit's choice of words was probably more appropriate.

My little friend couldn't just fall—she used her own wings to keep moving forward as she descended. Unfortunately, instead of landing on the pilot's helmet, she got caught in the slipstream off the front windscreen and ended up fighting her way through the tangled length of the pilot's long white scarf.

Zelda Fitzgerald spotted Chit and reacted, rotating in place to face backwards. I could tell because the peacock feather on her hat turned one hundred and eighty degrees. Then a seam opened in the side of the Pyr's "body" and a human arm stuck out. At the end of the arm was a hand holding a mini-sweetener.

I felt two close near-misses, and suddenly my body was vertical, not horizontal. I looked down and saw a pair of fliers hanging limply from the small of my back—the shots weren't misses after all. At my shoulder blades, the two Quirinx adolescents there were struggling to support a vastly increased weight. We were falling toward the ornithopter at high speed.

As we neared the flapping flying machine, I twisted my body so my back was to The General and his mini-sweetener, then smacked into the leading edge of one of the horizontal tail fins, chest first. Thank goodness for my pupa silk shirt or I'd have broken a few ribs.

I felt the two unsweetened Quirinx fliers release their hold and take the limp bodies of the other two off my lower back. They headed north toward the Ad Astra complex without sticking around to collect their one thousand galcreds. Chit and I were on our own. At least the angle made it difficult for the ersatz Pyr to suppress his line of fire enough to shoot me—not that he wasn't trying.

Luck is important in business and in chasing evil would-be galactic overlords. I realized luck was with me—I was in the right place at the right time. I pulled myself along until I got to the 'thopter's vertical stabilizer, then stood up behind it, holding on for my life. I put my feet on the elevator flaps on the horizontal fins and pushed. The tail rose and the 'thopter's nose descended. We were going down toward the roof of the parking lot at Atlantic Station.

The General, stuck inside the Zelda Fitzgerald Pyr costume, tried to sweeten me, but the vertical stabilizer blocked most of the energy of his shots.

"Chit!" I shouted, or a word a lot like that.

"I got this," said my little friend.

She managed to crawl up the white scarf all the way to the pilot's neck. I watched the body at the controls jerk and spasm as bolts of high voltage electricity shot out from Chit's stinger. The pilot's body fell forward, rendered insensible by the jolts of current. Unsurprisingly, the ornithopter went into a steep dive. I nearly fell off my perch on the tail.

"Maybe you should have tried another approach," I shouted to Chit over the roaring wind.

"Ya think?" the Murm bellowed back.

I moved out of the way of another barrage of sweetener shots from The General and used my legs and body to pull up on the elevators, changing the angle of our dive. It was working, but it wasn't enough. We were descending so fast we were likely to go through the roof of the AMC IMAX-VR Theater at Atlantic Station rather than making a gentle landing on top of the mall's newest parking structure.

"Cavalry's coming," my phone exclaimed.

Extending dozens of legs from its mutacase, my phone crawled forward along the fuselage until it reached the pilot's compartment. Once there, it hooked itself into the guidance and navigation systems using a standard port designed for that purpose on the instrument panel. In seconds, we'd leveled off and were on track to make a smooth landing. We weren't going to be an inadvertent IMAX-VR feature presentation after all. I was ready to cheer my phone's efforts but had forgotten about Murphy and his blasted laws.

After one last set of sweetener blasts my way, the arm with the sweetener withdrew into the Zelda Fitzgerald Pyr costume. I watched warily as the broad-brimmed purple hat with its distinctive feather rotated all the way back to its original position. I couldn't see exactly what happened next, but The General's arm must have grabbed the pilot's scarf and pulled. Whatever he did, the pilot's head was yanked back and slammed forward half a dozen times in quick succession, dislodging my phone from the instrument panel and Chit from the pilot's neck.

This wasn't good. The wings on the ornithopter snapped tightly into the fuselage and the aircraft went into a diving spin. Chit and my phone fell out of the 'thopter and the only thing that kept me from falling to my death was my foot getting caught in one of the thin wires connecting the horizontal fins to the vertical stabilizer on the tail. It wasn't fun hanging off the back of the ornithopter with my body blowing around in crazy whirls and arcs like the pilot's scarf. I had a sense of *deja vu*, like I was hanging on to the banner on Cornell's dirigible back in Vegas last Monday.

The worst of it only lasted for a few seconds. The ornithopter pulled out of its gyrations and resumed its usual slow, methodical flapping. That gave me time enough to catch my breath and lever myself up to resume my previous position behind the vertical stabilizer, standing on the elevators. I saw that The General must have had a duplicate set of controls in his compartment and had resumed his original course going south. It was time to try forcing him down by pressing on the elevators again—but I never got the chance.

My adrenaline surged as I watched the wings on the ornithopter reconfigure for fixed flight and a congruent engine screamed up to full power a few inches below my feet. Maybe the engine wasn't the only thing screaming.

The airship's formerly sedate pace shifted to bat-out-of-hell mode and The General launched it upward in a steep climb. This time, my foot didn't catch on a convenient guy wire. I lost my connection to the morphed 'thopter and began to fall.

I flipped over as I fell, blown in random directions by the turbulence caused by the ornithopter's rapid departure. My eyes watered from the rushing wind. I could sense the inevitability of death and tried to make my peace with the universe, but failed. I was too young to die—and Poly would never forgive me.

My vision was going haywire as the ground rose to meet me. All I could see below me was red.

I knew only one thing for sure—this would hurt.

Then I hit.

Chapter 38

"So, what would you say... to get a free ride on a blimp?"
— Lana Kane

I was wrong. It didn't hurt—much. And I hadn't been seeing red. The color overwhelming my retinas was pink—a saturated, fuchsia-pink on steroids.

I was resting on a resilient pink surface that felt like thick Mylar under tension. It yielded to my touch and I had bounced a few inches in the air when I struck it, like landing on a trampoline that's been pulled too tight. Clearly, I hadn't fallen very far.

I sat up and found I was on top of something hundreds of feet long. It was rounded, almost as if I was riding a humpbacked whale. I oriented myself to the compass directions using the sun and my own shadow, then got to my feet and looked south. I could see a black speck quickly disappearing in the distance—The General's ornithopter.

I started to tell the universe what I thought of the situation, using alien-language analogues of Anglo-Saxon mono-and-polysyllables, but before I could get very far I was interrupted by a high-pitched buzzing sound. A dark shape looking like a thick business card between two soft-drink-cup lids was circling my head. The buzzing was from the drone-style fan blades spinning at either end. It was my phone, with Chit on its back.

I waved at the pair and leaned forward. My phone and little friend landed on my head, then moved down to assume their standard perches on my shoulders. As usual, one played grumpy devil and one played informative angel.

"You really screwed things up *this* time, bucko," said Chit.

"What do you mean, *I* screwed things up? Who zapped the pilot and put the 'thopter in a power dive?"

"I had everythin' under control," my little friend asserted.

"Were you going to lever his body away from the control stick with your superhuman strength?" I asked, not bothering to constrain my sarcasm for the sake of our friendship.

"No way," Chit replied. "I was gonna zap the pilot again at the base of the spine so involuntary muscle contractions would sit 'im up."

"Hmmm," I said. "That might have actually worked."

"Thanks for the vote o' confidence, ya big doofus."

"I'm sorry for doubting you," I said.

Then I remembered Chit's original comment.

"Maybe *you* had a plan, but I don't know where you got off saying *I* screwed things up?"

"You approached from *above*," said Chit. "If you'd come up from underneath, The General never woulda spotted ya until ya climbed into his compartment."

"Hmmm," I repeated. That made sense. "Why didn't you suggest it?"

"I can't do *all* your thinkin' for ya, bucko."

She had a point.

Unfortunately, in making that point, we'd lost a chance to capture The General.

It was time to put my strategic errors behind me and figure out what to do next. I walked a dozen paces along the length of the pink surface I'd landed on, enjoying the way it put a bounce in my step.

"At the risk of sounding like an amnesiac trope," I began.

"Spit it out, buddy boy," Chit encouraged.

"Where am I?"

"You are on the dorsal surface of the royal Dauushan dirigible, *Matriarch of the Skies*," said my phone.

That made me do a double-take.

"I thought the *Sky Mama* was still in Las Vegas," I said. "What's it doing *here?*"

"Queen Sherrhi is here," said my phone, "therefore the royal dirigible is here, too."

"That's almost two thousand miles," I said. "How did it get here so fast?"

"The distance between Las Vegas and Atlanta is seventeen hundred and four air miles or nineteen hundred and sixty land miles," said my phone. "Over forty-eight hours have elapsed since we left Las Vegas early Thursday afternoon, so the *Matriarch of the Skies* would only need to average forty land miles a hour to get to Atlanta by five o'clock Saturday. The maximum speed of the dirigible, with all congruent engines operating at full capacity, is one hundred and thirty-three land miles per hour, so it is not remarkable for the airship to be here."

I was surprised and impressed. I hadn't heard my phone go on at such length before.

"Shut your yap and get with the program, bucko," said Chit.

Was she talking to me or my phone? Probably me. I hadn't realized my jaw was hanging open and closed it with an audible click of my back molars.

I was glad my phone had stuck to land miles for its answer. My brain hated the knotty problem of converting from nautical miles.

"Not to pile on," said my little friend. " But we've got another problem."

"What's that?"

"I can fly off the top o' this blimp," said Chit, "and your phone can fly, too—but how do we get *you* off?"

Poly might have some ideas on that, the prurient part of my brain insisted.

Enough of this foolishness, I told my brain. I put my foot down and it bounced against the *Sky Mama's* helium-filled envelope. I'd been given a problem I *could* solve and started riffing on possibilities.

"Could I climb down the side?" I asked.

"That might work for the upper half of the envelope," said Chit, "but not the lower part."

"Right," I realized. I'd be hanging out over a long drop once I got to the mid-line. "Are there any hand-holds in the surface I could use?"

"The *Matriarch of the Skies* is a marvel of airship engineering with the latest in low-friction streamlined coatings on its envelope," recited my phone, as if reading from a marketing brochure.

I threw my arms up in frustration and proved what my phone had just been saying when my feet flipped out from under me and I bounced on my butt. I was lucky I didn't start sliding down a sloping side.

"Okay," I said, carefully resuming my feet. "Climbing down is off the list. What about asking the crew of the *Matriarch* for assistance?"

"Someone just tried to blow up the royal family," said Chit. "Do you want to tell the crew there's a strange human on top of the queen's official dirigible?"

I considered the question. What if none of the Dauushans I knew were on board? It wasn't worth the risk.

"Point taken," I said. "Any other suggestions?"

"You could contact Mike or one of the other Xenotech Support Corporation team members and have them rent a helicopter or mini-dirigible to rescue you," said my phone.

"How long would that take?" I asked.

"At least an hour," said my phone.

"Put that idea in the parking lot for now," I said.

"The Atlantic Station parking structure is approximately twelve-hundred feet below this vessel and an equal distance to the northwest," said my phone.

"You're kidding me, right?" I said. "Your idiom interpretation subroutines are better than that."

"Correct," said my phone.

I laughed. It only made sense that *my* phone would have an odd sense of humor and use it to tease me.

"Any *other* suggestions?"

"There are parachutes located at the nose and tail of this dirigible's dorsal surface," my phone offered.

"Great," I said, feeling relieved. "Why didn't you mention them earlier?"

"Because the parachutes are designed for Dauushans," said my phone. "There would be no guarantee they would work as required for someone the size of a human."

"Gus could probably use them safely," I grumbled, hoping the easy-going Gojon was having a good audition downtown.

"Possibly," said my phone, "though the configuration of a harness meant for a hexapod would be difficult to adapt to a biped, no matter what his size."

"Duly noted," I said.

I considered trying to use one of the Dauushan parachutes to fashion a hang glider, but realized that would take a lot longer than an hour and would have a much higher chance of disastrous consequences. I was about to resign myself to calling Mike for help when I heard the sounds of a Vulcan lute. It was punctuated seconds later by a beeping horn that must have been lifted from one of the sixty-year-old *Love Bug* movies.

I turned my head in the direction of the beeping and smiled as I saw my favorite white car rising up around the curve of the *Matriarch.* In the late May light its lustrous paint job glimmered with waves of red and orange and gold from the slowly setting sun. Like Lola, Agent Coulson's beloved car from *Agents of Shield,* the white car's wheels had rotated down and were shooting out high-pressure congruency-powered jets of air to support its mass. Additional congruencies projected below minimized the backwash.

I spotted Chilly behind the wheel. His mask screen had changed from David Tennant to Harrison Ford.

"Anybody call a cab?" Chilly asked as he made the white car hover next to me.

I just grinned and stuck my thumb out like I was hitchhiking the galaxy. The gull wing door nearest me folded up and Chit, my phone and I got in.

"Thanks," I said, enjoying the car's incredibly comfortable seats again.

"Glad to help," said Chilly.

"Could you take me back to Ad Astra?" I asked.

"I could," said Chilly, "but I wouldn't advise it."

"Why not?" asked Chit.

"Well, you see…" began Chilly.

My phone hopped up on the dashboard and began streaming video from outside the Dauushan consulate. If one picture is worth a thousand words, one video is worth at least a million. There were fire trucks and ambulances everywhere. Multicolored light bars were strobing on scores of official vehicles from the Atlanta Police Department, the FBI, and Homeplanet Security.

My phone zoomed in on someone familiar. Clarisse Beatty, the Atlanta Fire Department officer I'd met when WT&F and Factor-E-Flor's buildings had been damaged, was in middle of everything. She was on her phone and giving orders simultaneously, ensuring her team was efficiently investigating the scene.

Reporters from the local, national, planetary and galactic press were there as well, milling about in large-scale Brownian motion. Cameras and blazing banks of LEDs were pointed in the faces of any being who looked like he, she or it had a clue.

Tomáso was near the entrance to the consulate with a forest of microphones stuck in his face. There were Tigrammaths, Pyrs, Pâkk, Nicósns, and a veritable plethora of other species looking on. Down the courtyard, I saw a pair of giant turtle-beetle Tōdons making their deliberate way up a wide path to see what was causing all the fuss.

In the branches of nearby trees, juvenile Quirinx fliers were gawking. Two of them looked stunned and another two looked like they'd soon be asking me for money. I was glad all four of the teens who'd helped me chase The General had made it safely home—and I always paid my debts.

Chilly cleared his throat to get my attention. "That's why I wouldn't advise returning to the Dauushan consulate."

"Thanks for the warning," I said. "I'd rather take a busload of sugared-up third graders to Disney World for a week. Did Poly, Emma Ann and Spike get away before the circus arrived?"

"Yes," said Chilly. "My remotes spotted them. They caught one of the scheduled sightseeing blimps that was headed for Stone Mountain to watch the sunset. It showed up just after you jumped."

Spike must have had an interesting effect on the blimp's other passengers.

"Can we pick them up, too?"

"Already on our way there," Chilly answered.

I looked down. We were passing over I-285, the circular interstate around Atlanta also known as the Perimeter, and were tracking the route of US-78, the Stone Mountain Expressway. Traffic was heavy, but moving at speed. *Thank you self-driving vehicle technology!* A few minutes later we reached the nine-hundred-foot, egg-shaped granite mountain. A garishly-painted blimp labeled Monadnock Tours was moored at one of the masts on top.

"What's a monadnock?" asked Chit.

"It's a mountain without any other mountains nearby," I replied. "Sometimes they're called *inselbergs,* meaning island mountains."

"Thanks, but that's too much information," said Chit. "You're starting to sound like your phone."

I didn't think that was such a bad thing.

"Poly reports they're on the east side," said my phone. "She says it's near where the main trail from the bottom comes out."

"Great," I said.

I knew where she meant and guided Chilly toward them with imprecise hand gestures.

"Hey," I said, reminded of a question I'd had when Chilly first appeared. "How do you get this incredible car around the state and federal restrictions on flying vehicles?"

Chilly grinned, or rather, *Harrison Ford* did.

"The finish on Baby is special," he said. "It doesn't show up on radar and is hard to pin down visually."

Baby, I mused. It certainly was a beautiful child. My van was just my van, though now I thought I might name it *As You Wish.* I promised myself I'd ask Chilly for his help creating a similar car for me someday, with all the same bells and whistles.

Chilly banked and I could see our prospective passengers standing alone on a dimly lit expanse of bare rock. The vehicle hovered a foot above the granite and Poly, Emma Ann and Spike climbed into the back. I kissed Poly over the top of my seat.

"I'm glad you're okay," she said when the kiss was over. "My heart nearly jumped off the side of the building when you took that flying leap."

"You'd have joined me if those adolescent fliers had known English," I replied, squeezing her hand.

"That's just it," Poly said. "They did. The rest of them were too full of pizza to fly safely."

"Must have been good pizza," noted Chit, who seemed to have recovered from her concern about the arthropod toppings.

"You're making me hungry," said Emma Ann, snuggling against Spike in the backseat.

My Dauushan feline friend had a new admirer.

"Who's a big boy? You're a big boy," said Emma Ann, rubbing the big cat's fur.

"You could tell he didn't want to leave Terrhi," said Poly, "but when we heard all the sirens from ground level we dragged him with us."

I'd been surprised Spike had left Terrhi's side, but perhaps the chance of chomping on The General was irresistible.

"I'll return you to the research facility expeditiously," said Chilly. "If you order dinner now, it should be ready by the time you get there."

"Wait," I said, "before we worry about ordering food—who *are* you?"

"Now is not the time to answer *that* question, kid," said Chilly. "Let's survive Sunday first."

There was something to that perspective.

"Will you be hanging around this time?" I asked.

"Maybe later," said Chilly. "Duty calls."

What sort of duty? And to whom, I wondered?

I realized I wouldn't get more information out of Chilly tonight, and turned to more practical matters.

"Okay," I said, "What do the rest of you all want for dinner?"

The answer, as I'd expected, was unanimous.

Chapter 39

"There is no magic substitute for soft caring and hard work..."
— The Outer Limits

It was just us humans—plus Chit and Spike—at the research facility for dinner, so we could get all our pies delivered from Fellini's instead of splitting the order with Galactic Pizza. Poly and I agreed that it would be smart to get several salads, too— and a tray of brownies. It was important to set a good example for Max and eat a balanced diet. At least we didn't have to worry about special toppings for Chit—she'd eat anything that didn't eat her first. I suspected she'd chew away on the innards of any creature who *did* eat her, for that matter.

Poly, Emma Ann, Spike and I had reconnected with Cornell and Rosalind at the facility's entrance. They had left the General's suite at Ad Astra soon after we did and made their escape through the underground parking garage before the place turned into a madhouse. Rosalind had been thoughtful enough to tell my phone they were coming so we knew how many pizzas, salads and sweets we needed for everyone at the table.

Spike wasn't technically *at* the dinner table—he was under it, happily gnawing on a nine-pound ham. Fellini's was kind enough to include it in our order instead of chopping the ham into small pieces to put alongside chunks of pineapple on Hawaiian-style pizzas. We were much happier having Spike's company than enduring the dour faces of Winfield and Johnson. Which reminded me...

"What happened to Winfield and Johnson?" I asked.

"I sweetened them and left them in the suite," said Cornell.

Max stopped tossing slices of pepperoni down to Spike and laughed. I don't think Cornell realized quite what he'd said. Sally either didn't hear the unplanned homophones or chose to ignore them.

"Don't give the cat spicy food," she said to Max. "We don't know how it affects his digestion."

Now Poly laughed.

"Are you kidding? A Dauushan trisabertooth like Spike can eat a peck of pickled Påkk peppers without any problem," my partner exaggerated. "Though I wouldn't want to stand too close to him afterward."

"Will pepperoni make him toot?" asked Max.

Poly held her nose and shook her head from side to side. She used the pizza slice in her other hand for emphasis.

"No," she said. "But it will give him really bad breath."

"Sorry," said Max, moving both his arms to the top of the table so we'd know he'd stopped feeding Spike.

"Don't worry," I said. "A few slices of pepperoni won't hurt."

"Thanks, Daddy. I won't do it again."

I reached over, plucked the only remaining round of spicy sausage off Max's current slice, and popped it in my mouth.

"Your punishment is having to give up your last pepperoni," I said with a mock-serious frown.

"That's okay," said Max. "I don't like it that much anyway."

"Neither do I," said Poly, giving me an arch look that took me a few seconds to interpret. Once I worked it out, I was glad I had toothpaste, mouthwash, breath mints, and chlorophyll gum back in our room.

"Got any more of those Parmesan packets?" asked Chit from her usual perch on an upturned tumbler.

"Here you go," I said, ripping open a foil pouch and sprinkling a few milligrams of finely grated topping on Chit's square inch of pizza.

"Hey! Watch it, ya big lummox," said my little friend. "You're gettin' Parmesan in my spiracles."

"Sorry," I said.

I hadn't meant to cheese her off.

Everybody looked at me—Max and I had used exactly the same intonation when we'd said that word. Our pitches were an octave or more apart, but the way we'd both said it identically was cool, and a bit eerie. *Sahr-rhee!* I liked having a son.

"Did you go back to bed after lunch?" Poly asked her sister.

"Uh huh," said Pomy, who was working on her third slice. Creamy dressing—the remains of a Caesar salad—coated a paper plate in front of her. A rich chocolate brownie was resting on a thick napkin a few inches away. I was glad to see Pomy's appetite returning. It was a good sign she was feeling better and rebuilding her reserves after her ordeal.

By unspoken agreement, none of us told Pomy about Winfield and Johnson's escape earlier in the day. She was asleep and didn't realize Sally was the only person watching the slippery pair. Pomy shared her sister's sense of responsibility and would have protested that she could have helped if she'd only known she was needed.

I didn't mind the two executives showing their true spots and running back to The General. I hadn't trusted them farther than I could throw them—unless I was throwing them off the roof of a sixty-story building without benefit of adolescent Quirinx assistants. I hoped I wasn't being overly optimistic, naive or stupid to trust Cornell, Rosalind and Sally.

I tried to remember which circle of Dante's hell was reserved for traitors, but couldn't summon up the answer. It was high, I knew that. I reminded myself to ask Pomy when she fully recovered. In the back of my head an obscure Beatles' song was trying to turn into an earworm. It kept repeating its lyric monotonously: *Number 9, Number 9, Number 9.*

Cornell had finished his salad and pizza and was eying his brownie.

"What's on the schedule for tomorrow?" he asked.

"I'm not sure, without hearing from Martin, Shepherd, Tomáso and Queen Sherrhi," I answered.

"The G70 activities start at nine o'clock at the Georgia capitol building," said Poly. "They'll be there and we should be, too."

"Is Shepherd part of the G70 dignitaries' tour?" asked Pomy.

"Who knows," said Poly, "but can you imagine him being anywhere else?"

Pomy removed a few crumbs of brownie from her napkin and pondered the question.

"Not really," she answered. "I picture him running a network of stealth surveillance drones from a gondola at the top of the SkyView ferris wheel."

Poly had a perspicacious sister. That was exactly how *I* pictured Shepherd.

"Let's all meet for breakfast at seven," I said. "I'll bring the donuts."

"Sounds good," said Rosalind. "Who's got Max duty tomorrow?"

"I'm not a duty, I'm an effin' pleasure to be around," said Max brightly.

His right hand was back under the table where I suspected Spike was licking it. Max's hand probably tasted like pepperoni.

"Where did you hear *that* wash-your-mouth-out-with-soap phrase?" asked Rosalind.

She glared at me but I didn't have to *play* innocent—on that count I *was* innocent.

After several beats and more glaring, Cornell reluctantly raised his hand and confessed.

"I may have said something like that in his hearing," Cornell admitted.

"Don't let it happen again," said Rosalind in protective mommy mode. "Little pitchers have big ears."

"Uh huh," said Max. "And good hearing, too!"

We all laughed. It felt good to release some tension.

"I'll watch Max tomorrow," said Sally. "If you're all going down to Centennial Olympic Park, maybe I'll take him to the Georgia Aquarium."

The aquarium was at the north end of the park. It was a huge structure, made even larger by a new addition housing a pair of jumbo tanks. The new tanks were orders of magnitude larger than the aquarium's original whale shark habitat. One of them housed ichthyosaurs and megalodons, while the other held a rotating collection of alien aquatic species, depending on what planetary ocean was connected to the tank's congruency this quarter.

If I remembered correctly, the latest exhibit of alien sea life came from Tōdos, the home of the giant turtle-beetle Tōdons. Until the end of June, part of that world's Great Western Ocean—and representative samples of its gigantic ferocious fauna—extended into Atlanta.

The most impressive monster of the Tōdos' deep was the star of the Georgia Aquarium's latest marketing campaign. All the posters I'd seen around town featured depictions of a frightening creature the size of a supertanker with the front end of a Terran killer whale, the back end of a giant squid, and the charming disposition of a hungry piranha. Max would love it.

"Great," said Rosalind. "If things don't get too chaotic, maybe Jack, Cornell and I can join you for lunch."

"I'm not holding my breath about things not getting too chaotic tomorrow," Sally remarked.

I nodded in agreement. There were several wise women at the table tonight—and the cafeteria at the Aquarium wasn't five-star dining, so it wouldn't be much of a loss if I had to take a rain check. Max could catch me up on his aquatic adventures later, if there was a later.

"The General is sure to try something to disrupt the tour," said Poly. "Any thoughts on what?"

She was looking at Cornell, Sally and Rosalind, but Max answered first.

"Blow stuff up?" he suggested in his high-pitched almost-five voice. "Like at Terrhi's place? I saw that on television."

"I'm not sure what that would accomplish," I said.

Poly had an answer in the form of a question that put one of our friends in jeopardy.

"Other than eliminating Queen Sherrhi so her sister could take the throne of the Dauushan empire?"

"Oh dear," said Emma Ann. "That means The General will have to kill Terrhi, too."

Spike sat up, put his massive front pair of paws on the table, and growled. I shared his concern.

"We'll get you back to Terrhi soon," I told the unhappy pink-striped feline. "I've got a great idea on how to ensure she's well-guarded. You'll like it."

I still wasn't sure how much Spike understood, but he stared at me with all three of his eyes for a moment, then resumed his spot under the table next to Max. Poly gave me a look and a secret smile. She could tell what I was thinking and liked it.

"You can call Martin after dinner," said my partner.

"I think we can count on Martin, local law enforcement and Homeplanet Security to handle conventional challenges like nova bombs," I said, wondering when congruency-powered nova bombs had become an everyday checklist item in my planning.

"You're going to focus on the stuff The General can do that's *unconventional?*" asked Emma Ann.

"That's how it's worked out so far," I said.

"Cool," said Emma Ann.

She got out of her chair and got down on the floor next to Spike, rubbing the fur on his back until a low-level purring hum filled the room. I could only imagine how loud the purring would be if Bavarian Kreem got her own trisabertooth. At least Spike wasn't suffering from lack of affection away from Terrhi.

Poly returned to her original question. I admired her focus.

"What *else* could The General do?" she asked the room. "What else unconventional?" she added.

"Giant robots?" suggested Pomy.

"We've got that covered," I said.

Poly nodded to back me up.

"A mercenary army?" offered Emma Ann from under the table.

"Homeplanet Security's problem," said Poly.

"From what I heard you had to handle a mercenary army yourself last First Contact Day," said Emma Ann.

Cornell winced.

"Now Homeplanet Security is on alert for mercenary armies," said Poly.

We could hope—though I wouldn't bet my life on it.

Chit blew grains of Parmesan out of her spiracles and buzzed over to the side of the table in front of Cornell, Rosalind and Sally.

"You three chumps have been awfully quiet," she said. "You worked for th' guy—whadda *you* think he's gonna do?"

"I'm afraid he's got something big planned," said Cornell.

"Really big," echoed Sally.

"There were rumors floating around the company," said Rosalind. "The General hates using non-Terran solutions, but corporate scuttlebutt indicated he might be planning to make an exception to that policy."

"Like he did with the Zelda Fitzgerald Pyr costume?" asked Emma Ann from the floor next to Spike.

"Something on a larger scale than disguising himself as an alien, I think," said Rosalind. "What I'd heard was along the lines of recruiting help from off-planet."

"Could they be referring to Lüzhiulterianne?" I asked. "She'd fit that description."

"Lüzhi seems like she'd be an off-planet resource who'd be mostly acting off-planet," said Rosalind, "and my rumor was about outside help for The General arriving here on Earth."

"Can you shake the tree and find out if your contacts can provide more details?" I asked.

"Of course," Rosalind replied. "I'll see if Mildred has picked up any additional information."

Mildred? Oh yeah. The receptionist at EUA's headquarters who'd called Rosalind *Rosey.*

"Great," said Poly. "Sounds like we'll have to be ready for any-thing."

"That seems to sum things up," said Pomy. "Given your lack of actionable intelligence, what are you going to do?"

"What we always do," said Poly.

I knew what came next, and completed her thought.

"Improvise!"

* * * * *

Poly had encouraged me to call it an early night, since we were both short on sleep and the next day would likely be interesting in all the various senses of that term. I'd called Martin to suggest something he could do to help us deal with contingencies. The two of us conferenced in Mike and he and the rest of the Xenotech Support team said they'd help get things ready.

Now I'd finished chewing on mints, brushing my teeth and gargling with strong mouthwash after chewing two sticks of chlorophyll gum. I was almost ready for Poly's inspection kiss. With luck, I'd pass and wouldn't have to request express delivery of a box of tiny Orishen arthropods to scour my mouth and eliminate any remaining hint of pepperoni. My amazing partner was already in bed, keeping it warm for my eventual, orally-sanitized arrival.

I rinsed and swirled with water and held my hand in front of my mouth. Then I breathed out through my mouth and sucked air in through my nose, trying to detect any presence of spicy sausage. So far, so good. I stripped and hung my clothes up on the back of the bathroom door. It was time for the picosecond of truth.

I knelt by Poly's side of the bed and leaned forward to kiss her. She stopped me with a hand between our lips.

"First things first, lover-boy," she said. "Exhale."

I did.

"Minty fresh," said Poly. "You pass phase one. Now kiss me."

I did that, too. Thoroughly.

"Get your butt in here," said Poly, patting the bed next to her. "I have plans for you tonight."

"Whatever you're planning, you know I'll just improvise," I replied, sliding under the covers and reveling in skin-to-skin contact.

"I'm counting on it," said Poly, "and expect to do some improvising of my own."

"Sounds like we're going to play jazz on a sax," I said, smiling.

"I'd prefer to change one letter," said Poly.

"Ploy?" I asked.

"Shut up," said Poly.

Soon I didn't have any need to talk. Before we'd moved from necking to any action *below* the neck, a tremendous booming knock rocked the door. It swung open with a crash and Terrhi and Bavarian barged in. Poly and I reacted with aplomb and pulled the sheets up to our chins. We'd been through this before. Using only our eyebrows we exchanged the obligatory *I thought* you *locked the door?* series of questions.

"Hi Uncle Jack, Aunt Poly," said Terrhi. "Where's Spike?"

"He's in Emma Ann's room," I said.

"Three doors down on the left," said Poly.

"Thanks," said Terrhi. "Bye."

The Dauushan girl started to leave the room.

"Wait," I said. "How did you get here? How did you even know where we were?"

"We took an autocab from Lenox Square Mall and Bavarian showed me how to track the transmitter in Spike's collar and got us out of the consulate without anybody seeing us and…"

Bavarian interrupted her friend.

"They don't need all the details," said Bavarian. "Sorry to bother you Mr. Buckston, Ms. Jones. Carry on."

I thought carrying on was what we'd been *doing!*

Bavarian had good manners, at least. She could have easily been a spoiled little rich girl. Instead, I was impressed she was so polite. Devious, but polite.

"Call me Mr. Jack," I said.

Really? said Poly's eyebrows.

Both girls left as quickly as they'd arrived. When I was sure they were gone, I got up and locked the door. I found a small triangular rubber doorstop and wedged it under the bottom of the door as well, just for insurance.

"We should have expected that," said Poly.

"Uh huh," I said.

"At least *now* we're alone and should stay that way," said Poly.

"Hold my calls," I told my phone, "for anything short of an Extinction Level Event."

My phone beeped in a familiar pattern. It was trying to figure out whether or not it should tease me and wisely decided not to.

I was glad I wouldn't have to disassemble it into its component parts tonight. I had more important things to do.

Chapter 40

"I owe it all to little chocolate donuts."
— John Belushi

I got up extra early on Sunday morning, took a shower and got dressed, being careful not to wake Poly. I timed things perfectly and could hear the whir of rotors from a small squadron of approaching drones as I entered the facility's lobby. They were transporting eight or ten boxes and bags with different company logos holding various options for breakfast—all paid for by Bavarian Kreem's generosity.

My phone and I had arranged things with Atlanta Drone-Hover Delivery for them to consolidate separate orders from Dunkin' Donuts, Krispy Kreme, Voodoo Donut, and Winchell's. There were even two boxes of Tim Horton's TIM-BITS for me that had been teleported into the Jackson Teleport Nexus straight from the store on Queen Street in Toronto. With their usual attention to detail, AD-HD had pulled all the disparate pieces together and gotten everything right—even the special high-protein donuts with no powdered sugar for Spike.

I'd requested most of my order to be made with the new patented Nicósn process that encapsulated donuts' fat molecules in insoluble shells *after* you eat them, so you could get the wonderful mouth feel of the ring-shaped treats without gaining weight. That was both a nod to the need to set a good nutritional example for Max and an appreciation of the fact that I didn't want to fall asleep in the middle of any adventures. Poly had reminded me of my tendency to zonk out shortly after consuming five or six conventional donuts. I didn't want any more incriminating photos of me napping with my mouth open posted on Spacebook.

Looking like a Sherpa hauling supplies to base camp, I carried the boxes and bags down to the conference room we'd been using for our meals and arranged all the goodies on the built-in counter. I laid out the donuts by type, not company, putting all the plain donuts on the left and the filled donuts to the right, with the frosted ones in between. It was difficult to resist sampling, so I compromised and popped a donut hole filled with galberry cream into my mouth, chewed, smiled and swallowed. Nobody would notice one missing donut hole, right?

There were three large tubs of fresh fruit on the far right, followed by a pink plaid box holding a volleyball-sized egg from some avian Dauushan, hard boiled, wrapped in spicy ground sausage, rolled in bread crumbs, and broiled. The plaid was the same pattern as the cummerbund on the tuxedo I'd worn to the awards banquet at the Teleport Inn a little over a week ago. It seemed appropriate for the alien equivalent of a Scotch Egg and I wondered if any of my friends would find that as amusing as I did.

Juice, milk, and soft drinks were already stocked in the conference room's capacious refrigerators. Coffee and hot water for tea were available from spigots on the wall attached to congruencies linked to Starbucks.

I removed a Diet Starbuzz from one of the fridges and used my phone to check the time. It was only six-thirty, so I sent a text to a friend and confirmed he'd be able to help with one of the contingency plans I'd figured out last night with Poly's help. She's great at brainstorming. Since I knew he was awake, I called Martin, double-checking he had everything in place to increase security for the G70 guests downtown.

"By the way," said Martin, "Tomáso gave me an update this morning. He said last night Terrhi and Bavarian insisted on coming on the tour today. I didn't object, since it would simplify logistics if they were all at Centennial Olympic Park. Terrhi was also adamant about reconnecting with Spike as soon as possible."

"She did that last night," I informed Martin. "Terrhi and Bavarian showed up here a few hours after dinner."

"What?" said Martin. "Tomáso thinks the girls are still sleeping in Terrhi's room."

"I'll let him know right away," I said. "He and Sherrhi are probably frantic. We'll bring them straight to the park with us."

"What a kid," said Martin.

"What *kids,*" I replied. "With both of them around, things get exponentially more interesting."

"Thanks for your help with the girls and Spike," said Martin. "Now we won't need the additional units from Emory to cover Ad Astra."

"They can be our reserves," I said. "Was my team helpful?"

"Incredibly helpful," said Martin. "Mike and CiCi and Ray Ray were great at calibration and testing, Shuvvath had an innate understanding of their morphic functionality, and Hither reactivated hundreds of octovac auxiliaries."

"Not bad for a talent management major, is she?" I asked, knowing the answer.

"Talent management?" asked Martin.

"The latest biz-speak for human resources," I replied.

"Right," said Martin. "I'd hire her any day."

"No poaching," I said, feigning indignation. "She's mine."

We laughed, but both of us knew good people like the ones Poly and I had hired were hard to find.

"Where are you staging the units?" I asked.

"Where you suggested—Mercedes-Benz Stadium."

"Will you keep the roof mostly open or closed?"

"Mostly closed," said my friend. "There will be enough room for them to move quickly if they're needed."

"They're only a hop, skip, and a jump away from the park," I noted.

"More like just a hop," said Martin. "We're talking seconds, not minutes."

"Great," I said. "Let's hope we don't need them."

"Let's hope," repeated Martin.

Neither one of us sounded very convinced we wouldn't.

"Where do you want us positioned?" I asked. "Should we meet you at the capitol building?"

"No, that's going to be enough of a zoo already," said Martin. "It's a more constrained environment and I think I have that part of things under control. I need you and your folks on the ground in the park. There's a lot more acreage to cover."

"Right," I said. "When do you expect the G70 dignitaries' motorcade to leave the capitol?"

"That depends on how much the top legislators want to milk their time in the spotlight."

"So somewhere around five in the afternoon?" I joked.

"The official schedule says they're supposed to leave the capitol building at ten."

I snorted my disbelief.

"Really?" I said. "What kind of odds do you give that they'll keep to that schedule?"

"Pretty good, actually," said Martin. "Homeplanet Security runs a tight ship."

"Getting hundreds of galactic bigwigs to follow a schedule will be a challenge even for them," I remarked.

"Less of one than you'd think," said Martin. "Most of the dignitaries are used to following tight timetables and being told where to go."

"Let's hope," I repeated. "What's the motorcade's route?"

"Mitchell Street to Central Avenue, past Underground Atlanta, up to Decatur Street, which turns into Marietta Street…" said Martin.

"…and Marietta Street runs right by the south end of Centennial Olympic Park," I completed. "Where are the delegates stopping first once they get there?"

"The World of Coke," said Martin. "Then the Georgia Aquarium—most of them, anyway. Some delegates are going to the Legislative Hall of Fame."

The Legislative Hall of Fame had replaced the College Football Hall of Fame when that museum had been enticed to move to Tuscaloosa, Alabama a few years back. Its building was across from the park, next to the CNN Center. I thought both museums were underwhelming, but legislators were a lot more popular with galactics than college football players, so it made sense some of the delegates would want to go there.

"We'll focus on the park itself and the two biggest attractions," I said.

I heard loud conversations in the background under Martin's voice.

"Thanks," said my friend. "Things are ramping up here. I've got to go. Good luck!"

"You, too," I said, but the line was already dead.

It was getting close to seven—the rest of the team would be here soon and I could enjoy some of the donuts without feeling guilty. I put my Diet Starbuzz down on the counter.

"Simon says, 'Reflective Mode,'" I commanded.

The smart wall changed into a mirrored surface. I didn't tell it to trigger its electrostatic cleaning function and eliminate Max's latest drawings—some of them were quite good and worth preserving. One resembled a circuit diagram and I resolved to talk to my son about proper electrical engineering safety practices in the near future.

I checked myself out and thought I'd done a good job of picking things to wear that would help me blend in with the Sunday morning tourists at the park. I was wearing khakis, tan socks, white Mutaswoosh sneakers, and a dark green polo shirt with a white collar and a small embroidered red dragon on the left breast. Mom had given me the shirt for Christmas a few years ago, after she'd returned from a consulting assignment in Cardiff.

To top off my look, I wore an aqua baseball cap with the Georgia Aquarium logo—a stylized capital *G* with a fish's tail. The cap was a *tchotchke* I'd received from the chief information officer at the aquarium two years ago after helping her people debug enrichment software for narwhals. Before I'd arrived, the software had enraged them so much that they were trying to pierce their tank with their tusks in hopes of returning to the sea.

Narwhals have excellent sight and hearing, so some geniuses had determined giving them a touch-based interface to pull up classic movies and music from the internet would make their highly constrained environment more tolerable. The only problem was that the developers tried to cut corners and used only ad-supported content. The constant annoying interruptions were making the narwhals so ticked off they would do anything to escape.

It only took me a few minutes to revise the code to point to commercial-free streams. I paid for the first year of the narwhal's subscriptions myself and signed up to keep doing it for the next several years as a tax-deductible contribution. The aquarium's chief information officer was impressed by the simplicity of my solution. She remarked—only somewhat in jest—that it was a good thing the developers never entered the narwhal's tank—they would have been skewered for sure.

As I left her office, the CIO got me with a zinger.

"What language is used to write most salt water aquarium software?" she asked.

I played along.

"I don't know, what?"

"C."

It took me a minute, because the code I'd just revised had been poorly designed Java. Then I got it.

"Ouch," I'd said.

I hadn't been back since.

I was pulled away from my reverie by Poly entering the room.

"You're looking spiffy," she said, meaning the opposite.

"You're pretty spiff yourself," I replied, meaning what I said.

Poly was wearing navy blue shorts, calf-high white cotton socks with little blue garter tabs, white Chuck Taylor All-Stars, and a jaunty white sailor shirt with navy piping. The shirt even had anchors embroidered on both sides of its broad collar. Her auburn hair was pulled back in a severe bun and a cute little sailor's cap was bobby-pinned to her head.

"Are you shooting for Sailor Moon?" I asked. I didn't know much about *anime*.

"No, silly," she said. "I'd need a blue skirt, red boots and a big red bow on my shirt for that."

"Okay," I said. "I give up. What *are* you trying to look like?"

"Me," she said. "I wore this the last time I went to the aquarium."

"When was that?" I asked. "When you were twelve?"

"Last Halloween," Poly replied.

She made a little moue that turned into a grin, gave me a peck and headed for the donuts. I had a lot to learn about my partner.

"Simon says, 'Reflective Mode Off,'" I told the smart wall.

It returned to normal. I didn't want anyone else to catch me looking at myself in the mirror.

Smart devices reacted to many different trigger phrases. My phone and my van had sophisticated language processing systems that knew when I wanted them to take action, but simpler systems needed more implicit key words. Most of the time, my phone just ordered them to act without me needing to say anything, but this morning I was feeling playful. Sometimes I'd use the *Computer* keyword, spoken with the intonation used on Star Trek to get the attention of the A.I. on the *Enterprise*. It was revealing to find out what other keywords my clients programmed their smart devices to recognize. *Safe word* made me scratch my head for a few seconds until my phone explained it to me.

"What smells so good?" asked Rosalind from the conference room door.

She didn't wait for an answer, but joined Poly at the counter, selecting the donuts and side items she wanted for breakfast. Cornell and Sally were close behind. From his expression, Cornell was one of those people who'd be grumpy until he had his first cup of coffee, while Sally looked bright-eyed and bushy-tailed, ready to meet the day without benefit of caffeine.

"Where's Max?" I asked.

Just then, my son made a grand entrance riding on Spike's back, holding on to the trisabertooth's ears for balance. For a moment I worried Max was bothering Spike, but the big cat seemed to enjoy having Max perched between his midlegs and forelegs. Maybe it helped loosen his spine. Bavarian was up on Terrhi's back and all four were trying to get through the door to the conference room at the same time. It didn't end well. Spike rolled back out of Terrhi's way, doing his best to protect Max.

Terrhi did a forward somersault—quite a feat for a hexa-pod—while Bavarian gracefully jumped up and out of the way, touching down just in front of Terrhi. Max was giggling as Spike lifted him back to his feet with a nudge from his massive head.

"That's a consensus 9.5 across the board except for a 7.5 from the Russian judge," said Emma Ann. She was close to the doorway, just behind the kids, and had witnessed the whole thing.

"It's not funny," said Terrhi, her dignity tarnished.

"Yes it is," said Bavarian. "Let's get some donuts."

"DONUTS!" shouted Max.

The kids rushed to the counter and filled their plates, while I reached over them to get the box of high-protein donuts for Spike. The cat stared at what I offered him, then faced me and gave me a you've-got-to-be-kidding look.

"Just try one," I said.

Spike lowered his head into the large box. When he emerged, all three of his extended incisors were different. A donut encircled each one. I kept my face impassive, knowing that if I laughed, Spike might never forgive me. I reached into the box and handed a donut to my long-toothed, furry friend. Spike chewed on it, moved it from side to side in his mouth, swallowed it, and started to purr.

"Told you," I said.

Spike's tongue rasped out and removed the donuts from his extra-long incisors one by one. The big cat was pleased and all was right with the world, sort of. He settled down with the box of donuts, taking his usual spot under the table next to Max. Rosalind graciously moved down a few chairs so Terrhi and Bavarian could be next to Max and Spike.

"Good morning, everybody," came a voice from the doorway. It was Pomy and she sounded like she was mostly back to normal. "Did I hear somebody mention donuts?"

"On the counter," said Poly after she'd swallowed a bite of French cruller. "There's fruit and a Dauushan Scotch Egg, too."

"Tea first, food second," said Pomy.

We only had teabags, but Pomy didn't complain. I got in line behind her, selecting a sturdy paper plate, a bowl for fruit, a couple of napkins, and an assortment of plastic silverware. I made my choices—an original glazed Krispy Kreme, an original plain-cake Dunkin' donut with a handle from Dunkin' Donuts, and in honor of Terrhi's new friend, a Bavarian Cream from Winchell's.

I filled my bowl with mixed Terran and galactic fruit salad and added a thick slice of Dauushan Scotch Egg to my already crowded plate. Carefully balancing my breakfast, I carried it to the table and sat between Poly and Max. I'd just gotten comfortable when I realized I had to get back up to retrieve my Diet Starbuzz from the counter where I'd left it earlier. For several minutes, everyone was focused more on eating than talking.

When most of us had finished and Spike was still noisily filling in the cracks, I reached out and tapped Chit's overturned tumbler with a fingernail to get people's attention.

"Hey, Daddy," said Max. "Where's Chit?"

I felt embarrassed I hadn't noticed my little friend was missing. My phone launched itself up to the light fixture in the ceiling and scanned the room. Then it jumped down to the table and walked to a stack of napkins near Chit's tumbler. It extended a pseudo-pod and carefully pulled back the top napkin, revealing a tiny carpet remnant left over from construction of the facility. Chit was on the carpet, comfortably snoring, as snug as a bug in a rug.

"Rise and shine, little buddy," I said.

"Go 'way," grumbled Chit. She made a sound like a yawn, though I don't think her breathing apparatus is designed to produce one.

"Okay," I said. "If that's how you want to play it."

I turned over Chit's tumbler so the opening was facing up and pulled out my Swiss Army knife, selecting the largest blade. Then I rapped the side of the glass sharply with the thick metal, sending high frequency sound waves in all directions, inches from Chit's ears and antennae.

"Alright, alright, I'm up, I'm up," protested Chit.

"Thanks," I said. "Grab some breakfast."

I slid my plate of crumbs toward my little friend and poured her a thimbleful of Diet Starbuzz.

"Martin wants us to concentrate on Centennial Olympic Park," I continued. "We need to pay special attention to any threats we can identify there. A few seconds of advance warning could make a big difference."

"Roger that," said Emma Ann.

"Cornell and Rosalind, please be on the lookout for anybody you know from EUA Corporation or one of their subsidiaries," I requested.

"Will do," said Cornell.

Rosalind nodded seriously.

"Pomy," I said, "You can hang out here and recuperate."

"No way," said Poly's sister. "I'm coming with you."

"Fine," I said, meaning it wasn't fine at all. "You can join us, but I would appreciate it if you could do me a favor first."

"What is it?" asked Pomy, tentatively.

"Can you take Bavarian, Terrhi and Spike down to the state capitol building so they get there just before nine? Terrhi needs to be with her family."

"I can do that," said Pomy.

"Can we leave right now?" asked Bavarian. "I need to pick something up on the way."

"Sure," said Pomy.

She stood up and brushed powdered sugar off her pale blue t-shirt. There was something printed on it in Latin.

"Cur etiam hic es?" asked Emma Ann.

"Why are you still here," said Poly.

"Huh?" said Emma Ann, looking a bit hurt.

"Not you," said Poly. "My sister's shirt. That's what it says."

"I'm leaving, I'm leaving," said Pomy. "Come on, kids. Let's go. Bye, everybody."

Pomy, Terrhi, Spike and Bavarian all left the conference room, heading up to the surface to catch an autocab.

I was confused and knew I'd missed something—then I remembered what I'd forgotten.

"Crap," I said. "I was supposed to let Tomáso know Terrhi was here with us."

"Already taken care of," said my phone. "They'll be expecting the girls at nine."

"Thank you," I said.

"What am *I* doing?" asked Max. He sounded unhappy to be left out of the action and less than pleased not to be going along with the girls and Spike.

Sally got up from her chair a and walked around to where Max was sitting. She leaned over and hugged his shoulders.

"Didn't I tell you? I'm taking you to the Georgia Aquarium."

"Wow!" said Max. His face seemed at least seventy percent smile. "Ichthyosaurs! Megalodons! Leviathantors!"

"What are Leviathantors?" I asked.

"They're from Tōdos and they're super-big and look like whales and squids and have so many teeth and tentacles and…"

"Got it," I said. "They're the ones on the posters."

"Uh huh," said Max. "And now I'm gonna see one!"

I simultaneously envied and didn't envy Sally taking Max to the aquarium.

It was time for the rest of us to leave. We closed the donut boxes and cleaned off the table, then headed topside to catch an autocab of our own.

Poly and I were holding hands and bringing up the rear as we walked to the lobby. Rosalind, Cornell and Sally were trying to keep up with Max with youthful assistance from Emma Ann.

"Hey," said Poly, intentionally bumping into me just for the sheer joy of additional contact. "What ever happened to Gus?"

"Good question," I replied. "I wonder how he did on his big audition."

Chapter 41

"All I need to make a comedy is a park,
a policeman, and a pretty girl."
— Charlie Chaplin

Our autocab turned left from Marietta Street onto Baker Street and dropped us off next to the Georgia Aquarium in the northern part of the park where the museums and major attractions were located. A dozen or more medium gray school-bus-type buses with opaque black windows were parked at the curb along Luckie Street.

My first thought was that they were for elementary students on a field trip, but there weren't any school names painted on their sides and Georgia school districts would never authorize the added expense of tinted windows. Besides, it was Sunday.

Poly nudged me—she'd seen them, too. Each bus probably held forty or fifty Homeplanet Security troops in full kit. I wasn't sure if that made me feel more or less comfortable. Still, it was nice to know the government wasn't taking any chances.

Our little clump of seven humans and a Murm stayed together as we walked along the south wall of the aquarium building. Giant posters in frames bolted to the wall advertised sea lions, belugas, penguins and more exotic aquatic creatures from Earth's past and across the galaxy. When the wall finally ended, we could see the entrance was down a level on the left, near a large courtyard. I'd never seen it from this side before, since I'd previously approached from the parking garage. The sunken open area was where people were waiting to get in. It was only nine in the morning and there was already a long line.

"Come on," said Max as he tugged on Sally's arm. "See you Daddy. Say hi to Terrhi and Bavarian and Spike for me!"

"Will do, sport," I replied. "Have fun, and no sushi for lunch."

"Ick," said Max.

"I thought you *liked* sushi?" remarked Rosalind.

"Uh huh, but not at an *aquarium!*"

I admired my son's sense of what was and wasn't appropriate dining in specific surroundings.

"Good hunting," said Sally.

Max was pulling her along like a Tibetan mastiff straining at a leash.

"Don't get eaten by a Leviathontor, kid!" shouted Chit to Max's receding back.

"I'm too little to make much of a meal for one of them," Max called over his shoulder. "But I'll watch out for ichthyosaurs and megalodons!"

At least *Max* would have a good time today.

"What now, Jack?" asked Rosalind. "Do you have a plan?"

"Yes," I said. "I think we should manage our investigation by wandering around, like Tom Peters advised in his book, *In Search of Excellence.*"

"Where did you dig up *that* old chestnut?" asked Poly "Everything in it has been disproved."

"Not quite everything," I said. *"Management by wandering around* is still a thing. I found the book in the chief engineer's office at the Aswan Dam when I was nine."

"Peters didn't originate the concept, you know," said Poly. "Hewlett Packard and a few other companies in Silicon Valley had been using it for years before his book came out."

Poly spoke on the topic with the confidence and authority of a newly minted M.B.A.

"I didn't claim he did," I protested.

"Some say Abraham Lincoln invented the style when he dropped in to check on Union troops during the Civil War," said Rosalind.

Her observation surprised me and made me realize I didn't know anything about Rosalind's formal education. I'd have to remedy that lack.

"It wasn't Lincoln," Cornell asserted. "It was Twain back in the Gold Rush days when he…"

Rosalind, Poly, Emma Ann and I started laughing. Cornell stopped short and looked miffed.

"Sorry, bro," said Rosalind. "There's an old joke about attributing everything said in the nineteenth century to Mark Twain."

"And everything out of the eighteenth to Benjamin Franklin," said Emma Ann. "I learned about that in my Internet Skepticism class last year."

Cornell shrugged, giving up. I think he knew he'd lost.

"All you lunks are wrong," said Chit. "It was Ahksedhet, the head of construction on Cheops' pyramid. He used to take a bag of sweet dates around with him and share them with the guys on the crews so they'd tell him what was really going on."

"Yeah, right," said Cornell. "How would you know? There weren't any aliens on Earth until First Contact."

Chit guffawed. Crackling wheezy noises came out of her spiracles.

"Believe what you want, but I was there," said my little friend. "Though that scarab beetle outfit I had to wear itched like the blazes when it got hot, and it was *always* hot."

"Wait," I said. "Hold on. You're almost five thousand years old?"

"Over five thousand, buddy boy."

"Why didn't you tell me?" I asked. "There was so much I could have learned."

"Ya never asked," said Chit. "Your momma raised your right, so you knew never t' ask a lady her age. An' it's not somethin' I was just gonna volunteer."

I glanced at Rosalind and saw she had a big smile on her face.

"This means the wackos were right," she said. "Space aliens *did* help build the pyramids."

"Incorrect," asserted Chit. "I never lifted an appendage, though I may have offered ol' Ahksedhet, the head project manager, some common-sense advice from time t' time."

"Fascinating," said Rosalind. "Like what?"

"Well, back in the day, there was a major problem with too many workers chewin' khat," said my little friend. "They would forget t' eat and wouldn't be strong enough t' move stone blocks."

"Khat?" asked Emma Ann.

"The African equivalent of coca leaves in the Andes," I said.

"Anyway, Ahksedhet could see things were fallin' behind schedule, and he didn't like contemplatin' the Pharaoh's probable reaction t' project delays, so he needed to act quickly."

"Go on," encouraged Rosalind.

"I did some reconnoiterin' by wanderin' around and identified the *bast*ard who was providin' the *khat*," said Chit. "The joker was the supervisor in charge of the hydraulic system for liftin' the blocks on the east side. He had contacts with traders down in Sheba who'd bring the drugs in, then he'd handle distributin' the vile stuff."

Bast-ard? Bast was the Egyptian cat goddess. I'd have to come up with a good one to pull on Chit later.

"Hydraulic system?" asked Emma Ann.

"Look it up," I whispered. "Keywords are *pyramid* and *water shaft theory.*"

"What he said," confirmed Chit. "Anyway, I left a scrap of papyrus for Ahksedhet lettin' him know about the pusher and he took the appropriate steps t' solve the problem."

"What did Ahksedhet do?" asked Emma Ann.

"Let's just say Jimmy Hoffa wasn't the first person to be incorporated into a major construction project," said Chit.

I couldn't tell if Chit was feeding us a line of b.s. or not, but my little friend sure knew how to spin a story. If it was true, *requies-khat in pace* for the hydraulics supervisor.

Rosalind had a harder time swallowing Chit's tale.

"Yeah, yeah," she said. "Next you'll be telling us about Atlantis."

"You mean Akrotiri on Santorini," said Chit. "The ancient Cycladic civilization on the island of Thera before it blew up."

"Whatever," said Rosalind.

She turned to me.

"It sounds like your plan is not to have a plan," she said.

"That's about it," I said. "We'll just have to observe and improvise."

"I can do that," said Rosalind.

"And you're *good* at it," said Cornell.

"This is going to be *fun!*" said Emma Ann.

I hoped she was right.

The four of us walked into the concrete-covered area between the aquarium and the World of Coke. Not far away, caterers were setting up what promised to be a lavish buffet for the G70 visitors and their guests. I smiled when I saw a dozen or more white vans unloading tables, chairs appropriate for diverse species, table linens, coolers and hotboxes. I wondered if Mike had gotten the bullet holes in my white van repaired yet. Its glass was bulletproof, its side panels not so much.

It was a beautiful day with only a few fluffy clouds in the sky and temperatures in the mid-seventies. Large birds or Quirinx fliers soared high above on rising air currents. Centennial Olympic Park was twenty-one acres of lush, well-tended grass crisscrossed by dozens of interwoven concrete paths. The buildings housing the park's top attractions congregated at its north end like a small herd of grazing Ubercows. To the east, across Centennial Olympic Drive, brooded the black bulk of EUA's corporate headquarters, while the CNN Center and the mile-high needle of the SLN Tower were on the far side of Marietta Street to the south. A small stage used for public concerts anchored the far south end of the park.

Poly and I would focus on the area around the aquarium and the World of Coke. After a quick discussion, it was agreed that Rosalind and Cornell would check for suspicious activity close to EUA HQ. Emma Ann would head south and see if she spotted anything odd down by the stage. I asked her to text me if she saw any signs of the motorcade approaching. She left with a wave and a bounce in her step. For her, this was just an adventure. Rosalind and Cornell left too, and Poly and I were alone.

Scratch that. Poly, *Chit* and I were alone. I didn't expect any delegates to show up for at least an hour.

Poly took my hand and the two of us strolled the park, two young lovers enjoying the day—while surreptitiously scoping out the other beings in the vicinity. Chit crawled under my shirtcollar so she didn't distract from the idyllic image Poly and I were projecting.

"Homeplanet Security agent at six o'clock," said Chit.

"I see her," said Poly.

"So do I," I agreed.

Reflective buildings like the World of Coke make spotting tails a lot easier, except that I didn't think the woman in dark sunglasses was intentionally following us. From what I could tell, she was doing what we were doing—checking out the area and assessing potential threats to the visiting dignitaries. That was standard procedure.

"Homeplanet Security agent at eight o'clock," said Chit. "And four o'clock."

"There's five of them at eleven o'clock waiting outside the World of Coke," said Poly, "and one more beyond them standing on a brown sewer maintenance access disk at one o'clock."

My mind distracted me, wondering if it was a chocolate-covered manhole cover.

"How can you tell they're agents?" I asked

"They're all wearing identical sunglasses," said Poly.

"Standard government issue?"

"Correct," my partner replied. "With built-in access to facial recognition systems and law enforcement databases. The guards at the Terran ambassadors' parties my mom dragged me to off-planet all wore them."

"You were an observant young lady," I said.

"I'm still all three," said Poly with a grin.

"Just not quite as young as ya used t' be," said Chit.

"Hey," said Poly. "Look who's talking, grandma."

"That's great-great-*great*-grandma to you!" Chit retorted.

Poly squeezed my hand and we all laughed.

"Chit, would you mind doing a short flit?" I asked. "There's some personal stuff I want to discuss with Poly. Take a quick flight up by the Civil Rights Museum or something."

"Sure, bucko," said my little friend. "I'll give ya your privacy. Remember t' hold out for at least three cows, five goats and a plow."

My face turned red. So did Poly's.

"That's *not* what I want to talk about," I said.

"I'm glad to hear it," said Poly, managing to look simultaneously relieved and a bit disappointed.

"See ya, chumps," said Chit.

She buzzed off my shoulder, heading northeast.

I tugged Poly farther along until we reached a park bench. We sat together, still holding hands.

"What did you want to talk about?" asked Poly.

"Living arrangements," I answered.

"I prefer living to the alternative, don't you?" teased Poly.

"Your apartment is tiny," I began. "And Pomy is—or at least *was* living in it."

"Uh huh," said Poly.

She wasn't making this easy.

"I've got plenty of room at my place," I began.

"Which is currently serving as the business office for Xenotech Support Corporation," Poly observed.

"Well, yes, but that's temporary," I said. "We can find some real office space once we deal with The General."

"I certainly hope so," said Poly. "All the best startups begin in garages, not apartments."

"Yes, but," I said, trying to get the words out. "Since you're already spending a lot of time at my apartment…"

"And since my classes and homework projects are over," Poly encouraged.

"I thought you could move in with me."

Poly kissed me and did a very nice job of it, with my enthusiastic cooperation. I'm sure she convinced any agents observing us that we were just what we seemed to be—a pair of young lovers enjoying the park.

"Of *course* I'll move in with you, Jack. I thought you knew I was fine with that. We'd talked about it. I was just waiting until I finished all my classes because I didn't want the distraction."

"I'm a distraction?" I said, smiling.

"Stop fishing for compliments. Of course you are," said Poly, "and I plan to distract you right back."

"Sounds wonderful," I said.

"When it comes to the logistics—like when we can get Xenotech Support real office space—we'll just have to improvise and figure things out as we go," said Poly.

"That gives us extra incentive to get new space for the corporation quickly," I said.

"Absolutely," said Poly. "I don't want to go back to my old apartment. Pomy is welcome to stay there until she can find something better."

"If she can *afford* something better," I said, knowing how little the Carlos Museum paid its professional staff.

"When we have to clear out of the research facility," I said, "we can move into a suite at a hotel in Ad Astra. We can afford it."

"That would be fine," said Poly, "so long as we're not there for six months or something."

She kissed me again. It was nice.

My phone climbed off my belt, extended its humanoid pseudo-pods, and stood with a foot on each of our legs. It waved its pseudo-arms to get our attention, which took a while.

"Internal emails to the Ad Astra management company report that several tenants are using the explosion at the Dauushan consulate as a reason to exercise the escape clauses in their leases," said my phone. "There's a space that would work well for XSC not far from the consulate that would be a good fit for a growing consultancy."

Poly and I spoke at the same time.

"Reserve it."

"Already did," said my phone. "It will be available in a week. The current tenants are moving to a new facility near Hartsfield Port. Also, the new negotiated rent is below market levels because Ad Astra doesn't want the space sitting empty and giving other tenants ideas."

"Thank you, thank you," I said, rubbing the back of my phone's mutacase like it was a kitten.

"I'm so glad you know when to exercise initiative," said Poly.

She picked up my phone and kissed it in the middle of its screen, which promptly turned red. When she put it down again, my phone chirped happily.

"One more thing," it said. "Emma Ann just texted. She's spotted the motorcade."

Chapter 42

"I accept chaos, I'm not sure whether it accepts me."
— Bob Dylan

I sent Rosalind a text about Emma Ann's report. Poly and I would join Emma Ann to watch the motorcade's arrival while Rosalind and Cornell continued to observe EUA for anything fishy. My brain suggested they'd be more likely to find something fishy at the aquarium, but by now I was getting used to its foolishness. From their vantage point on a patch of grass just south of the World of Coke, they could spot inimical activity from EUA while also scanning for would-be tourists who weren't what they seemed.

Poly and I dropped hands and trotted across Baker Street and down an arrow-straight north-south path that led to the stage. Two of the Homeplanet Security agents stared at us, but they didn't seem to consider us a threat. The motorcade was noisy—sirens were blaring and lights were flashing—so quite a few park visitors were moving in the same direction we were.

As we hurried along, my phone chirped.

"Incoming call from Shepherd."

"Put him on speaker."

"Jack? I can see you and Poly. Be aware that there are barricades in place to keep the spectators back from the delegates. You won't be able to get very close."

"Understood," I said. "It's more important that Poly and I scan the crowd for troublemakers."

"Where are you?" asked Poly. "In the top gondola of the SkyView ferris wheel?"

The giant rotating structure was just north of EUA headquarters. I turned my head in its direction and saw its slow spin.

"Why would I be there?" asked Shepherd. "Half the time I'd be too low to see properly."

Why indeed? I wondered.

"So where *are* you?" asked Poly.

"On the roof of the CNN Center," replied the Pâkk. "I can see everything from here with binoculars—I don't need drones."

"Sometimes low-tech is best," I said.

"You've got time to check black hats," said Shepherd. "Once all the delegates and their guests arrive, Martin tells me there's going to be a huge photo op with everybody on the stage."

"Except the Tōdons and Dauushans," said Poly.

"Except them," confirmed Shepherd. "Martin says they'll be at ground level."

"The photographers better have really wide-angle lenses," I quipped.

"Not our problem," said Shepherd.

The grizzled Pâkk's sense of humor was somewhat limited.

"What's your take?" asked Poly. "Will there be some sort of attack or disruption during the photo op? When they are moving from their vehicles to the stage? On their way up to the World of Coke and the aquarium?"

"I don't know one way or the other," said Shepherd. "Neither does Martin. All we've heard is the meeting will be disrupted when the G70 delegates are in the park."

"That does imply there won't be an attack on the motorcade," I offered. "After all, it won't technically be *in* the park."

"I doubt The General and his minions will be overly concerned with fine points of nuance," said Shepherd.

"So we have no idea when, where, or if something is going to happen?" asked Poly.

"Correct," said Shepherd. "You'll just have to wing it."

"Right," I said.

What else is new?

Poly and I had reached the row of waist-high metal barricades separating the crowd from the stage. We were seventy-five yards back and had a good view of the delegates walking in from Marietta Street. The Musans came rolling up on their Segway-like transports, observing their surroundings from Plexiglas hamster balls mounted on long titanium poles that lifted them up to human eye level. A clutch of J'Vel came next. They were mouse-sized, but lizard-like aliens shaped like miniature velociraptors riding in their own *balls-on-sticks* conveyances.

Behind the Musans and J'Vel crawled three craggy, rock-like Thortans, each about twice as big as a Roomba automated vacuum cleaner. They flowed along the path on a layer of superheated steam below their magma-hot ventral surfaces. Thortans usually got their water supply from congruencies linked to bodies of liquid on their planet. The first two, leading the way, appeared to be the parents of the third, a juvenile. He was carrying a small riveted copper water tank on his back and had attached dozens of gears to his upper surface. I smiled, remembering back when *I* was into steampunk.

Two Pâkk contingents—one for each of their philosophical camps—came next. A buffer of Pyrs came between the Pâkk and the Tigrammath delegations. Poly and I spotted Roger Joe-Bob Bacon in with the Pyrs, while Bart Urrrson and Niaowla Murriym, professors at Georgia Tech and Emory, respectively, walked with the tall felines. I'd known Roger Joe-Bob was a mover and shaker, but didn't realize Bart and Niaowla were held in such high esteem by their own species. We waved, but they were too far away and too preoccupied to see us.

"Isn't this exciting?" said Emma Ann.

She startled me. I'd been so focused on the parade of G70 dignitaries that I hadn't been paying proper attention to my surroundings and hadn't noticed her joining us.

"It certainly is," said Poly. "Do you recognize all the different alien species?"

"I know the Nicósns," said Emma Ann, pointing at the incoming stream of life forms moving toward the stage. "And isn't that lady somebody famous? Are those her pets?"

I took a look at where Emma Ann's finger directed. Mistress Marigold was a prominent member of the Nicósn delegation, with several mini-Drees running in and out around her legs. The mischievous mobile plants had gotten bigger in the past week.

"Yes," I replied. "She runs a big company down by the Atlanta Botanical Gardens. Mistress Marigold is an XSC client."

"And no," said Poly, "they're not her pets. They're more like attractive nuisances."

"They're cute," said Emma Ann.

"Until you get to know them," I said.

Next in the procession were three odd looking machines, like heavy-duty forklifts specially modified for transporting thick metal rings. The rings were about ten feet in diameter and seemed to be circular frames around Harry Potter-style portraits with moving images inside them.

"What they heck are…" I began.

"I know what they are," broke in Emma Ann. "They're mobile congruencies. I'll bet there are species on the other side that can't handle Earth's atmosphere or gravity."

She seemed pleased to be able to enlighten me about something other than popular culture. I could see gilled, vaguely humanoid aliens inside the nearest ring. They were surrounded by a greenish haze I supposed must be from trace amounts of chlorine. When I thought about it, I was glad there was a sheet of sturdy polymer separating them from Terran air.

We patiently watched as rank after rank of delegates and their guests processed in. I had to stop myself from laughing as a quorum of elderly Quirinx waddled up the walk like a so many emperor penguins. Behind them came the Dauushan delegation, with Queen Sherrhi and Tomáso in the lead. A pair of royal bodyguards marched a few steps behind them, and an assortment of what I assumed were Dauushan business leaders came next, in rows two abreast.

Wait! Where was Terrhi? And Spike? And Bavarian? Where was Pomy, for that matter?

"Hi, Uncle Jack!" said a familiar piping voice behind me.

I turned around, finding several of my questions answered.

"Hi Terrhi! Hi Spike!" I said. "How did you get away from your family?"

"And your bodyguards?" added Poly.

Terrhi was a few feet away from us, with Spike by her side. The big cat didn't look that happy. The Dauushan girl didn't have a chance to answer before Bavarian pushed her way through the crowd. Actually, she didn't have to push—the throng parted in front of her. I soon saw the reason why. The biggest dog I'd ever seen—if it was a dog—was irresistibly pulling her along. The creature's head almost came up to my shoulders and its white coat was covered with black and brown blotches.

"What. Is. *That?*" asked Emma Ann.

The young woman backed away, eying the huge beast warily.

"He's an *epicyon,*" said Bavarian.

Poly, Emma Ann and I stared at Bavarian, then at the beast, moving our heads from side to side like we were trying to follow a tennis match.

"His species existed five to twenty million years ago," Bavarian continued. "Scientists brought them back through genetic engineering."

"Wouldn't it have been wiser to let them remain extinct?" I asked.

The huge beast cocked its head and gave me a look that made me wonder if it understood what I'd said. Then it tugged on its chain and made me worry about whether or not it wanted me for dinner.

"Heel, boy," said Bavarian. "I was going to get a Dauushan trisabertooth, then I saw a picture of an epicyon in an oligarch's catalog and knew I had to have one. Pomy helped me pick him up on our way to the capitol building. He's from ITBB Corporation."

"ITBB?" asked Emma Ann.

"Impossible Things Before Breakfast," said Poly.

"They're the company that engineered the ichthyosaurs and megalodons for the aquarium," I said, remembering an article I'd read in the *Atlanta Business Journal* while I was recuperating from my injuries back in April.

"Woof," said Poly respectfully.

The big prehistoric dog nodded at her. Spike looked at her sideways, keeping at least one of his three eyes on Bavarian's new pet at all times.

"He seems well trained, anyway," Poly noted.

"The company did that before I could get him," said Bavarian. "They said it wouldn't be safe otherwise."

"I can believe *that,*" said Emma Ann.

"Your new companion explains why you don't have bodyguards around, Terrhi," said Poly.

"Sort of," said the Dauushan girl. "Mom and Dad were kinda busy when we got to the capitol building and security there wasn't happy about letting us in with an epicyon, so we didn't stay."

"Oh," I said, sensing Bavarian's influence at work.

"Terrhi's parents expected us to be with you," said Bavarian, "and we figured you'd be at the park, so here we are."

That made sense, from a child's perspective. I'm glad we were able to link back up with the girls. I'd need to give Tomáso a heads up on their whereabouts as soon as the photo op was over.

"What did you name your new pet?" I asked the human girl, not knowing what to expect.

"Looking at him, I think I know," said Poly.

She let the beast smell the back of her hand then rubbed his mottled coat.

"His name is Spot," said Bavarian.

Spot and Spike, I thought. *How perfect.*

"*There* you are," said Pomy as she rushed up to join us. "I told you to wait for me while I paid for the autocab."

"Sorry, Aunt Pomy," said Terrhi.

"He started tugging and I had to follow him," said Bavarian, indicating Spot.

I remembered what she'd said about her new pet being well-trained and smelled another one of Bavarian's machinations. Spike rubbed his head against Pomy's hip in sympathy and collected a few scritches.

"Woof," said Spot.

My thoughts exactly.

We all turned back to watch the last delegation enter the park and lumber to the area in front of the stage. The four members of the Tōdon contingent positioned themselves behind the Dauushans at ground level. A delegate-wrangler with a bullhorn did her best to move all the dignitaries into good positions for publicity photographs.

One of the Musans rolled his or her ball-on-a-stick conveyance out onto the carapace of the Tōdon closest to the stage. There was a joker in every crowd. The wrangler convinced the Musan to return to position, then congruency-powered flash bulbs began to strobe.

I closed my eyes to prevent the bright lights from blinding me. When I opened them, hundreds of shock troops in black Macerator armor were pouring out of every manhole in the vicinity.

Chapter 43

"...the good thing about chaos is you don't get time to think much."
— Nomadic Wonderings Blog

"I've got a bad feeling about this," said Poly, only half in jest.

"Pomy, Emma Ann, please get Terrhi and Bavarian to cover," I said.

The armored shock troops were massing around the stage, confronting small contingents of city of Atlanta police. The space on the other side of the temporary metal barriers was a milling tangle of black and blue, while more Macerators and green-armored Homeplanet Security forces were moving toward us at high speed from the north. I estimated those two forces would collide close by, leaving us caught between hammer and anvil.

"Where should we go?" asked Pomy.

"We're cut off," said Emma Ann.

"Make for the trees," said Poly.

Three tall oaks stood near our current position. Their crowns were vividly green with new spring leaves. It only took us a few seconds to reach them, but I quickly realized the oaks wouldn't provide protection.

Bavarian pointed eight feet up the trunk of the nearest tree, where the branches began to split and, well, branch.

"Spike could climb up there," she said, "and so could I, but I don't think Terrhi or Spot could make it."

The big cat leapt up into the lowest branches as if his body was made out of springs, just to prove Bavarian's point. Spike hid his striped form in the shadows of the leaves.

I looked back at the metal barricades—they might work as ladders for differently shaped species, but there was no way we'd get Terrhi's hexapod Shetland pony-sized form up one of the trees, even with a makeshift ladder.

Dozens of Macerators were running past the oaks, charging toward the stage, and larger numbers of Homeplanet Security troops were catching up to them. So far, none of the Macerators had attacked us, but it was only a matter of time until we were noticed.

"You're right," I said, scanning frantically for a way to escape.

"Look out, Uncle Jack!" shouted Terrhi.

I turned and saw a couple of figures in black Macerator armor trotting toward us. They were stragglers from the main group and one of them must have spotted us—or more likely, spotted Terrhi. I suspected they had orders to look for her. Pomy and Emma Ann positioned themselves in front of the girls, with Spot crouched behind Bavarian. Poly and I stood side-by-side and drew our mini-sweeteners. They wouldn't be much good against anyone in armor, but they were all we had for weapons.

Our attackers weren't so limited. They carried dual-barreled over-under slug-thrower and sweetener rifles and came in under the trees with us, their weapons pointed our way. With our Orishen pupa-silk shirts, Poly and I might be able to survive a slug to the torso or shrug off a shot from a sweetener's molasses chill field, but none of the rest of our party could.

"Hands up," grunted the lead Macerator.

"Yeah," said the second one, sounding like he would have been challenged by two syllable words.

I dropped my mini-sweetener and raised my hands. So did Poly and Emma Ann. Pomy, however, remained frozen in place for a couple of heartbeats. The two Macerator operators stared at Poly's sister—or at least their heads faced in her direction. It was hard to tell because of their opaque visors.

Pomy began to whimper and wring her hands, imploring the Macerators not to hurt her. Emma Ann played along and did the same. The young women had a good act. Once Pomy was sure she had their attention, she fell to her knees, feigning terror. Emma Ann, with all her Remote Hands training, mimicked Pomy's movements. They both bowed low until their heads touched the grass. It seemed like they were performing an obeisance to Allah or doing a yoga pose named after some contorted animal.

With Pomy and Emma Ann's screening bodies out of the way, Spot made a flying leap over Bavarian and Terrhi, striking the lead Macerator with significant force, the product of his two-hundred-and-fifty pounds of mass and all the acceleration his muscular legs could impart. I remembered that Macerator armor had a stability problem, and this unit was no exception.

The lead Macerator fell on his back with Spot's full weight on top of him. The weapon he'd been holding flew into the air. The second man couldn't react fast enough before a similar fate befell *him*. Spike jumped down from his concealed perch in the tree, turning the second armored attacker into an overturned turtle as well.

Poly caught the first attacker's weapon before it hit the ground. She pointed it at the second man, who was still holding his double-barreled rifle. It was awkwardly wedged between his chest plates and a hundred and fifty pounds of unhappy trisabertooth. I extricated the weapon from his grasp and removed the man's helmet. He was a real loser, probably plucked from a prison somewhere. His face was covered in Chinese character tattoos and I didn't have the heart to tell him what the tattoo artist had pulled on him.

Pomy came over with our mini-sweeteners and zapped the man, freezing him in place for at least an hour. I shoved him on his side and Emma Ann removed his power pack cylinders, turning his armor into an effective prison. We repeated the process with the other attacker. It seemed that The General hadn't improved his hiring practices in the past fortnight. The forces of Good will always triumph over the forces of Evil so long as Evil insists on only paying its minions minimum wage.

"Everybody okay?" asked Poly.

"Yes," said Bavarian, a bit more subdued than usual.

"That was *fun!*" exclaimed Terrhi. She was excited enough for both of them.

"Maybe for *some* definitions of the word," I said.

"Don't be a stick in the mud, Uncle Jack," said Terrhi.

"He has to be a stick in the mud," said Pomy. "So does Poly, so does Emma Ann, so do I. We're adults. We protect kids."

Bavarian pulled a shiny metal tube that looked like a toy fife from her pants pocket.

"This kid can protect herself," she said.

She pushed a small button on the tube and a beam of red light sliced off a branch above us, sending a dozen leaves to the ground. I realized her toy fife must be a variable beam congruency-powered laser and felt both more and less worried for Bavarian's safety.

"Jack and I still have to get you kids out of here," said Poly.

"But we want to *help!*" said Terrhi.

"The best thing you two can do to help is get to someplace safe so we don't have to worry about you," I said. "Once that's accomplished, Poly and I can pitch in to help Martin's people save the G70 dignitaries."

"Jack," said Pomy, tugging on my sleeve. "We may be in for more trouble."

Emma Ann had seen something, too. She was pointing at a white van speeding our way from the north. Poly and I put our captured rifles to our shoulders and stood tensely at the ready, awaiting the new threat, while Pomy, the girls, and their pets hid behind tree trunks. I knew it wasn't *my* white van, which meant the unknown vehicle could be trouble. When it got close enough for me to read the letters printed in reverse on its hood, I put my hand on Poly's forearm.

"We can stand down," I said. "I think it's friends of ours."

Poly smiled when she recognized the van. She slung her rifle out of the way over her shoulder. Bavarian put away her laser.

"What's a Teleport Inn catering van doing at Centennial Olympic Park?" asked Bavarian.

"They're probably setting up a buffet for the G70 attendees and their guests," I guessed. "I saw the tables near the World of Coke."

"Kijanna!" shouted Poly when the van reached our deciduous refuge. "Pierre! And François!"

The young human woman at the wheel hopped out and gave Poly a quick hug. She was wearing an elegantly cut little black dress that I assumed was her working uniform as a greeter.

"Good to see you, Mademoiselle Poly—and Monsieur Jack," said Pierre Auguste Escoffier, the tuxedo-wearing Pyr and *maître d'hôtel* of the Teleport Inn where Poly had once worked translating menus. He'd descended from the passenger seat and flowed over to us on his mobility cilia.

"It is a pleasure to be of service to you and your associates," said François, the Inn's top waiter. He was always a consummate service professional. François had come from the back of the van and left its double doors open.

"Thanks for your help," said Poly. "This is Emma Ann, a friend and business associate of Jack's.

Emma Ann curtsied, putting a finger to her chin at the end.

"Enchanté, dear lady," said Pierre, bowing in return.

Poly continued. "You remember my sister, Pomy, and Terrhi the royal princess of Dauush?"

"But of course," said Pierre, "and her clever cat, Spike, as well."

Spike acknowledged the complement with a bob of his massive head.

"This is Terrhi's friend, Bavarian and her pet, Spot," continued Poly.

"Mademoiselle and *nice doggy,"* said Pierre, diffidently.

Spot had moved closer to check out the little alien. His broad shoulders were higher above the ground than the top of the Pyr's pointy head.

"I'm glad we brought enough ubercow steaks to feed an army," muttered François softly.

"What was that?" asked the Pyr.

"Nothing," said François.

"How did you know we needed you?" asked Poly.

Kijanna looked puzzled.

"Jack sent me a text."

"Right," I confirmed, giving my phone an appreciative squeeze. I *loved* its initiative.

"Can you get my sister, the girls, and their pets out of harm's way?" asked Poly.

"We can get them to our buffet location," said Kijanna.

"That will have to do," said Poly with a thin-lipped smile.

"Wait a second," said Pomy. "I want to help, not be out of the action."

"Me too," said Emma Ann.

"You can both help by making sure the girls are safe," I said.

Then I remembered a famous quote. "They also serve who only stand and wait."

"Don't I know it," said François under his breath.

We reclaimed our mini-sweeteners from Pomy—they had plenty of firepower with Bavarian's laser and Emma Anne's weapons. They also had plenty of muscle with Spot and Spike. Terrhi used her arms to lever herself into the back of the van. The rear compartment was crowded with two large animals, a juvenile Dauushan, and four humans, but they fit. We waved as Kijanna shut the loading doors and they drove away, the G-below-Middle-C drone of their van sounding like a mellow cello, not my van's familiar bassoon.

Poly and I tried to make out what was going on down by the stage. It was a blur of black and green dotted with blue. I could see the Tōdon delegates—they were hard to miss—and a knot of three or four Dauushans, but we didn't have the right angle or enough altitude to see more.

"Climb one of the trees to get a better view?" I suggested.

"Too many leaves in your way to be useful," said Poly. "Why not ask your phone to play drone?"

"That's why," I said, pointing at a dozen camouflaged Home-planet Security hunter-killer drones painted to look like turkey buzzards. "They have air-to-air missiles."

"Got it," said Poly. "So why did you encourage Chit to go airborne?"

"She's not big enough to attract their interest," I said.

I hope, I thought. I wished I had my backpack tool bag. If I had my climbing tools, I could shimmy up one of the nearby light poles.

Then something tickled. My phone was crawling up the front of my torso along the strap of my spoils-of-war rifle until it got to my shoulder.

"Binoculars-mode is a specialty," it said in a voice imitating C-3PO.

Poly gave me a you-should-have-known-that look and we both checked out my phone's screen as it showed us more details of the confusion near the stage. Now we could see what was happening in the pink blur. Tomáso and Diágo, the head of the queen's security team, were on either side of Queen Sherrhi, trying to protect her from attacking Macerators. They'd used one of the Tōdon delegates as a substitute for a wall, so they had one less side to defend.

I watched as an attacker slipped past Diágo, requiring Sherrhi to grab him in her sub-trunks and send him sailing back twenty yards or more into the milling mass of Macerators. Homeplanet Security's forces were much better trained, and were trying to help the queen, but they were outnumbered by four to one and had to protect *all* the delegates, not just the ones from Dauush.

"We've got to get down there," I said. "Our friends need us."

"I agree," said Poly, "but how? We can't fight our way through that meat grinder."

"There is a way," said my phone.

"Enlighten us," I requested.

"Before congruencies changed things, all the attractions at the north end of the park were heated by steam from a generating plant a few blocks south," it said.

"I'd heard about those old steam tunnels," I said, "but won't they be full of Macerators?"

"I don't see any more Macerators coming out of manholes," said Poly. "The tunnels are probably empty now."

"What sort of probability do you attach to that *probably?*" I asked.

"He never wants to be told the odds," said my phone to Poly, still using C-3PO's voice.

Poly laughed. I made a Grumpy Cat face.

"Where's the nearest entrance to the steam tunnels?" I asked.

"Five feet ahead of you," said my phone. "Look down."

I did. It was grate.

"Mutakey service, please," I requested.

My phone jumped down to the six-foot steel grate installed flush with the ground. It was secured by a simple padlock hanging down at the near side. I assumed the grate was originally placed here to help moderate the temperature in the park during the winter by allowing some steam to escape. In seconds, the padlock was open and my phone was happily congratulating itself on its own resourcefulness.

I had to tug extra-hard to get the grate to move. I think the hinges had rusted in the past decade or so since the widespread use of congruent energy. Finally, it moved, with a sound a lot like those ominous creaks you hear when doors that should remain closed are opened in horror movies. At least now it was daylight.

I put my fears aside and located the metal rungs of a ladder made from bent reinforcing rods embedded in the wall of the shaft leading down into the steam tunnel.

Hadn't they made a Dungeons & Dragons movie about adventures in steam tunnels?

"Flip you for who goes first," I offered.

"You're standing there," said Poly. "Just go."

I had a foot on the first rung when Chit came buzzing in, gesticulating wildly with her forelegs. She settled on my shoulder so I could only see her using my peripheral vision.

"Jack! Poly! You've gotta look," Chit shouted.

Poly turned and followed where Chit's forelegs were pointing. I looked where she looked—it was easier than trying to figure out what Chit intended when I could barely glimpse her out of the corner of my eye. She was pointing to the southwest. I could see a collection of large, black, vaguely-humanoid shapes a thousand feet up, approaching at high speed.

"The robots are coming, the robots are coming," said my little friend.

Yes, I thought. *They certainly were.*

Chapter 44

"He's a piece of hardware… a weapon, a big gun that walks."
— Dean McCoppin, *The Iron Giant*

Six of the two-hundred-and-fifty foot robots the octovacs had taken apart last week were now reassembled and flying toward Centennial Olympic Park from the nearby mothballed Mercedes-Benz Stadium. Five of them landed near the stage with *thuds* we could feel from half a block away. The sixth hovered above where Poly and I were located by the steam tunnel grate, then lightly and almost soundlessly touched down on a broad concrete walkway twenty feet away. The thuds from the other landings must have been intentional, to get the combatants' attention.

"Incoming message from Mike," said my phone.

"Put him through."

"Cavalry's here, boss," said Mike's familiar voice. "We'll sort things out."

"Excellent," I said. "You're just in time. Don't squash any delegates or Homeplanet troops by accident."

"We'll try to keep that to a minimum," Mike replied. "CiCi, Ray Ray, Shuvvath and Hither send their regards."

"Make sure they're careful, too," said Poly.

A chorus of confirmations from the rest of the Xenotech Support team came over my phone's speaker. I hadn't realized we were on a conference call. It was good to be working with everybody again.

"See you soon," I said.

"Better hurry up, or you'll miss all the action," said CiCi in an upbeat girls-just-wanna-have-fun voice.

"We're on our way," I said.

I extended my arm toward the sixth giant robot, sweeping my hand out at the end.

"Your chariot awaits, dear lady," I said to Poly.

She smiled, but looked at me dubiously.

"How do we get up to the head?" she asked.

Four octovacs skittered down from the robot's kneecaps and pairs of them grabbed our shoulders.

"Oh," said Poly.

With Chit flying ahead, we were rapidly hoisted up the robot, dangling from the octovacs' metallic, tentacle-like arms. Soon we were at the access hatch at the neck. The entryway opened without our intervention and Poly and I were gently placed inside. Chit joined us and found a safe spot to sit on top of a monitor. The octovacs dogged the hatch and went who knows where. I got into the pilot's harness, while Poly strapped herself in at the weapons' console.

The tactile memory of how to operate the robot came rushing back to me. I rotated our robot's head so we could see how the the other five robots were doing. Three of them were bending over and separating clumps of Macerators and Homeplanet Security troops from G70 delegates.

When they didn't need to defend alien dignitaries, the well-trained Homeplanet Security squads made short work of the black-armored bargain basement berserkers. The other two robots were isolating collections of Macerators through deft side kicks, then stepping on them, forcing their armored bodies deep into the soft grass. Roger Joe-Bob Bacon, Bart Urrrson and Niaowla Murriym, assisted by several of Martin's police colleagues, removed power pack cylinders from the Macerators, leaving them helpless.

The tide of battle was turning, even before Poly and I could join in. The remaining active Macerator units, sensing their cause was lost, executed a strategic retreat and ran for access grates connected to the steam tunnel system. I was glad we hadn't tried them—they'd soon be crowded with unhappy and well-armed opponents.

"Look," said Poly. "Homeplanet Security troops are on their heels."

The troops were also disappearing below ground in pursuit of their opponents. Soon the south end of the park was cleared of any armored figures in either black or green—except for the

Macerators squashed into the turf. Blue-clad Atlanta city police and Georgia state capitol police were regrouping and forming up around G70 delegates and their bodyguards, but there were a lot fewer members of law enforcement around now than there had been earlier.

"Does the Macerators' retreat make sense to you?" I asked Poly as we tried to puzzle out what had just happened.

"Well, they were getting creamed and they'd accomplished their mission," she replied.

"To disrupt things for the G70?" I asked.

"Uh huh," said Poly. "It gives Earth a black eye to be so violent and out of control."

I trained the robot's telescopic gaze on an area near the stage. Dozens of reporters from Galactic news organizations and their camera crews were still filming everything.

"It may not be that bad," I said. "Galactics love heated political debate. I'm betting their delegates are riding high, publicity-wise, for being caught up in a spontaneous, over-the-top expression of Terran political exuberance. At least that's how I'd spin it."

"Maybe," said Poly. "But I didn't like the way all the Macerators left at the same time. It looked more like a pre-planned maneuver than panic."

"What do you think *that* means?"

"It means another shoe is about to drop," said Poly.

"Hey," she said, drawing my attention to the monitor showing a close-up of the stage. "What's that green thing?"

I saw it, too. It wasn't the mottled olive green of the Home-planet Security troops' armor—it was a more vivid green, with lots of texture.

"That's Gus!" I said. "What's *he* doing here?"

"I wonder how his audition went," said Poly.

I zoomed my main view-screen in on my favorite Gojon.

"I don't know," I said, "but he doesn't look so good."

My scaly green friend had the same spaced out, disassociated expression that I remembered from the drugged executives at the power station near Hoover Dam in Las Vegas. I considered calling 9-1-1 to get Gus medical help—Atlanta had some outstanding specialists in xenomedicine available—but didn't have time to ask my phone to do so.

Gus was growing.

He went from six feet to sixty in seconds, then twice that, then twice again. Now he was as big as the robots around him. Delegates and police, frightened by the appearance of a monster, began running away from the stage, heading north to the Georgia Aquarium and the World of Coke.

Gus wasn't done growing. He didn't double to five hundred feet, but increased to three hundred in two heartbeats.

"Rrrrawrrrr!" Gus bellowed.

Spurred by the roar and the threat of a giant green scaly dinosaur behind them, the delegates and their guardians ran north even faster. My friends and team members in the five other robots didn't react—they must have been too shocked. Gus rotated his tyrannosaur-like body and flipped three robots off their feet with his tail. With deafening *clangs* of metal striking concrete he brought one of his massive feet down on the heads of each of the robots, stunning them—or their operators—into immobility.

Poly and I hadn't been able to react, either. Everything had happened in the space of a few eye blinks. I hoped my friends operating the three damaged robots were okay. The Gojon wasn't done yet, however. He rotated his longer-than-a-tyrannosaur's arms and struck the remaining two robots at the south end of the park mighty blows to their jaws simultaneously. They fell backwards onto the now-empty stage like a pair of redwoods toppling in slow-motion, crushing it beneath them.

I'd read in the Atlanta Journal-Constitution that the mayor had planned to replace the stage with more modern construction in the next year or two—now she'd have to accelerate her time table. Thank goodness the falling robots missed the Terran and Galactic camera crews and reporters, or the lawsuits would be astronomical.

Gus was turning now. He spotted us in the sixth robot.

"Any suggestions?" I asked Poly and Chit.

"Bug out?" offered my little friend.

"Strategic retreat?" said Poly.

"Any *other* suggestions?"

Lives were at stake. Delegates, their guests, law enforcement officers, and members of the press were in danger. The Tōdon delegates had spread their beetle-like wings and were beating their way north. Several smaller species were riding on their backs, putting as much distance as they could between them and the rampaging Gojon. Many of the escaping dignitaries were running up the path toward where Poly and I stood on guard in the sixth robot.

"There's Tomáso, Queen Sherrhi and Diágo!" shouted Chit.

Our Dauushan friends were almost even with our robot's legs. Gus was chasing them, his giant feet like seventy-league boots. I knew Gojons were masters at changing their size, but I was pretty sure they couldn't fly. I had my robotic avatar bend down and scoop up the three Dauushans, cradling them in its arms, and triggered the robot's boot jets. *Lèse-majesté* be damned.

I managed to get high enough fast enough so that Gus couldn't grab me, though it was close.

"Get me Shepherd," I said.

"I'm here, Jack," said the Pâkk through my phone's speaker.

"Where can I drop off my precious cargo where they'll be safe?"

"You could put them on the next starship to Dauush leaving Hartsfield Port," said Shepherd.

I wasn't in the mood to be teased—especially by Shepherd, but maybe he wasn't joking.

"Or," Shepherd continued, "you can drop them off with me on the roof of the CNN Center."

"On my way," I said, angling to the south.

A lone Macerator in the middle of Marietta Street took a shot at us with his slug-thrower as we passed over him. Poly hit him with a special round from one of the weapons at her command. Before it struck him, its shell casing broke, dousing him with chemicals that foamed up and glued him to the asphalt. I loved that weapon—it was almost a molasses chill field for armored opponents.

I hovered horizontally above the roof of the CNN Center, afraid to land, because I wasn't sure if the roof was strong enough to hold the weight of a giant robot. Queen Sherrhi, Tomáso, and Diágo stepped down from the robot's arms to be greeted by Shepherd. I made the robot wave and they all waved back. Then I regained altitude and turned back to deal with Gus. Poly adjusted one of the monitors to show the view behind and above the CNN Center—the huge pink bulk of the royal dirigible, the *Matriarch of the Skies,* filled the screen. My Dauushan friends should be fine.

"Nice shooting," I told Poly as we circled Gus a couple of thousand feet up.

"Thanks," she said. "Watch out!"

Gus had found a large chunk of the stage's foundation and was launching it in our direction. I was able to dodge the missile, but it reminded me that being able to fly didn't make us invulnerable. I contorted to nudge the flying concrete into a nearby fountain with a boot jet. It made a splash, but didn't hurt anyone.

"I'm glad you saw that," I said. "I'm not fond of close encounters."

"Not one of Spielberg's best," said Poly.

"What?"

Poly hummed a familiar five-note pattern.

"Oh," I said. She meant *Close Encounters of the Third Kind.*

"Mike just sent us a text," said Poly, checking her phone. "Everybody's okay—a little shook up—but okay."

"Thank goodness," I said.

I'd been worried, but had been too busy surviving and rescuing to touch base with the team. Surviving and rescuing were still my top priorities. We needed to get Gus back to normal fast, to up our odds of success at both. As usual, Poly was a step ahead of me.

"Do you remember how we cured the drugged and programmed executives back in Vegas?" asked Poly.

"Chocolate and caffeine," I said, "but I don't think we're going to be able to feed either to Gus. There aren't enough Nicósn truffles in the city of Atlanta to make more than a morsel for Gus at his current size. Caffeine may be a different matter—the World of Coke is here in the park."

"I was thinking about something else," said Poly.

"Cool," I said.

"No," she said. "Cold."

Bells began chiming in my head. We'd deprogrammed the executives—including Queen Sherrhi and Tomáso—by putting them in an extremely cold environment. Given that it was Atlanta in May, a sudden cold snap was unlikely, so we needed another option.

"Could you reprogram those mobile congruencies?" I asked my phone. "The ones for species from planets with non-standard air or gravity?"

"It shouldn't be difficult to crack their encryption," my phone replied. "How fast do you need it?"

"Ten seconds from now," I replied.

"That shouldn't be a problem," said my phone. "It's practically an eternity in nanoseconds. How do you want them recalibrated?"

"To Niflheim's atmosphere," I said, "about five thousand miles out from the planet's center of mass."

"Where the pressure is twenty times Earth normal, got it," said my phone. "Asgard system. Five planets out from Midgard colony."

"Right," I confirmed.

"Can you reprogram them remotely, or do you need to be physically near them?" asked Poly.

"If they're connected to Galnet—which they are—they can be hacked at a distance," said my phone.

"Good to know," said Poly. "Where are the mobile congruencies now?"

"Just west of the wreckage of the stage," my phone replied. "They were abandoned when the Macerators showed up."

Gus had been following my robot's movements as it flitted back and forth across the sky like a big metal Peter Pan. Then he gave up and scanned the ground to the north, looking for new victims in the knot of dignitaries congregated near the catering tables between the aquarium and the World of Coke.

While Gus's back was turned, I dove for the area by the stage and scooped up the three mobile congruencies, popping the rings and forks off the forklifts so I could wear the congruency interface rings like, well, rings. My phone worked fast. I could see roiling white and icy blue clouds twisting on the other side of the congruencies' protective polymer shields. I put one ring on each of my robot's huge hands and tapped the third into the middle of its metallic forehead.

"Can you target the polymer covers?" I asked Poly.

"Already locked in with guided mini-missiles," she replied. "Just say the word."

"Will do," I said.

I kicked in the robot's boot jets and afterburners, zooming toward Gus at a speed approaching Mach 1. I stopped abruptly, just before I reached him, and landed with a very satisfying thud, leaving dents in the concrete walkways.

"Gus!" I shouted, using all the decibels my robot's speakers could push. He turned to face me.

"Word!" I told Poly.

Small cigar-shaped objects trailing sparks zipped from launchers at the center of my robot's chest and collided with the mobile congruencies, shattering their polymer covers. Blasts of chilled gasses close to a hundred degrees below zero shot out of cone-shaped nozzles at high pressure. I reached up and directed the streams from the rings on each hand at the sides of Gus's face, then tilted my head back so the chilly wind from the ring on my forehead struck him between the eyes. My Gojon friend stopped—cold.

I held the robot's hands and head in place for nearly a minute, until frost rimed every scale above Gus's neck.

"I think that should do it," I told my phone. "Cut the interfaces."

The freezing blasts abruptly stopped. Gus stood frozen in place. I was afraid I'd damaged him permanently when his extra-long tyrannosaur arms quivered, then twitched. I sighed and my connected robot body relaxed its vigilance temporarily. I was examining Gus's eyes and noting the pair of nictating membranes protecting them when Gus's arms shot out and began to squeeze my robot body hard enough to break it in half.

"Easy, Gus!" I said through my speakers. "You'll break my robot!"

"Oh Jack, thank you, thank you!" said my scaly friend, hugging my robot again. "I felt like an underwater sleepwalking marionette with someone else pulling my strings—but you saved me!"

I gave up trying to parse Gus's metaphor when I heard 3D-printed components in my robot's torso creak from the strength of his hug.

"Not so tight," I protested.

Gus relaxed his hold.

"Sorry," he said. "Sometimes I don't know my own strength."

"Don't worry about it," I said. "At least you're back to your old self now."

"How did your audition go, Gus?" asked Poly.

"There's good news and bad news," said the Gojon.

"What's the good news?" asked Poly.

"I got the part," Gus replied.

"And the bad news?" asked Chit.

"This was it."

Crap. My friend's audition had been a scam to program him for The General's nefarious purposes.

"That sucks," I said.

"Sorry about the other robots," said Gus.

"It wasn't your fault," said Poly. "And don't worry, their robots are trashed, but they're all okay."

"That's wonderful," said Gus. "I'm not the sort of guy who goes around hurting people or destroying property."

"We know," I said. "Your mind was being controlled."

"And I hadn't had anything to eat today," said Gus. "I'm not myself when I'm hungry."

Poly snickered.

"Incoming call from Rosalind," said my phone.

"Put it on speaker," I said.

"Jack," said Rosalind. "Look at EUA headquarters. You're not going to like this."

I rotated the robot's head until I could see the black and brooding structure just east of the park. When I'd first seen it, the place reminded me of a gigantic version of Darth Vader seated in a massive chair, complete with a head like Vader's flared helmet. The central part of the seventy-story structure was shifting, standing, rising to its feet. It was another giant robot, twice the size of Gus and ten times more intimidating—and it was heading this way.

Chapter 45

"Everybody's out there wrestling like a robot."
— Hulk Hogan

"You've got to be kidding," said Poly.

"I wish," said Rosalind via my phone. "Cornell and I are going to try to get inside it."

"Good luck," I said, "and remember not to get stepped on."

"We'll do our best," said Rosalind.

I extended the robot's hand, like one of the statues of Isildur and Anárion at the Falls of Rauros, and pointed at the gigantic new player entering the field. Gus turned to follow my gesture.

"O. M. Gee, that thing's big," he said.

"Coming from you, that's sayin' somethin'," said Chit.

"Can you get large enough to stop it?" I asked.

The seven-hundred-foot robo-building was striding toward us, scanning us as potential opponents and scoping out something on the ground as well—the G70 delegates.

Gus pressed his fists together and assumed a look of concentration that I only saw in the mirror when I needed to pass gas. For the sake of the people on the ground, I hoped that's how he summoned the extra mass needed to grow larger.

It was. As the robo-building approached, Gus doubled in size again to over six-hundred feet. He was still shorter than the building-that-walks, but not by much. He'd need help to take on The General's biggest threat, which I'd decided to name G.D. for General Destruction or maybe some other, more blasphemous phrase.

"Do you have anything you can throw at that thing?" I asked Poly.

"Get me closer, and I'll try lobbing a few nova bombs at its knees," said Poly.

"Great," I said. "And I've got a few ideas of my own."

The G.D. robot was larger, but slower than my robot. It also couldn't fly, and I could. I triggered my robot's boot jets and did my best Superman impression, shouting "Up, up, and away!" while Poly and Chit looked at me like I'd lost a few screws. Maybe my robot had, after Gus's last hug, but I hadn't. I wanted to try something that might slow the G.D. robot down.

While we were airborne, Poly launched a couple of missiles from our robot's forearms. They struck the G.D. robot at mid-thigh and latched on like remora fish sucking up to a shark, but the seven-hundred-foot robot brushed them away with its huge mechanical hands before they could explode. The nova bombs went off in midair, not attached to the robot's armored skin, and did minimal damage.

"Drat and drat squared," said Poly. "I was aiming for the backs of its knees."

So was I, but I didn't have time to tell her.

After a short ascent, I touched down across the street on the east side of the park, next to the two-hundred-foot SkyView Atlanta ferris wheel. Back in the park, I could see Gus had blocked the path of the monstrously large robot and the two behemoths were now in a battle of truly Brobdingnagian proportions.

The General Destruction robot's back was to me, so I had my robot tug on the SkyView's wheel until its axle popped off its mooring. My robot stood there, holding the wheel in its out-stretched arms like a Salvador Dali-esque version of daVinci's Vetruvian Man. The wheel was almost as tall as my robot, but it was mostly made from cables, which made it light enough to lift and easy to move around.

I rotated my robot's hips and made it crouch so I could lever-age the strength of its leg motors as I moved the wheel back and forth in a tick-tock motion. At each *tock* I moved the wheel farther and farther back, rotating it closer to horizontal in the process. Finally, as I moved forward for the last time, I released the giant wheel and sent it spinning into the park like an oversized Frisbee headed straight for the back of the G.D. robot's knees.

The wheel hit the EUA robot precisely on target, forcing the multi-story monstrosity to kneel, its metallic patellas hitting the ground with enough of a shock to bounce G70 delegates a hundred yards away several feet in the air. I also watched in horror as several tables holding the Teleport Inn's beautiful buffet toppled, sending what I was sure had to be delicious food onto the pavement.

Poly sent four more limpet missiles screaming in to latch onto the EUA robot's shoulder joints, but once again they were ineffective. Odd-looking creatures resembling Alaskan king crabs made of obsidian—EUA's version of octovacs, I assumed—skittered out of cracks in the G.D. robot's back and detached the nova bombs before they could go off. The bombs exploded high in the air and the ugly black crab-things waved their segmented legs at us defiantly.

The G.D. robot hadn't lost its grip on Gus when it knelt, either. The big Gojon was also on his knees and didn't seem to be doing well. His bright green scales were fading to a bilious hospital-walls green and his eyes were bugging out. The giant EUA robot was choking the life out of my friend.

"Hang on," I shouted.

Poly, Chit and my phone grabbed whatever they could to help maintain their stability while I pushed our robot's boot jets up to maximum power and sent it flying directly at the G.D. robot. Realizing, almost too late, that it wouldn't be wise to smash into the EUA robot with *our* robot's head—since we were in it—I put out our robot's arms and assumed a flying superhero pose, planning to slam into the center of the G.D. robot with the entire weight of our robot concentrated in the minimal cross section of its fingertips.

It would have been a good idea, too, if Gus hadn't lost consciousness and suddenly returned to humanoid size. The G.D. robot bent forward involuntarily, as the giant lizard-alien it had been choking shrank away to nearly nothing. My robot went careening over the EUA robot, forcing me to pull up at a very steep angle so my robot wouldn't crash into the twenty-fourth, twenty-fifth, and twenty-sixth floors of the Omni Atlanta Hotel.

"Everybody okay?" I asked, as I reoriented our robot and directed it back to the park.

"As Terrhi would say," said Poly in a completely uninflected, deadpan voice, "Whee."

Everyone's a critic.

"You sure you don't want *me* to drive this thing?" asked Chit.

"I don't think you have the right size or number of appendages to pull it off," I replied.

"I'm not sure you do, either," said Chit.

"Point taken," I agreed. "Now what?"

The G.D. robot had returned to a standing position, leaving the wrecked cables of the ferris wheel behind it. Macerator units were pouring out of the EUA robot's feet, rounding up G70 dignitaries and herding them inside the G.D. robot. We were too late to rescue them.

I had our robot circle above the park on autopilot, trying to figure out what to do next. Maybe I could use the cables from the SkyView Atlanta ferris wheel to wrap up the G.D. robot's legs, like Luke Skywalker taking down Imperial Walkers?

At least Tomáso, Queen Sherrhi and Diágo were safe—but what about Terrhi and Bavarian? And Max and Sally—were they still inside the aquarium?

We had to stop the G.D. robot before any more people were captured.

"Brace yourselves, here we go again," I said.

"Go for it," said Poly.

I landed our puny two-hundred-and-fifty-foot robot in front of the G.D. robot, feeling like a hobbit standing up to a troll. Poly launched a dozen more nova bombs, but they were all countered by the obnoxious black octocrabs. I tried to get our robot to punch at the G.D. robot's knees, to bring it down closer to our level, but that brought me too close to its arms. The G.D. robot's fist crashed into our robot's head so hard we went flying independently while our robot's torso remained rooted to the ground.

"I know there are independent thruster controls here somewhere," I said, searching the command console frantically.

"Better hurry, bucko," said Chit. "Nine point eight meters per second per second ain't nothin' to sneeze at."

Poly, wisely, didn't comment and distract me. It's one of the many many reasons I love her.

"Got it," I said.

The parabolic arc our robot's head had been describing changed to a vertical line.

"I love you," said Poly, now that it was safe to do so.

"Love you, too," I replied.

I instructed the robot's head to hover well out of reach of the G.D. robot and tried my favorite guided meditation to lower my heart rate—without much success. Then my phone beeped.

"Jack," it said. "You're going to want to see this."

"What is it?" I asked.

"A multimedia text message from Rosalind's phone. A photo."

"Put it on the main monitor," I said.

"Oh no!" said Poly when she saw the screen.

"Crap," said Chit. "Crap squared."

It was a picture of a conference room. Our friends—Rosalind, Cornell, Pomy, Emma Ann, Terrhi, Bavarian, Spike, Spot, Mike, CiCi, Ray Ray, Hither, Shuvvath, Roger Joe-Bob, Bart Urrrson, Niaowla Murriym, Mistress Marigold, Kijana, Pierre, and François—were all tied to chairs or otherwise bound on the floor of a large conference room. Even Mistress Marigold's three self-mobile plants were held captive under bell jars in pots positioned near the far wall.

The photo was high definition, so we could make out the fear on our friends' faces. It had a caption that made my blood run as cold as the atmosphere of Niflheim.

Room 6660 in ten minutes or they die.

Chapter 46

"I suppose you're all wondering why I've gathered you here today..."
— Standard Summation Trope

There are times when it doesn't pay to get up in the morning. This wasn't one of them. We finally had The General right where we wanted him.

Yeah, right.

"Is there a landing pad on top of EUA's headquarters?" I asked.

"You mean the big-ass robot?" asked Chit.

"Yes, that's what he means," said Poly. She sighed.

"There is a landing pad large enough for you to set down just behind the rounded top of the EUA robot's head," said my phone.

"You mean the Vader helmet?" asked Chit.

"Yes, it means the Vader helmet," I replied.

I quickly maneuvered our robot's head over to the specified pad and made a gentle landing. I counted it as a win that we weren't blown out of the sky in the process. We climbed out through the hatch near where the robot's neck had been. Chit rode at my collar, hidden by my hair.

As soon as we left our robot's head, dozens of obsidian-black octocrabs swarmed over it and began its disassembly. We wouldn't be making our escape by the roof, unfortunately. Poly, Chit and I boarded the landing-pad-level elevator and Poly pressed the button with double sixes.

Things were tense in the small enclosed space of the elevator as we descended. Poly and I held hands to reassure each other and help cope with our jangled nerves. Chit started humming the music from Final Jeopardy. Poly and I both laughed, then told Chit to shush. I reached for my phone to see how we were doing on time, but it wasn't on my belt. Just as well it was exercising its initiative again—it would probably be confiscated if it was on me when we reached our destination.

The normalcy of hearing an elevator chime its arrival on a designated floor felt surreal under the current circumstances. Poly and I stepped off and looked in both directions down a long, empty corridor. Nobody was around, though I could hear the chitter of octocrabs echoing off polished marble walls and floors in the distance. A sign pointing to the right directed us to Room 6660 and Media Production.

"Better step on it, bucko," said Chit. "Only two more minutes left on The General's deadline."

Poly and I sped up our pace. I saw an open door on one side of the corridor and couldn't resist a quick look inside. It was a television recording studio and the single fixed camera near the back wall pointed at the upper torso of a faceless mannequin in a dark suit. *Curiouser and curiouser.*

We continued walking and finally spotted signs of habitation. Two solidly built security guards in stiff black uniforms with epaulets stood outside a door. They weren't the type to work for minimum wage. I was pleased to see the numbers 6660 were incised into a small rectangle of black marble affixed to the door.

"Assume the position," said the larger of the pair. His partner covered us with a heavy-duty sweetener, the kind that's jokingly referred to as a *sugar shocker.*

I'd seen enough cop shows to know what to do. I spread my feet apart and leaned toward the wall, resting both palms on its smooth surface. I was patted down professionally and felt heartsick when my Swiss Army knife was confiscated.

"Be careful with that," I told the guard. "I'm going to want it back when this is over."

"I don't think so," said the guard.

"Do it anyway," I said.

My comments didn't make him change his expression and he returned to his work, taking my mini-sweetener, but missing Chit because she could shift away from his hands. I stayed in my awkward, splayed position while his partner repeated the process on Poly.

The other guard was equally thorough and every bit as professional as her larger associate. She managed to find where Poly kept her cell phone, something I hadn't been able to figure out in several months. The not-quite-so-large guard also discovered a long thin knife Poly had hidden in the waistband of her navy shorts. I was pleased to confirm that Poly and I both subscribed to the Boy Scouts' *Be Prepared* philosophy. Somehow both guards missed our Orishen pupa silk shirts, but that made sense. The shirts only turned rigid in response to a solid impact.

The larger guard said, "You can go in now," making the command resemble a request, but we knew better.

His partner was flicking her sugar shocker toward the door in an urgent manner that my brain interpreted as "Schnell, schnell!"

Poly and I entered. The room was an extended rectangle with tall windows along one of its long sides. Our friends were still tied to chairs around a light-oak conference table almost the size of a Dauushan Model-43 3D printer. Two more uniformed guards dragged us to a pair of empty chairs and duct-taped our arms and torsos in place. I could see the disappointment in our friends' eyes when they realized Poly and I were also captives.

I scoped out more of the details of the room. I was sitting next to Poly, opposite the windows. I rotated my chair and studied the wall behind me. It was a smart wall displaying an intricate Microsoft Project plan for galactic domination, with boxes labeled things like *Kidnap Princess Terrhi, Sue Melpomene Keen-Jones,* and *Leverage Dauushan Production Capacity for Conquest.* I had to stifle a chuckle when I saw yellow sticky notes over certain tasks on the complex work breakdown structure. It was hard to find people who really understood how to update project plans properly. I took comfort in knowing my own efforts were responsible for parts of The General's master plan being off schedule.

Alban White was also present, taped to a chair like the rest of us. The old man looked at me without any glimmer of recognition and I wondered if this was the original version, not his android human-duplicate doppelganger.

Adolphus Kone seemed to be presiding over the conference room with the *don't give me any crap* attitude of a judge in a courtroom. He was standing by the far wall, checking a large tablet. There was a door behind him. Yet another pair of human guards flanked Kone, sugar shockers at the ready.

"So glad you could join us," said Boss Kone. "The General will be pleased to see you. We only have to wait for a few more guests to arrive."

"Guests?" I said, practicing my ironic tone.

"In a manner of speaking," said Kone, doing the same, only better.

Someone knocked on the door behind Adolphus.

"Come in," he said.

One of the guards opened the door and Pablo Daniel Figueres entered with Camilla Moultrie right behind him. Camilla had her right hand in the side pocket of her suit jacket, which made me wonder if she was holding a mini-sweetener or slug thrower. Camilla was behind SLN's leaks, of course.

"What's going on, Uncle Dolph?" asked Figueres. "Why are all these people tied up?"

Uncle Dolph?

"All in good time, Danny," said Boss Kone. "I'll explain everything as soon as the last few stragglers arrive."

"You'd *better* have a good explanation," said Figueres. "I don't want to have anything to do with holding people captive."

"I guess I was wrong," I told Danny. "I thought you were one of the good guys—but you're on *his* side."

"I *am* a good guy," said Figueres. "And I'm sure my Uncle Dolph is, too."

"You're related?" asked Poly.

"Not by blood," said Figueres, "but we're as close as family."

Danny looked around the captives at the table and stopped short.

"Hi Rosey," he said. "Hi Cornell. Why are *you* taped up?"

"Great question," said Rosalind. "I asked Uncle Dolph the same thing myself."

Rosalind's Uncle Dolph, too?

"How do you know Rosalind?" asked Poly.

"Dolph and Freya adopted Rosey and Cornell after their parents died," said Danny. "They also sort of adopted me too, unofficially. Remember the lawyer from Atlanta I tried to hustle in Old San Juan—the one who helped me get into Georgia Tech?"

I vaguely recalled Figueres sharing that story when we'd met in his office.

"Dolph and Freya took me under their wing when I moved to town," said Danny. "Later, Uncle Dolph helped me get the financing I needed to get the Sirocco Legislative Network off the ground from my dorm room. We agreed to keep our relationship quiet since it made a better story for me to be a completely self-made, up-from-the-streets kind of guy."

"But you lied to us about not knowing anyone on the EUA executive team," I said.

"I know," said Danny. "I'm sorry, but like I said, I've been keeping my relationship with Dolph quiet since before First Contact. By now it's almost a reflex."

Poly's brows were furrowed.

"Who's Freya?" she asked.

"My late wife," said Adolphus Kone. "May she rest in peace."

Danny lowered his head in sympathy.

"Rosalind," I asked, "how are you and Cornell related to Boss Kone? Danny said Kone adopted you."

"He did," said Rosalind. "Our parents were Dolph's business partners back when EUA Corporation was still *Terra of the Galaxy, Incorporated,* a small e-commerce company selling Earth-legislators' memorabilia."

"What happened to your folks?" asked Poly gently.

"They were crushed near the current site of the Ad Astra complex," said Cornell. "Some dim-bulb from an on-line brokerage thought it would be a good idea to have an uberbull twice the size of a Tōdon walk down Peachtree Street for a First Contact Day parade. It was supposed to celebrate the rise in Earth's stock markets or something. The uberbull went berserk when he saw a family of Musans watching from the curb. Our parents never had a chance. Rosey and I were down the block with Uncle Dolph and Aunt Freya getting cloud candy. We saw it happen." He seemed numb as he relived the painful day.

"I'm so sorry," I said.

I'd been so love-struck when I first met Rosalind, and in so much shock when I first met Max that I'd never asked Rosalind about *her* family.

"Now you know why EUA Corporation is dedicated to establishing Earth's hegemony over the mongrel species of the galaxy," said Boss Kone. "The General showed me his vision of a Terran-led empire where things like that can't happen—where the human race is in charge!"

That wasn't the lesson I would have taken from the wild uberbull incident, which seemed like a classic case of human stupidity. Unfortunately, Boss Kone and *his* boss didn't seem to be playing with full decks and interpreted things differently.

Kone scanned down the table and fixed Cornell and Rosalind in his increasingly crazed gaze.

"I can understand those fools from C&C switching sides," Kone said, "But why did *you*—my own *family*—turn against The General?"

"After Winfield and Johnson's jet was shot down," said Rosalind, "we thought he wanted to kill us."

"No," said Kone, "he wanted to kill Winfield and Johnson for their many failures."

"But he shot missiles at our shuttles going to and from the *Charalindhri,*" said Poly.

"He wanted to send a message, but he didn't want to kill you," said Kone. "If he'd wanted to kill you, you'd be dead."

"What a cheerful thought," said Pomy.

"Hah," said Kone. "The *other* sister heard from. You made a good distraction, my dear, with your little mockery of a trial. It kept you and your meddling friends from realizing The General's plans for the pink princess and the G70 delegates."

"My mom and dad are going to stomp your butt!" cried Terrhi from her spot on the floor.

"Silence, child," said Boss Kone with icy calm, "or I'll send your parents one of your sub-trunks—or your kitty-cat's tail—to help them understand the gravity of the situation."

Terrhi closed her mouth and began to tremble. I wished I was free so I could hug her and tell her I'd make everything better, but neither one of those was a viable option at the moment.

Danny Figueres had moved a few steps away from Boss Kone. It seemed like the more he'd heard from his mentor, the less he'd liked. Camilla Moultrie stayed near Boss Kone, watching Danny closely and keeping her hand in her suit jacket pocket.

I felt pressure on the duct tape holding my torso to the back of my chair and remembered Chit had sharp mandibles. I took a deep breath and felt the tape on my left side start to give. Surreptitiously freeing my body was one thing, but it would be a lot harder for Chit to release my arms without being seen.

Someone else knocked on the door behind Kone. They didn't wait for an invitation to enter. The Bulldog strode in like she owned the place. For all I knew, maybe she did. She gave her father a dutiful peck on the cheek and crossed to give Danny a hug and a much longer kiss.

"Welcome!" said Adolphus.

"Shush, Father, I'm busy," said his daughter.

"*Te amo,* my little Valkyrie," said Figueres.

"*Te amo,* Dani*el,*" said Brunhilde Dagomar, accenting the last syllable. "I've missed you."

She kissed him again.

The two were mismatched for height, but seemed a good fit otherwise. I kept thinking there was something familiar about Kone's daughter, but didn't know what. I knew I'd figure it out eventually.

After a ten-count, Daniel and the Bulldog came up for air.

"Who are all these people and why are they taped to chairs?" said Brunhilde Dagomar in her witness-interrogator's voice.

"I'm glad you asked," said her father, "and I'm glad you're here to see The General's plans come to fruition at last."

"Daddy, you're sounding nuttier than a fruitcake," said the Bulldog. "Why are you still listening to that megalomaniacal Terran chauvinist?"

Boss Kone was spared the need to answer by the door to the outside corridor opening. I heard a voice I knew well.

"Get your hands off Aunt Sally!" shouted Max.

"Shut up, kid," said the larger guard from outside.

He was limping as he dragged Sally and Max into the room. *That's my boy!*

"Mommy! Daddy!" said Max.

I was closest so he ran to me, climbed into my lap, and cuddled ferociously. Chit took advantage of Max's body screening one of my arms to start cutting the duct tape holding it to the chair.

"Dad?" said Sally, looking at Adolphus Kone.

She saw the Bulldog holding hands with Danny Figueres.

"Sis?"

"Hiya, Squirt," said the Bulldog.

"Who are you calling a squirt, munchkin? I'm two inches taller than you and and have been since we were twelve."

"It would have been more fun to be identicals than fraternals," said the Bulldog.

"Yeah, but then Daddy would have insisted on *me* being a lawyer, too," said Sally.

"Right," said the Bulldog, "just to psych out opposing counsel by double-teaming them."

"I'd rather be dancing," said Sally.

"Some days, so would I," the Bulldog replied.

"So you finally fell for Danny?" said Sally.

"I did that years ago," said the Bulldog. "I just had to make my case to *him* so he'd look at *me* instead of those models he was dating."

"Just because a quantitative PhD looks good in a bikini doesn't make her a model," said Danny, grinning.

"Just because you tried to hide your attraction to me doesn't mean you were any good at it," said Brunhilde Dagomar.

"*Nolo contendere,*" said Danny.

"Excuse me," said Boss Kone. "That's quite enough. I suppose you're all wondering why The General gathered you here today."

Poly, Pomy, and Emma Ann unsuccessfully tried to stifle giggles at Kone's melodramatic trope. I encouraged Max to move his body with subtle shifts of my chest and shoulders so he hid my other forearm from view and wondered what my phone was up to.

"Mr. Kone," said Poly. "You can stop the masquerade. We know who The General is."

"We do?" asked Pomy.

"Who is it?" asked Emma Ann.

"He is," said Poly, pointing at Adolphus Kone with her chin. It was the only part of her body she could currently point with.

Everyone—even the guards and Camilla Moultrie—stared at Kone.

"If you're The General," said Cornell, "who's Manny?"

"Don't you get it, bro," said Rosalind. "*He's* Manny. Remember, *Manuel Garcia O'Kelly-Davis* was *human,* not an A.I.*"

"Damn," said Cornell. "Uncle Dolph *is* The General."

"You're kidding," said the Bulldog. "Gudrun, tell Rosalind and Cornell they're wrong."

Gudrun? Was that Sally's real name?

"Dad," said Sally, "Why are you pretending to be some sort of senior military officer?"

"I never said I was in the military," answered Kone.

"But Rosalind says you're The General," said Brunhilde Dagomar.

"*The General Counsel* of EUA Corporation," her father replied.

A series of exclamations based on the letter between *N* and *P* circled the room.

"You mean you really are?" asked Sally. "You're the megalomaniac? Looks like I was smart to move to Vegas."

"You and Rosalind and Cornell still work for the company," said Kone.

"I work with Rosalind and Cornell—I don't work for *you,*" said Sally. Or was it Gudrun?

"Daddy, why do you want to take over the galaxy?" asked the Bulldog.

"It's the only way for Earth to be secure and ensure a healthy Terran economy," said Adolphus. "I'm doing it for you and your sister and Rosalind and Cornell—and my grandson."

"Nonsense," said the Bulldog. "You're doing it for yourself—and Cornell and Rosalind can barely stand you anymore. She doesn't want Max to have anything to do with you."

"But think what Terra's hegemony will mean for business," Adolphus protested.

"Balderdash," said the Bulldog. "Thanks to free trade with other species, the economy has never been stronger."

"And besides," said Sally, "if you conquered the galaxy, you'd have to *run* it, and that's a thankless task if I ever heard one."

"I think he's got control issues," said Cornell.

"Shut up," said Adolphus. "But you're right. I *do* have control issues. Thankfully, I am in complete control of the current situation. Once I present my ultimatum to the G70 representatives and eliminate the queen of Dauush, her sister will become queen. She will build me the weapons I'll need to enforce my rule."

"Over my dead body!" shouted Terrhi from the floor where she was bound.

"That's the plan," said Boss Kone.

Terrhi didn't shake this time. She stared back up at Kone, looking resolute.

"Why did you ever buy him that biography of Napoleon?" Sally asked Brunhilde.

"I didn't buy it," said Brunhilde. "It must have been mom."

"It doesn't matter who bought it," said Adolphus. "The man had vision. Look!"

The smart wall shimmered and changed from showing a project plan to displaying views of other rooms in the seventy-story EUA General Destruction robot. Other conference rooms held collections of G70 attendees bound with duct tape. Yellow sticky notes still blocked small squares of the screen and made me smile despite the circumstances. As the smart wall switched from view to view I even saw what looked like a loading dock holding the Tōdon delegation.

"These delegates will make excellent hostages for the good behavior of their planetary governments," said Kone. "As will your friends and *their* friends here with you."

"Dad," said Brunhilde. "It will never work."

"Thankless child," said Boss Kone. His face was as red as Mistress Marigold's. "If you and your sister and Rosalind and Cornell are against me, you can face the same fate that's in store for the Dauushan girl, Scott Winfield and Josephine Johnson."

"Death to traitors?" I asked.

"Precisely," said Kone.

And I thought Poly and Pomy's father was bad...

The door behind Kone eased open quietly and I watched my phone scuttle in at floor level. Winfield and Johnson were behind it. Two more guard-types *not* wearing EUA uniforms were with them. My phone must have been relaying what was said in this conference room out to the former Chapultepec & Castle executives and their hired bravos. Winfield and Johnson held sugar shockers in their hands and slug throwers stuck in their belts. The guards with them were similarly armed. The four newcomers sweetened the four guards and Camilla Moultrie in five quick bursts. All their targets stood as still as frozen statues.

I took advantage of the confusion to stand up, ripping the weakened tape from my chest and arms. Max slid off my disappearing lap, ducking down, and running under the conference table. I dove under the table to join him. I could see Poly's feet moving as she pushed off and sent her chair careening back-first in the direction of Winfield and Johnson. I heard a blast from a sugar shocker, but could still see Poly's legs kicking.

Bavarian rolled her chair close to me and whispered. I reached up and found her variable beam congruency-powered laser where she'd told me to find it. I used the laser to cut her bonds, then freed Terrhi, Spot and Spike on the floor without being noticed in the chaos. More carefully placed beams of coherent light sliced through the glass of the bell jars holding Mistress Marigold's mobile-plant pets.

I looked up from under the table and saw Roger Joe-Bob Bacon extruding extra tentacles and using them to rip his own tape off while the mini-Drees were releasing Mistress Marigold. Shuvvath flexed to lift his front limbs off their protective metal covers and used his scimitar-like forearms to free himself and the human employees of Xenotech Support Corporation. The two Tigrammath professors, Bart and Niaowla, found their own approach to escape their bonds. They used their freakish feline-like strength to snap lengths of duct tape and rip it off their bodies, along with two-inch strips of striped fur. Boss Kone's irrational hatred of aliens had led him to underestimate them.

I poked my head above the tabletop, ready to zap Winfield and Johnson's weapons with Bavarian's laser when I froze without being hit be a sweetener. Josephine Johnson had pulled Emma Ann's chair to her and was holding a slug thrower to her head. Winfield was doing the same to Boss Kone.

"Come out, come out, wherever you are," said Johnson.

I duck-walked out from under the conference table and stood, leaving Bavarian's laser on the floor and putting my empty hands over my head.

"Here I am," I said. "Now what?"

"Now you and Poly and your phone can witness Adolphus signing over full control of EUA Corporation and all its subsidiaries to us," said Winfield. "That was the deal."

"That was the deal?" I asked my phone, which was now on top of the conference table.

"Correct," it said.

I extracted Poly from her duct-tape cocoon, then took my Swiss Army knife back from the frozen guard who'd confiscated it.

"It's got a pen," I said. "Do you have the documents?"

"We will in a second," said Johnson.

She pointed her slug thrower at the nearest window and pulled the trigger. The window shattered and the drone waiting outside came in, dropped an envelope on the conference table, and left.

Winfield forced Boss Kone to sit at the table with the papers in front of him. My unbound friends stood away from us and quietly helped untape the others. I couldn't see Max, Terrhi, Bavarian or their pets but assumed they were keeping out of sight under the table.

"You know that any contract signed under duress is not binding, right?" asked the Bulldog.

Johnson stroked her slug thrower. "He's *not* signing under duress, though, is he?"

"I guess not," the Bulldog, eying Johnson's gun uneasily.

I heard a whirring sound outside the open window.

"Are you expecting another delivery?" I asked the C&C executives.

"No, these are all the required documents," said Winfield.

"Good to know," I said.

I saw a familiar white flying car hovering just outside the room. Chilly—looking like Ryan Reynolds—was driving. And my mother was riding shotgun.

Chapter 47

"I once defenestrated a guy. The cops got all pissed off at me."
— John Sandford

Winfield and Johnson didn't see the car hovering outside the window. They were too focused on persuading Adolphus Kone to sign the agreements and didn't have the right angle to see the vehicle once it pulled a few feet back from the shattered pane. Poly had spotted my mother and Chilly, however, and she squeezed my hand to confirm she'd seen them.

Adolphus Kone was sitting at the end of the conference table near the broken window. He slumped down like his favorite sportsball team had just lost a championship. Wind whistled in through the empty space where the tinted window glass had been, forcing Winfield to rest one palm on the loose documents so they wouldn't blow away. His other hand held the muzzle of a slug thrower against Boss Kone's left temple.

They hadn't needed the pen in my Swiss Army knife—Winfield had a Mont Blanc pen and thought a fine writing instrument was a better choice for such a high-priced transaction. I thought the symbolism of using a pen that was also a knife made a lot of sense, but it wasn't my decision.

Johnson was providing the Secret CEO of EUA Corporation with more incentive to sign. She had traded Emma Ann in for the Bulldog and was standing to Boss Kone's right with the point of *her* slug thrower under Brunhilde Dagomar's chin. The two guards who'd entered with Winfield and Johnson were covering Poly and me with sugar shockers. Every few seconds they would wave their weapons around to ensure none of the other sentients in the room caused trouble.

"Just sign," said Winfield. "You won't be broke. You've got to have money stashed away."

Adolphus moved his head from side to side in a slow rhythm, as if he didn't want to hear what Winfield was saying.

"Listen up, Kone," said Johnson. "I'll put this in simple terms. Your company or her life."

Johnson jammed her slug thrower into the soft skin of the Bulldog's neck, making Brunhilde Dagomar cry out.

"Well?" said Johnson when Adolphus didn't respond.

"I'm thinking, I'm thinking," Kone said.

"Think faster," said Winfield.

Enough time for two deep breaths passed without anything happening. When I inhaled a third time, I thought I smelled something burning—then everything happened all at once.

"Yeeeeeowch!" screamed Johnson.

She had dropped her slug thrower on the conference table and was hopping up and down on one foot, clutching the other foot with both hands. A second later she tugged off her smoldering pump and threw the offending shoe across the room.

Winfield screamed a beat later, an octave lower, and ten decibels louder. Adolphus Kone had put the tip of the Mont Blanc pen through the center of Winfield's left hand, nailing it to the conference table. Instead of dropping his slug thrower, Winfield's arm swung out and his finger involuntarily contracted, sending two shots into the pane to the right of the previously shattered window. More glass rained out and down on the park and made me hope nobody was dumb enough to be standing too close to EUA's giant General Destruction robot.

Poly and I reacted to the noise and chaos by extracting our guards' slug throwers from their belts and using the threat of shooting them at close range to confiscate their sugar shockers as well. We zapped them into immobility with the heavy-duty sweeteners and turned to look for the former Chapultepec & Castle executives. I sweetened Winfield, a much easier shot because he was nailed to the table, while Poly took on the more difficult task of zapping a moving target. Johnson was still hopping around on one foot half the length of the table away. She was frozen while off balance and toppled to the carpeted floor.

Someone was tugging on my pants leg. I looked down—it was Max, holding Bavarian's laser and beaming.

"Did I help, Daddy?" asked my son.

"You helped a *lot,* buddy boy," I said, bending down to help him up and giving him a hug.

"Jack!" shouted Poly.

I heard the crackling sound of a sweetener blast hitting a wall, not flesh. Adolphus Kone had pushed back from the table and was running toward one of the open floor-to-ceiling windows. Poly had tried to zap him, but her blast had gone wide.

I vaulted up on the table and took two quick steps before leaping for Boss Kone where he stood by the window. The force of my momentum carried us both over the edge and out into empty space.

* * * * *

This was becoming a habit—and one I really wanted to break, if it didn't break me into hundreds of tiny pieces first.

I'd landed on Boss Kone's back, but he twisted as soon as we were in free fall. The two of us grappled, which made it a lot harder for me to figure out how to save my own skin, let alone his. The wind was whistling past us and the concrete below was coming up fast. I couldn't count on octovacs with parasails to save me this time.

Then I remembered my mom and Chilly and the cool white flying car and relaxed for a moment.

I shouldn't have done that. Boss Kone broke free and slammed the heel of his right hand into the point of my jaw. That action had two effects. One was to snap my head back and make me see stars. The other was to separate me from Kone by a few feet.

I shook my head to clear my vision, which was already not what it should be due to the wind. I watched Boss Kone remove a mini-sweetener from the breast pocket of his flapping suit coat and felt him zap me in the chest. He aimed at something above and behind me and shot again. I wasn't in any position to turn around and see what he'd hit. My Orishen pupa silk vest had saved me from the worst of the blast, but it would take twenty minutes I didn't have for my arms and torso to unfreeze.

Boss Kone didn't seem to be interested in self-preservation after dealing with me. Instead of keeping his body spread out and horizontal to maximize wind resistance, he pointed himself straight down and fell even faster. The ground was looking entirely too close for my own survival, let alone comfort.

Then comfort was the farthest thing from my mind. The bad news was that it felt like something was trying to pull every hair on my head out by the roots. The good news was that my progress toward the origin on the y-axis was slowing. I saw the white flying car come up alongside me. The rear gull-wing door on the passenger side folded up and over and the car tipped to the left. I was gently lowered inside the vehicle, then the rear door closed and the car leveled out and circled.

My body leaned to one side, but I could briefly see out the white car's left rear window. A dark, man-shaped splotch was on the pavement not-far-enough below. Kone hadn't made it.

"Are you okay, Jack?" asked my phone as it switched from helicopter drone-mode to its arms-and-legs configuration.

"I'll live," I said. "Thanks for the save."

It was hard to breathe with my torso sweetened and my words came out in difficult rasps.

"No problem," said my phone.

"I don't know how I'll ever make it up to you," I added.

"You'll find a way," said my phone.

I knew I would. I owed it one. Heck, I owed it a lot *more* than just one.

I glanced in the front seat. It was hard to see very well because my body was tilted, but it looked like my mom was now driving. Chilly was leaning against the right front window the same way I was leaning against the left rear. Kone's last sweetener blast must have hit him. I would pay for a video of mom moving Chilly out of the way to take the wheel.

"Thanks for rescuing me, Mom," I said slowly. "And Chilly, too."

"Our pleasure, Jack," said my mom as she lifted the car back up 'til we were even with the conference room again. "I'm glad we were in the right place at the right time."

I forced words out of my sweetened lungs. "So. Am. I."

"And Jack," she said, using the serious voice she used when I was a kid telling me we were moving again. "Chilly has something important to tell you."

I wondered about her timing, but wasn't in a position to do more than listen. Chilly exhaled twice as if to build up enough air or enough courage to say what he needed to say. His words came out deep and raspy, like he was breathing through a helmet. They hit me like a sledgehammer between my eyes.

"Luke," said Chilly. "I am your father."

Chapter 48

"The world will be yours and everything in it…"
— Rudyard Kipling

"Who's Luke?" I asked, not quite realizing what I was saying. How could I, of all people, miss a Star Wars reference?

"It's a joke, son," said Chilly.

"It's a joke that you're my father or it's a joke you called me Luke?"

"The second one," Chilly replied.

"Okay," I said. "We can talk about this later."

I needed time to process.

The white car was now next to one of the broken EUA conference room windows. Bart and Niaowla used their wiry feline strength to carry me into the room and plant me in a chair near the end of the table like one of Mistress Marigold's horticultural experiments. They crawled back in the car, repeating the process for Chilly and putting him in a chair across from me and a few down. Cornell was at the head of the table in the chair formerly occupied by Adolphus Kone. The Bulldog and Danny Figueres were immediately to his right with Sally and Rosalind to his left.

Poly was standing by an empty chair where she could hold my hand once she sat down. My phone had extruded a chair for itself along with pseudo-arms and legs and Chit was in her usual post on top of an overturned tumbler near a carafe of water in the center of the table. My mom stood behind Chilly's chair.

Max jumped in my lap, landing a bit harder than I preferred on a sensitive part of my anatomy. It was a small price to pay for the joys of fatherhood. He seemed to take pleasure in the fact that my sweetened self couldn't hug him, just like I couldn't when when I'd been taped down. I gave him a stern paternal look that meant, "Don't you dare tickle me when I can't defend myself." I was lucky I had a good kid—he just cuddled.

"I'm sorry about your father," said Poly to Brunhilde, Sally/Gudrun, Cornell and Rosalind.

The quartet didn't answer. In order they looked sad, stunned, numb, and angry.

"Let's send Mike, CiCi, Ray Ray, Shuvvath and Hither out looking for G70 delegates to rescue," Poly continued. "I hope they won't have any problems with EUA's guards."

"I can help with that," said Cornell.

He touched a button on the surface of the conference table that I didn't know was there. A microphone rose up out of the polished oak of the tabletop. Cornell ran his fingers over a few more keys, then spoke.

"Attention all personnel, attention all personnel," he said. "Stand down. I repeat, stand down. This is The General's chief lieutenant, Cornell, authorization code Epsilon Upsilon Alpha Forty-two. I regret to inform you that The General and Adolphus Kone, the head of our legal department, both lost their lives in a tragic accident a few minutes ago. I am now acting CEO and Brunhilde Dagomar Kone, the older daughter of Adolphus Kone, will be our acting general counsel."

He turned off the microphone.

"That should do it," said Cornell. "The guards and Macerator troops should stop fighting until it becomes clear who's going to pay them."

"Thanks," said Poly.

"No problem," said Cornell. "Let me make things easier on your team, too."

He turned the microphone back on.

"Attention all armed personnel. Please engage the safeties on your weapons and put them on the floor. If you are responsible for any captives, please remove their restraints and assist designated representatives coming down from the sixty-sixth floor with the captives' orderly exit from this mobile facility. Thank you, and stand by for further announcements."

Cornell turned the microphone off.

"I think your people won't have any trouble getting the G70 delegates and their friends out of the giant robot building now," he said.

"Thank you," said Poly. "What about the Macerators in the tunnels?"

The door to the corridor opened. Shepherd and Martin walked in. Martin was smiling and Shepherd looked pleased, for a Påkk.

"They're under control," said Martin. "Homeplanet Security is taking care of them. Quite a few took off their armor and ran for it once they realized they were outnumbered."

"Good help is hard to find," said Poly.

"Especially when you pay minimum wage," quipped Emma Ann.

"That was never *my* philosophy," said Alban White.

His speaking voice sounded just like his android's, though I guess that was the point.

"I always believed in finding the best sentient for the job, paying them what they're worth, and giving them the resources they needed to be successful."

"An excellent approach," I said. "Poly and I run Xenotech Support the same way."

"What's Xenotech Support?" asked Alban White.

"Our company. We provide technical support for organizations using galactic technology," I replied.

"Did you say 'the best sentient for the job' a second ago?" asked Poly.

"Of course," said Alban White. "White House & Home is an equal opportunity employer and always will be."

"Did you know The General replaced you with an android and switched to xenophobic hiring practices?" I asked.

"The cad," said Alban White. "Where's my shovel?"

"Your shovel?" asked Poly.

"Yes," said Alban. "I've got to get back to my excavations."

"What are you digging?" I asked, a bit worried about his answer.

"The Panama Canal," said White.

Perhaps Alban's android wasn't a precise duplicate of him after all.

I could see why it was easy for The General to step in and run White's companies.

Mistress Marigold took Alban White aside and gave him a pill. I was glad White wasn't carrying a bugle.

"Do you think you can operate this robot building and move it back to its original location?" asked Shepherd. "It is blocking access for emergency responders getting into the park."

"Sure," I said, "When I can move my own arms again in fifteen or twenty minutes."

"My apologies," said the grizzled Pâkk spy master. "I hadn't realized you'd been sweetened."

"I'll live," I said.

"I hope so," said Poly.

"Remote robot mobility controls accessed," said my phone.

It imitated Cornell's voice and sent an announcement to every loudspeaker in the giant building.

"Stand by. Stand by. Initiating movement. Please sit down and strap in. Starting in five-four-three-two-one."

"Let's hope they hadn't gotten too far in untaping the captives," I said.

The seventy-story robot building began to move more smoothly than I'd anticipated. It took less than two minutes for the giant self-mobile construct to resume its "seat" between the wings of EUA's headquarters. It settled into its original position with a thud and the clang of steel interlocks reengaging.

"That was fun, Daddy, can we do it again?" asked Max.

"Maybe later," I said. I was starting to get a pins-and-needles feeling in my upper arms and shoulders.

Bavarian stuck her head out from under the table.

"Is it safe to come out now?" she asked.

"By all means," said Poly. "Join the party."

Bavarian, Terrhi, Spot, Spike and two mini-Dree plants appeared near the center of the room. Spike took advantage of my inability to move to put his front pair of paws on my knees, lean over Max, and lick my face with his sandpaper-like tongue.

I protested, sort of, but was glad to see the big cat, too. Pomy and Emma Ann fussed over Spot and rubbed his belly while the big dog kicked his legs with pleasure. The mini-Drees found the documents Winfield and Johnson wanted Adolphus Kone to sign and were turning them into paper airplanes with their manipulating tendrils. As they finished folding, they released the planes into EUA's austere courtyard through the open window not blocked by Chilly's car.

Pushing Spike out of the way, Bavarian gave me a hug around the neck, then kissed Max on the top of his head.

"What was that for?" I asked the little girl who'd grown up too fast.

"For being a good guy and knowing what to do and being Max's dad," said Bavarian.

She gave me another hug, then jumped down from my chair and put her arms around Poly's waist.

"Thanks," said my partner, "but what did *I* do?"

"You kept your head and stayed smart and you love Jack and Max," said the girl.

"You've got me there," said Poly. She put her arm around Bavarian's shoulders and hugged her back. "You've done a good job of keeping *your* head for the past few days too, you know."

"Thanks," said Bavarian. "It's hard."

Poly didn't say anything. She just hugged the little girl tighter.

"Uncle Jack, Uncle Jack, Aunt Poly, me too, me too," piped Terrhi.

For the fourth time in three minutes I got attention from a child or a pet. Terrhi spun my chair toward her and hugged me with all nine of her sub-trunks. It was a weird sensation—and a pleasant one.

"Thanks, Terrhi," I said. "Well done. You were as courageous as the Cowardly Lion defending Dorothy when Boss Kone threatened you."

"I wasn't scared, Uncle Jack," said the Dauushan girl. "I knew you and Poly and Uncle Shepherd and my mom and dad would make everything right."

"Speaking of Queen Sherrhi and Tomáso," said Shepherd. "The *Matriarch of the Seas* is moored at the top of this structure and ready to accept passengers."

Looks like I'd been wrong about not being able to make our escape via the roof.

Two phones chimed. Martin held his to his ear and turned away.

"You have a call from Pierre Auguste Escoffier," my phone announced.

"Put him through," I said.

"Madames et Monsieurs, friends of Poly and Jack," said the Pyr *maître d'hôtel* from the Teleport Inn. "We have recovered much of the luncheon feast planned for the G70 dignitaries, but it looks like lunch for the delegates is off. Therefore, it would be my great pleasure to host you at the Teleport Inn in one hour."

Poly looked around the table and saw only nods of assent, except from me, Chilly, the C&C executives, and the sweetened security guards—and the last two groups weren't invited.

"Sounds great," said Poly. "We'll be there on the *Sky Mama* soon. I hope you'll have enough for us *and* some hungry Dauushans."

"We have plenty of food on hand, my dear, even for Dauushan appetites. The more the merrier," said Pierre.

"Excellent," said Poly. "See you in sixty."

"Merci, à bientôt!"

Pierre closed the connection.

"I could use some grub," said Chit. "Donuts don't hold a girl that long. I'm starving."

"You should have tried one of our high protein varieties," said Bavarian.

"Maybe later, kid," said my little friend.

It was clear Chit needed to refuel. She wasn't normally that abrupt with children—just with me.

"I've got more good news," said Martin as he put away his phone. "Mike and my officers report that the G70 delegates are not distressed by what's happened. They're thrilled to be caught up in Earth's 'exuberant political process' and pleased to have great stories to tell for the next several decades. Most of the excitement was broadcast out to the GaFTA networks and their own political capital on their home planets has gone way up. They're all in great moods coming into tomorrow's opening session. Tomáso says Queen Sherrhi's status is huge for suggesting the G70 meet here."

"It was Queen Sherrhi's idea?" said Poly.

"More like Tomáso's, actually," said Martin. "He's developed a very strong working relationship with diplomats and trading partners here on Terra."

"Good for us," said Poly.

"Tomáso also reports that Lüzhiulterianne took her personal shuttle off the *Charalindhri* ten minutes ago. She's probably at the Jackson Teleport Nexus right now trying to figure out how far she can jump to get away from Sherrhi."

"Knowing the queen, that's a wise move," said Shepherd. "I'd suggest somewhere in the Andromeda galaxy."

Martin showed a hint of a smile.

"Families are complicated," said Poly.

"You can say that again," I confirmed, looking at my mom and Chilly.

"You're my dad, Rosalind is my mom, Sally and Cornell are my aunt and uncle, Bavarian and Terrhi and Spot and Spike are my friends, and Poly is my step-mom," said Max.

"Not exactly," I said, seeing Poly smiling, "but close enough."

Being shot with a sweetener affected my muscles, but not my hearing. A diffident knock came from the door to the corridor.

"Come in," I said.

It was Gus the Gojon at human-normal size.

"I hope you don't mind me popping in unannounced," he said. "I got a text message telling me you were here."

I looked at my phone. It was showing a smiley-face on its screen.

"I wanted to apologize," he said. "I didn't mean to cause so much trouble. I just wanted an acting gig."

"It's not your fault," said Poly. "You were drugged and brainwashed. We know it wasn't your idea."

Roger Joe-Bob Bacon stepped over to the despondent Gojon, extruded a few more feet of tentacle, and put it around the scaly green being's back.

"If you're lookin' for a part, I know some people over at Toho Productions in Tokyo. You'd be perfect as a *kaiju.*"

"Thank you, *thank* you!" said Gus.

"I can take you on a hop over to Japan on Monday in my private jet," said Roger Joe-Bob.

"Is Japan near Las Vegas?" asked Gus. "And what's a *kaiju?*"

"Close enough," I said. "And don't worry about it. Now stick with us, we're going to lunch."

Chapter 49

*"Note on a door: Out to lunch; if not back
by five, out for dinner also."*
— Unknown

"Pass the microchips," I said, glad my arms and upper torso were working again.

"Here you go," said Poly.

She pushed a red plastic basket in my direction. It kept a fixed height twelve inches above the table, its weight perfectly balanced by four helium balloons. When I took a handful of chips it lifted higher until the sensors on the balloons could release some of their noble gas.

The chips weren't called microchips because they were made of silicon and etched with integrated circuits. They'd been given that name because they were cut with a microtome into slices thinner than a sheet of cellophane and zero gravity flash-fried in a mist of hot Quirinx float-tree oil. They were incredibly light, crisp and delicious. Nobody could eat just one. It was hard not to eat a hundred of them, but they were so thin it took a thousand to make you feel full.

We were back in the Teleport Inn's large species dining room where the banquet after the awards ceremony had been held. The restaurant was closed for lunch today because all their staff had planned to be at Centennial Olympic Park on their big catering job. Pierre had turned it into a private party for us, and the Matriarchy of Dauush was footing the bill even though Pierre had offered to feed us for free. Queen Sherrhi had told Pierre *there ain't no such thing as a free lunch* and the little *maître d'* had looked puzzled until Poly explained it to him.

Chit was sitting on an overturned tumbler in front of Poly and me, drinking something that that smelled like lemon-scented paint thinner from a glass thimble. My phone was gleefully pounding on another overturned tumbler with two halves of a broken chopstick. It had been playing the *Yub Nub* Ewoks' celebration song from the end of *Return of the Jedi* until Poly had threatened to drop it into a pitcher of Diet Starbuzz. I told my phone it was in bad taste to seem too happy after The General had just died.

At least The General hadn't returned as a force ghost.

Terrhi, Bavarian, Spike, Spot, Max and the mini-Drees were sitting at a kiddie table close enough to the adults' table for us to keep an eye on them. François kept them busy eating so the kids and pets couldn't get into too much trouble, though it was a challenge keeping the self-mobile plants in their training pots during the meal.

Martin had seen to it that Alban White had psychiatric care, so we didn't have to worry about Teddy Roosevelt appearing, blowing his bugle, and shouting "Charge!" I wondered if I could talk White into digging a couple of graves in the Ad Astra courtyard for Winfield and Johnson, but knew that was only wishful thinking. Martin's people would see the pair got what was coming to them. Camilla Moultrie was also being held. Chit's testimony about Moultrie's industrial espionage for EUA should put her away for several years, if it was admissible.

Tomáso and Queen Sherrhi filled thirty degrees of arc of the big round table on the far side from the kiddie table. Their bodyguards, Diágo, Lohrri and Naddéo, kept watch a dozen Dauushan paces behind. Martin and Shepherd sat close to the Dauushan royal couple, talking shop. Mistress Marigold, Pomy, Niaowla and Bart were discussing plants grown from ancient seeds found in sealed jars in the ruins of Old Pyr. Roger Joe-Bob Bacon was regaling Gus with stories about visits to the sets of movies he'd funded.

Poly and I were near Rosalind, Cornell, Sally, Danny Figueres and the Bulldog. A few degrees farther around, Emma Ann was listening avidly to Mike, CiCi, Ray Ray, Hither and Shuvvath run through descriptions of the client calls they'd made while Poly and I had been away in Las Vegas. I looked at my partner and smiled. We were both thinking it wouldn't be long before Emma Ann would be joining the company.

Chilly and my mother were sitting near Martin and Shepherd, lost in conversation. I couldn't tell if their discussion was foreplay or just old friends catching up and I really didn't want to know either way. I still wasn't ready.

I overheard Roger Joe-Bob tell Gus about his plan for underwriting a new galactic television show based on the events of the day called *Real Delegates of Terra*. Several star-struck alien G70 dignitaries wanted to stay on Earth and room together in a set of apartments in Ad Astra. I hoped they'd end up somewhere at the other end of the complex.

Then I heard Brunhilde says something about probate and my ears perked up.

"What?" I asked.

"One of my father's A.I. systems just emailed me his will," said the Bulldog. "He's indisputably dead, so that triggered the message."

"Already?" I asked.

"Pay attention, Jack," said Poly. "Hildy has been telling us about the details."

Hildy? Oh, right. From Brunhilde.

"Could you catch me up?" I asked.

Brunhilde Dagomar rolled her eyes, but started over. I slid the basket of microchips her way to say thanks.

"It's simple, really," said the Bulldog. "I'm appointed the new general counsel, with ten percent of the company. Cornell is the new chief executive officer and also gets ten percent. Gudrun gets ten percent and control of the EUA Charitable Trust, and Rosalind gets another ten percent and the portfolio of her choice. Father wasn't sure if she wanted a corporate job since she's more of an independent agent."

I looked down the table. Brunhilde, Cornell, Sally, and Rosalind all seemed pleased by the news.

"That's only forty percent," I said. "Who gets the other sixty?"

"Max," said the Bulldog.

"Yes?" asked my son from the kiddie table.

"Nothing, buddy," I said. "We're just saying good things about you."

"Okay, Daddy."

Wow. My son was heir to sixty—no, seventy percent—of one of the largest fortunes on the planet.

"Max Buckston," whispered Poly. "Who knew how apt that name would be?"

"You're all okay with this?" I asked.

"Yes," said Cornell. "Until Max turns twenty-one, his shares are controlled jointly by the four of us, giving us each twenty-five percent."

I did the math. "So you need at least three of you to agree on any big decisions?"

"Correct," said Cornell. "That should keep us focused on consensus, not conflict."

"I'm giving Jack and Poly joint proxy for my shares," said Rosalind, tossing a verbal hand grenade on the table.

"What?" said Poly.

"Why?" I added.

"Shepherd's made me an offer to work on an undercover project for a year," said Rosalind. "It's off-planet."

"Please don't! I'm just getting to know my son."

"That's one reason why I'm leaving," said Rosalind. "After all the years you didn't have with him, it's only fair he should live with you full-time for a while."

"But…"

"Don't worry," said Rosalind. "Cornell and Sally will be in Atlanta to back you up—and Hildy wants to spend time with him, too."

I was in shock. So was Poly.

Tomáso's voice boomed out from the other end of the table.

"You never got to see what *I* had planned," said the royal consort to Martin and Shepherd. "There's a giant robotic Dauushan exoskeleton I'd planned to wear into battle at the park, but it wasn't done on time."

He projected a hologram of something that looked like a massive pink-painted AT-AT Imperial Walker with six legs into the middle of the table.

"It would be cool to see *that,*" I said.

"You can," said Tomáso. "It's being assembled in a dirigible hanger near Hartsfield Port."

"Please let me know when it's finished," I said.

Tomáso waved a couple of sub-trunks in acknowledgment.

"You're on-board with this?" I asked Rosalind. "And Max?"

"Max is nuts about you," said Rosalind. "He's also used to me being away for long periods on business. This will just be longer than most."

I turned to Poly and took her hands.

"How do *you* feel?"

"Happy that you're happy," she said. "And interested in getting to know Max better myself. He's a cool kid."

"He is that," said Rosalind. "And he likes you a lot—he's told me so several times already. You heard him call you his step-mom."

"Yeah," said Poly.

I couldn't read her reaction. She squeezed my hand.

"When are you heading out?" I asked.

"In a month or so," Rosalind replied. "Shepherd has to set some gears in motion first."

"That gives me more time to prepare," I said.

"It gives *us* more time to prepare," said Poly. "I'm your partner, remember?"

"I remember," I said. "I'll always remember."

"Good," said Poly. "Now let's talk about something else and enjoy our lunch."

"Pass the flatfish roll-ups," I said.

"Not the half-pound ubercow cheeseburger sliders?" asked Poly.

"No," I said. "I'm not that hungry."

Poly saw me glance over at my mom and Chilly.

"What's going on, Jack?"

"I don't want to talk about it."

I turned away and stared at my plate.

One of the reasons I love my partner is that she knows when to leave me alone.

* * * * *

I must have had a black cloud over my head to signal people away because nobody tried to talk to me. I was sitting with my back to Poly, my head bowed, and the base of my palms pressed to my forehead. I stayed in that position while Pierre's team served red-gold strawberry-galberry trifle, pink Dauushan bread pudding, and lavender jathberry-plum shaved ice.

I was upset, nervous, and angry. My head was pounding. I was angry at my mother and Chilly and frustrated because I knew I was behaving like a child. I was so mixed up I didn't taste any of the delicious-looking desserts. Okay, maybe a spoonful of the trifle. I was just about to kick my own butt for behaving like a nine-year-old when a *real* nine-year-old tugged my hands down and gave me a hug.

"Thanks, Bavarian," I said, hugging her back gingerly.

"Don't be sad," she said. "I don't *have* a mom and dad anymore and *I'm* not sad—at least not very often."

I hugged Bavarian tighter.

"Your mom asked me to ask you to talk to her and her friend in the Stone Mountain Room while everybody's having coffee and stuff," said the girl after she disengaged from our hug.

I took a deep breath and centered myself.

"That sounds like a good idea, thank you," I said.

I pulled Bavarian closer and gently kissed the center of her forehead.

"Thank you so much," I said. "I'm going to try to be a grown up, but it's hard."

"It's hard for me, too," said Bavarian, "but I'm a kid. I know *you* can do it."

A hug from a sweet kid did a lot to brighten my mood, but I still wasn't looking forward to what I had to do. I scanned the large-species dining room to procrastinate. My friends were talking and laughing and nibbling on this and that from Pierre's luncheon feast, filling in the corners. Tomáso and Queen Sherrhi had polished off an entire tray of three dozen pink, cantaloupe-sized Dauushan caviar eggs with seaweed garnish, leaving only the silver serving platter behind.

The wait-staff at the Teleport Inn were consummate professionals. They weren't trying to clear any plates, glasses or half-eaten dishes because they didn't want to rush us. It was just as well they hadn't tried, since my friends were so absorbed in their varied conversations that prematurely disturbing their discussions while trying to prep for dinner might have broken the spell.

A bald human waiter in a poorly fitted tuxedo was bent low, wheeling a cart toward the table. He was broad-shouldered with protruding brow ridges and appeared to be bringing something under a large, chrome-plated metal dome toward us. I wondered if Pierre had something special planned for anyone still hungry, like flaming *crêpes suzette* prepared table-side.

The cart was almost to the table, only a few feet from me, when alarm bells began ringing in my head. The bald, broad-shouldered and brow-ridged waiter wasn't just a random temp Pierre had brought in to help with a big catering job—he was a phony. This Neanderthal was the same fake waiter who had tried to disrupt a meeting of religious leaders at the Teleport Inn last March when Poly and I were on our first date.

"Do you still have your laser?" I asked Bavarian, who hadn't moved from my lap.

"Uh huh," said the girl. "Max gave it back after he had his fun in the conference room."

"May I borrow it, please?"

"Sure."

She removed the slender tube from somewhere on her person and handed it to me, making sure the business end of the weapon didn't point at either of us and somehow knowing not to let the waiter see it. The laser didn't weigh much, but I knew its congruency-powered coherent light could generate a lot of heat quickly.

I was sure the waiter was up to no good, so when he reached for the polished dome on his serving cart I directed the laser beam at the handle on top of the dome. The waiter screamed when the bare flesh of his left hand touched the now searing-hot handle. He threw the chrome-plated metal dome backwards but still managed to reach forward with his right hand and press a button on the device beneath the dome—a nova bomb big enough to blast this section of the restaurant into smoking rubble. I could hear the bomb counting itself down over the waiter's cries of pain.

"Ten. Nine. Eight."

I shouted six words louder than I'd ever shouted anything in my life.

"MARTIN! WINDOW!"

"TOMÁSO! PLATTER!"

"EVERYBODY! DOWN!"

I'd never been more glad to have intelligent, competent friends. Martin used his sidearm to turn the upper half of a large window at the back of the dining room overlooking the river into so much open air. Tiny grains of safety glass pattered down just outside the large-species' dining room.

Tomáso picked the silver serving platter up off the table and held it in two of his sub-trunks, ready for anything.

I took the football-shaped nova bomb from the serving cart and tossed it as far as I could in Tomáso's direction. The Dauushan consul intercepted the bomb with his platter when the device said, "Five." Rotating his powerful upper body, Tomáso did an alley-oop, launching the nova bomb in a graceful arc through the shattered window and out into the Chattahoochee river.

The bomb said, "One," in a soggy voice, just as it sank into the flowing water. I wrapped myself around Bavarian and fell forward under the table.

What happened next must have made quite a spike on seismographs down at Georgia Tech. The boom—even muffled by the river—was loud enough to wake sufficient walking dead for twenty-six episodes of a zombie show. The building shook, plates on the banquet table rattled, and glasses turned over, dripping their contents over the edge.

I missed it when it happened, but when I looked at the security camera footage later I saw that the plume of river water produced by the nova bomb's explosion rose three times higher than Old Faithful at Yellowstone.

When the shaking stopped, I crawled out and looked around. Bavarian wanted to look, too, but I told her to stay put since I didn't know what had happened to the fake waiter and would-be suicide bomber. It turned out I didn't need to worry. Poly was sitting on top of him, holding him down. She had her mini-sweetener against his Adam's apple.

"Freeze, asshole," she said.

I smiled at her un-Poly-like language. It's a good thing when the person you love can still surprise you. It's a great thing when you know your partner will always come through in a clinch.

Tomáso and Queen Sherrhi were unharmed. It takes a lot to damage a Dauushan. Diágo, Lohrri and Naddéo had been closer to the explosion, however. The shock wave had knocked them over, so they had a few bumps and bruises, but the glass in the remaining windows stayed intact so they didn't add cuts to the list.

The other adults were getting up, too. Humans and non-humans alike seemed none the worse for wear. We were lucky the kids' table was on the far side of the banquet table, away from the bomb. Max, Terrhi, Spot, Spike and the mini-Drees were scared, but unhurt. Bavarian treated it as an adventure and helped Max and Terrhi get over the trauma.

The Stone Mountain Room wasn't near the river, so my mother and Chilly, waiting there, had missed most of the excitement. They did stick their heads out and my mom waved across the huge dining room, trying to get my attention.

I was even less interested in talking to my bio-father than I was in coping with a hundred EUA Macerator units charging through the dining room's front door. Unfortunately, no Macerators appeared to distract me further. Just as well. They're pushovers.

Martin had taken over for Poly in guarding the fake waiter. He'd cuffed the man to a chair and called the Atlanta police to take him into custody. I noticed Martin had cuffed his right hand so he could suck on the burns on his left. I wondered if I'd show that much compassion to someone who'd tried to kill me and my friends and was pleased to realize I probably would.

I stepped over to Martin and spoke softly.

"Will you be handling the interrogation?" I asked.

"Yes," said my friend. "This one is personal."

"You might want to hold off for a day," I said. "I'll ask the folks from Hu Zahn Fierst Corporation in Provo to fly out with a stock of their telepathic nanoparticles. Poly and I can meet them on Tuesday. I feel bad for blowing them off last week."

"I can do that," said Martin, "and I'll make sure Homeplanet Security doesn't hear about it."

"Thanks," I said.

I felt like I needed either a six-pack of Diet Starbuzz or a twelve-hour nap.

My phone chimed. I looked at its screen and saw it not only had a confirmation from Hu, Zahn, and Fierst—it had handled their travel arrangements and booked them rooms downtown in the SLN Tower's five-star hotel. I didn't know what I'd do without my phone.

Pierre's efficient staff was already cleaning up the spilled wine and broken crockery. The little Pyr was wringing his tentacles and lamenting what this latest round of damage would do to his insurance rates when Queen Sherrhi, Roger Joe-Bob Bacon, Cornell, and Bavarian all offered to help cover the cost. They could pay for the repairs out of petty cash.

Poly had come back to stand near me and was talking to Hildy. I distracted her with a kiss on the cheek and told her I was heading for the Stone Mountain Room.

"Do you want me to come along?" Poly asked.

"No," I replied, "but I expect I'll need a hug or three when I'm done."

"I'll warm up my arms to get ready," she said, moving her shoulders in circles.

"Love you," I said.

"Love you, too," said Poly.

Nothing like the threat of imminent death to make you think about family.

Chit picked that moment to flit down to my shoulder.

"Go on, bucko," said Chit. "Stop stallin'—it's time to git."

I got.

Chapter 50

"Sing, O muse, of the rage of Achilles..."
— Homer, *The Iliad*

The Stone Mountain Room was off the main large-species dining room. About the size of a basketball court, it would count as an intimate space for Tōdons and Dauushans. Teleport Inns around the galaxy named their private dining areas after local landmarks and Stone Mountain was one of the biggest things in the Atlanta area, so the room's name made sense in context.

Pierre and his team had shown their usual care, efficiency and customer service by setting up a small, human-sized square table and stocking it well. There were several bottles of water, wine, and Diet Starbuzz in one corner, along with a small bucket of ice and associated goblets and tumblers. There was even a parfait glass with strawberry-galberry trifle and a long spoon there to tempt me.

My mom and Chilly were sitting at the table with mostly full glasses of red wine in front of them. They'd been talking, but stopped and turned my way when I entered. Given the size of the room, it was a hike to get to the table. I felt their eyes were on me every step of the way and my stomach was tossing like a small boat on a restless, wine-dark sea. I took a seat across from my mother and got right to the point.

"When were you going to tell me?" I asked, the way a French prosecutor might say, *"J'accuse!"*

"Today," said my mom.

That slowed me down. I'd been expecting apologies, or an answer like, "Never."

"Go ahead," I said to my mom. "Is Chilly really my biological father?"

"Chilly?" my mom asked.

"That's what he told me to call him."

"Okay," she replied. "Then yes—just look in a mirror for confirmation."

I reluctantly looked at Chilly's real face for the first time. He wasn't wearing his programmable mask this time and did look rather familiar. I compared his face to my memory of the one I saw in the mirror when I shaved every morning. We clearly shared a lot of genetic material. He looked back at me, his face warm, open, and welcoming. I turned away.

"What *is* his name?" I asked my mom. "I expect it's not Chilly."

"No," said my mom. "Chilly is the reception you're giving me and your bio-father."

Mom always knew how to make me smile. This time was no exception. The corners of my mouth turned up involuntarily and I almost laughed. Goodness knows I needed to release *some* tension.

"No fair," I said, giving her a mock glare.

"My name is Achilles," said the man. "Achilles Theranos. I need your help."

That wasn't fair, either. My brain was hard-wired to help people who needed my assistance.

"You're not my father," I said, fighting back against my desire to learn more. "My father is Thomas Jefferson Buckston. You're just a sperm donor."

Chilly's face fell and my mother gave me a stern look and a word of warning.

"Jack!"

She said my name with the tone she'd used after one of my engineering experiments had resulted in property damage. It made me feel about nine.

"I'm sorry, mom," I said, "but this is a lot to process. I haven't even told T.J. about Max yet."

"Don't worry about it, Jack," she said. "I have and he's thrilled."

"Okay," I said.

I'd wanted to be the one to tell him.

It felt like my skull only had room for two gigs and somebody was trying to cram it full of forty gigs of information.

My brain was spinning faster than a thirty-millisecond pulsar. I took a deep breath and did a mental reset. Unreasoning hostility wouldn't necessarily get me anywhere. I put a calm I wasn't feeling into my voice.

"I'm sorry, Mr. Theranos," I said. "That was out of line. All in all, I'm pleased to have the random assortment of genes I've inherited from you. They've served me well."

Theranos nodded—not giving me anything to trigger more anger.

What could this total stranger I shared DNA with need from me? A kidney? Doubtful. Galactic medical technology had that covered. I tried to retain my zen-like attitude but couldn't manage it and shifted back to prosecutorial mode.

"I have three questions," I said. "Why did you leave? Why did you come back? And what's your problem?"

Theranos started to speak but my mom held up her hand.

"Wait," she said. "There are some things *I* have to say first."

I sat back in my chair, crossed my arms over my chest, and tried to center myself into active listening mode. It wasn't easy.

"I know now that Achilles wasn't supposed to fall in love with me," said my mom. "It broke all the rules. Understanding that after the fact makes it somehow even more romantic. Achilles and I were literally star-crossed lovers. I thought he was just an exchange student from New Zealand or something."

"Or something," said Achilles.

My mom kept going. "We fell for each other in a big way and got married after a whirlwind courtship."

She looked at Achilles with what I interpreted to be a wistful smile.

"You got started shortly thereafter," she said, "Then Achilles just disappeared, without leaving a note or text message or anything. I hadn't even told him I was pregnant."

Mom's wistful smile got tighter.

"I was worried that he'd been killed or kidnapped or I don't know what. It made me a wreck for months."

She reached out and patted Achilles arm. I shook my head.

"Now I know *why* he left, Jack, and it wasn't his fault. He didn't want to go, but received emergency recall orders and had to leave immediately. I didn't know any of that until yesterday. He wasn't allowed to tell me before he left."

I looked at my mom, then looked at Achilles, then turned back to my mom. She may have forgiven him, but I wasn't ready to.

Emergency recall orders from where? New Zealand?

"Got it," I said, my anger flaring. "Abandoned his family. Didn't mean to. You didn't have a husband. I didn't have a dad, but there were extenuating circumstances. As far as you're concerned, all is forgiven. Next?"

"Don't take that tone with me—I'm still your mother."

"I know, Mom," I said. "But can you blame me for my reaction?"

She didn't seem particularly maternal when she glared at me.

"Just be civil," she said.

"Okay," I said. "Sorry. I'll dial it back."

I recrossed my arms in the other direction. Hate led to the dark side, so I tried not to feed it, but it kept begging for scraps from the table. I put it on a leash so only a little seeped through and focused on calming my mind.

"What's the story?" I said. "Do you want to tell it or should he?"

"It's probably better coming from me," said Achilles. "Let me tell it to you straight—I'm an alien."

I looked closely at my bio-father. He seemed every bit as human as I was.

"What does that make me?" I asked. "Mr. Spock, with a human mother and an alien father?"

"You told me he had a flare for the dramatic," said Achilles.

"He got that from reading too much Shakespeare as a child," said my mom.

"Not just Shakespeare," I said, thinking of all the adventure stories I'd read.

"I'm an alien, Jack, in that I'm from another planet—but I'm human, too. You're not half Vulcan."

I looked a bit disappointed and made both of them smile by saying, "Fascinating."

A little more tension evaporated. Then I thought through the timing of Achilles' presence here on Earth before I was born.

"Hey," I said, "You were on Earth before First Contact Day. I thought Terra was off-limits."

"It was," said Achilles. "My presence wasn't sanctioned."

"My father was an *illegal* alien?"

Now all three of us were smiling. I quickly shifted my face back to Vulcan imperturbability.

"I didn't know there were humans anywhere else in the galaxy," I said. "Where are you from?"

"My planet is called Akrotiri," said Achilles.

"Akrotiri? Like the ruined village on Santorini?" I asked.

"Correct," said Achilles. "Exactly like that. A G'nandrian trader was making an illegal water stop on Terra about thirty-six hundred years ago when his instruments told him the Thera volcano was about to explode. Against all GaFTA regulations he loaded the citizens of Akrotiri into the hold of his freighter and took them with him when he left, saving all their lives."

"Nice guy," I said. "Sometimes you have to break the rules to do the right thing."

My attempts at nurturing serenity were starting to work—and Achilles' story was interesting. I wondered if the trader's water stop was to pick up aquatic life forms with promising pharmaceutical possibilities.

I poured some Diet Starbuzz into a glass and sipped.

"Remember," said Achilles. "No good deed goes unpunished."

"Ain't *that* the truth," I agreed. "What's a G'nandrian, by the way? I don't recognize the species."

"That's because there aren't any G'nandrians left anymore," said Achilles. "The reason is sadly ironic—but I'm getting ahead of myself."

I spooned up a bite of strawberry-galberry trifle and waited for Achilles to continue.

"The trader realized he could get in a lot of trouble back home with the GaFTA authorities if he showed up on a GaFTA planet with a cargo of pre-congruency sentients," said Achilles. "Being a good hearted being, he dropped the Akrotiri citizens off on an uninhabited Earth-like world several thousand light-years from here. The humans named their new planet after their original village. The trader figured he'd done a good deed and there'd be no way to pin anything on him. It didn't hurt that Akrotiri's system was hidden deep inside a dense nebula and hard to find."

"A sentient after my own heart," I said.

"Then he got bad news—the G'nandrians' sun had just gone nova, slagging their planet and destroying all life in their system."

"Ouch," I said. "I see the irony."

My mom patted my hand and encouraged me to have more trifle while I listened.

"Wouldn't a space-faring species be dispersed across enough systems to come back from such a disaster?" I asked.

"You'd think," said Achilles, "but the G'nandrians had rigid roles for each gender. Males were the traders—they went out into the galaxy. Females stayed home and ran the governments, factories, farms, and families."

My mom was shaking her head slowly.

"Those poor people. Those poor, poor people," she said.

I agreed.

"All the G'nandrian females were gone," said Achilles, "and the remaining males—mostly other traders—hadn't figured out how to create new females using genetic engineering. There were religious taboos in their culture that discouraged that line of research."

I thought about similar problems we'd had here on Earth and found I was getting deeper into his story, my anger replaced with interest. I waved with my spoon, encouraging Achilles to keep talking.

"The trader who rescued the Akrotiri folks—my ancestors—quietly got the word out and hundreds more G'nandrian traders were able to join him on our hidden planet. The lonely males adopted the humans as their children and successors, teaching them how to use and expand on congruent technology. They also made it *very* clear that we would not be welcome in the Galactic Free Trade Association of the time because we didn't invent congruent technology—it was handed to us."

My mom took up the tale while Achilles had a few sips of wine.

"Eventually the G'nandrian traders all died," she said, "leaving the people of Akrotiri with an empty, resource-rich planet and humans' built-in compulsion to be fruitful and multiply, along with all the technology of an advanced galactic civilization." She hurried her words along to get them out in one breath.

"Let me guess," I said. "Doing that violated GaFTA's Prime Directive."

"Exactly," said Achilles. "The trade sanctions for doing something like that are draconian, including complete quarantines."

"From what my Murm friend Chit says, the Prime Directive is more often treated like the First Suggestion."

"True," said Achilles. "Let me just say that some species are more equal than others when it comes to stretching the law."

"A universal truth," I said. "But you're talking about stuff that happened thirty-six hundred years ago. You're an established congruency-using civilization. Why wouldn't they just think you figured things out on your own? And since you're hiding from the rest of the galaxy now, how much worse could it be to get stuck with a quarantine?"

"It isn't that simple," said Achilles. "There's more to the story."

"Humans don't *do* simple," I noted. "Go ahead, drop the other shoe."

"Akrotiri's culture inherited the desire to trade and explore from both our human and G'nandrian sides," said Achilles. "My original ancestors did a lot of trading around the Mediterranean. For the past three thousand years we've been surreptitiously visiting planets with pre-congruency civilizations and rescuing members of other species slated to die in natural disasters."

"I can understand why, given your own history," I said. "So you relocated the survivors elsewhere on their planet. What's wrong with that?"

"What's wrong is that we didn't move the rescued sentients elsewhere on their original planets," said Achilles. "We followed the original G'nandrian trader's example, brought them back to Akrotiri, and taught them how to use congruent technology. That means Akrotiri isn't guilty of just one violation of GaFTA's Prime Directive—there've been twenty-seven of them."

"Less than one a century," I said. "That's not too bad."

"Tell it to the Galactic Free Trade Association Council," said Achilles. "They'd lock up our system and throw away the key."

"Are we talking about the same Galactic Free Trade Association?" I said. "In my experience, they'd be more interested in trade than quarantine."

"How long as Earth been in GaFTA?" asked my mom.

"You know the answer to that," I said. "Just over fifteen years."

"How long has Akrotiri been observing GaFTA in operation?" she went on.

"Ummm… Over three thousand years?"

"Uh huh," said my mom. "We've been a bit naive and shielded from GaFTA's worst politics."

I thought about the recent Pâkk-Orishen War and the Pâkk-Tigrammath War thousands of years ago. There was a lot I didn't know. Come to think of it, I'd never heard of the Galactic Free Trade Association Council.

"Okay," I said. "Point taken."

"The member species of the Galactic Free Trade Association would have been willing to look the other way if a planet full of humans appeared using congruent technology they didn't invent," said Achilles. "We've got entertaining legislatures, too. But they can't easily condone us abducting small populations of twenty-seven other species and giving *them* congruent technology in violation of their number one rule. It's too much."

"I'm beginning to see the scope of the problem," I said.

This wouldn't be easy.

"What's your current planetary population?" I asked.

"Five-point-three billion," said Achilles.

"How many of them are human?"

"Three-point-three billion."

"The second largest concentration of humans in the galaxy," I said.

"To my knowledge," said my father.

"Right."

"So you have two billion non-humans on the planet?"

"Across twenty-seven different species, right," said Achilles.

"And they all share a common technological culture?" I asked.

"Pretty much," said Achilles, "though many species retain aspects of their original cultures. We're more of a mosaic than a melting pot."

"Sounds like Canada," said my mom.

"Good analogy," said Achilles.

"Okay," I said, "that makes things more complicated."

"Achilles was visiting Earth incognito before First Contact to see if there was any way some of his people could become legitimate GaFTA members by getting hold of Earth credentials and passing themselves off as Terrans," said my mom.

"You mean he was spying on us to see if the human Akrotirians could exploit us?"

"Po-tay-to, po-tah-to," said Achilles.

He'd done a good job learning Terran idioms.

"Then what happened?" I asked.

I scraped the last bit of galberry-flavored cream from the bottom of my parfait glass.

"Then I was called home," said Achilles.

Perhaps he hadn't learned as much about Terran idioms as I thought. There'd be time to explain it to him later.

I raised my eyebrows.

"All of us had to pull out," said Achilles.

"Thank goodness not before I got started," I quipped.

"Jack!" said my mom, more laughing than chastising.

"Our senior people were concerned you were too close to discovering congruencies on your own and we didn't want to be on-planet for First Contact," said Achilles. "The galactics' sensors can overlook a few preexisting congruency signals—there are always species trying to jump the gun with new candidate civilizations—but we didn't want to risk the possible scrutiny."

"An understandable precaution," I said. "But we didn't invent congruencies for another eleven years."

"There's no way to tell when or if an R&D project is going to work," said my mom.

"Akrotiri's operating philosophy is based on caution, Jack," said Achilles. "And compassion. We've stayed hidden for millennia. If we're discovered, GaFTA's enforcement arm might try to knock our technology back to pre-congruency levels. We've gotten really good at flying under their radar."

Another good idiom. Despite myself, I was beginning to like Achilles.

"You pulled a turtle and locked yourself up tight inside your shell for the past fourteen years, I get it," I said.

"No, we just stopped having agents on the ground," said Achilles. "We still kept an eye on things on Terra from a distance. And we have a few allies."

"Right," I said. "So what changed? Why are you back on Earth now?"

"My unit..." said Achilles.

"Akrotiri's Espionage Division?" I suggested.

"Close," said Achilles. "We refer to it as the Reconnaissance Corps. My unit called for volunteers to return to Terra and I raised my hand. I wanted to see what had changed since First Contact Day—and I desperately wanted to find out how you and Nory were doing. That's not so easy to do remotely."

"Understood," I said. "Were you one of the people bugging my apartment?"

Achilles didn't say anything, but he did smile. Good enough. His non-answer prompted my self-protection circuits to kick back in hard.

"How do I know any of this is true?" I asked. "You could be a flimflam man trying to seduce my mom now that there's money in the family."

"There's money in the family?" asked my mom.

"I'll catch you up on that later," I said. "Max is a billionaire."

Mom looked stunned—as if she'd just been sweetened.

"Shepherd will vouch for me, Jack," said Achilles. "He knows the score and is one of the allies I'd mentioned."

"I'll talk to him," I said.

Boy, would I talk to Shepherd. I wondered if Rosalind's project for him had anything to do with Akrotiri?

"Shepherd says you, your partner and your team are the best, Jack," said Achilles. "I need your help. An entire planet needs you and your friends' creative approach to problem-solving."

"Let me get this straight," I said "You want me to help you cover up a thirty-six hundred-year-old violation of GaFTA rules, plus twenty-seven more violations over three millennia? Then you want me to figure out how to legitimize three-point-three billion humans and two billion uplifted aliens on a hidden planet before the GaFTA Council finds out you exist and takes action?"

"Pretty much," said Achilles.

"I told you he picks things up fast," said my mom.

I may be quick on the uptake, but this time, I was overwhelmed. It was too much. I'd only learned I had a son on Thursday. Now my biological father was in the picture and he—and a planet with billions of sentient beings—needed my help.

I desperately needed hugs from Poly, time to think, and a good night's rest.

This meeting needed to be over.

"Let me sleep on it," I said. "I'll talk to you on Monday."

Chapter 51

"All's well that ends well."
— William Shakespeare

My friends were all congregating near the large-species dining room's wide exit when I came out of the Stone Mountain Room with my mother and Achilles. My meeting hadn't slowed anyone down, since Martin had insisted they all write up statements after lunch, even Max and Bavarian. I promised I'd get mine to Martin before five today and so did Achilles and mom.

Poly had arranged for most of us to spend one last night at the research facility before finding other lodgings. It made more sense than trying to pack up now, only to unpack into other temporary housing. Danny Figueres offered us luxury suites in one of his hotels starting tomorrow if any of us needed extra time to locate suitable, more permanent quarters.

By some unspoken arrangement Poly and I ended up alone—just the two of us—in an autocab heading back to the facility. Chit decided to ride in a cab with Gus. The Gojon promised to shrink down to the Murm's size to leave more room for Spike, Spot, Terrhi, and Bavarian in their vehicle.

When our cab's door eased closed behind Poly, I pulled her to me and the two of us embraced, holding each other tight.

"How did it go with your mom and Chilly?" asked Poly. "You seemed in better spirits when you came out of the meeting than when you went in."

"I learned a lot," I said.

"Want to talk about it?"

"Not right now," I said. "I'd rather cuddle. It's going to take a long time to explain and I'd rather just hold you."

"Fine by me," said Poly, snuggling close. "You can fill me in after we get to the facility."

"Right."

We sat silent for several seconds, soaking each other up.

I had a lot to think about and wanted to blissfully *not* think for the next ten minutes.

"Jack?" asked Poly.

"What, darling?"

"Why do you think Rosalind is leaving Max with you for the next year and making us *both* responsible for voting his shares?"

I had to rouse my relaxed brain to fire more neurons and answer. Luckily, my response didn't take much thought.

"She really does want me to have more time with Max," I said, "and she wants to stress our relationship."

"Uh huh," said Poly languidly, seeming nearly as relaxed as I was. "That's my read, too."

"People fight over kids, sex, money, and in-laws," I said. "This hits three out of four."

"It's four out of four if kids get in the way of good sex," murmured Poly.

"We'll make sure Max has an early bedtime," I said, laughing.

"You'll be a good father," said Poly. "And lover and business partner and…"

I kissed her.

She tasted wonderful.

She tasted like more.

"It's not going to work, is it, Jack?" asked Poly when we took a break from kissing.

"What's not going to work—Rosalind trying to mess us up?"

"Uh huh," said Poly. "I'll try my best not to let her get to me."

"So will I," I said, "but you didn't sign up to be with a single father with an almost five-year-old son. It's not going to be easy."

"I know," said Poly. "We'll figure it out as we go along."

"Together," I said.

I invited Poly to cuddle again so we could reassure each other all was right with the world. It wasn't long before we were ever--so-politely interrupted

"Jack," said my phone. It sounded oddly diffident.

"What?" I said, wondering what it wanted.

"Has this unit provided you with good service?"

"Stop fishing for compliments," I said. "You've saved my life as many times as I have fingers and toes."

"Two more than that, actually," said my phone.

"But who's counting," I said, laughing. "No, you have *not* provided good service. You've provided outstanding service. I'd pin a medal on you if it wouldn't damage your mutacase."

"A medal would be superfluous," said my phone, "but a near-perfect human duplicate android that can interface with…"

"Jack," Poly interrupted. "Your phone wants to be a real boy."

"Correct," said my phone. "If the service delivered by this unit is worthy of such a reward."

"You don't need to beg," I said. "Of *course* you're worthy of an android body if EUA's still set up to make them. We can figure that out next week. But wouldn't a humanoid body be a step down from what you can do with your mutacase?"

"Yes," said my phone. "The android body would only be for special occasions."

"How would you interface with an android?" asked Poly. "They're organic human analogues, not cybernetic."

"An excellent question," replied my phone, "and one that can't be answered until more details about the program are available."

Poly nodded. I could see her thinking through potential designs.

"Are you cool with this, fellow EUA stockholder?" I asked Poly.

"I support the motion one hundred percent," said my partner.

"Then it passes unanimously," I said.

"Thank you," said my phone.

"Approaching destination," said our autocab.

* * * * *

After our huge lunch at the Teleport Inn we grazed on leftovers for dinner. There were plenty of them. Earlier, Poly and I had spent the balance of the afternoon distracting ourselves from our worries by playing games with Max and Bavarian on the conference room table. Spot took up a lot of room by our feet, snoring with enough decibels to force us to speak louder.

Playing games helped keep Bavarian and Max from missing their new friends Terrhi and Spike too much. Bavarian helped Max when we played *Monopoly* and contrived to have *him* be the one with hotels on Boardwalk and Park Place. I went bankrupt first and used the time when I wasn't playing to write up my report for Martin. Then Poly landed on Boardwalk with three hotels and joined me. Bavarian pronounced Max the winner and showed him how to put all the tokens, money and properties back in the box neatly. She was great with Max and made me wish I had grown up with a big sister.

Note to self: check with Achilles to find out if I have any half-siblings on Akrotiri.

After dinner, the kids wanted to play more games. Bavarian didn't protest when Max asked to play *Candy Land.* We moved from there to *Life*—the board game, not the one with cellular automata. Poly and I were surprised when Max suggested playing *Cards Against Humanity* until Rosalind told her there was a G-rated kids deck available. I won the first hand with *Simba Eats The Roadrunner.*

Rosalind was reviewing information on a tablet at the far end of the table while we were playing. Every now and then I caught her looking at our idyllic family scene and smiling. I wished I could figure her out, but knew that wasn't likely.

After Max and Bavarian beat Poly and me three games to two at *Othello,* I yawned. It had been a long day and I was ready for bed. Poly resonated with my yawn and repeated it.

After I yawned a second time, I realized I still hadn't told Poly about Akrotiri and promised myself I'd catch her up on the details in the morning.

"Looks like it's time for the grown-ups to go to bed," said Bavarian.

Then Max yawned.

"And small boys," said Rosalind.

Rosalind helped us put the games away. Earlier in the afternoon, my phone had used its initiative and arranged to have a box full of classic games delivered. They really helped pass the time and were yet another mark in its favor. *Ten points to Gryffindor!*

That reminded me I wanted to take Max—and Bavarian—to a Quidditch match someday soon. Congruent technology had finally been able to get the flying brooms working right and SLN was expanding into sports by broadcasting professional Quidditch matches to a growing list of planets. The Atlanta *Phoenix* were even leading their division.

"Good night, buddy boy," I said, giving my sleepy son a hug.

"G'night, daddy," he said.

Max gave Poly, Bavarian and Spot goodnight hugs, too, just to extend his bedtime, then Rosalind led him out to their room and his bed.

"Excuse me," said Bavarian.

"How can we help?" asked Poly.

"I know I come off as all grown up," she said, "but I'm really only eight-and-three-quarters."

"Oh?" I said, smiling. "I thought you were nine."

"I round up for my corporate bio," said Bavarian.

"That's understandable," I said, smiling softly. "Anyone would do the same."

She smiled back, enjoying the gentle teasing.

"You know what kind of a day it's been," said Bavarian, "so I was wondering if you and and Poly could please tuck me in?"

"We'd be glad to," said Poly. "I'll help you get ready, then Jack and I can read you a bedtime story."

"I'd like that," said Bavarian.

Poly and I read her the first few chapters of *A Spell for Chameleon*. She hadn't heard of it before, explaining that she spent most of her time reading the *Wall Street Journal* and economics text-books. Bavarian loved the story, especially with Poly and me and my phone acting out the various characters. When we finished the third chapter, Poly said it was time for little girls and their big dogs to go to sleep. Spot was already snoring at the foot of the bed.

We leaned in from either side and kissed her forehead. Before we could leave, Bavarian held our hands tightly and tugged us down to sit on either side of her.

"I have a business proposition for you," she said in a very grown-up voice.

"Okay," I said, paying close attention.

"You know I'm only eight-and-three-quarters…"

"You mentioned that," said Poly.

"And you know I can be tough and hold my own with adults when I need to," Bavarian continued.

"We saw the video of you facing down Boss Kone," I confirmed.

"But I really want a mom and dad," she said. "Can I pay you to adopt me and be my new parents?"

"No," said Poly. "You can't pay us."

Poly looked at me. I looked back. We both nodded.

Bavarian looked so vulnerable. Her chin began to quiver.

"You can't pay us," I said.

"We volunteer," said Poly.

Bavarian's eye grew wide and so did her smile.

"So long as you know what you're getting into," I said.

"I do," said the girl. "I do, I do."

"Parents have to be strict sometimes," said Poly.

"Uh huh," said Bavarian. "I know. I'm counting on it."

Tears of joy were streaming down her cheeks. I got her some tissues.

"I'm going to be a handful."

* * * * *

After a very long day, Poly and I were finally in bed together, cuddling. I'd double-checked to make sure the door to our suite was locked and didn't expect Tomáso and Queen Sherrhi or their bodyguards to let Terrhi off the *Charalindhri* any time soon. I understood that the royal family planned to stay on the *Chara* until Tomáso's apartment next to the Dauushan consulate was repaired. It was reassuring to know that a cute, but frequent source of interruption was in orbit twenty-two thousand miles overhead and likely to remain there for a while.

Poly fluffed her pillow and turned on her side to face me. I loved looking at her eyes.

"You know," she said, "if we're going to be Max and Bavarian's parents, there's something we should consider doing first."

"What's that?" I asked. "Get married?"

"Well, sure," said Poly. "Getting married would be fun, if we don't make too much of a production out of it. But that's not what I was thinking."

I nodded my agreement and slid my hand along her side, under the covers.

"Ummmm," said Poly. "That's nice."

"What *were* you thinking?" I asked.

"I was thinking we'll need a bigger place to live than your apartment."

"As you wish," I said with a grin.

Poly hit me with her pillow—then she kissed me.

Please visit

www.XenotechSupport.com

for more details about
the universe of Xenotech Support
and the Galactic Free Trade Association

Jack & Poly's adventures start in

Xenotech Rising

Xenotech Queen's Gambit

Xenotech What Happens

and will continue in

Xenotech Versus the Galaxy

Sign up for the Xenotech Support mailing list
on the web site to get advance notice of publication
and receive a free short story.

You may also enjoy a related novelette:

Xenotech First Contact Day

which tells what happened on April 1, 2015

www.ingramcontent.com/pod-product-compliance
Lightning Source LLC
Chambersburg PA
CBHW070800030726
47504CB00003B/631